The Co...
RICHARD...
Volume Six

Demo
Teeny Bopper Idol
Glam

S.T. Publishing

The Complete Richard Allen Volume Six: Demo, Teeny
Bopper Idol, Glam (pbk)

© Richard Allen, 1997

ISBN No. 1 898927 35 9

First editions of the three books in this omnibus edition
were published in 1971, 1973 and 1973 respectively.

Published by S.T. Publishing, Scotland.
Printed by Progressive Printing, England.

S.T. Publishing
P.O. Box 12, Lockerbie, Dumfriesshire. DG11 3BW.
Scotland.
S.T. Publishing - the original street publisher

The Complete
RICHARD ALLEN
Volume Six

Demo
Teeny Bopper Idol
Glam

INTRODUCTION

Of all the Richard Allen novels, *Demo* is perhaps the hardest to find in its original NEL paperback format. And for good reason too. Despite going on to be a million seller, *Skinhead* got off to a slow start (barely shifting a thousand copies in the first six months) and there was little to suggest that it would go on to spawn other youth cult paperbacks like *Suedehead*, *Boot Boys* and *Mod Rule*.

Richard Allen was of course one of the many pen names used by Canadian author James Moffatt, and rather than drop it completely, it was decided to publish any other youth related titles by Jim using the new name. *Demo* was published in March, 1971, just as *Skinhead* eventually took off. It told the story of the sons and daughters of wartime have-a-go heroes taking on the student demonstrators who were having their strings pulled by the puppet masters back in Moscow. The kids flocking to buy *Skinhead* had little or no interest in the long haired types manning the barricades, and when *Suedehead* was released to cash in on *Skinhead's* success, *Demo* was quietly forgotten.

Demo is actually quite a good book, although whether it lives up to the original back cover blurb of "a masterfully researched novel that probes behind the scenes of today's university unrest" is open to debate. The story line often borders on the unlikely - bad guy Stanley Edmond must be the only 43 year old in history who could pass for 19 - and the temperature never really rises above lukewarm, but we're talking pulp fiction here, not pretentious literary award material, and it does hold your interest from beginning to end.

It's actually quite interesting to see how little has changed since 1970. Tribal warfare in Africa, street demonstrations in the UK, and even the argument for and against having to buy a TV licence to fund the BBC are as topical today as they were then.

Substitute the real world for the music world, and the same is true of both *Teeny Bopper Idol* and *Glam*. Both offer a cynical glimpse into the world of manufactured pop that dominated the charts back in '73 (when both books were originally published) just as it does now with The Spice Girls and friends.

Pop star Johnny Holland is a character in the Joe Hawkins mould and is central to both books. Not content with documenting the changing faces of British youth, Richard Allen does his best to influence it by creating the Roundhead cult. It never left the pages of these two novels, but Johnny Holland's decision to sing racist material like *Aggro Addict* certainly pre-empted bands like Skrewdriver by a good few years (funnily enough, there is even a character in *Glam* called Ian Donaldson). What's more, some of the glam bands in the two books could easily have been prototype punk outfits, and this underlines the link between glam and punk that definitely exists, but is often forgotten by the Malcolm McLaren created punk brigade. In reality punk was both a reaction against and a natural continuation of what glam and manufactured pop represented.

This is the sixth and final volume in the Richard Allen series, and with its publication, all 18 Richard Allen novels are available simultaneously for the first time. Some of the books are better than others, and everyone will have their personal favourites, but what is beyond dispute is that Richard Allen truly was the king of youth cult fiction. Richard Allen's creator, Jim Moffatt, sadly died in 1993, but his memory lives on in this and the other volumes in the series, and with those who have held onto the original editions and bought these reprints. It'll be interesting to see which goes first - the Beeb's licence fee or Richard Allen's collectability. My money's on the former.

George Marshall, 1997.

DEMO

By Richard Allen

FOREWORD

DEMONSTRATION is an ugly word today. And demonstrators are automatically associated with militant student bodies or those 'foreign' elements pandering to Maoist-Communist slogan-chanting malcontents. Within a decade, the peaceful right of protest has drastically become an issue with the British public. Liberals tend to downgrade the disruptive effect of violent demonstration. Right-wing advocates simply shrug and criticise the leniency shown by Courts to those 'caught in the act'. But to the working man with his long traditions of fair play, Britain is Britain and to hell with the world generally, abhors the very word 'demonstrate' nowadays.

Unlike 'skinhead' violence which is apparently the vicious outlet for lower-class status-seeking, demonstrators are a unique creation of a Cold War-'Bomb' fascination. From simple beginnings - the right of youth to refuse parental guidance and become fodder for global slaughter - the demonstration now encompasses every form of protest imaginable. Let a body take exception to any facet of national life and there *must* be a demo!

No sane individual would refute youth's right to protest. Regardless of generation or era, youth has always rebelled against established authority - either parental or legal. Yet never quite like today's mass parades and anti-police hysteria.

Law-abiding citizens deplore the senseless cry of 'Pigs', those needless injuries, the inhumane treatment of innocent police-horses, the deliberate destruction of property that follow so-called 'peaceful demonstration'.

Elements are at work under cover of legitimate organisations to disrupt essential services; to encourage working men to consider employers as bloody-minded bastards incapable of understanding lower-class problems; to foment a desire for total anarchy. Scotland Yard's 'Special Branch' have the names and backgrounds of dozens of known 'terrorists' engaged in undermining anything even remotely approaching a peace-purpose demo. These same professional demonstrators can be hired by other militant units to encourage strikers, to supply the much needed 'backbone' for paid political disturbances, to support any cause no matter how tenuous, how just or unjust; how disastrous for Britain as a whole.

There is an awful lot to be said for that ancient British sense of justice that these people can be allowed their freedom. The very slogans they shout suggest an alliance with Iron Curtain diplomats, or at the least with communist ideologies. One does not have to wonder very long to arrive at a conclusion concerning their monetary support. Nor does one have to think hard about their fate if they tried those self-same tactics in a strict communist state. The insults, the destruction of property, the empty-headed denial of a man's right to express his opinion would not be tolerated for a split-second in Russia, China, Cuba or North Vietnam. It speaks highly of a capitalistic democratic system that pays social security benefits and grants to those seemingly dedicated to the complete overthrow of that which feeds and nurtures these vipers.

The majority of British youth are against violent demos. The preponderance of students believe that study is their grant-given duty. Unfortunately, democracy permits militants and those debased power-seekers to infiltrate and control aspects of community life - be it a student council, a shop steward's committee, a political party. Their weapons are words, oratory, fear, brute force when all else fails. Twisted facts, plausible arguments, uninhibited sexuality - these are the thin edges of their wedge. Pot and disregard for set standards are the broader knife-thrust. Abuse of social security, claims of police brutality, infiltration of news media are the final involvements.

Awareness is the only alternative to their insidious sneak attacks. To be forewarned still holds true. But apathy and whispers that all is well can bring Britain - and, indeed, the Western world - to its knees. It is up to youth - those intelligent searchers after a better Earth - to fulfil their bright-eyed, zestful promise to make this a much better land for you, and them to live in.

The challenge is theirs - youth's. Either they elect to stay within a democratic framework or utterly destroy what has taken centuries to construct; and with it the dreams of lost generations of teenagers who have sacrificed life itself for a cause they believed would endure all outside attacks.

Richard Allen,
Gloucestershire, 1970

PRELUDE

OUTWARDLY, the van looked innocent enough. The name gaudily painted on each side helped convey an impression of legitimate purpose. *Richardson & Stafford, Light Removals* had every right to be parked outside a block of exclusive flats on this Saturday afternoon. Admittedly, close scrutiny would have revealed a sad lack of removal activity but the majority of those passing the parked van had neither time nor inclination to investigate its presence.

Inside, the van was a massive electronic communications complex connected to various vantage points through closed circuit television and two-way radio. Its soundproofed sides effectively stopped incessant chatter from reaching the pavements; its ingenious aerials could not be seen; its purpose and location a carefully kept secret even from those divisions most closely involved in law enforcement.

Inspector John Trust was not unduly worried as he watched a silent monitor-screen. He had six tough detectives on guard; a squad of mounted-police within two blocks - and, his joker, twenty uniformed patrolmen inside the flats adjacent to their vehicle. Special Branch were taking no undue chances with their ultra-modern 'secret weapon'. The fight against highly organised professional agitators demanded the latest scientific arsenal and this van was the nerve-centre of the Yard's defences against an all-out assault on Grosvenor Square.

And Trust was absolutely certain of that!

Already, he had seen seventeen known faces in the crowds - features he had committed to memory when he undertook the assignment giving him complete charge of the Branch's anti-demo squad.

In a way he detested himself for being here. Somewhere out there - an innocent victim of militant pressure - was his own son. He admired the boy. He respected a man's right to hold views at variance with established logic. Parliament was not always right. Like anywhere, parliamentarians were subject to influences that directed their lives. Be a man Conservative or Labour he was under the Party whip; governed by headquarter dictates rather than constituency wishes. In Trust's view, Parliament had ceased to be the voice of the people. It was now the voice of a few directing traffic from Party sanctuaries. People voted for men they hoped would have courage and gumption to stand up for their local issues - and got machines bowing a knee to a Prime Minister elected by 'mysterious' behind-the-scenes fiddles. It was his opinion that neither Wilson with his gimmickry nor Heath with his constant smile would have been chosen by the People had the choice of P.M. been theirs - as it should have been! He wasn't in favour of the American system with its graft; corruption down to dogcatcher levels. He just wished there was an in-between method of being represented - a vote for local candidate and another for Prime Minister. It wasn't good enough to be presented with *a fait accompli* - pipe-smoking Harold of the many tongues or silent Ted the faceless, voiceless director of a nation's affairs.

'Christ, no wonder the kids want changes!' he blurted.

'Sir ?'

He turned from the monitor and grinned. He was a cross between Richard Widmark and Rock Hudson - an enigmatic type. He possessed the phlegm of a Welshman, the cunning of a Scot, the haughtiness of an English aristocrat, the guile of an Irishman. Somewhere, too, hidden behind five generations born in England, there existed a touch of French romanticism and a little Spanish mañana-ness. 'Nothing, sergeant. Just speaking aloud to myself!'

Sergeant Barrington smiled understanding. It was one of those job hazards that men engaged in constant preparedness should begin to discuss problems with themselves. He did it, too. His wife often accused him of speaking more to a subconscious than her.

'Milligen here . . . the main body are approaching the Square!'

Trust brushed aside further conversation, concentrated on his monitor. Milligen was placed at the extreme limits of the police cordon overlooking what Trust had called 'Flashpoint Intersection'. If the howling crowd got past this vital spot there was bound to be serious trouble.

Grabbing his microphone, Trust growled: 'Send in units five and six. Cut off those waving that damned 'FREEDOM IS MAO'S AIM' banner. They're the bloody ring-leaders!' Immediately he uttered the words, John Trust wished he could recall them. His eyes bulged and there, directly behind the chanting, slogan-shouting mob, was his son - hair long, wearing Levis and floppy sweater, a placard protesting about American war atrocities carried proudly aloft. Through a desire to save the boy, Trust bit his lower lip until blood flecks appeared, and hoped that a miracle would prevent the lad's capture . . .

James Trust - Jim to his many friends - knew he was doing wrong. His father had warned him. His mother had pleaded in vain for him to forget this demo. But he was only 'wrong' inasmuch as his parents did not approve. His conscience *demanded* he make this appeal to Britain. He loathed war, sincerely believed that American intervention in Vietnam had escalated death, corruption, genocide. He wished he could find one glimmer of hope in democratic processes - yet admitted that Mao's thoughts seemed more in keeping with global requirements than anything the Western powers could offer youth. As the chanting mob moved towards the Square, Jim felt less sure of his right to be here. What had been promised as a peaceful demonstration of solidarity against warmongering was quickly developing into a hate campaign directed against the 'pigs' and those responsible for upholding the dignity of British institutions. He had heard violent threats yelled into his ears - threats which, if carried out, would turn Grosvenor Square into a battlefield to compare with the worst slaughters of the Far Eastern conflict. Just before the squeeze prevented anyone from leaving he had seen Julius Gold speaking to several known militants and was certain that weapons had changed hands.

From his refuge far behind the surging demonstrators, the man called Julius Gold smiled wistfully and relaxed. His job had finished when he handed over the 'tools' his pupils needed to make this the bloodiest battle yet in London. He had taken no chances. The Canadian government building was directly on the route taken by the mob and, if stopped by police, he had his passport, his reasons for visiting the area and an internationally respected agency to justify the briefcase he carried. It didn't matter a damn now if he was stopped or not. The powerful air-pistols, the thunder-flashes, the ball-bearings had been dispensed. And, too - so had that one Very-light pistol which would signal a concentrated assault from several quarters.

In a way he was sorry he could not get closer. *What will the U.S. Marines do when a Very flame ignites their precious Embassy?* he thought. He hoped they would open-fire on the mob. That alone would trigger a greater explosion than even he had dared anticipate.

Inspector Trust watched his snatch-squads move into action. Until the last minute they were indistinguishable from the demonstrators. Then, suddenly, those militants known to be most eager for an eruption within the Square were surrounded - whisked off to one side and quickly pulled inside the safety of a heavily-guarded building.

Uniformed police appeared magically; a solid blue line confronting the disorganised hard-core hate merchants.

And, less than fifteen feet away - pressed forward by the crush - was James, his son!

'God, don't let him get too involved!' he whispered to himself. Parental torment pulled at his mind. Sympathies twisted his logic. 'Disperse them,' he roared into his microphone. 'Break up that crowd - keep 'em moving away from the Square!'

Almost like a military force advancing into its private 'valley of death' the mounted men moved forward - easing into the mob, trying to convey their message without undue discomfort.

Trust squirmed. His screen showed the spontaneous reaction in all its barbaric disgust. *God, how those horses suffered!* he thought. *The rotten bastards! What harm was the horse doing? It followed instructions - like it had been trained to do! Christ - don't they draw a line anywhere? Is this what their bloody Mao taught? Is it an exchange for war to have anarchy shoved down our throats! An anarchy that neither respects humanity, animal life or those common, ordinary decencies the British people have fostered during the course of their turbulent history!*

'I'd like to use a cigarette end on those bastards myself,' Sergeant Barrington snarled, bending over Trust's shoulder.

'Enough of that talk, sergeant!' Trust compelled himself to be the efficient, unbiased officer every policeman was paid to be. Personal opinions could be thought - not spoken. The law demanded equality, strict adherence to duty - not an inch more. 'Get your lads forward. We've got a fight on our hands . . . ' He gazed sadly at his monitor . . . saw the streaming, brutal crowd surge forward and burst into Grosvenor Square. He was glad their closed-circuit system taped evidence. That policeman going under a vicious group of kicking, punching young thugs deserved to be revenged. And yet - he doubted if a magistrate would give the culprits more than a £10 fine. It wasn't his place to argue against legal thinking on how to deal with offenders but it seemed a crying shame that a policeman doing his duty to protect the public property should be beaten to a pulp and the punishment dished out was a fine - a small fine - probably paid out of a council grant or a social security kitty!

It was a crazy world, he mused. A world of demo and violence and artificiality. A world gone stark raving mad with the power of its own ability to object, protest, out-shout any opposition. Where would it end? When? And who would be left to reap the bitter harvest of anarchy ?

CHAPTER ONE

EVERYTHING was arranged and Colonel Brett Hart viewed his preparations with a critical eye. Many years had vanished behind history's curtain since he last held one of his 'gatherings'. He could recall the old days with fondness, nostalgic hysteria. God, what wouldn't he give to be *that* age again! Retirement had drained vital fluids from his heart, made him over-cautious. And damned fussy. He frowned, adjusted the meticulously sharpened pencils so that each lay neatly beside its notebook. He felt the coffee percolator - James had grown old with him and could not be trusted to remember minor matters. It was hot - just how it used to be when . . .

'Excuse me, sir . . . '

The colonel's military bearing had lost none of its zip. Neither advancing years nor tweeds could take away that career stiffness nor dim his penetrating gaze. 'What is it, James?' he asked impatiently.

James smiled weakly. He was weary. It had been one of those infernal days when regimentation got him down. He hadn't minded when the old man had been a serving soldier. They'd had much to occupy them, spring in their step to sustain a heavy work-load. 'Will the gentlemen be staying long, sir?'

'I hope so, James. I sincerely hope so!' Hart waved his hand. 'Take a pew, James.'

Immediate obedience was not essential. They had friendship now to override malingering. James slowly walked to his favourite chair knowing it was also Hart's. He loved this room with its familiar objects - maps, weapons, model soldiers ready for battle-games, ancient reminders of Roundheads and Drake. As he stuffed tobacco into his worn briar, James felt the tension multiply. He understood something important was due to take place in the room - it showed in the colonel's mounting impatience, his jumpiness.

'What would you say if I told you we were going back into business, James?'

The ex-batman gasped, clung to his briar. 'We're w-what, sir?'

Hart laughed. It was good to see James react so strongly again. He felt - well, satisfied now. They had buried themselves in Surrey's green-belt for too long. 'If I name our guests you'll know exactly what I mean.' Lifting both hands, Hart began to tick off fingers as he spoke. 'Rolande Aubin, Frank Sommers, Bob Thomson, Claire Porter, Eric Nimmo, Konrad Bluther, Mai Bedford.'

Their eyes locked. Each had sparkle and renewed appraisal of life in rejuvenated gazes.

'It will be nice, Colonel.'

'You always were a deliberate cuss, James. Don't you ever express yourself with more than a becalmed five-word sentence?'

James smiled and jammed his briar in his mouth, sucked contentedly. 'You trained me, sir. Remember that day when you accused me of allowing emotions to bubble on the surface?'

Hart nodded thoughtfully. He could recall it. Perfectly.

'Well, sir - I've kept things so bottled up inside me for . . . how long is it, sir?'

'Thirty-one years, James.'

'How time does scoot past, sir!' James shook his head unbelievingly.

Hart ignored the obvious. He did not care to dwell upon passing years. At seventy-two he had neither inclination nor precious seconds to spend in retrospect. And, anyway - there was the coming 'gathering'. They would discuss times best forgotten; memories taken from concealed places and paraded for old friends to munch over.

'Would you like us to get back into the swing again, James?'

'I would indeed, sir.'

'Even if it meant . . . ?'

James interrupted quickly. This was important. Vital for his peace of mind. He'd had enough of this tranquil country existence. At sixty-four he deserved better than stagnation. An active man would always hunger for fresh fields to harvest. 'Even if I had to take to the service, sir?'

Hart's eyes clouded. 'Impossible - and you damned know it, too. No. I have an idea but I'd prefer to elaborate when the others arrive.'

'I'll listen outside the door - as usual, sir.' James laughed. His memory was sharp.

'No need for subterfuge - you'll be here in the room with us.'

'Thank you, sir!'

'Don't speak too soon, James. I'm getting past administrative work. You're officially nominated as my assistant.'

James stuck his scrawny chest out, smiled beatifically. 'I'll do my best, sir. And now - if that's all?'

Hart nodded.

'I've got a few chores . . . '

'Their drinks?'

'Why, yes, sir!'

'You know what each has?'

'I've never forgotten, sir,'

As James attended to the drinks, Hart measured the floor with absent-minded paces. He was like that - always needing something to occupy his brain. No matter how trivial the task he had to have this mental stimulation.

Ten feet . . .

Will they have altered much?

Eleven feet . . .

Are they too old for what I have in mind?

Twelve feet . . .

Will Frank object? He always had reservations!

Thirteen feet . . .

What shall we call ourselves? That's important - a name is everything to a group!

Fourteen feet . . .

Operation Smokescreen? A blasted horrible title that! What else?

Fifteen feet . . .

That sunshine! On the drapes and carpet . . . like golden dawn on the Rockies with graceful eagles soaring over crags and forest. It had been so long he could hardly recall how they looked in an Alberta morning. A lifetime away. Even his accent had changed. The army had seen to that! A British Colonel should not talk like a Canadian farm boy.

'Drinks ready, sir.'

He ceased his pacing. 'Excellent, James. They should be here very soon . . . '

In a way, Hart was glad they'd arrived together. His memory must be slipping, he thought. Why hadn't he suggested a pre-gathering drink in their old pub off Marble Arch? They had not failed to capitalise on a full-dress march down memory lane. But, perhaps it was better they renew their particular camaraderie before confronting him. A commanding officer was not a man one invited to a celebration party. Not even one as close to them as he had been!

'See any changes in us, Colonel?' Frank Sommers asked.

They were comfortably seated in the lounge and James was already handing out the prepared drinks. Looking from face to face, Hart wondered how he should reply. They had all altered. As he had, too. Dare he tell this one, or that, how unkindly the passing decades had treated them?

'Bloody hell!' Bob Thomson tasted his drink a second time, glanced at James with admiration in his eyes. 'You old so-and-so. You got it right first time!'

James smiled happily. He watched each sample his or her drink and saw the pleased expressions when his 'prescription' met with approval. Only Hart's glass contained a different mixture from the one he used to drink. Lime and soda now liquor was out according to the doctor's latest pronouncement.

'To Hart's Heroes!'

The colonel felt pride wash over him as Mai Bedford lifted her glass high. It was a distinctive appellation - like Flying Tigers and Desert Rats. But for sheer guts and courage none of those others could begin to match a Hartsman, or Hartswoman as they had fondly been called in those final days of Europe's torment. These were the backbone Britain and the Free World had needed when dark hours clouded the horizon. They had been a strange mixture of bravery, nervelessness, patriotic neurotic so vital in that ancient game called espionage.

'Come on, Colonel,' Frank begged. 'Tell us how we've aged!'

Hart nodded grimly, adjusted his gold-rimmed spectacles. They would not appreciate platitudes from him. So . . . 'I'll leave the ladies until last,' Hart bowed slightly to Claire and Mai. 'You've all put on weight. You're slower, less frivolous, inclined to treat our gathering as a social occasion instead of asking my reasons for calling you here. That shows a falling-off process in your inquisitiveness. I'd imagine all of you were content with the present, recalling other days with unease. Mai - you haven't changed much but there are signs of frustration. Claire surprises me. Not an ounce extra and the same sleekly dangerous excitement burning in those green eyes. After that, I think I was wrong getting us together.' He sighed.

'Department Seven was about to reform?'

James glanced warily at Rolande Aubin. The Frenchman had no sense of humour and his face expressed distrust for Hart's grandiose scheme - if he was right in assuming that was the plan. For the ex-batman, Aubin presented an enigma. He had never understood what made the French patriot tick. Killing Germans had been an accepted aim of all underground fighters but Aubin's hatreds for Germany went deep. Too deep for even Hart to unearth.

'I had considered the possibility - unofficially, of course,' Hart admitted.

'And why not?' Thomson asked. He was the playboy; a lover of fast cars, sensuous women, adventure.

'I can see we are too old for what I had in mind.'

Konrad Bluther rolled his eyes and adjusted his fat frame within the confines of a rather cramped wing-chair. 'Nein, Herr Colonel - not old. Smug, complacent, inactive perhaps. But not old.'

From his corner seat, Eric Nimmo asked, 'What was the plan, sir?'

Hart thanked the heavy-set man with a glance. Clearing his throat he concentrated on James - the dependable James; the mirror of all their combined emotions, feelings, fears. 'Like me, I'm sure you all detest what is happening to this generation. Students paying more attention to political affairs than their education. Young people claiming in court that their vocation is professional demonstrator. Others engaged in creating disturbances because some silly ideology says that we, the democratic capitalistic nations, are decadent. I have never glorified war nor the supreme sacrifices our department made to uphold the dignity of mankind as a whole. I deplore violence for violence's sake. I have a horror of global conflict as a solution to international differences. I engaged in espionage because I knew where my duty lay - because I honestly believe in freedom under a duly elected government. Not mob rule. Not having a man shouted down simply because his views are not our views. I have examined every article, every speech, every individual I could connect with this modern trend towards anarchy. My findings are shocking . . . '

'May I interrupt, Colonel?' Mai Bedford leant forward. Small and fragile looking, she did not convey outwardly the strength that had brought her through some terrible, dangerous escapades. She was a Dresden doll - dainty, immaculately dressed, more immaculately formed. Her neckline hung loose to reveal her small, perfect breasts.

'My God! She's still showing 'em,' Frank grinned.

Hart glared as Mai laughed lightly. She didn't mind her wartime comrades joking about her ability to reveal more than decency called normal. Her sexuality had won many a battle; destroyed many a tough German officer's determination not to disclose secrets.

'If we have heard the last comment you may proceed, Mai,' Hart growled.

'I only wanted to make a guess at what you've discovered, Colonel. The reason we're here is because you believe there is global plot against democracy and that these uprisings and demonstrations are master-minded from Moscow. Am I right?'

Hart stared at his former agents one by one. He was proud of Mai - and them. Not one dissenting expression showed in the room. 'True, Mai,' he said softly. 'I swear that a pattern exists!'

'I'm of the same opinion,' the woman remarked. 'I have teenage children . . . '

'You've what?' Frank asked startled.

'Did you expect me to remain single all my life, Frank?'

'No - but . . . '

Hart's mind clicked into high-gear. Suddenly, he saw hope! His voice held that mystic quality of enthusiasm they all remembered from the Forties. Each had reason to remember, too. More than one mission had been undertaken only because Colonel Brett Hart had made it *sound* right.

'How many of you are married with teenage children?' he asked.

'I have a daughter aged sixteen,' Claire Porter said, 'And my name is now Gresham.' She smiled mysteriously across at Bob Thomson as if to cancel out an old affair.

'Unmarried. Free, white, twenty-one plus,' Bob grinned.

'Two sons - 14 and 18,' Sommers cut in.

'I have a beautiful daughter called Nanette. She's nineteen,' Aubin informed them.

'My son is twenty-three,' Bluther said.

Nimmo frowned, added the data, 'Son Joseph, aged twenty.'

Hart rubbed his hands together gleefully. 'My boy Tim is twenty-two. How old are your children, Mai?'

'Tom is 18 and Wanda is 19. I'm Mrs Collins - not Mai Bedford.'

'You know,' Hart remarked sagely, 'we were the old brigade. This is a problem for young people to face. I propose we call ourselves "Network Forty" as that was the era in which we found companionship. Our children are "Network Seventy", their age of sanity. If there are no objections I would like the remainder of our stay to be pleasant, social. I suggest we bring the children here a week from today and ask them if they will be guided by us . . . '

'From the States?' Frank asked with mild astonishment.

'I'm sure an expenses paid visit to Britain would not be refused,' the colonel replied hurriedly. 'The same applies for Rolande and Konrad. If anyone else requires assistance . . . ?'

'I'll buy my tickets myself,' Mai laughed.

Nimmo came to his feet, marched into the centre of their loose circle. His face reflected apprehension. 'I have nothing against personal involvement but I strongly object to my son getting mixed up with what we fought to destroy.'

Claire clapped her hands excitedly. 'I was waiting for this, Eric,' and she spoke directly to Nimmo. 'If I am correct our children will possess the same spirit of adventure that guided us when we were their ages. My Gloria is a tomboy, full of fun; ready to tackle anything providing it has spice, danger. Why don't we invite the kids, present them with a straight proposition and let them make the final decisions? We could offer our experience as a guideline for them to follow. We could stay in the background in case they get in over their heads.'

Nimmo shrugged his defeat. 'Joseph and I shall be present. No influence from me - he makes his decision for himself. But I warn you, Joseph is headstrong and - ', he made them wait, 'quite addicted to demonstrations as a means to his end.'

CHAPTER TWO

'I don't like it, dad. We're playing with fire trying to make pigs smell like roses. Joe Nimmo isn't in the least interested in proving that student unrest and the youth revolution are Moscow inspired. He's one of *them* - an enemy.'

Brett Hart inhaled menthol smoke. For a sixty a day cigarette man he found the cooling menthol caused less cough, less comment from his doctor. Death, at seventy-two, did not worry him. But he had this one job to finish and he did consider medical instructions as vital for the completion of the work. His qualifications did not include a detailed study of the human anatomy, clinically speaking. Female figures had been his subject when he was Tim's age - and for years afterwards. But that study had been directed by biological urges, not the curative nor the diagnostic. And so he smoked *Everest* and prayed nothing else would limit his span until Network Seventy had uncovered their enemy - youth's enemy!

'Dad, suggest something,' Tim pleaded. 'This isn't my forte. I'm not a secret service ace. I've been trained for the diplomatic corps - not a subversive.'

Looking at his son, Hart found the young man a carbon copy of himself at age twenty-two. There was that same long, tapering nose, those grey eyes and the hairline already starting to recede. Tim was six-one - as he had been then. And strong as a virile bull. He smiled to himself. How he'd showed the girls his virility during the war. The First War! There had been precious few French girls who hadn't experienced a sample of Brett Hart's passion. He supposed Tim was no different. The boy was handsome, charming, dipped in the mould that screamed 'sexy' to young girls.

'Joseph Nimmo's father is a friend of mine, Tim. I'd hate to lose that friendship now. I do not disagree with you, boy. Young Nimmo is too far gone to be brought back. But humour him. Give him minor assignments. Let him work alone - as his father did. Ask for reports. See how biased he really is. Don't keep him informed unless it has to do with a particular task he is supposed to handle. Make absolutely sure he can't get information from your squad and, above all else, treat him sympathetically. Let him attempt to indoctrinate you - not the reverse.'

Tim Hart relaxed. He had been thrown in against his better judgement. He hadn't known what was expected of him when he had attended the 'gathering' that week. None of the youngsters had. But, with parental glee they had all volunteered - all except Joseph Nimmo. Now, Tim found himself commanding a secret organisation code-named Network Seventy - an illegally formed counter-revolution group dedicated to principles youth totally disapproved of. He felt as if he was betraying his generation. And, regardless of the logic put forward by his father and Mrs Collins he was unprepared to accept the tenet that Moscow had inspired the post-war population to reject their parental guidance. He preferred to believe that youth had rebelled against policies that were outdated, no longer capable of holding water under modern circumstances.

'What if we - you and the older members of the Network are wrong?' Tim asked.

'I hope to God we are,' Hart replied sincerely. 'I'd hate to think that we fought for a wrong cause during the war.'

Tim smiled generously. 'Not you, dad. Your cause is always just. You know, the only reason I accepted this bloody job is because I have never found you, as a person or father, to be less than scrupulously fair.'

'For that, Tim, I thank you.'

'No thanks to me, dad. It's your code. And I'm bloody glad! Most kids fear their fathers or think of them as ordinary people. I'm unique,' and he grinned. 'I can honestly point to you with deep-down pride and truthfully state: "My dad's the best man in the country".'

Hart grunted, stubbed his cigarette in an ashtray. Getting to his feet he smiled wearily, avoiding meeting Tim's proud gaze. 'I'm going to bed, son. Think about Joseph Nimmo. Don't let him spoil the organisation. One rotten apple - and all that.'

'Good-night, dad. I'll take your advice. That's why we have you old geezers behind us, isn't it?'

Hart hid his feelings in an artificial yawn. He glowed. He wondered why the world was in such a state when there were young men like Tim in it. God, how good it made a man feel when he could think of his son, or daughter, as a chip off the old block!

Stanley Edmond sat in his hotel room listening to the sounds of Los Angeles rippling past the continuous crackle of a neon sign. Lights flashed, blanked out, flashed anew. The vibrating colours reminded him of strobe-lights in some junkie haven along Venice. The glare hurt his eyes and he slipped Polaroid's on to combat the steady flick-flick, click-click of the changing neon. He could have stayed in a select hotel far from the hustle-bustle of this weird, demented city. He could have paid a fortune for Beverly Hills privacy. But he hadn't. He never did. His expense account was meticulously balanced - always correct. Not once had he ever spent a dime more than was necessary to provide bed, shelter, a place to hang his hat.

According to his passport, Stanley Edmond was forty-three, Canadian born of émigré Russian parents who had, by deed poll, changed their name. He looked like a youthful nineteen especially when garbed in student clothing. Tonight, after seventeen hours aloft and a fifteen thousand mile journey safely behind him, he was far from youthful looking. He was beat. Sick of having his life dictated by faceless men seated in a top-secret room behind guarded doors.

The wail of a police car - or ambulance - disturbed his reverie. He swore - in Russian. A not unnatural expletive for the son of Russian parents!

Climbing from the sagging bed he undressed to the buff. Carefully, he hung his clothes where no contact was made with furnishings. He had been in a flea-bag before. Baltimore to be precise. If he was going to have bed-bugs for company he preferred them to attack his flesh, be washed away in the morning and to know that his clothes were free of their biting presence. *For two dollars fifty what more could a man expect*, he thought.

Throwing the bedclothes back he examined the sheets. Not a stain; not a sign of nocturnal predators. He'd been lucky. This joint was one of the clean pads in town.

Hands behind his head, he stared at the dancing patterns thrown on the ceiling. They reminded him of what had been, was now, would ever be until . . .

He mentally shuddered. Exposure was an intolerable conjecture. His 'cover' would stand the stiffest investigation. Human rights covered a huge field of endeavour and the 'foundation' paying his salary was recognised for its work in promoting brotherhood. His masters had been vigilant. Nobody could connect International Studies with Moscow-dominated enslavement.

A sudden repulsive thought struck him. He'd been guilty of democratic thinking. Enslavement was not a word he was expected to use when referring to the 'foundation'. Nor was it a word a *loyal* socialist agent would dare consider, let alone voice. Even mentally!

Was he falling victim to the insidious propaganda of the West! Had he swallowed too many clichés for his Soviet soul to digest?

He couldn't sleep. His body ached for release from this seventeen-hour torment. Yet, he was incapable of closing his eyes and passing beyond the barrier of thought . . .

He remembered Moscow . . .

That fateful day back in 1949 . . .

Moscow was having its best Spring day for decades. People walked the streets of Leningrad, Kiev, Odessa unaware that the capital was enjoying sunshine. Outside the Kremlin overcoated Red Guards patrolled conscious of the heat, the officers who kept them clad in heavy uniforms when, instead, they should have been attired in lighter-weight jackets.

He had been in the third limousine to park outside Commissar Gregorov's office. The others - those carrying V.I.P's had continued on to the Kremlin doors themselves. But not the likes of him - not a mere Ivan; a soldier called lgor Gruginshof.

There had been wonderment when he entered a famous hall with its magnificent murals, its artistic ceilings and crystal chandeliers. He had sat wide-eyed, stupefied as the elite of Soviet Russia had given their speeches, their welcomes, their blessings to a project dedicated to intrigue, subversion, the overthrow of tyranny. He had believed it all that day. That simple day when the sun shone brightly and Mother Russia seemed kissed by the Unknown's love.

It hadn't been until after the gathering had dismissed he discovered what his mission was to be. Commissar Yushilo had wasted neither time nor words. His briefing had been brevity itself. 'Comrade Gruginshof, the Supreme Soviet have decided to make you their instrument of total destruction . . . '

He had listened to the tirade against a Western Alliance that had supplied arms and equipment for hard-pressed Soviet forces with less understanding than a sparrow has when a cat jumps upon it. His teaching had warned him how decadent the West really was; how Mother Russia could not trust any powers but herself. He had been brainwashed into accepting communism as the only true ideology, even although the undemocratic West had been forced to help save his native land by running in supplies. But that, his teacher had smugly explained, was not because they wanted to help Russia. They wanted Russian blood staining the Steppes, the Ukraine, Moscow's doorway but not beyond a certain degree. They wanted Hitler exterminated and then, after they had regained strength, they would turn their hatred against Stalin's domain.

When the ranting had ceased he had been sent immediately to a special school. He already spoke fluent English. Now he was taught how to pronounce words with a Canadian accent. He was indoctrinated with capitalistic slogans, taught how to overcome every argument with logical lies proclaiming communism as the natural order of humanity. He got a political background that few trade unionists in Britain, Canada, America ever had. He could name the leaders of Free World unions, their secretaries, their functions and the men pitted against them in management, government. He was perfectly attuned to the difficulties of youth, too. How young men and women were underpaid when studying; how university staffs obeyed dictates handed down through the ages; how their masters acted in accordance with Establishment orders. He got to know the several student malcontents already working for his KGB unit and was trained in the use of home-made bombs, how to fight civilian police with cobblestones and use arson to gain an initiative.

Fifteen weeks later, private Igor Gruginshof ceased to exist. In his place stood Stanley Edmond, Canadian citizen - man with a mission.

Angrily, Edmond got to his feet and tried for the third time to draw the flimsy curtains across his hotel window. They were rotten and tore in his hands. He swore, strode back to his bed. Throwing himself across the bed he fought to erase the sounds from this demented city with its way-out ideas, its immorality, its ghostly memories of halcyon days when famous stars roamed the celluloid jungle demanding, and getting, special treatment. He twisted and turned, tormented with what he had to do. The years had drastically altered his concept of right and wrong, of the ideological conflict between two systems that - on close examination - presented little different for the common people.

Slowly, physical weariness overcame him . . .

His mind still roiled; his displeasure with the tasks he was supposed to accomplish still bothered him; his frustration mounted . . .

But the need for sleep swallowed all thought, all desire to see a path that was pure, humane . . .

CHAPTER THREE

NETWORK SEVENTY, had a decided advantage over most 'committees' formed by student bodies. It had the backing of experienced masters in the various forms of sabotage, intrigue, infiltration. Its members were tutored by experts who knew intimately the characters, frustrations, ambitions of their pupils. Parents were not always the best teachers but for Network Seventy's role there was no mistaking the value of a father's, or mother's, instruction.

Tim Hart fully understood the necessity of having a meeting place classified 'beyond suspicion'. It was his request that the unmarried Bob Thomson should supply that venue.

'My God, you're not actually suggesting I turn my nightclub into a drug-addicts' den, are you?'

Looking at the exotic club Tim felt like telling his father's friend that he was already the owner of a 'dive' - a haven for Establishment degenerates. He didn't. He used the diplomacy his father had used when 'conning' his agents to undertake an onerous assignment. 'You're a smart businessman, Bob. You know the way your clients dress. Well, we won't seem any different. Maybe one or two *friends* we bring will be loud mouths but your staff can soon dispose of them. That would heighten the innocence of where we congregate.'

Bob uncoiled his tall frame and flashed his mysterious signet ring with its entwined B-M motif. Nobody quite knew who the 'M' was, or had been, although Colonel Hart suspected that Bob wore the damned thing for vanity reasons unconnected with a serious affair. 'Tim - I want to help the kids. I honestly do.'

'Then let us use the club.'

'Isn't there a coffee joint where you could meet?'

'Name one where we could discuss plans in private!'

Bob grunted, signalled his barman to pour fresh drinks. Although the club was closed during the day certain members of the large staff were paid to report early. Bob had a thing about his club - it must always appear freshly cleaned, smelling of pine soap and air-freshener. 'Okay - so you operate from here. That's agreed!'

Tim grinned, finished his *Skol* lager. The difference in ages between them was not so apparent. Bob had preserved his vitality to a remarkable degree. Those cool, blue eyes had a devilish sparkle to captivate women; his handsome features accentuated by blond hair that had a groomed casualness a certain breed of upper class female found exciting, adventurous.

'But a warning, young Hart - don't get the idea your old man can apply screws to make me hop through hoops. Those days are gone. *Kaput! Finis!*'

'I'll bet,' Tim said solemnly, 'you'd leap at any chance dad offered. In fact,' and he affected a thoughtful expression, 'I was toying with a proposition to do with this investigation.'

Thomson tensed. Whatever he said made no difference to how he felt inside. He *knew* that danger was the tonic his ageing body and mind needed. He hated to think of himself as a playboy - and nothing else. The war had effected him more than he cared to broadcast. Excitement, living on nerves, watching every corner for a hidden danger had left its indelible mark. That was why he drove fast cars, preferred sleek women, high living. He stuck his neck out in business, in those trips to a Continental casino, in visiting French and Italian bistros known to cater for criminals. His refusal to make the 'Candelabra Club' Tim's happy hunting ground had not been influenced by any fear of teenage, hippy-style invasion. He had always been able to take care of himself, his property, his affairs. He had been loath to *see* others inviting, courting disaster knowing that he, aged, was exempt from partaking in the mission.

'Some of our girls would consider you a dreamy customer,' Tim grinned. 'They're hot little bits eager to climb into bed with any man they reckoned was extraordinary, capable of stimulating orgasm.'

'My God - not you, too?'

Tim relaxed, sipped his fresh *Skol*. 'What prompts that cryptic remark?'

Thomson shrugged, signed the barman's chit. He insisted on this for every drink served outside legal hours. It helped keep 'bent' help from dispensing free shots, beers during the evening. Also, he regularly tested the specific gravity of bottles. He had experience of the North American habit of using a hypo-needle to syphon-off whiskey and squirt in water. When the barman departed Bob tasted his drink, nodded to himself, said, 'Nothing, Tim. I was idly recalling some of the escapades your father asked me to do.'

'And that's precisely why I mentioned it,' Tim smiled.

'Like father - like son, eh?'

'You could say that! I wouldn't. Dad is a stick-in-the-mud. He still remembers the Empire. He's a native-born Canadian, you know.'

'I do! And I was very proud to serve under him. Your father Tim, had more guts than a regiment of the line. He never once tried to disguise his Canadian background. He spoke like an English officer and gentleman but he felt we should all know where he was born. He didn't try to defend his birthplace. He just wanted his subordinates to understand that he thought quite differently from us. And, whether or not you agree, Canadians are not misplaced Britishers. Nor are they American. They have a nationality of their own; a definite thinking process that touches on old links, new frontiers whilst keeping a separate, positive path.'

'Which means?' Tim egged.

'Your father loved the idea of a British Empire. He could not foresee the changes coming after the war. He stuck with Australia, New Zealand, South Africa, Rhodesia, Newfoundland, Canada as the mainstay of colonialisation.'

'Quite so! And now?' Tim asked sarcastically.

Bob drummed fingers on the table. 'I sometimes wish there had been more men like your dad!' He scowled, sipped his drink. 'I'm not anti-this-or-that. I'm a believer in freedom for all. But I remember comrades who fell during that so-called war to end wars. Men from Cape Town, Durban, Bulawayo, Salisbury. They volunteered to defend Britain. Now look where they are - outside the Commonwealth; ostracised because they dare uphold the British belief that conquest is right - that those who brought wealth, industry, stability to tribal communities are entitled to govern according to their local light.'

'Do you operate a colour-bar in this club?' Tim asked tightly.

'No! And don't paint me with a socialist brush, son. I invested the money I made fighting for England in this club. I have other wealth but this place is paid for by sweat, blood, tears. I refuse to entertain unions because I risked my cash and no bloody miner's son is going to tell me how to manage my affairs. I refuse to listen to what a Race Relations Board official says I must, or must not, do. I'm still a free man. This is my castle. I admit those with whom I feel inclined to associate. Nobody else. The colour of a man's skin doesn't interest me. But his politics do. If somebody couldn't feel Britain was worth fighting for I

27

don't want him here. If an African wishes to call white Britishers names that's his privilege - but he can make his point in Hyde Park, not on my premises.'

Tim Hart got to his feet. 'You're prejudiced,' he accused.

'No, son - I'm me! That's the important point we all fail to see. Me - I - you. Each man is entitled to his viewpoint. If a new immigrant feels inclined to complain then that is his choice. If I, as an individual, refuse to associate with strangers that is my choice. We don't need laws in Britain to tell us with whom we must, or must not, associate. We are free men - or were until government decreed that a minority had the right to dictate to their elected majority.'

'That's an Enoch viewpoint,' the young man declared.

'Yes - and no, son. I don't hold with white is best, black is evil. But I do believe that British is British - not a melting pot conglomeration of nationalities, creeds, races, colours. I have seen what happens when white and black Americans are in the same base area. Fights, slaughter, antagonism that fetches its fetishisms into our standard of living. I don't like seeing this ancient, peaceful kingdom turned into a colour-battleground.'

'Peaceful?' Tim laughed scornfully. 'We've had nothing but war within these British Isles since time memorable. Saxons, Normans, Romans, Picts, Welsh, Irish, Danes and Vikings - they've all had a go and been demolished or digested.'

'And what colour have our invaders been?' Bob asked belligerently.

Tim mused thoughtfully, 'White! I see what you're getting at but I disbelieve your reason.'

'Ah, ask the man in the street. Ask him, too, what he thinks about the Common Market deal. He'll tell you - keep blacks out, stick to our own kind. No Afro-Asian integration; no European union that lets a million Italians swarm after British jobs. Sorry, Tim - you and I must agree to disagree. I'm not your generation. I sympathise but I'm not going to alter. I'm me - and to bloody hell with those who would push their modern ideals down my throat.'

'Mind, if I excuse myself ?' Tim replied.

'Not at all, son.' Bob laughed. 'Don't go away mad - just go away! That's what you youngsters say, isn't it?'

Tim grinned, waved aside his own feelings. 'Sorry, Bob. We don't particularly care for our *elders*,' and he stressed the word with a sarcasm Bob tasted, 'spouting off on old-fashioned, unbrotherly sentiments. We've seen what war can do. And we don't bloody care to have our generation wiped out by a missile barrage.'

'Who the hell does?' Bob growled.

'No sane person, admittedly. But what you people forget is that African and Asian nations could develop the bomb. If they hate us,' and he shrugged, 'then, by God, we've got more troubles than any between Uncle Sam and Uncle Joe's new boys.'

'Tell me, Tim - how the hell are you going to carry out this assignment when you're in sympathy with those your dad has ear-marked for ridicule?'

Leaning back, smugly confident, Tim replied: 'Easy. I'm organising the kids to investigate the *possibility* of an undercover plot to disrupt youth's thinking. I'm not saying such is the case. I'm free of preconceived notions. I'm doing a job as any policeman would - collect evidence, present the facts and let a jury be the judge.'

Bob nodded his approval. 'Nice thinking, Tim. Okay - use this place for your meetings. Introduce some of your sizzling little minxes to me if you can't handle 'em. Maybe I can convince their mini-skirted mentalities their ideals are crazy.'

'You've got some hope!' Tim laughed. 'It wouldn't surprise me that after a few sessions in the hay you changed. Those girls have more than brains. They've got sex with a capital "S" - much better operatives than your wartime women had.'

'Hark at Hart!' Bob laughed back. 'You weren't around then, Tim - but those so-called outdated dames we hustled into a hotel were the hottest creatures on two legs. They knew we were "danger men". They expected that night to be the last - and they gave their all. But all, man!' He sighed, memories flooding back.

Tim didn't stop to argue. He could have told Bob that the modern girl gave more than her all; she gave herself in a 'pot' rush, drifting on an emotional tide that turned solid, respectable lovers into fluid excitement devoid of artificiality, social taboos. The oldest thrill had lost none of its ancient 'goodness' but it sure had taken a new slant; a new bliss in equal sharing. That was the major difference. Girls didn't wait to be satisfied. They shared, they insisted, they invented to capture every last dreg of sensation. And God help the man unwilling to follow their lead . . .

'See you around, Bob. Don't wait for the world falling apart. We won't let it!'

As Tim reached the exit, Thomson called: 'Ask Finian what to do, son - just follow the dream. Your dad's dream . . .'

CHAPTER FOUR

'MAX, these pigs goddamned nearly tagged me!'

'Cool it, Cy!'

Cy studied the newcomer with a critical gaze. He wasn't seeing too clearly but the guy didn't appear to represent a threat. Fuzz never looked like this! 'Shit! He ain't a pig,' he yelled, gesturing to Tim Hart, making room at their table. Get involved, fella. Here . . . ' and he patted a cosy cushion by his side.

'I'm splitting!' The one who had ordered Cy to cool it climbed unsteadily to his feet, stuck a joint in his slack mouth and weaved dreamily towards the exit. He was a tall, gangling lad with shoulder-length red hair, a straggling Van Dyke, a huge nose and narrowish eyes. In his hand-painted Levis, T-shirt and sandals he looked every inch what he hoped people would take him for - a hippy-orientated student. It didn't give a damn he carried I.D. stating he was twenty-six, married with five kids, and was currently employed as a caterer for a minor studio. He belonged with 'loose' guys. The up-tight world he daily strove to serve didn't interest him. It provided bread, a pad, the dough to buy what he wanted. Nothing more.

'Get your ass back here, Chick!' Cy glared, waggled a disjointed finger at his retreating buddy. 'I ain't about to integrate alone!'

Chick hesitated. Cy and he had shared many a scene. They'd this thing between them - a deeper regard for personalities than a guy even felt for some doll.

Tim could sense the dark, tense atmosphere in the corner. He had given himself the hardest chore of all - infiltrating the California 'chapter'. Whatever California did today - so the saying went - the world did tomorrow. And they weren't far wrong when it came to the youth revolution. He didn't buy those key-club happenings, the Manson kicks, the cults, the swaps between frustrated nine-to-five jokers peddling talents for some big concern. He bought Berkeley, UCLA and generalised episodes that resulted in Watts and similar blow-ups

'Man, you're stubborn,' Cy admonished as Chick still menaced the exit door.

'Fuckin' right, pal!' Chick swung back to face them. His lax features spoke of the extent of his kick. 'Who is this bastard?' His finger jabbed air in Tim's direction.

'You'd call me a Limey,' Tim replied forthrightly. 'My father's a Canuck, my mother was Irish.'

'Sounds Limey,' Cy ventured.

Chick returned to the table. None of the forty or so habitués of their hangout seemed to notice anything unusual. In the smoke-hazed room it was a feat to distinguish abnormalities. A corner couple were feverishly groping under loose robes; beaded girls were engaged in an anatomical painting lesson of the naked body of a 'tripping' fifteen year-old; two solemn young men were wrestling with a chess problem; four coloured kids angrily discussed the merits of a Mexican girl's poetry as she read for a disinterested audience; a boy sat strumming a mournful melody on a battered guitar; two girls lay on their backs, naked young bodies glistening under a thick oil coating as they studied the interchange of lights high in the smog wrapped ceiling; and, as if cut off from humanity, a couple copulated under a table that bounced to the rhythm of their exertions.

Cy banged an ebony hand on their table. 'What's your name, Limey?'

'Tim Hart.'

'Okay, Tim - how come you're in L.A.?'

'If you want to know,' Tim grinned, relishing the amazement he reckoned would follow his announcement, 'I'm here to prove that you kids are suckers for a world conspiracy masterminded by a foreign power.'

'Oh, Christ - spare us!' Chick moaned.

The coloured youth grinned with his Pepsodent white teeth. 'Man, you're way out, Tim.'

'Am I?'

The noise from the copulating couple had reached crescendo. Gasps, grunts, bangings wetly melded to fleshily inspired squelches erupted from under their table. Chick glanced at them, swore, kicked a cushion in their direction and turned his mind back to Tim.

'Look, it's like this, man . . . ' Cy gave his attention to the furious final throes of lust as he spoke. 'Every sonofabitch screaming against our freedom to do as we goddamned like has this fuckin' commie link going for him! It's dead, D-E-A-D! 'Cause we don't dig war and don't wanna be like our folks don't make us pushovers for a Red plot. Those Russian kids are doing the same as us - trying to bust loose. And nobody can tell me they're being primed by Kremlin bossmen!' He rubbed his hands gleefully, hollered: 'Don't let her get away, bud . . . keep it going!'

Tim covered his embarrassment. He'd been to a few wild Mayfair parties where fornication had just happened naturally from an overdose

31

of pot or alcohol. Sex wasn't something private and modest for him although he personally preferred to mate behind doors. But he did not enjoy having Cy shout encouragements and offer suggestions when the copulating youth apparently had mastered his partner's erotic urges.

'Mind if I say a few words?'

Tim smiled to the girl who had been squatting to one side of Cy. She was very young - he gave her sixteen at most and probably two years less - and wore the standard costume of her associates; long, loose dress to her ankles that could not hide budding maturity, and a Navajo belt with beads draped round her neck. A huge silver medallion swung from a chain, its Mexican motif catching and distributing light in shooting glints. She had jet-black hair - long to her waist and uncombed - with a pert, cupid's face and the minimum of make-up.

'Go ahead - it's a free country,' Tim replied, capitalising on American youth's phraseology.

'Cy hasn't covered all the points but he's an inarticulate bastard anyway!' She smiled dreamily at the frowning Cy. 'First, though - are you a pig?'

'No, I'm not!'

'A newspaper reporter?'

'Nope! Not that, either.'

'What then?'

Tim considered his reply with lightning mental gymnastics. He had come into the open to a degree. He didn't want his mission to fail but neither did he intend letting word of Network Seventy's investigation spread to Europe, Africa, South America, Asia, Australia. He was aware that students kept each other informed. This alone had worried him. It seemed to confirm his father's opinion that a top-secret outfit existed to correlate data. But, on thorough checks he had unearthed what was, for him, a plausible explanation - students out of step with the Establishment were as entitled to form a world governing body to pass along information as the international agencies were. He cursed his initial revelation and devised a cover.

'I'm an author. Or I hope to be.'

The girl examined his eyes as he spoke. She seemed satisfied. 'Your father has money, eh?'

'Enough,' Tim laughed.

'So has mine. More than sufficient. Would you believe me if I said I'd been educated in private schools and still have a tutor?'

'I might.'

She extended a slender hand, showed him a massive diamond ring. 'That was for my fourteenth birthday. Daddy is very generous but not tolerant.' She sulked momentarily. Recovering her equilibrium she affected a 'black sheep' frown. 'I hate my tutor. He's a beast. All hands and excuses when he can't make it. He got me going but I cut loose. Shook him off fast for these stupid creeps.' She stroked Cy's shoulder proving that she liked creeps better than uptights and maulers.

The coloured youth brushed her hand away. 'Goddammit, Syl - try Chick!'

Chick was far from interested. He reclined on his cushion, eyes tight shut, a blissful expression on his face as he crooned a dirge to some folk-hero. A joint slowly burned down to his fingers - pain unheeded, unfelt.

'See what I mean?' the girl smiled distantly.

Tim nodded. The copulating duo had finished their 'thing' and lay separated under Cy's bright, admiring gaze. The female kept staring at Cy as if she was unable to comprehend that her thrills had reached their ultimate conclusion. It was as though she were encouraging Cy to continue the fleshy delights.

'Look at him,' the girl said, indicating Cy with a sympathetic gesture. 'He's got her impregnated already. Soon, he won't have the strength to refuse and he'll jump into the saddle. He's like that - a horny bastard!' She shifted position until Cy was a sensation near her, not an attraction. 'You don't wanna mess with us,' she told Tim solemnly. 'Get lost! Get back to England. Things there are more organised.'

'We've got scenes going there, too,' Tim warned lightly.

'Yeah, sure! I've been in London. My tutor thought a world cruise would broaden me. It did - underneath him!'

'What age were you?'

Her face contorted with the difficult question of counting back. 'Thirteen, I guess. You know the old saying - if you're big enough, you're old enough! I was big okay - thanks to my tutor's perverted sense of loyalty to my old man. He used to tell me how daddy wanted me to be a worldly woman. By God - he got more than he bargained for.'

Tim wanted to yell his lungs out. Sex was sex was sex. He had nothing against young couples experimenting when the urge was strong. But this tale sickened him. He could have killed the tutor with bare hands for what had been done in the name of *education*.

'I'm sorry . . . '

The girl laughed bitterly. 'Sorry? That's wrong, man. You're out-dated expressing trite sympathies. You should be saying "terrific" and trying to strip me.'

'I might if . . . '

'If you're encouraged?'

Tim nodded.

'The English!' She opened an Indian purse, took a joint and lit it. Her eyes got dreamy. 'I'm a knock-over for these,' she confessed. 'One puff and I'm ripe, man. But ripe!' She raced her eyes up and down his body. 'You could be exciting, Tim.'

'I could be if I had accomplished what I'd set out to do,' he reminded her.

Cy growled. 'Screw her, Tim. She's yours. Me - I'm gonna split!' He began unbuttoning himself, crawling across to the partly naked female whose eyes had never once left his since completing her disintegration of her first partner.

Tim was mildly surprised that Cy had been conscious of the conversation. He had thought the coloured youth was too engaged in mental telepathy with the semi-depleted female to bother with their chit-chat. He wasn't surprised, though, to see Cy cover the girl with his virile body and make the preliminary plays so vital to complete conquest.

'Goddam that coon!'

Tim grinned automatically as the girl, Syl, got to her feet and glared at Cy.

'Let's blow this den,' she snapped. 'I've got an apartment.' Her eyes focused on Tim. 'Want me?'

'If I said no?'

She shrugged casually. 'There are lots of guys.' She walked away, not in the least deterred by Tim's hesitation. Like she said - there were lots of guys. In Los Angeles there were always men. All sorts . . .

She lived high above street-level and the apartment had cost somebody plenty. It was furnished in modern style with little attention to decor. Some of the walls were outrageously hued, the paintings hung at crazy angles a complete mixture of Old Masters and neurotic moderns. Underwear littered the deep pile carpet seeming to shout that the owner was confused, muddled, frustrated, without volition.

'If it's pot there's a supply in that humidor. If you prefer liquor there's some in that cabinet. And if you're straight - go home!' She flung herself along an outsized divan, dared him to make a decision.

Tim walked to the liquor cabinet, poured a generous Scotch. 'Want one?' he asked without looking at her. He opened a ginger, added a measured quantity.

'No thanks. I'm a drag. I only drink tonic.'

He sampled his drink, nodded approval. She was waiting for him when he approached the divan. Clothes he remembered her wearing at the hangout now rested untidily on top of other discarded apparel. Her nudity only heightened her youthfulness - the blush of adolescence firmly etched on her small, growing breasts. The Mexican medallion still hung round her neck, its shimmering circle resting on her navel.

'Don't mind me, Tim. I'm over-anxious, I know.'

He sat beside her, conscious of her thighs edging slightly open as she rolled partially on one side to face him. 'What's bugging you, Syl? You're compensating for some deficiency or else there's a gear missing.'

'Gear missing?'

'Low - you can't proceed at a steady pace. You've got to rush and get it over with before conscience stops you.'

A single tear trickled down one cheek. 'You're a louse! Don't analyse - just do!'

'Not yet, baby . . . '

'God, you're way off beam. Haven't you Limey's got hep to our scene? Baby dates you, Tim!'

'Sorry!' He grinned, finished his drink, climbed to his feet.

'Another? Am I that bad?'

He studied her nakedness. She was pretty good when taken in comparison with some Mayfair birds he'd had the dubious privilege of making. Somehow, when viewed with sex in mind she didn't appear that young. Everything was there - where it should be. Everything - including a forest that should have been soft, curling down.

'So?' Her body twisted, on its back now with arms up, knees bent, thighs parted.

'So you were telling me Cy hadn't covered every point . . . '

Her hands moved up, down, up her nudity. 'I haven't covered a goddamned bit of me,' she complained.

'True!' came his admiring reply.

'Shit!' She closed her thighs, sat erect. 'Am I just all encyclopaedia to consult before plotting a book?'

'If you were, Syl . . . ' He found the same bottle of Scotch, poured a hefty measure . . . I'd thumb a lot more pages than I normally do.' He added ginger, carefully again, turned and walked through yesterday's underwear to her side. 'Listen to me, Syl - I'm not a virgin. I'm experienced with what we British call "dolly-birds". They're a set a shade lower than a snake's belly but with wealthy parents. They inhabit plush nightclubs and seduce anything wearing pants - the cruder the man the better they enjoy sex. When they mature and become wives of successful City tycoons they have affairs with dustmen, window-cleaners, tradesmen galore. They're empty-headed sex-machines and no power on Earth could make them think higher than their pubic hair.'

'We've got that type here,' the girl declared triumphantly.

'They're everywhere, unfortunately,' Tim said. 'Don't be classified as one of them, Syl.' His eyes stared into hers avoiding more distracting erotic areas.

'What are you? Some kind of religious maniac?'

Tim laughed. 'Not me, Syl. I'm just a shade above those guys you usually sleep with.'

'Then make it, man. It's all yours . . . '

'*After* we discuss . . . '

'We discuss *after,* you mean!' Her hands seized his head, drew his mouth down to hers. Like a viper, her tongue darted forth - poisoning his resistance; driving home her insatiableness. Like smooth silk her voluptuous flesh slid across his hands; inviting further exploration - demanding its gratification. In her arms he festered sores that could not be healed without adequate medication . . . the slow-drawing poultice that was her body functions; her natural attribute.

During those precious minutes it took him to undress she bayed at the moon of his sex; crazy coon-like sounds with staring eyes fastened lecherously on her pleasure; body writhing in total surrender; passion-bloated face contorted into a hideous mask of uninhibited sensuality. Then, he was down with her again - feeling her thighs surging, wrapping, opening, offering entirely. Her mouthed obscenities did not shock him, simply sickened his mind to her depravity. Her suggestions went untried - and he was above her willing hot flesh, driving hard against her youthfulness; conscious of that experienced desire for mutual completion.

When it came he was raised on a plateau far superior, far higher than any he had walked before. The vigour of her frenzy, the frantic way she carried him along with her flowing, gushing lust left him sated - depleted, exhausted.

'God, you're good!' she gasped, hands refusing to relinquish his body. 'Don't stop, Tim . . . keep doing it to me!'

He thrust away from her and rolled on his back. *'Don't!* Let me rest . . .'

'No, no, no!' She twisted over him, kissing, touching, cajoling.

His feet thudded on her carpet and he pushed from her greedy grasp. Looking down at her he moaned. 'You could . . .'

She chuckled. 'Pregnant? Not me, Tim - I'm on the Pill. Relax, man - come back here. I haven't finished with you.'

'I need a drink!' He stumbled across the apartment, helped himself.

'Want to talk for a while?'

He swallowed two ounces of fiery liquid, coughed. 'Yeah!'

'What about?'

'Demonstrations.'

'Man,' she chortled happily, spreading her body on the divan, 'that's for me. Ain't I just demonstrated what a lovely girl I am?'

'Not that type, Syl.'

'God, I know what you mean. Tim - haven't you got a sense of humour?'

He felt in need of a hot bath. His skin crawled with drying perspiration. 'It wasn't funny what we did, Syl. It was exciting, wonderful, accomplished from your side. But not funny.'

'I thought it was fantastic myself.' She swung her feet to the floor, sat erect.

Even like that, he thought, she was a sex kitten.

'Okay, lover-boy - what's eating you?'

'You, your friends, this Californian scene.'

'You still harping on this international conspiracy thing?'

'I don't rightly know, Syl!'

'Forget it, man. We don't play for commie kicks. This is for real - our thing!'

'Do you ever attend meetings?'

She considered his point, shrugged so that her breasts did a small dance. 'Some,' she admitted ruefully. 'I've been with Cy and Chick a few weeks. They're avid protesters. Anything goes for that Cy, Tim. He's part Panther, part anti-pollutionist, part anti-Vietnam. You name it, he's in there pitching against established order. He hates pigs, too,' and she laughed uproariously.

'Is he violent?'

'Could be,' she stopped laughing, frowned. 'He's got guns and nitro.'

'Does he ever mention one specific individual he accepts as a leader?'

'Nope . . . hey, wait a minute!' She concentrated, added, 'There's a guy he calls Jason. I've never met him but I believe he's a Canadian working for some big foundation or other. Cy says he's got 'em all tagged - from the White House to a dogcatcher.'

'Think hard, Syl. What else does Cy say about this man?'

The girl snorted, stretched along the divan, waved to him. 'Nix, Tim. I'm ready again . . . '

Tim sighed, poured a fast drink, swallowed it in one long, desperate attempt to replenish his energies. He walked across to Syl - stood looking down at her worldly-wise adolescence and moaned. God help the next generation if this was an example of motherhood to be. One day her Pill would quit working and she'd pass along nymphomaniac genes to some other pathetic little bastard . . .

'Quit having an eyeful and let's get down to what really counts in this game . . . '

He lowered himself onto her, eager to please, ready to *suffer* for her beliefs . . .

CHAPTER FIVE

YVETTE MIRADOIS needed no passport when she entered the Left-Bank refuge known as 'Cochon'. Suspicious eyes followed her down ten steps into the centrally-lighted entrance then passed her through a stout portal. Once inside, she sensed the changed atmosphere - the fervent desire to share friendships, wine, lovers. She was always glad of those vigilant guardians outside the dimly-lit premises. The last thing she wanted was to be discovered here. Just knowing they all had various avenues of escape should the *gendamerie* invade gave her a feeling of security.

Accordions played softly from a dais before which couples swayed, lost in one another's passion. The hands that moved to the sensuous muted music did not care who was watching or why. They were guided by instinct; motivated by desire. Those intimate caresses, those daring familiarities all came from knowledge that nobody here would object;

that what was happening this second would occur a dozen times when the place emptied.

For a fleeting space of time Yvette pitied the musicians. Their job was not easy catering for swollen lusts - knowing they could not partake of the excitements being so blatantly displayed under their collective eyes. Then, she forgot the men. They were paid - and entertained royally afterwards. There were always girls who considered a musician more to their liking than adventurous-handed boys. And, too. there was the heightened desire burning in their veins. All that playing and viewing until, finally, the release came with a sudden rush. No, she should not pity the players. She should envy them!

'Yvette, *mon cherie!*'

She smiled as Paul approached. He was a handsome youth in his American-style jacket with its fringed-ends and those 'Midnight Cowboy' sideboards visible under his Paris-made Stetson. She wanted to tell him his Levis were too tight, too revealing but he probably knew that in advance. Paul didn't miss a trick when going after girls.

'I was beginning to wonder if you'd come tonight,' he said, kissing her deeply, racing hands lightly over her buttocks and breasts before releasing her.

'I can see you've been starved, Paul.'

He laughed. 'Don't tell M'sieur Pettu, *mon petit!*'

'Is he here?' Yvette searched the room for sight of the man.

'Mais oui, certainement! Come - follow me!' Treading carefully through the dancers and those standing in close proximity so that their ineffectual fondlings could go for dancing, Yvette caught sight of M. Pettu. She didn't like the man - considered him an intruder. There was something strange in the way he cold-bloodedly refused to become enmeshed in their amorous affairs and confined himself to politics and discussions on how to antagonise the authorities.

'Bon soir, Yvette.' The man held out a hand which she touched quickly. It was cold, devoid of human qualities.

'M'sieur . . . ' She accepted a chair, sank into it gratefully.

At least she was directly opposite the man, not beside him as was so often the case.

'We are discussing the possibility of arousing the Citroen workers again,' Paul informed her excitedly.

'Mon dieu!' M. Pettu exploded angrily, brushing aside Paul's apology. 'Must you be so hasty? Haven't I warned you not to broadcast our plans in advance?'

'Oui, m'sieur . . . J'ai beaucoup de regret!'

Yvette wanted to scream at Paul. He didn't have to greatly regret anything. Wasn't she a member of their elite circle? Wasn't she entitled to have their plans detailed? *'M'sieur* what is so wrong with what Paul said?' she asked angrily. Two could play at that game, she thought with some satisfaction.

'Nothing, Yvette - except that if he will speak aloud here there is no telling where he will draw a line.'

'Trust us a little, *m'sieur* Pettu.'

'Trust no one,' the man replied quickly.

'Not even you?' Yvette smiled sarcastically, challenging the older man. Perhaps, she mused, that was why he did not seem to fit. He was much older than any of them. He may have looked young at first but she sensed his 'antiquity' from little escapism things he mentioned.

'Not me!' replied the man solemnly. 'Not you. Not anyone.'

'What a world we are building,' Yvette remarked.

'It is not what we are attempting to construct, Yvette. It is what we have been left. Our inheritance is rotten to its core. We move amongst evil people and we must exercise caution if we are to survive.'

'I'd rather be dead than untrusting of humanity, *m'sieur.*'

Pettu glared at the girl. She was a dominant character in this group and he had to mollify her before Paul, Robert, Andre, Charles and Celeste broke away from his stranglehold over them. He smiled. He forced himself to sound contrite. 'Bravo, Yvette. Well spoken. We agree, naturally. Humanity is what we are fighting for but remember the words of a famous Frenchman - not all humanity is worth sacrificing liberty for!'

Yvette searched her intelligent mind for the quotation, failed to get a response. She refused to be drawn and said: 'All right, *m'sieur* - let us proceed?' She deliberately made a question.

Pettu nodded thoughtfully. The girl was a disturbing influence in every way. Pretty without being a ravishing beauty, her chestnut hair, grey eyes and pouting lips combined with a voluptuousness of body to make her presence a distraction. Her high I.Q. bothered him, too. She accepted little without wanting to probe beneath the surface for hidden motivations. More than once she had uncovered bias in their schemes and foiled his plans to foment trouble where it could damage the economy most.

Yvette knew she was the object of his thoughts. She sensed his reluctance to speak until their group settled. It gave her ample time to study him - and she was far from satisfied with what she saw. On close examination his youthfulness faded, became middle age. The tell-tale

40

signs were there for a discerning gaze to behold. Wrinkles round the eyes, nose, mouth. Deep furrows between thick brows. The hands creased, the voice deep with maturity - not just naturally baritone. Only his clothing was of their generation and that reminded her of an aged disc-jockey keeping his job by affecting styles he did not honestly like.

'Citroen have offered their workers a two-year contract guaranteeing an increase of approximately fifteen per cent,' Pettu said finally. 'The majority of the men are in favour of this deal but some militants are against on basic principles. These are the ones we must encourage.'

'Why?' Yvette asked.

Andre glared at her. He was a hot-head with a penchant for leading rebellious students to the barricades. He enjoyed violence - especially when directed against his favourite target: gendarmes: He made no effort to conceal his anarchist leanings. Nor did he have the slightest interest in their sworn declaration to make the students' life a happier, more fulfilling one.

Pettu grinned, spoke directly for Andre's benefit. 'Why? you ask. I would have thought everyone of us knew that answer.'

'Tell me again, *m'sieur,'* Yvette insisted tightly.

'Student power is disruptive,' Pettu replied with mounting anger. 'Students are not producers nor do the people have sympathy when we simply stay away from classes to make our protest. Therefore, students are forced to take remedial action; to incite workers and others so that their voices can be heard in every corner of France. Car production is an important factor in the economy. If we get Citroen to strike, Renault will follow. It is simple fact - we must recruit those militants and offer support for their cause.'

The girl smiled at Paul. 'Do you agree?'

'Mais oui, cherie. It is the thing to do!'

'You've forgotten that we have justice now. Our former uprising accomplished much of what we wanted. The authorities are slow to act but they seldom object to hearing our demands. What are we fighting for this time. M'sieur Pettu? Tell me that!'

Paul and Andre felt uncomfortable. The others were not intimately involved as yet and could sit back to watch the infighting between Yvette and Pettu. But neither boy could enjoy the battle. Certainly not Andre. His face flushed, his hands banged on their table. 'Liberty - that's what!' he shouted. 'We're the new revolutionaries. France does not need this government. France is being ruined by capitalist pigs. Unless we overthrow them all France is doomed. I, for one, shall not cease to strive for liberty.' He jumped to his feet, trembling as agitation built to its crescendo.

'I'll go with you, Andre,' Paul remarked. He glared at Yvette, nodded to Pettu. 'If you agree to discuss actual methods for giving more than vocal support to our comrades let us know.'

Yvette kept a straight face as the two youths departed. Pettu's flinty gaze bored through her - accusing, suspicious, doubting. She smiled at last. 'Sorry, *m'sieur*. It was not intentional but I do have rights to question decisions affecting me.'

'Naturellement!' He slowly got to his feet. 'If you'll excuse me . . . '

Yvette hurried after him. She did not want the man catching up with Andre or Paul. She wanted him for herself. 'M'sieur . . . '

He swung, waited until she was beside him.

'I'd like to speak with you alone - if you wouldn't mind.'

'Come along, girl.' His attitude was most discouraging yet she insisted on following him from the 'Cochon'. It had been raining and street-lights formed luminous pools on glistening pavements. Scattered droplets fell from the canopied chestnut trees as couples strolled oblivious of discomfort or dampness.

'Why do you take such an avid interest in student affairs, *M'sieur*?'

Pettu smiled to himself as they strode towards the Seine. *If only she knew!* His silence matched the stillness that permeated the river shimmering like a silken ribbon in the immediate distance. The outline of Notre Dame caught against city-glow clouds did not stir him. Churches were mere constructions to him. Not repositories of sacred music, prayers, hopes, peace.

'You haven't answered, *m'sieur* . . . '

They reached the embankment as another downfall washed the streets. The plip-plop of rain beating its incessant tattoo on the river had an eeriness one could almost taste. Quickly, Pettu darted under a tree, hugged its thick trunk as Yvette joined him.

'M'sieur . . . '

'Call me Armand, Yvette.' His eyes held hers with a tenderness she could not fathom. 'You're a pretty girl - but a dangerous opponent.'

'Thank you, Armand. I appreciate truthfulness.'

Rain bounced off the pavement, wetting their feet. Now the deluge swirled down gutters, gurgling obscenely as it sluiced into a drain. From the swollen river the sound of drumming drops increased in volume; heard above the traffic's growling.

'If we could get a taxi,' the girl suggested.

'And where would we go together?'

She shrugged. 'Your apartment. Mine. It makes no difference.'

'Whatever gave you the notion I want to accompany you?'

She snuggled against his side as rain cascaded down from overladen branches. 'You're not married and you're not meeting a mistress so why not me?'

'You're very sure of yourself.' He said it lightly but inwardly cursed the day he'd permitted Yvette to join their group. It had been a major error and one he would rectify soon. She was too astute to continue being a threat.

'Armand - don't you ever think about girls?'

'Certainement! I'm human, *n'est pas?'*

Yvette laughed. 'Kiss me and I'll confirm or deny that.' Her face tilted upwards, her hips moistly parted.

Suddenly, he could control his animalistic urges no longer. His arms swept her tight against him, his mouth hungrily devouring hers. The heat of her, the subtle gyrations of her hips, the way she fondled his neck drove him wild. It had been months . . .

Against a background of moonlight music, Bob Thomson watched the five youngsters finish their meal. He was pleasantly surprised to see how well-behaved they were; how they fitted into his clientele. None of them wore outlandish garb. In fact, Tim Hart was elegantly dressed in a lounge suit while Nanette Aubin's gown was positively radiant. He wanted to approach them but discretion being the better part of intrigue he compelled himself to quell that old inquisitiveness. This was their 'show'. If they needed help they'd shout. Until then . . .

'I enjoyed that steak,' Tim remarked. He poured a second glass of wine, waited whilst the others declined before replacing the bottle to one side of him. 'If anyone wants a sweet . . . '

'Not me,' Nanette laughed, patting her stomach. 'Since arriving in London I've gained three pounds. A girl must be careful of what she eats.'

Brad Sommers leant across the table, whispered loudly: 'Honey, I go for you fat or thin!'

'Oh, la-la! Your name should be M'sieur Armand Pettu!'

Tim glanced at their nearest neighbours, lowered his voice.

'Right, as Nanette has brought us back to reality I think we should discuss Pettu - and some others about whom I've formed opinions. Frankly, I'm not yet convinced dad is correct in assuming we have an international conspiracy although some ramifications do worry me.'

Nanette Aubin rested her elbows on the table, sighed. 'There is a mysterious organisation behind the unrest, Tim. I think I have proof of that!'

Her bombshell startled them all. Brad Sommers especially. He leant back, wiped perspiration from his forehead, said: 'Either it's goddamned hot in here or else I've got an attack of nerves!'

He concentrated his attention of the French girl. 'If you're sure, Nanette . . . '

'Not one hundred per cent but almost,' she replied.

'Then I vote we ring in the old "network".' He searched their faces for confirmation.

'Not yet,' Tim said dubiously. 'I'd rather we got a few facts straight first. Go ahead, Nanette. Tell us your story.'

Rolande Aubin's daughter liked holding the spotlight. She was a born actress. Before her father had requested she join this group she had been studying drama - and the situation was tailor-made for her talents. 'Armand Pettu is, I think, the man behind French student unrest. Tim,' and she smiled gratefully at Hart, 'suggested I infiltrate the Sorbonne chapter which I did - successfully so. I used the pseudonym Yvette Miradois . . . '

Wanda Collins laughed understanding. 'Forged papers and all?'

'Certainement! We have resources most people do not. Father made a beautiful set within an evening. *Sacre bleu!* how they trained agents in *those* days!'

Karl Bluther inclined his head, asked, 'Have we all used an alias when dealing with our compatriots?' When the group remained silent, questioning mentally, he continued: 'It would appear our parents have been successful in part. If we resort to undercover tactics we must surely suspect they have called the tune correctly!'

'I'm not sure I like that assumption,' Tim said defensively.

'Nor I!' Brad declared vehemently. 'I'm not saying I agree or disagree but my mind is blank - no decisions made yet!'

'How about you, Wanda?' Nanette asked then.

The English girl sighed, steepled her slender fingers and gazed at them across scarlet-painted fingernails. 'When my turn comes I shall enlighten you. Not before! But, please, let Nanette continue . . . '

Tim grunted approval. As their chosen leader he was bound to make the final analysis. If their reports indicated a subversive element associated with demonstrators and student unrest he would critically and logically examine every facet of the *outside* interference and make plans accordingly. 'Go ahead, Nanette,' he said firmly.

Ever conscious of their neighbours and those dancers whirling past their table, Nanette told her story. She left nothing out - not even her sexual involvement with Armand Pettu. Her description of the man got totally unexpected reactions, however.

'He could be Jason,' Tim mused.

'I was thinking he is a ringer for a guy at L.S.E.'

Karl frowned, asked Brad, 'Attending the college or on the fringes?'

'Fringe only,' came the quick reply. 'Why?'

'As a full-time student he could not be everywhere at once. He does sound very like Hans Mannlicher to me!'

Tim felt excitement race down his spine. 'Look - let's construct a picture of Nanette's Armand Pettu. I'm not sure how to go about it, but - . . . '

'Ask Bob Thomson,' Brad suggested.

An hour later, Bob placed his pencil on a desk and handed his sketch to Nanette. His private office was hardly large enough for their group meeting but under the circumstances he had thought it advisable to bring the youngsters in there.

'That's Armand,' Nanette declared positively as she examined the drawing. 'He looks younger than he actually is.' She smiled. 'I should know. I've slept with him!'

'A slight change of hair style and it's Jason from California,' Tim grunted.

'Hans Mannlicher!' Kurt remarked.

'Julius Gold - friend of L.S.E's militants,' Brad said.

'That's Stanley Edmond,' Wanda said acidly.

Thomson leant back and looked at each thoughtfully. 'You realise this pretty well confirms our theory,' he mentioned. 'I think it's high time Network Forty got working on Mr Edmond-Gold-Pettu-Mannlicher-Jason.'

'No, not yet,' Tim interrupted quickly. 'We undertook to do this job on our own.'

'True, Tim, true! And you've done better than expected already. But guys like this joker don't play infantile games. They're top agents following orders, creating situations off the cuff, stage-managing youngsters everywhere. This one . . . ' and he tapped the drawing, 'must be excellent. He's world-wide - Paris, London, Los Angeles, Berlin, God knows where else. He needs handling with kid gloves and experience.'

'Don't tell my father for one week, Bob. We won't do anything hasty nor scare off the suspect . . . '

Thomson shrugged. 'It's your show, kids but my advice is stay clear of this man. If he gets the slightest idea you've twigged his caper he won't hesitate to eliminate the danger.'

Wanda shivered. 'I wonder how mum felt when she was cornered? Did she think of her life being in jeopardy or did she pray?'

Bob got to his feet, said grimly: 'Mai Bedford knew what she was doing. We all did - and that's the difference between the Forty and Seventy networks. We were engaged in a war for high stakes. You kids can't begin to understand that this is the same thing simply because soldiers are not engaged in combat. But don't kid yourselves. The Russians are convinced that espionage and disruption of every lifeline in a capitalist society is an act of total war. They're not acting roles; they're locked in an ideological struggle with us that decides their fate - and ours. That's why I'd like to call upon the older generation,' and he grinned then. 'Sure, we're old but not defunct. Not decayed. Not relegated to pensionable ineffectualness.'

'You're trying to warn us, aren't you, Mr Thomson?' Wanda asked.

'I am, girl, I bloody well am!'

'Thanks! Consider I've been told off.' She smiled and took his arm, gazing up into his handsome face. 'Now, if you've finished trying to scare the pants off me, I'll have a drink - for courage.'

Bob slapped her bottom playfully. 'It's on the house. One drink each and no flashing eyes at me, Miss Wanda Collins. Your mum would slay me alive if I seduced her daughter.'

'Ha!' came back the immediate response. 'What a parent doesn't know . . .' She laughingly accompanied Bob back into the nightclub. Two lone clients sat huddled in a corner with a disgruntled waiter hovering over them. Other members of the staff placed chairs on tables and swept the floor, doing everything possible to tell the tardy duo that it was time to depart. Wanda felt Bob's body tense against her, asked, 'Something wrong?'

'Bloody right!' he growled. 'Excuse me . . . ' He pulled away, went directly to the hand-holding pair and bent over them. Wanda couldn't hear what was said but it was effective. Like bullets from a gun the duo rose, hurried to the foyer - their every move watched by an appreciative staff. As he approached their group, Wanda saw the hardness that was so carefully hidden beneath Bob's pleasant, care-not facade. And she tingled expectantly. She would have this man - regardless . . .

CHAPTER SIX

As a 'Bantu' refugee from Vorster's apartheid policy, Jan Hugens qualified for membership of any Black Panther group. That he had taken temporary residence in Harlem made him a natural for inclusion in the chapter dominated by those most dedicated to the armed overthrow of established American government. Unlike many South African 'natives', Jan spoke perfect English with just a slight trace of North American language. His associates did not notice this deviation nor did they care. In Jan they had the *example* they so desperately desired - the incitement needed to inflame other coloured inhabitants to take up their violent cause.

For Jan, the Panthers went about their rebellion the wrong way. Insurrection, destruction was not - for him - the way to gain sympathy. The coloured man had a legitimate grievance. That in itself was tantamount to forwarding a claim to social equality in today's world. Martin Luther King's 'peace marches' had not accomplished any noticeable advancement of the problem simply because most whites did not wish to be forcibly made aware of their governmental shortcomings. But external pressures brought to bear in an United Nations predominantly Afro-Asian in membership could have swung the wedge in their favour. Violence, threats to 'Whitey' and calling law enforcement agency men 'pigs' did not endear a black cause in white hearts.

Jan believed - in all sincerity - that progress could only be made through education. The bitterness caused by segregated schooling did not solve the issue. What was needed were more black teachers willing to forego the 'white' monetary gains to offer their talents to educating poverty-line 'nigger' students in the Deep South. Guns could not send the walls of Whitey supremacy tumbling; but that pen which was mightier than a sword could.

Unknown to his Black Panther group was the fact that Jan Hugens was not one hundred per cent *black*. His father had belonged to Colonel Brett Hart's 'Department Seven' crew - a white South African whose whole life had been spent trying to 'free' his native countrymen from Dutch-church domination. When his father had seen fit to take M'golu of the Zulu tribe for his 'woman' he had automatically been castigated, kicked out of white society. That his son - Jan - had been more black than white had not bothered the father. He had been proud to spawn a 'breed' that was a 'native-son' of the African continent.

Often, Jan wondered how Hart had traced his ancestry. In South Africa he had been 'Bantu' - although he hated the word. He was Zulu - and white. A curious mixture but one he was proud to have. The whites who had conquered the vast plains, velds, mountains, deserts, coastlines of what was now the Republic had his admiration. The Zulu race who had fought so valiantly against overwhelming odds deserved historic recognition - and gratitude. Their struggle to maintain independence had forced the white invaders to assume a mantle of greatness they could not otherwise have claimed.

From his window he looked across the Bronx with its stench, its old brownstones falling apart at the seams, its garbage-littered streets, its pathetic poverty and wondered how this 'land of plenty, opportunity, give-me-your-poor' could condone such misery. For all that was said about South Africa such neglect, distressing circumstances, abjectness did not exist. There were no written laws saying that all men were equal, deserving of opportunity, justice, liberty. S.A. had its segregated code - and the *African* (not the Afrikaaner) knew where he fitted. Not here. Not in America's polyglot community that considered a Polak, Bohunk, 'Nigger', Irisher an inferior being. The Pilgrim Fathers still ruled America's thinking. Boston and the 400 controlled society. Even California with its integrated millions did not realise how unjust the system really was. Only Watts stood as proof of that State's tribulations.

The memory of Colonel Hart's beautiful country residence returned to taunt him . . .

'Jan,' Hart said as he poured coffee into a delicate cup, 'I'm making a confession I do not wish you to repeat. Your father saved my life and I owe his son a debt. I'm an "EMPIRE" enthusiast - and that *excludes* those of coloured blood. Whilst I readily admit to having a prejudice I still decline to go whole hog and condemn every black nation seeking its future apart from the Commonwealth, or Colonialism. I believe in every man being equal, but some being less capable of governing themselves than others - if you get what I'm trying to say?'

'I do, Colonel Hart,' Jan readily admitted.

'You realise then that I'm going to be a hard taskmaster?'

'Yes, sir.'

'And that I'm going to throw you in where all your African notions of black identity will be subjected to severe testing?'

'Yes, sir!'

'And you're willing to work under my orders?'

'I am, Colonel.'

Hart smiled then, sampled a whisky, poured two drinks and relaxed opposite Jan as they sniffed the delicate aroma of the amber liquid. 'Forgive me if I make a symbolic gesture,' Hart mentioned. 'I'm under doctor's orders not to imbibe.'

'That's alright, sir. Thank you, sir. Cheers, sir . . . ' Jan got ready to drink his Scotch, hesitated when he saw Hart's face tense. 'Something wrong, sir ?'

The Canadian swore. 'Goddam! Is that what they teach you in Cape Town? Sir this, sir that, yes sir, no sir . . . ?'

Jan grinned. 'I'm sorry . . . '

'Sorry nothing. I admit to wanting respect for my rank, son. I like a lad who can speak to an elder with deference. But I'm goddamned if I want sir thrown at me every few seconds. Cut it out, eh?'

'Yes, sir.' Jan laughed, drank his whisky, apologised, 'Sorry, Colonel - I won't snap to attention so fast again.'

Hart shrugged off their exchange. 'I'm not going to fill your head with modern daydream stuff, Jan. Your father's old - and I mean old - department is kaput as far as the British government is concerned. If we are to believe fiction authors and those spectacular motion pictures there still exists an outfit with a 00 prefix licensed to kill. That's for laughs, I can assure you. Professional spies don't go around slaying one another. If they did there'd be none left. We have a lousy budget for espionage in Britain. At one time, the British Secret Service was second to none in the world. Today, thanks to petty governmental cuts and the need for more and more social security *chaps* and union dictatorship, the spies have been almost eliminated. But not in Russia, or Czechoslovakia, Rumania, Bulgaria, Albania, China, Hungary, Poland, East Germany. They know that men are needed and that men cost money. They realise the value of diplomatic, economic, industrial espionage. They've got unlimited budgets. Not us. We muddle along and when the crunch comes we'll scream "why weren't we warned in advance?". Well, if you're alive then you tell those fucking unions and Left-wing advocates why we weren't. Excuse the language, son - I'm from a mould that cannot be broken. I believe in freedom - and the necessity of keeping our defences as strong as possible against subversion whether it be from a foreign army or malcontents within the system.'

Jan helped himself to another Scotch. He liked the smooth blending of those old, fine products incorporated under the label: *Teacher's Highland Cream.* He considered the masterblenders in the same light as he contemplated Colonel Hart die-hards to tradition; proud of their product and its acceptance to the majority.

'What has this got to do with me, Colonel?' he asked.

'Everything, lad. Everything!' Hart sniffed his glass for about the fifth time. He was sorely tempted but the doctor knew best - or did he? 'I've formed a youth division of our old organisation. I am proud to state my son, Tim, commands it. But I'm not ready to let him know you are one of them. Not yet. Not until you finish your assignment . . .'

'Which is?'

'To infiltrate the Black Power adherents!'

'That,' Jan laughed, 'would be extremely unlikely. I'm a known Whitey sympathiser in Cape Town . . .'

'With new papers, and *official* documents stating that you are suspected of being in league with a liberation movement you'd be a natural, son!'

Jan inclined his head. He didn't doubt that Hart could perform the 'miracle' he had mentioned. His father had drummed into him Hart's invincibility. 'If that was possible . . .'

'It is, son. I happen to have the papers and documents here.' The colonel reached inside his sporting jacket, withdrew several officious envelopes. 'You can be on a plane to New York within . . . ' He consulted his wrist-watch, said, 'Ten hours - if you're willing?'

Jan shrugged. New York was a 'mecca' he had wanted to visit for many years - a haven denied him because of his colour. 'I'll accept - on one condition.'

'Name it, son.'

'I don't betray those with whom I feel kinship.'

Hart walked round and round his elegant study. Jan loved the leather-bound books, the antiques, the Persian carpets and those polished boards that had seen so much British history trampled beneath heavy boots. 'All right, Jan Hugens - you've got my word on that. I want the leaders of Black Power. I want them catalogued and classified. I want the names of their foreign contacts - the people who supply them with ideas, arms. I want them in my files - and not because I have anything against their struggle, either. I - as you - appreciate what they're fighting for. But I detest their methods. Especially, I loathe the white people using them for personal, or national, gain. They're really the ones I'm after, Jan. Those,' and he smiled disarmingly, 'Whiteys making the black man look like a bunch of ignorant savages.'

'May I ask one question, Colonel?'

Hart nodded, his active mind leap-frogging ahead for the answer he was sure would be needed.

'They say every man has his price and does good works for gain. What do you get out of all this?'

'Satisfaction, son,' came the immediate reply on schedule. 'I have spent a lifetime fighting one evil after another. Twice against a military-indoctrinated Germany. Other places you've never heard about. I've sent men to certain death on a slight chance we got enough information to save a thousand other lives. I've seen an Empire - a proud, God-fearing, just Empire, ruined. I've watched from retirement as the world I helped preserve lowered its standards of decency and degenerated into a drug-crazy, lazy caricature of human goodness. My son doesn't want the wealth I have accumulated - doesn't honestly need it. So, if it costs me every penny to offer youth yet another opportunity to climb out from under the snake's-belly unscrupulous men have constructed above their heads then I shall be satisfied.'

'My father was right, Colonel Hart - you're the greatest!' Jan laughed, held out his hand. 'I'll do my share, *sir!*'

'I'm sure you will, Jan Hugens. And there'll be a million Africans who'll owe you a debt of gratitude, too.'

Thinking about that day spent at Hart's English home gave him the shakes. Compared to the view from his window, heaven could have been a day-trip to the countryside. And while he wouldn't call Hart omnipotent he was as close to being God as he could surely meet. Only one facet of the old man's character lacked shimmering-silver lining - his straightforward declaration that there were second-class world citizens and they were mostly coloured. Yet, in himself, Jan knew what Hart had meant. The Canadian did not erect colour bars against black men. He simply could not comprehend the changes his loss of Empire had brought. Nor could he assimilate self-governing black nations with his old-fashioned British justice is best notions.

Grim-faced, Jan stretched his six-foot frame and slipped into an old sweater. Somewhere under a pile of discarded clothes was his leather jacket. Tonight, he could howl across the river. For the first time in weeks he did not have duties to perform for his 'cell'. And relaxation was going to be really sizzling something with that high-yeller chick from Brooklyn. If ever a gal got his hormones all agitated and unbalanced it was pretty Lena . . . '

Sergeant O'Dell lived on Third Avenue right where all the Irishers and Germans congregated. Often, he swore to move from the neighbourhood and find a small bungalow over on Queen's but his wife stoically refused to shift her fat ass. She had friends, she claimed, and no sonofabitch called Mike O'Dell was about to deny her the only companionship she'd ever had in New York.

Sitting back with a cigar smouldering, O'Dell prayed he never had to ride with Grutzmann in heavy traffic. The man was a menace on the roads - swerving in and out of easy-flowing bridge-bound cars as though he was intent on committing suicide or causing one helluva pile-up.

'Look at that bastard!' Grutzmann snarled, flicking his siren into action, gunning his patrol car with signs of entering the oncoming lane.

'Watch it, you goddamned idiot!' O'Dell shot forward, sat tensed. He peered through the windscreen. 'Crissakes, wait until they move aside.' Every nerve jangled hysterically.

Grutzmann was impatient. Normally, he took things easy. He didn't enjoy driving in or around New York and all his fears of an accident seemed to control him when O'Dell sat beside him. The sergeant and he didn't hit it off; a five year old incident having established a working agreement between them to avoid one another like twin plagues. He was sorry now he'd mentioned the motorbike. But that was life - a magazine, and a lotta errors.

Their siren had cleared an avenue and Grutzmann careened alongside the motorcycle. O'Dell leaned from his window, gestured for the driver to draw against the kerb and waited as the patrol car almost sliced the poor bastard in two in Grutzmann's haste to issue a ticket.

'Stay here,' the sergeant growled, heaving his ample frame from the car, walking sedately back to where the motorcyclist had halted.

'Anything wrong, Sergeant?' Hugens asked, shoving his goggles over his protective helmet.

O'Dell tensed anew. He hated niggers. That came from a stint in a Harlem precinct and the current wave of cop-baiting. When he started to mention the infringement that had upset him so much he suddenly realised that Grutzmann hadn't made any reference to what this kid had been doing. Frankly, it didn't matter a damn. There were at least a dozen logical offences he could throw at the smiling, calm nigger. He'd soon wipe the goddamned smile away. He had a lulu . . .

'Let's have the licence and registration certificate.'

Jan opened his billfold, extracted both and reached them to O'Dell. As he did, a twenty dollar bill slid from the leathercase, drifted down to hit the road by the sergeant's feet.

O'Dell grinned sadistically, nudged the bill. 'Trying to bribe an officer of the law, eh? Okay, punk - off the heap. You're coming with me.'

Jan stiffened. He knew that hate-filled look, the flushed features, the ruthlessness that could shelter behind a blue uniform. 'No bribe, sergeant,' he said softly, reaching for the money.

O'Dell's foot locked, caught Jan's wrist. 'Leave it, nigger. That's evidence . . . '

Sixty per cent of those coloured inhabitants of The Tombs were lying, Jan believed. The forty who weren't gave an indication of the enormous problem confronting those who wanted to work for social justice. Heavy footsteps reminded him of the guards prowling back and forth along the tiers of this city prison which had, for age and filth, few equals anywhere on Earth. All around - hemmed into cells a pig would find disgusting - were the drunks, junkies, hippies, coloureds, pimps, homosexuals, pornographers, drifters, bums that New York collected each and every day. Some would get a free ride to Jersey on the morrow; some would languish as a shyster attorney tried to make a name for himself on a lost cause; some would feel the majesty of law descend on them and face years decaying behind bars; and others, like Jan himself, would sweat it out and pray that O'Dell (or a hundred other vicious, tough, inhuman cops) would relent over night.

Jan had no illusions regarding the severity of his chargesheet. Attempting to bribe an officer, assaulting an officer, speeding, failing to stop when signalled, failing to give right of way to a police car. He had heard O'Dell mention a vagrancy charge, too - although how the sergeant hoped to make that stick alongside a bribery attempt was laughable.

All those guys he had heard discuss police brutality and corruption came back to haunt him now. He had been disbelieving. Not because he didn't know how people hated others of different religions, colours, opinions. But because this was supposed to be the 'land of democracy and liberty'. Now he knew - things were no different in New York than, say, Cape Town, the Negro got a raw deal either way.

'God,' he thought, 'how they make a bed of nails for themselves!' Staring at a cracked, dirty ceiling - the slats he was lying on digging into his spine - he thought about *their* plight. The Negro plight! No wonder kids grew big hating whites when the cops did everything possible to make the hatred worse. He didn't go along with the Panthers or Power militants but he could see why they reckoned it was the only solution. He remembered one huge Panther screaming: 'They've gotta pay, brothers. They steal us blind; rob our kids of an education and expect us to lick their white asses. Well, we ain't gonna. No more. You hear? No more! I gotta lovely ass and it's gonna be licked - jest like that bastard captain wants our chicks to perform for him!'

CHAPTER SEVEN

TIME meant nothing for Jan Hugens. It flew on multi-hued wings, drifted along clouds that swiftly changed into silken cushions. He was suspended above a swirling mass that had once been his world - and the predominant colour was white; a white smeared blood-red mingled here and there with black battered blobs

Sound had meaning, though. Sweet noise rising to crescendo proportions; wailing into jazz; singing from a curved, ivory throat; lost in baritone negroid belly.

Feeling had never been so acute. Those caressing hands working down his sweating nakedness . . . touching . . . exciting; arousing to an intensity as nothing had ever been aroused. And, too, he could feel - oh, how he could feel: silken flesh slithering through his palms; erect nipples jutting eagerly to be kissed; flanks of ebony textured pleasure moving to signal another delight as he fondled . . . probed the forested haven . . . prepared her for that supreme moment when they would join, unite . . . he penetrating her moist goodness . . . she accepting, coaxing, begging for that spontaneous release . . . those flesh-dissolving erratic thrusts to send them spinning off their cloud-being.

Unconsciously, he rolled with her, their limbs a symphony in sensation, sound, exhortation. Like crawling insects they entwined, arms doing fantastic things as hands sought to heighten already Olympian contacts. Then he was inside her very life, drawn up into the void of her ecstasy - sharing her supersensitive emotions, lusts, perverted desires; fulfilling his reason for being male, her's as a woman.

The torment erupted in a torrent that flooded thought, energy, need of communication. They were one - ONE in harmony. In soaring pleasure. Voluptuously titillated into newness - the old liquid fire slithering away where nobody wanted it any more . . .

Slowly, draggingly, the effect wore off and he moaned. She lay by his side, eyes wide open, dreamy expression not yet dampened by reality. She had taken a larger dose, of course. She had warned him not to sample more than a minimum.

Something about the trip worried him. Behind the foolish escapism, the phantasmagoria, the hyper-void through which they had rushed in unison as passion swallowed all but its jungle joys there had been a feeling of tragedy, wrong, evil.

Little by little his faculties returned. He wondered how everything had appeared so fantastically beautiful when he saw the dingy room with its cracked wash-basin, its peeling walls, its cheap Goodwill store furniture, the sagging bed they lay upon. Only Lena looked respectable, lovely. And she was respectable according to current standards, too. She didn't let just any man accompany her into passion's hinterland. She had to feel something; had to want the guy before tripping; had to be wooed like they did back when Capone was going strong in a coonskin coat.

She had a near perfect body - high, firm breasts with uptilted nipples still showing desire, flat stomach with a thick pubic bush adorning her mount, long slender thighs that could wrap round a man like twin steel bands. Her face lacked none of those attributes of a beautiful negress. Her lips pouted just right, her large deep brown eyes shimmered exactly as they were supposed to, her nose was flaring at the nostrils almost as if she had white blood somewhere in her genes and her hair was soft, straight, clean. The longer he studied her, the more convinced Jan became that Lena was not the hundred per cent negress she claimed. And this suited him. They could share a secret - once he got what he wanted from his 'cell'.

Not until then, though. He dare not risk disclosure before his mission was finished. As it was, the threat of deportation hung over him like an angry wasp. He had been fortunate he came from South Africa. The judge had shown mercy, leniency; issued a stiff warning along with the information that, naturally, the Immigration authorities would be notified of his misdemeanour.

Frankly, all he asked for now was an opportunity to ingratiate himself with the Black Panthers and uncover the man behind the scenes. Hart had been right in this. There were whites actively engaged in supplying facilities, legal advice, aid for the 'cell'. Liberals they were called. Some were honest citizens trying to carry through the mayor's instructions that peace depended upon total, unbiased co-operation between New York's polyglot millions. Others had a stake in anarchy, destruction being their aim, civil strife their immediate target. And, too, there were the Mafia with tentacles waving for a share of the lucrative drug traffic. Pot and acid were not enough for the pushers. They wanted 'H' and coke, the mainstemming narcotic that every militant used.

One Whitey, however, stood out like a proverbial sore thumb in a haggle of geese. He had not been pleasured with the guy's company but he knew of him.

'You, Jan, are fantastic. Man, like raindrops on a Spring morn. Like sugar on a pill. Like wow. Great. Sexational. Do it to me again, lover-boy!'

He rolled on his side, gazed down into her awakening eyes. She unlimbered - all of her resilience elasticating into a marvellous formscape of sensuality. She stretched, purred, clawed kittenish approval of his hand circling each breast, flicking each nipple, moving down the gentle slope of ribcage and stomach into the valley so mysteriously wrapped in its precious foliage. He witnessed her reaction - the quickening of breathing, the rise and fall exciting her to grasp his wrist, holding his hand on her.

'You'se it, man,' she panted. Then, laughing, she leapt off the bed, stood with arms akimbo, hips shaking, thighs apart. 'An' it has flown away on foolish wings!'

Mentally, he estimated her addiction by grains slowly falling from a sand-timer. For seconds she seemed to have snapped out of her trip - and then, zoom; back to wide-eyed fantasia.

'I gotta go, Lena. There's a cell meeting tonight.'

She gyrated obscenely, hands doing sweet sentimental things across her torso.

'I'll get dressed!'

'Crap! Ain't no use you attending, man. They're gonna kick your lush ass outta the U. S. of A. but fast.'

He winced as the acid kept her gutter-high. He kept telling himself - 'she's decent. This is the stuff talking', yet he couldn't quite match personalities.

Letting her wander aimlessly round the room he got into his clothes, hearing those sob-croon notes filter through the turmoil inside his head. She rocked back and forth - off on another colourful ride, her velvet brown body ecstatic; jerking into a mental orgasm that would drain her as effectively as any physical stimulatory experience . . .

Flashpoint hadn't reached Harlem yet but given time it would explode larger than Watts. Before Malcolm X and CORE and a hundred other break-away groups, Harlem was fun-town, U.S.A. It still shook nightly but now the jazz bands had guns tucked under their loose shirts and the cops steered clear of anything short of a full-scale riot.

Not far from the Apollo Theatre on West 125th Street sixteen dark bodies slithered through the night and found their individual way down a flight of steps into a stinking basement dive. Up top, the big 'chocolate brown entertainers of some renown' lashed out the jazz, song, jokes for tourists. Down here, amid broken crates and rat-infested boiler-rooms the sixteen listened avidly to Whitey expose yet another weakness in the System.

Thankful for the weak light that swung directly above the man's head, Jan studied him - creating a never-to-be-forgotten picture he could take back to Colonel Hart. He listened with one ear, recording the instructions, catching every inflection - the thickness when certain words were spoken; the melodic lilt of voice when emotion seemed to stir it. Yet, he felt sure, the man was unemotional - doing a job he neither liked nor disliked enough to work up enthusiasm for their cause.

The old slogans sickened him. He wanted something new and shining with which to encourage his race to take a rightful place in an integrated society - not the mumbo-jumbo of rabble-rousing hypocrites. It showed on the other fifteen faces - that listless dance of the macabre; that stereotyped facade presented without thought, logic, understanding. It reminded him of how the Nazis brainwashed kids into believing Hitler was next door to God. It stank of secret police closing in on an African township with orders to create a disturbance so that the world at large would have proof of 'nationalistic antagonism towards the established White government'. He felt sick to his stomach and wanted out. Right out. His mission was complete now. Lena was deader than last trip's acid-drops. He had nowhere to go here. Somewhere to head for - and a country mansion set amid green fields and shady lanes with birds singing their silly beaks off because they didn't have a care.

CHAPTER EIGHT

NOBODY had issued a warning. Nothing had come through from Moscow deploring this present period of anti-climax and recovery. His superiors knew only well enough that the pressure could not be maintained continuously. In the years since his recruitment, he had accomplished more than any one man dare hope to see bear fruit. Admittedly, those so-called conferences of international student bodies and the many-sided sponsored organisations *dedicated* to race relations, labour solidarity, justice for all committees had been worthwhile, too. They had taken leading malcontents and those fellow travelling 'pinks' into a communist influence and strengthened passions that could not otherwise have been nurtured. It was not good to have 'pinks' lazing about in a capitalist country. They were never dependable until their colour changed to a deep red hue. And the conferences did just that.

Walking through Hyde Park, Stanley Edmond breathed the slightly-polluted air of London's greenery. He enjoyed London. More than Paris, Berlin, Madrid, New York, Los Angeles. He detested North America, in fact. Not because it was the antithesis of Russian ideals. Living an existence supposedly sympathetic to the American notion of democratic government had altered his Soviet-orientated suspicion of anything smelling of capitalist intrigue. The Americans were incapable of intrigue, in his opinion. They were much too brash, self-centred, given to boasting to be worthy espionage material. The British, on the other hand, needed watching. Their secret service had been active for more generations than rebellion had ruled Russia. But capital was lacking for the British units and this made them ineffective to an extent. Also, there was that tendency to promote old-boys from Harrow and Eton into the limelight. Not into front-line jobs but as backstabbing Civil Servants seated in plush Whitehall offices. That's where Britain's counter-espionage faults lay - in the quarter where they should have been strongest.

No. he liked London best simply because it happened to brush aside petty jealousies, shelve major issues under a cloak of frivolity. Anyone who thought the average Englishman was a frigid reserved being had a shock when they saw what made London tick. It certainly wasn't the tourist, nor those highpaid American stars entertaining in theatres and clubs. It was the Average Londoner - be he Cockney or Mayfair socialite.

The lights were red!

Inside where he lived, Stanley Edmond knew the traffic flow had come to a dead stop. He was completely unsure where it was going wrong - but he was positive that something had happened to take the ball from his court and place it in . . .

He frowned at a passing rider exercising her horse along the Row. Nobody had unearthed a single reason for those set-backs he had suffered within the last three months. His superiors had shrugged off a few failures under the heading: 'You can't win 'em all!'

Age showed when he smiled at his assumption that Moscow would ever use such a decadent Western phrase. He was conscious of the passing years. It was getting more difficult to fool the young rebels. In a year he had gained ten of his missing decades. Even a 'baby-face' had to mature in time. He hoped Moscow would not get a recent photograph of him. The result would be catastrophic.

He paused, swung angrily and entered the Bayswater Road. History was full of individuals such as he - men who had come to regard the society into which they had been placed with more affection than native land. He told himself that Russia alone counted. And contradicted himself with a fleeting thought of how nice it would be to have a flat in which to spend his fading middle age in this lovely, quaint London of his.

Of his? He shuddered although it was a sunny afternoon. Here was his dilemma - to be or not to be. A suitable question and not one Moscow's educational committees could claim. That belonged to England - and Stratford.

'I'm a seedy little man in a cold world,' he thought. 'A spy who can't come in.'

Was he a spy?

He wasn't in any position to make a decision. He believed himself to be an instrument of salvation. Youth needed him. Negroes needed his valuable help. But he was acting for a foreign power and inciting these people to destroy their established traditions. For what? For an ideology that didn't give a damn whether or not youth got its chance, its head, its rightful place in a war-torn, corrupted globe.

Crossing the road he entered a pub. A pint, a sandwich and a 'slash' would put his thinking processes straight. Time was when he considered vodka the only civilised drink. When a sandwich had all the earmarks of depraved mentalities. And a slash was handled against a brick wall - not in an enclosed urinal with armpit high guards to stop the nearest pervert from catching a glimpse of his next delight . . .

Joseph Nimmo entered his flat and flung his braided jacket on the floor. Everything in the two-roomed retreat bore the same stamp of untidiness. Dishes from last night's meal unwashed; pots and pans littering the carpet; a pair of gaudy knickers draped triumphantly over a bed-rail; a ripped brassiere hanging from a pseudo-chandelier testimony of a struggle that had ended in passionate victory. Kicking aside a volume of Hood's poems, he stepped across a stack of L.P.'s and sat on the creaking bed.

'Christ - it's bloody getting worse!'

He waved drunkenly to his reflection in the cigarette-fugged mirror beside the wash-basin, lay full-length on the groaning bed. *The music this piece of furniture had played!* he thought. Creak . . . creak . . . bounce . . . creak! Action for duet. Chords struck at random creating a marvellously harmonious recital. If he had a quid for every dolly he'd directed into those Elysian heights on this bloody bed he'd be a rich man . . .

Riches? He didn't want wealth. His old man had money but that hadn't altered his way of thinking, his life's dedication. He hated wealth-laden bastards. Money should be abolished. It belonged where it did most good - and that wasn't in a government's patronising hands nor in a bank account. It belonged to the People. To struggling artists, poets, musicians, revolutionaries. They alone counted for something. Fuck the politicians and those pig bastards.

He was drunk - and he knew it. When he couldn't get the urge and find a dolly-bird he had to be pissed. God, they were so available. Within three houses he could have his choice of a dozen willing screws. University types with more between their hairy legs than was brooding in their demented minds.

Staggering to his feet, he hurried from his flat. In the toilet he sicked up his drunkenness and wiped froth-stained lips. He wished somebody would find a way to vomit without getting sick on beard and moustache. Back in his flat he wiped water across the stained hair, dried his face on a filthy towel. He felt immensely better. Now - where were those damned screws?

Jean Beckett had a steady boyfriend but that didn't stop her from enjoying the occasional side bit. Johnny knew, anyway. He played in bed with other girls. She'd actually caught him in the act once and been pleasantly surprised when he invited her to share the sport. It had been a revelation - a fab hour threesome.

At nineteen she had experienced every perversion, every sensation a woman three times her age should have sampled. Her own mother had never been treated to such orgiastic splendours as Jean had managed in two years at Essex University. It wasn't that the campus as a whole indulged in depravity. There were elements here that summed up youth's explosiveness. Sex, pot and sharing seemed right somehow when taken in its broader view.

She was naked beneath her lonely sheets when Joe knocked. She knew it was Joe. No girl in this street could fail to recognise that impatient, *I'm here* knock.

Joe grinned at her nudity, asked, 'Expecting the boyfriend?'

Jean turned away, giving him an unadulterated view of her swinging, prominent derriere. Few men could have ogled that provocative delight without seeking more intimate contact with its satin curves. 'Lock the door, Joe!' her sleepy voice said as she climbed back into bed.

'Crissakes, you're a cold bitch,' he complained, undressing.

Enigmatic as Mona Lisa, her smile shattered him. There was a laughing secret hidden behind those clear, blue eyes. Ruffling Titian hair she propped against a pillow and let him see her large, cantaloupe breasts in unfettered glory.

'Okay, what's so bloody funny, Jean?'

'You, Joe. God, don't you ever wash?' She sounded annoyed. 'Look at you - thin, bones sticking out everywhere and your dirty mind projecting its lusts at me. But you've got a surprise coming . . . I can't. It's that time of the month!' She folded her arms across her breasts, laughed silently at his frustration.

He snorted, threw back the covers, got in beside her. 'So what? There are ways . . . '

'Not with me - not for you, Joe!'

'Ah, Jean,' he pleaded, trying to snare a breast.

'Take your dirty hands off me,' she warned. 'I don't mind company. I hate sleeping alone. But no funny business. I know what you're like so don't try turning me around and getting hot. It won't buy you a bloody piece tonight, Joe Nimmo.'

'He mulled over his predicament. If only she would relax. Talk . . . maybe that would mollify her determination not to have him caress her gorgeous body. 'They're going ahead with plans to invite Amos Platt to the Union next week,' he mentioned offhandedly.

She tensed. Like Joe, she was a dedicated Young Socialist. Amos Platt was a name to make any loyal Red Flag-waving adherent go crazy. His view on the colour problem, racial distrust, a 'white Britain fit for old war heroes' rankled. It made little difference that the man was intelligent, dedicated, honest. She preferred gimmicks and untruths and vote-catching mockeries to forthright statements reflecting the nation's mood. To hell with what the common bastards wanted. They the students, liberals, internationalists - knew best. Nobody should rock their boat. And nobody would providing they could always break up a meeting so that things which were needed saying could not be said.

She didn't even 'feel' Joe's hands insidiously working under her lush, firm buttocks as she chewed over what he'd said. She was semi-aware of urges that had nothing to do with politics building within her seat of emotion.

'I know where we can get a canister of C.S. gas,' Joe mentioned, slipping a finger where it should not be.

Her body reacted to his probing automatically - not unfavourably. And she was completely innocent of helping his hand reach its desired target. 'That's lethal stuff, Joe,' she warned.

'Oh, bloody hell!' He made his subtle move seem like part of his explosive derision. Now he had her going! He could *taste* her sympathetic surrender as flesh flowed over his hand and offered itself for more strenuous efforts. Gently, he altered her position, guiding her onto one side so that her back was to him. 'You've been listening to our own propaganda, Jean. We don't blast off against tear gas and C.S. isn't that much worse.' He fingered diligently.

An involuntary moan escaped her lips; her hips heaved; and she presented more of herself for his pleasure. It was a build-up to depravity. Suddenly, she was conscious of where he was gaining entry and tried to pull away.

'No, Jean . . . don't. I won't go all the way but you enjoy this . . .'

She shuddered. What a rotten bastard! She didn't mind the perversity. It was nothing new for a man to attempt this - and, occasionally, get it. But he was a slimy bastard all the same. She tightened her muscles, gritted, 'Bloody right you won't! That's *verboten* territory tonight - or any night as far as you're concerned, Joe Nimmo!'

'I'm warned off. Okay! About Amos Platt . . .'

She wriggled uncomfortably. His finger hurt. But there was something highly suggestive in *its* wriggling that pleased her. She suffered the discomfort, remarked, 'We could force his car to detour.'

'Not on! Others have tried that and the bastard sneaks in a back door.' He grinned. *How like Platt he was now!*

'I'm not in favour of gas, Joe. What do the committee say?'

'Split down the middle.' Another double-entendre. It gave him great pleasure insinuating when she wasn't fully conscious of his meanings.

'And does Julius agree?'

He chuckled. Julius Gold could thank him for being safe from Network Seventy . . . what a bloody stupid name, he mused. Those stupid kids play-acting at being spies. And his old man actually going to bat for him and believing that his son would not squeal on their organisation. He had news for Mr Nimmo, senior. When he personally met Gold he would spill the beans - but good!

'Julius doesn't know yet. He will, though. He's due at our next meeting.'

Jean groaned, flung herself onto her stomach. 'You horrible pervert!' Her thighs widened, her bottom lifting ecstatically. 'All right - go ahead. Get it over with . . . '

For one hesitant minute Joe rose above her, staring at those white, lecherous buttocks. Then, with a sigh, he came down on her, grinding his thin body against her plumpness - feeling her total surrender; hearing her softly muted moans into the pillow . . .

CHAPTER NINE

BRITISH plans to supply arms to South Africa gave him a cast-iron motive for visiting Zambia. The 'toothless bulldog' had done it again. Facts could be twisted. Planes were always a controversial subject. Nobody could swear that a specific aircraft was only fit for coastal defence. What flew could fly across sea or land with equal freedom and anything suitable for dive bombing a submarine was capable of dive-bombing a group of nationalists. Also, frigates were just as likely to train their guns on an inshore target as they wore to bombard another vessel.

In his heart of hearts, Stanley Edmond did not want to see all Africa black. In Russia there was lip-service to equality, racial integration. But that was just lip-service - the true facts bore no resemblance to actuality. Many ethnic groups had been forcibly ejected from their homelands; others systematically decimated until they no longer posed a threat to centralised government. Fortunately, Mother Russia had not been confronted with a serious colour problem. There were no Africans, no ebony blacks within her domestic sphere of influence to make the situation critical. China, too, faced no such internal strife. There were divisions within the Chinese-Tibetian-Mongolian hierarchy but a question of dark skin never arose. Like so many nations free from the insoluble question of integration, Russia and China felt it necessary to promote racial disharmony as an aid to world domination.

And Stanley Edmond - Igor Gruginshof - had a sickness that amounted to rebellion in himself. He was absolutely certain now that the years had finally caught up with his mental ability to ride roughshod over established facts. The ideological training, his frequent returns for further indoctrination and examination had failed to provide tap-roots. He hadn't been home since undertaking his assignment but there were other sectors of the world where full-scale Soviet infiltration made that nation a subsidiary of the Motherland. In all but name the Eastern Bloc were Russia without being within the elite states of the union.

Listening to frenzied natives promising to overthrow Ian Smith, threatening to have Britain ruled out of the United Nations, denying the U.K.'s right to control their Commonwealth gave him the shits, to put it mildly. He wanted to tell them how much they owed to Britain, the British taxpayer; how they could not survive without annual loans from that country they delighted in tormenting. Perhaps the bulldog had lost some of its dentures but it wasn't dead yet. The 'old lion' upon which the sun never set had a bite - a damned good appetite when starvation seemed nigh. When left alone he had a lethargic nature; when aroused he could always prove why he ruled as monarch of every jungle.

Naturally, he was treated with deference due to his position with the foundation. As a dispenser of monetary hand-outs and an able lecturer in economics, international affairs and the ever-inflammatory subtle race theory he was a welcome guest in any black African community. His hotel had been paid in advance by the authorities - more sumptuous than he personally would have chosen. His meals were gratis, free, on the house but he ate simple foods, declining the *splash* that was urged upon him. It was a considered opinion that beggars should not be munificent hosts. Pleading poverty, striving to negotiate foreign loans did not walk hand in hand with laying a splendid table for the banker.

Alone in his suite, he contemplated his future. He verged on that rebellion he had encouraged others to take. But, for him, a revolution would be the reverse of all he had preached during his sojourn in the West. He was ill-suited for the role of instigator nowadays. His ideological fervour had diminished until it no longer sustained his effectiveness.

Then, too, the memory of what that Essex University student had told him lingered. 'Network Seventy' - a dangerous enemy. He did not underestimate the power of youth. He had been using it for communist advantage long enough to know how fickle, how treacherous it could be.

Youth had its ideals, and rightly so. But it had an inherent distrust of adult guidance that, come the moment of truth, seemed to blow-back in the faces of those eager to exploit young energies, young enthusiasms.

What he did not like particularly was the fact that Network Seventy had on call its parent organization, Network Forty. He was versed in the courage, ability, unswerving loyalty of those WWII agents who had been responsible for Germanic collapse. All the soldiers, sailors, airmen could not have accomplished invasion and defeat had it not been for the diehard men and women of Allied special services. Much credit was due them for Russia's own safety. And the thought of being confronted by such an outfit scared the hell out of him. He did not relish the thought of languishing in gaol, regardless of KGB's record in gaining freedom for her key men.

No, the time was fast approaching when he had to make a choice. Either he could continue his activities to that bitter, cell-door end or decide to cut-loose and fly high, free, unshackled by ideologies, sentiments, duty.

He was close to telephoning the British High Commissioner when a knock shook him from catastrophe. His gaze swept the room. Automatically. There was nothing visible to connect him with subversion. He smiled, opened the door.

The woman was in her middle thirties; ebony, slender, attractively dressed in a flowing gown of Viennese design so that her shining flesh was revealed right to the upper swells of firm, high breasts. She wore a hair-piece crowning swept-back styling and a string of expensive natural pearls round her velvet throat. Dark, flashing, intense eyes fixed him with slightly mocking innuendo. Diamonds sparkled on her hand as she gestured at the partially closed door.

'I'm Ullime N'gola,' she said huskily. 'May I come in?' He stepped aside, smelling exotic perfume as she swept regally by him. He liked the provocative sway of hips and buttocks beneath the Austrian creation, the manner in which she turned - defiant, feminine, willing to be compromised and those so-expressive eyes that dared him to comment upon her beauty.

'You're wondering what I am doing here, no doubt?'

He inclined his head, affecting a care-not stance.

'My husband will be entertaining you later,' she continued unabated. 'He's a slow man - quite unable to come to a point.' She laughed uproariously. Swinging her capable hips into action she crossed the hotel room, stood outlined against a setting sun that had no equal for sheer brilliance. Watching the play of artful colours across her city, she spoke directly to his reflection in the picture-window overlooking natural splendour. 'We need your help, Mr Edmond. Our economy is facing ruin unless we arrive at some solution to the Rhodesian crisis.'

'What makes you think I have any solutions?'

She slowly swung to face him. Her hands did mysteriously sensual things down her hips, flanks. 'I have heard rumours, Mr Edmond. We have sources in London . . . '

He stiffened. Had it got to that stage?

' . . . and they confirm that you are in favour of united action by the African nations. For that we require funds. Patriots do not exist on a handful of rice today, sir. They need clothing, arms, ammunition, communications equipment and a logistics support.

'That, Mrs Ngola, is outside my province. I'm from a foundation - not an organisation supplying funds for insurrection. My work is the alleviation of suffering, providing medical and education facilities so that native populations can work towards self-sufficiency.'

Sheba used her volatile charms then.

For an instant, Igor, the Russian, almost reverted into his native language. Then *Mr Edmond* assumed mastery . . . He closed his eyes to the voluptuousness of her enticements, those proffered charms, the insatiableness glinting in her dark, hot gaze. He ignored her mobile gyrations, the hands that could not be quietened as they roamed her lush curves in preparation for a 'native' festival.

'Please, don't!'

Ullime N'gola did not lessen her ultra-sensuous assault on his mind. Her hands swiftly encompassed her jutting breasts, went to her hips, her thighs, curled suggestively into her abdomen and buttocks, snaked back to her breasts and throat. Her eyes festered, begged, cajoled. Her flesh beckoned, created a canker in his soul.

'*Mrs* N'gola - stop!'

She hesitated, hands on breasts.

'I have no intention of authorising funds for subversive activities against another sovereign state. It would mean my neck on a chopping block if I did.' He laughed. 'And there isn't anything you can offer to make that prospect a lesser evil!'

'No?' she moved across the room, stood inches from him. 'I have been told . . . '

'Not by me, *Mrs* N'gola.'

'Why must you stress the missus?'

'A simple reason. You are married. I am single. Your husband is an important man in the hierarchy here and I have no intention of getting myself involved with an ambitious man's wife.'

'You prefer a single girl then?'

'Naturally!' He moved aside so that her perfume, her beauty could not detract his determination to steer clear of her enticements.

'That's decided!' She dropped her seductive manner, walked to the door. 'If you have a caller don't treat her as you have me. You see, Mr Edmond, I happen to love my country. I believe that - with money - we can overcome!' She left no doubt in her expression she expected him to bow three times to the protester's song.

'Forget it, N'gola. I'm not prepared to have a prostitute soften my resolve. Especially . . . ' He stopped, trying to look beyond her to where the fast-sinking sun etched palm trees and tall buildings in its hurry to escape this land.

'Especially if she's black?'

'I didn't say that!'

'You meant it, Mr Edmond. Aren't you showing prejudice?'

'Hardly, since I didn't make a comment.'

'Ah, but . . . '

'But nothing, Mrs N'gola. What is left unsaid is not for speculation. What if I tried to suggest I meant *especially if she's a common trollop?'*

'She isn't - and that I guarantee. My daughter cannot be classified as common, sir!'

He felt for his chair, slumped into it. 'Daughter? Your daughter?'

'Yes!' She didn't show the slightest inclination to make excuses for her daughter proposing to visit a white man in his hotel room with fornication the ultimate outcome of that visit.

'You must be mad!'

'No, Mr Edmond - just devoted to my husband's ambitions and his aspirations for Zambia's future. We are black but that is not a crime. We are an incomplete nation and that *is* a crime. You see, Africa is beset with tribal problems Europe has never faced. You have nationalities fighting against one another for supremacy. Here, within a national boundary, we have tribes stressing their right to rule their own domains. This has got to cease. And my husband is the man who can accomplish that feat. He is trusted, respected, known to favour autonomy within a federal jurisdiction. That's why I want your money and why I'm willing to sacrifice myself or my daughter to make that dream come true.'

The man was devoid of any intelligent reply. He understood her innermost convictions. That she was willing to offer her daughter's flesh upon the altar of her husband's ambitions for national reasons was an unanswerable argument. He had heard of such women, men. He had not believed they existed. Those with whom he dealt seldom bothered to go beyond stereotyped idealisms and those fleshy attendants called pot, sex, superficial freedoms. Permissiveness did not appeal to him. Although he was supposed to support, encourage the depravities of Western Culture he did not believe it did humanity any good to have nudity, licentiousness, drug-induced looseness set upon the entire globe. The backlash must come and he did not relish his Russia bathed in a blood-bath of violence such as had been turned loose upon Los Angeles, Berlin, Paris, London, even Zambia. He preferred nations to co-exist, fight their boundary wars between soldiers paid to throw away their lives and let the civilians rest in peace - not under a tombstone - or have differences settled in a congress of neutral ideologies. Preferably, he wished the world could agree to a single military force under an international commandature subject to a global presidency.

'I'm sorry, Mrs N'gola. I don't want your daughter sharing my bed. In fact - and it might surprise you - I don't happen to want any woman sleeping with me unless I chose her myself!'

'If I undressed . . . '

He raised a hand apologetically. 'Don't. It wouldn't change my mind. I would have seen your nakedness and probably laugh at your foolishness afterwards.'

She sighed. 'I admire your sincerity, Mr Edmond. I shall not insult your intelligence by offering other alternatives. I respect a man of integrity - like my husband. Don't feel he is brushed by the same paint as a lot of African leaders. He wishes to promote tribalism to a height where it no longer sees itself as a society apart from the country-wide citizenship. If that does not demand full sacrifice then I'm unable to comprehend what makes a white man think he is entitled to dictate to us.'

'Mrs N'gola - don't worry. Not all Europeans feel inclined to knock African efforts. What you say about tribalism is your disaster. It is your problem - not ours. Get rid of the tribal customs, those witch-doctor medical treatments and you might just reach a low-level of civilised government. But until then I'm sorry to state - you are backward nations; incapable of rallying your people into a single unit under a single flag.'

'How true!' She walked to the door, smiled beatifically at him. 'My daughter will accompany you to the luncheon tonight, Mr Edmond. If she is wanted . . . ' She rolled her expressive eyes, gave him a sample of what to expect by smoothing down her Austrian gown with hands that moulded her exciting figure and quickly touched that portion of her anatomy which men desired most.

'Your daughter will be home immediately after the reception,' he remarked acidly.

'I trust you - but not my daughter,' the woman replied . . .

Putsch was a word associated with Hitler, Mussolini and other fascist dictators. It apparently applied to African nations. Stanley Edmond did not have concrete proof that his hosts were guilty of the infamous word but he was surprised to learn that several liberals he had hoped to meet were now *persona non grate*. Other less democratic Black states did not make such an attempt to cover indiscretions behind a fabric of invective but those with whom Edmond spoke to all sympathised strongly with the missing diplomats whilst criticising their mistaken ideals. There was no error in his assumption that the men he wanted to meet had been effectively eliminated before the 'conference' began.

During the dinner - he had expected a small luncheon - he found that an army of informants came to him with their petty requests for aid. Then, when the speech-making had ended, the last drinks dispensed, he was escorted front the huge hall by Tom N'gola, his wife and daughter. The plot had thickened!

'Have you ever had the feeling that events had taken control of plans?' N'gola asked as they relaxed in the Rolls-Royce supplied for their return to his hotel.

'Many times,' Edmond admitted.

'I'm curious about your reactions to our missing representatives.'

'Don't be,' the Russian replied. 'I take such events in my stride. Here today - gone tomorrow is an old adage.'

'Those men were traitors to our country,' N'gola persisted. 'They would have you believe that we were only bent on invasion of a neighbouring territory. We do not condone the illegal Smith regime but we do not *actively* support any violence.'

Edmond smiled. 'Is the word active a lesser evil than moral?'

'Mr Edmond,' N'gola said sharply, sitting forward with an intensity of purpose Edmond could feel through his being. 'I suggest you discuss this with our young people. Your foundation actively encourages youth to submit their minds and hearts to the ideals of international brotherhood. You sponsor projects designed to increase harmonious working together. Whilst I must admit you are anti-action there is, sometimes, justification for non-passive intervention. I'm not,' and he smiled toothily, 'advocating direct military forays across the border but neither shall I decry those who make punitive excursions in the name of total freedom.'

Edmond compelled himself to take the approach step by step. He did not wish to appear overly eager. 'I suppose it would do no harm to speak with some of your hotheads.'

'None at all! I'm sure we would all welcome an opportunity to hear your advice.'

'Ah, there's the rub - as Shakespeare said!' Edmond laughed lightly, setting the man at ease with his slick, friendly delivery. 'I do not like adults present when I'm discussing adolescent themes. I find that parents have a habit of making their children over-conscious and as a result the message is lost.'

'I understand,' Tom N'gola remarked pleasantly. 'You may rest assured everything shall be done to provide privacy . . . '

For the most part, his plans went according to the manual. A spy could not have taken his words and used them out of context to convict him of rabble-rousing. The years spent gathering data, offering suggestions behind a phalanx of do-good instructions, distorting issues until those militants in his audience began to believe he was speaking only for them had given him a masterly touch. Whilst pretending to abhor violence he actually preached its merits. Whilst being critical of demonstrations he supported those who walked straight from his lecture and staged a protest.

Everything depended on the subject - and his appeal was most effective for those egotistic morons who thought in terms of action.

Moron was an inappropriate word for the gathering he had addressed. They belonged to those Negroid elite attending a university. It didn't make them less susceptible to his inflammatory subtleties; those hidden barbs. It simply took violence a higher notch up the educational ladder.

Now, from his hotel window, he could see the aftermath of his 'discussion'. N'gola would be sadly disappointed . . .

Especially if the man knew what was happening in that room. Then again, maybe he wouldn't give a bloody damn! His wife had been adamant in the interests of national advancement even a husband had to sacrifice something.

Yona N'gola had beauty going for her - in an African way. She possessed a striking figure, intelligence, a warmth that made mating the cementation of lasting friendship. She had no hibitions, few taboos, could be classified as an exhibitionist par excellence. Her childlike smile when she strutted naked exposing all of her gorgeous black sleekness - did not lessen her seductiveness. It served, instead, to heighten bestial thoughts and make him realise how some men considered young girls so excitingly fresh, unsoiled, sweetly desirable. The safe knowledge that Yona was old enough for what they *had* to share saved him from denying her his manhood.

Her hands fondled his shoulders as he watched the street scene. Burning cars on their sides bore evidence of the violence he had unleashed. In the distance, a struggle was taking place outside, inside the High Commissioner's office. Two energetic students climbed the flag-pole, lowered the Union Jack, tossed it to the chanting mob. Within seconds it, like the cars, was ablaze. Crashing sounds followed an orgy of stone-throwing; police whistles shattering the beautiful noises of insurrection at work.

'They won't be stopped now,' the girl murmured.

'Do you want them to stop?'

'It doesn't matter to me.' Her hands dropped, to his chest, fingers lightly touching his nipples. 'Please - take me to bed!'

He faced her, conscious of her sharp-nippled breasts, her silken abdomen. 'Are you a virgin?'

Her head inclined, her eyelids drooping modestly. 'Yes.'

'Haven't you ever . . . ?'

'I've played with men,' she replied hurriedly. 'I know what to do.'

'It might hurt.'

'Let it.' Her head shot back, lips parted now as she gazed at him anxiously. 'Don't keep me waiting.'

A pulse beat alarmingly in his temples. Her woman scent rose in assailing waves, gorging his desire. Her flesh slipped through his avid hands; her tongue hot, snaking, demanding as they kissed. Cupping her delightful buttocks, he lifted her - lips still fastened to hers - carried her like that to the bed. His weight on her went unnoticed. There was just flesh on flesh; hands feeling, experimenting, exploring depths of passion neither could resist. And, suddenly, she moaned, collapsed on her back

- a willing object of his manhood, offering pleasures men seldom found in this age of devirginized permissiveness . . .

And, in the streets, the eruption of brutality shared his savage love-making. Fires burned brightly amid cavorting students; inside the hotel room. For every thunderous roar of mob approval for another vandalistic act he surged ahead to greater destruction of innocence. It was as though a parallel existed between those bent on demonstration and his demonstration of what carnal appetites could accomplish. There was no let-up on that hotel bed. Like an untamed tiger he ravaged the girl consciously struggling to gratify her own insatiable desire for complete fulfilment.

They were jungle animals engaging in a death embrace - sobbing, gasping, panting into the final stages of exhaustion . . .

CHAPTER TEN

COLONEL HART paced back and forth across his living-room carpet, hands clasped behind back, shoulders bowed under the weight of responsibility. Like shadows occupying darker nooks, his audience waited patiently for his decision. Even Joseph Nimmo was conscious of the man's powerful character of his strength to bludgeon any opposition into dust.

Eventually, the colonel halted, took his seat and gazed at old friends, youthful recruits with fatherly compassion. He wanted a cigar - to have fragrant smoke coil and wreathe round his head as he issued his proclamation. But the doctor had been very adamant - no liquor, no cigars. Conceding medical defeat, Hart opened his *Everest* packet, lit a menthol cigarette.

'Twenty years ago I could have ordered this man's death,' he announced. 'Some of my people would agree to this edict even now.' He smiled gratefully at Bob, Eric, Karl. Memories lasted longer than changing times! 'But our children would object . . . '

'I certainly would,' Joseph Nimmo declared vehemently.

The youth's father winced. *God,* he thought, *how could I have conceived such a hopeless son?*

Nanette Aubin smiled wistfully. 'I refuse to be so positive but we - Network Seventy - deplore violence as an answer to violence. There has got to be another solution. James Bond may have a licence to kill but fact is not fiction. We are fact. Parents and children. Stanley Edmond is fact - not a mythical monster we can slay and ask for sainthood.'

Hart nodded his understanding. He liked Nanette. She was a sensible girl - and, if his wife had lived, he couldn't have asked for a dearer daughter of his own. 'There are many alternatives, Nanette. We do not necessarily have to be hangmen nor executioners. Certain nations have a death penalty. We could plant information and let the law there take its appointed course. We could also have Edmond exposed in a newspaper. Or see him imprisoned for thirty years in this country. All possibles - but not very appealing. Frankly, I would like to have Mr Edmond as my guest here.'

Young Nimmo jumped to his feet, cried: 'A trick! You would kill him!'

'Sit down, Joseph!' his father commanded.

From a far corner of the huge room, James Simpson studied the characters in this drama. For him, the colonel had bitten off more than was chewable trying to regulate these youngsters as he had their parents. They weren't military, nor did they feel that wartime 'belongingness' so vital to a mission's success. It was his opinion that this anti-demonstration campaign was doomed to failure. That any attempt to present youth with proof of its sucker-status would be received by catcalls and vicious laughter.

'Just a moment,' Hart barked, fixing Joe with his penetrating gaze. 'Right from the beginning I've been warned that you, Joseph Nimmo, would betray us. That you were antagonistic to our motives. I believe you have told this Russian-born agent we are on his trail. But I have faith in parental genes passing down into unborn generations. Somewhere deep within you there must be a single spark we can fan into a warm flame. If only you could get it into your head - we are not against youth's democratic right to protest against our system. We are prepared to change certain of our standards to meet this fresh outlook. But we cannot sit idle whilst Russia and China propagate dissention in our ranks. And that is what this man is doing. For years, our young people have been brainwashed to accept permissiveness, demonstration, drug-taking, perversion, abortion, State hand-outs as their natural inheritance. That is terribly wrong. In our eyes, at least. It is not the duty of older citizens to provide for the young - it is the youth who should be concerned with making things easier for those who have contributed to society and provided schools, opportunity, jobs for their off-springs. We have our values mixed up. Age should command respect, assistance. Not age being liable for youth's bankruptcy.'

'You brought us into a sad world,' Joe yelled. 'It's your responsibility - not ours!'

'In certain respects, agreed,' Hart admitted softly. 'Where we went wrong was in being too soft. We wanted peace at the price of our children's welfare. We should have insisted on stiff terms. We - the West - won the war. Not the Russians. Germany could have overrun Stalin's land if we hadn't supplied arms, material, sent convoys to their doom, running the gauntlet of Nazi bombers, created diversions by launching other fronts to extend Hitler's supply-lines. In the Pacific, we had Japan on her knees when Russia sneaked into the backdoor to grab more territory. And this after years of phoney manoeuvres where not a shot was fired in anger. I'm afraid, Joseph, we sold your birthright for a barrel of pipe-dreams and gave the Soviets every golden opportunity to destroy all that was decent, good, democratic in Britain.'

'You forget one important aspect of this,' young Nimmo remarked with sarcasm. 'Russian youth is on the march, too. How do you explain that?'

Bob Thomson crossed different knees, flicked a lighter and said through coiling smoke: 'Simple. Their movement has backfired. What they tried to do to us has now come home to roost. But let's examine their methods of curtailing rebellion. Stiff prison sentences - years at a time. Secret police paying midnight visits. Mothers and fathers treated like criminals because their kids dared opt out of society. We don't treat a dog like that, Joe - and I'd advise you to remember it, too.'

'Talk is cheap. You're quoting from a capitalistic Press. Russia has high standards.'

Bob grinned. 'Care to live there for a few years, Joe? We could arrange it - documents in order, faked passport . . . '

'Shit on you!' the explosive youth shouted.

'Hart leapt to his feet, eyes flashing danger signals. 'Enough of that language! There are women present . . . '

'Christ - listen to the old goat!'

Like a flash, Tim Hart covered the distance between Joe and his seat. His fist landed with a satisfying plop on the other's bearded chin and Joe sank back, eyes glazing over, his body sprawling full-length on the carpet.

'Thank you, Tim!'

All eyes turned to Eric Nimmo. His thick lips trembled and those hard grey eyes seemed misty, apologetic.

'I'm sorry, Mr Nimmo . . . '

'Don't be, boy. I should have done that when he was ten!'

'Oh, hell!' Wanda Collins suddenly laughed. 'Excuse me, Colonel. I didn't mean to be abusive but that Joe makes me sick. And no offence to you, Mr Nimmo.'

Eric shrugged pathetically. 'I understand, Miss Collins.'

'I don't for a minute think you do but it's nice hearing you say so,' the girl remarked. 'Anyway, what I wanted to say was if Joe has betrayed us why are we sitting here getting ourselves worked into a lather about what he does, or does not, believe to be the truth of our situation. He's just one against . . . ' and she rapidly counted the number present, 'seventeen.'

'Eighteen,' Hart announced stridently. He got to his feet, walked to the door. Hand on knob, he smiled at Mai. 'Remember Jan Hugens?'

A ripple raced through the older members but more so through Mai Bedford, now Mai Collins. She had good cause to recall Jan - another ten minutes undisturbed by the S.S. and perhaps her children would have been his. It had been close that night. So bloody near she could still 'feel' his body pressing hers down into that French haystack; still taste his kisses; still search for the orgasm that never materialised.

'Jan married and his son is here,' Hart said softly, opening the door. 'Jan . . . come in with us,' he called, standing back to allow the coloured youth a clear passage into the room.

For what seemed an eternity, Mai held her breath. She couldn't trust her eyesight. Not Jan! Not her handsome lover!

Eric Nimmo, surprisingly, was the first to stand, hold out his hand to the newcomer. 'Welcome, Jan Hugens. Your father was my closest friend.'

Suddenly, everyone in the room crowded round the boy. It seemed as if they all were trying to forget the past, trying to associate the South African with this dark-skinned youth who did not in the least resemble his father.

The sons and daughters had never known Jan Hugens, senior. To them, the coloured descendent of an old comrade was little more than another recruit - a gratifying taste of brotherliness insinuated into what had been an all-white society.

'Jan has been doing some undercover work for us in Harlem,' Hart said. 'His findings are confirmation of my preconceived verdict that our youth is being subverted by foreign elements determined to disrupt our civilisation.'

From the floor, where he sat nursing his bruised jaw, Joe Nimmo studied Jan with what amounted to cynical disapproval All his arguments had been demolished by the appearance of this stranger. Yet, could he capitalise on some of those older antagonisms. He felt sure that the members of Hart's wartime team did not honestly accept this bastard breed into their elite reunion.

'You pathetic nigger,' he growled. 'Can't you see what they've done to you?'

Jan walked forward until he stood directly over Joe. A silence enveloped the group as Hart watched the in-play with undisguised approval. He was depending heavily on Jan. On the lad's ability to place young Nimmo in a ridiculous situation.

'Nigger?' Jan asked menacingly. 'You say nigger and expect me to be your prop?'

Joe climbed to his feet - unkempt, dazed, stunned by Jan's rejection of him as the black man's messiah.

'Don't talk to me, man,' Jan said firmly. 'Don't hand me platitudes. Don't soft-soap me with tales of how your type love us and how all other Whiteys detest the ground we soil with our black feet. You're trash, man. Pure garbage. You belong in a zoo where real people can see your antics and get a belly-laugh. God, you creeps make me sick!'

'You sanctimonious bastard!' Joe howled. 'You're a traitor to your colour!'

'You know,' Jan replied with an effort to control himself, 'it's your kind who are traitors to yourselves. There isn't any law that says a black can't abide by white laws. We don't have to wear loin-cloths and swing from trees, boy. We don't have to listen to every long-haired drug-addict to know which side our bread is buttered on, man. We've been exploited for centuries but that is preferable when the exploiter offers some justice. What does your bossman propose? Slavery again? Chinese commies trampling over us? Russians sending us to Siberia if we don't behave? No, thanks, Hippy! We don't need tolerance and advice. Not cash with strings.'

'Hear, hear!' Tim shouted.

'Amen!' Eric Nimmo muttered.

'I'm getting out of here,' Joe screamed, pushing viciously at Jan.

When the coloured youth slammed him back against Karl Bluther, young Nimmo laughed hysterically.

'That's it! Be one of them! Torture me. Make me talk. Show us how your witch-doctors paralysed their victims!'

Jan stood aside, permitted Joe to stride brazenly to the door.

'Just a moment, lad!' Colonel Hart advanced a few paces, gestured for the others to be silent, spoke with utmost sincerity. 'I'm sorry if we've treated you roughly. I wouldn't want you to feel unkindly toward us but I will make this promise - defect and I'll personally hound you until I die. That's not an idle boast, son. I'd promise the same if you were my son. I happen to have high regard for what our country stands for and no individual, no friendship, no tie of blood will ever make me forget that. I'd like you to leave but I'd also like to know you felt kindly disposed to our aims.'

'Aims?' Joe sneered. 'You haven't got an aim, Colonel. You're old-hat. Stuffed for a museum. You don't reckon us kids - never will. You see yourself as a guardian angel trying to undo all the injustices we have suffered. But it's too late, Colonel. You had your chance. You could have bargained with Joe Stalin, with Adolf Hitler. You could have stopped that bloody bomb from being dropped on innocent Japanese citizens. You're guilty, Colonel. My old man is guilty. You're all guilty. You've given us a fucking awful world and you still insist on trying to dictate to us when we're only sorting out the mess you made.'

Before Brett Hart could reply his son stepped forward. 'We're about the same age, Joe. I can't be accused of sharing responsibility for the Bomb. But I wish to hell I had one now. I'd drop the bastard on you - and all those idiots who think like you. You're so bloody stubborn and all-right. You can't see that aggression and invasion must be met with strength. Where would our free world be if it hadn't been for American initiative in Korea, Vietnam, Israel?'

'American brutality and slaughter. You're forgetting Mai Lai, aren't you?' Nimmo taunted.

'I'm forgetting nothing. The murders there were drug induced. Your type of society, Joe. Not mine!'

'Like hell . . . '

Jan Hugens stepped forward until he was practically breathing into Joe's mouth. 'I've tripped, man. I've blown my cool and I can't say I enjoyed it. If those G.I.'s at Mai Lai murdered because they'd been taking pot then I've got one thing to say - the sooner we have global control of drugs with stiffer than stiff penalties for its use the better I'll feel!'

'You bloody would!' Joe snapped, opening the door. As a parting gesture he thumbed his nose at Colonel Hart. 'Get stuffed - the lot of you,' he snarled and slammed the door behind him.

'No comment!' Jan grinned, glancing at Wanda. He had noticed her early on and liked the way she gave him her full attention.

Mai noticed this, too. She didn't shudder; she didn't make the slightest attempt to deny her daughter the privilege of attracting the man she wanted to bed-down. It was Jan's son. He was black - and it still wasn't a major issue. She wondered momentarily - how she would have felt had the boy been a Negro without having a father she knew? Would colour then have counted as a deterrent?

CHAPTER ELEVEN

BOB THOMSON had many recollections of disobedience. There had been times when he figured Colonel Brett Hart would toss him out of 'Department Seven' with that most inglorious stigma: 'dishonourable discharge'.

Tonight, he was again actively disobeying orders. For the record, he believed in what he was doing. Believed it strongly enough to make the younger generation look like fools. There was an old saying - 'too many cooks spoil the broth' - and he considered that Network Seventy had too many inexperienced chefs to make this particular stew palatable. What it needed was an expert cook; one of the old school style of chefs. An experienced, artistic, master prepared to dedicate his career to a single dish.

And what a dish!

Bob knew his magnetic personality. Knew that he attracted beautiful women to his lair like a spider does flies into a web. He had a gift of the 'gab', a *savoire faire* few moderns could compete with, a way of handling starry-eyed dolly-birds that would make an uncouth hippy cry into his unwashed beard. He didn't grab a girl, throw her back and expect penetration as a natural follow-through thrust. He courted her, dazzled her with smile and charm, and - once the preparatory meals had been consumed - *retired* to a sanctuary where their mutually electrified desires could find sparking mate.

Wanda Collins was his first choice for a bed-mate. But Wanda was on his side. That ruled her out - until after their mission had been successfully terminated. He *never* mixed business with sheer pleasure although pleasure was a fleeting extension of business more than often.

Dot Clarke happened to be next in line and rated his bed that night. As an example of modern dolly-bird escapism she topped the totem pole. As a miss with a secret she more than figured in his schemes . . .

Dot was dark-haired, olive-skinned, small, fragile, shapely and vivacious. She exuded character, humour, a flair for affairs. She could charm a man with words, gestures, a batted eye. She did excite in her low-cut dress, her tight-fitted belt, her walking from the hip.

'You know,' Bob remarked as they finished the prawn cocktail, 'I've seen a lot of women eat in this club of mine but none with your style. I mean it, Dot - you're terrific.'

She placed her napkin on her lap. 'I've got an awful suspicion you're going to seduce me before dawn.'

'How right you are!' He laughed easily, signalled a waiter for refills. He appreciated Dot's insistence on having rye and ginger with everything she ate. He loathed those snobs who declared that a specific wine went with this, or that. He could not abide the waiter who suggested a special brand of wine, brandy, aperitif to match the order. He always reckoned it was up to the individual. *Name your poison* was a rule he followed religiously. His own brand was *Teacher's Highland Cream.* And if *that* was poison, then let him die contented!

'It's my contention a man wines and dines a girl for what he can get from her. Let me warn you, Bob Thomson, I'm an extremely sensitive person. I neither condone permissiveness nor veto its pleasures. I'm me. Nobody else. I enjoy a man because he excites my curiosity and my hormones. I sleep in his bed after he has satisfied my basest urges providing, of course, in the first place he has aroused certain inclinations in my flesh.'

He examined his interest in her. There was, firstly, the fact she was the only known female acquaintance of Julius Gold. Secondly, she was attractive - but how! Thirdly, she had a certain humorous way of covering herself that made the conquest all the more appealing. And, fourthly, he believed she knew his motives! He suspected that Joseph Nimmo had called the tune on his club.

When he had separated the wheat from the chaff he asked, 'Do I incite your imagination to such a degree that you'd honour me with a visit to my lonely, masturbatory pad?'

'Oh, Lord!' She chuckled. 'The day you resort to handling yourself will be a red-letter one. Of course, I'd love to visit your bed. And I mean bed, dear Bob!'

'Agreed then?'

She raised her fresh drink. 'Agreed! Guaranteed . . . in the flesh!' Her eyes twinkled mischievously . . .

Her perspiring body churned beneath his. There was a struggle here - not of his making but from her refusal to accept his readiness as a signal for her orgasm . . .

Somehow, at his age, she sustained him through a second climax and retained his vitality. Sweat poured from him, formed an obscenely sounding pool between their lathered bodies. The noise stimulated him to further efforts . . . driving deep into her willingness . . . co-operating with those frenzied gyrations she felt were necessary to accomplish what he had reached within the fateful first ten minutes. Then, like a geyser erupting, she reached the pinnacle of her attachment - melting, flowing, adhering to him in a fantastic culmination of lustful searching.

'You wonderful bastard!' she moaned. 'The day you resort to self-gratification name me a virgin!'

His life hung on a thread - temples throbbing wildly, lungs screaming for huge gulps of humid air, heart hammering to beat any band. 'You take your time,' he panted.

'To enjoy each and every second requires perfect co-ordination of mind, muscle, physical sensation. I appreciate a terrific bit . . . ' She rolled from under his dead-weight. 'Relax, Bob. I'm not going to hurry for another sample. That'll last me a month.'

'I've expended my annual supply of energy,' he gasped.

'Not as young and virile as you once were, eh?'

'Lord - no!'

'Want me to sleep beside you?'

'Damned right! After that bloody effort I deserve the warmth of a trim ass pressed against my belly.'

She stretched like a taut bow. 'I'm exhausted. Care to massage my spine?'

He stared at her frontal beauty, grunted. 'I couldn't raise the muscle power.'

'Okay. Rest your head on my shoulder then . . . '

He snuggled against a turgid teat, loving the readiness of the mammary gland; the sensuality associated with its rigid tip. He refrained from arousing it further although his tongue darted forth and curled round its hardened fleshy nub.

'Cripes - you do like it!'

He stopped teasing. 'I adore beauty - be it you or a painting in the Tate. One could call me a gourmet but I prefer the word "admirer".'

'Why have you taken all this trouble for me, Bob? I'm nothing extra-special. There are a hundred young birds equally attractive, equally proficient in bed. I don't imagine you make a habit of entertaining women less than twelve years your junior.'

He rested on one elbow, gazed down at her puzzled face.

'You already know why, Dot.'

'Julius?'

'That - and other matters.' He felt better for his confession. This wasn't the old Bob Thomson. When he'd operated for Hart he'd been a mean bastard. What happened to a woman after he extracted sex and information had never come back to haunt his conscience. Now - maybe he was getting soft as well as old! He refused to deliberately hurt Dot and that bothered him. Were his plans to be ruined because he sympathised with this plaything of a Russian agent?

'Do you expect me to blow the whistle on Julius?'

'Only if you wish,' he heard himself reply.

'I don't, really . . . but . . .'

He waited with bated breath. This was the crucial moment.

'I think you're trying hard to be honest with us both,' she said solemnly, a semi-modesty driving her to cover her genitals with a spread hand. 'I appreciate honesty, Bob. I make no allowances for my nature. I'm unashamed of the men I have had - and enjoyed. There is nothing quite like satisfaction arrived at with a man you find attractive. And you're attractive to me. No - more. You're bloody dangerous for me.'

He frowned. 'Don't read more into our mating than sex, Dot,' he warned.

'I do - and that's the trouble, Bob. This began as a game. I wanted something satisfying inside me and you looked the type to give a girl all those pleasures she dreams about in a lonely bed. I knew you had chosen me because I am an intimate of Julius Gold. But it didn't matter. I told myself I'd have you, find solace, retire undefeated champion of Thomson's boudoir and that would be that. It hasn't worked out exactly as I planned, though. I'm still attracted to you. I'd like us to have a relationship that included sex for years - and years. I'm not seeking a husband so don't worry on that score. I just want a steady man. A man I can trust. Or admire for his honesty. You'd never have to be faithful, just make sure I got the necessary enjoyment when we agreed the mood was right.'

Grunting, Bob stumbled from their soaked bed. He felt disgust for his former outlook on life. He wanted to tell how horrible he felt. For the first time, he *respected* a girl. And her right to seek pleasures he considered a male prerogative. It was a shock - more so when taken with what she proposed. The real trouble was - she was damned attractive! And so vitally alive! Few women had demanded as much from him as she; fewer still had kept him attuned to their raging passions, their seething sensations.

Physically, he wanted to accept her proposition.

Mentally, he rejected any compromise.

He poured two stiff drinks, returned to the bed. 'Dot, I'm not your man,' he said kindly, offering her a glass. 'I've been around too long to let myself fall in love - and that's about what you're suggesting.'

'No, Bob!' She sampled her drink, nodded approval. 'Love is a four-letter word beginning with "F". I'm not seeking a "F-man". I want a genuine "C-man' . . . ' and she laughed at his amused dismay. *'Companionship,* Bob,' she explained airily. 'I'm a university graduate. I like to call myself intelligent. I don't want a man whose topics only include the size of my breasts, my alcohol intake, my penchant for fashionable clothes. I want to discuss the economic situation in far-flung lands; the geographical hazards of having a border with an industrial giant as Canada has with the States; the problems of human rights, equal pay for women, parliamentary boundaries and how they affect the state of those parties in power or opposition; and, if you're equal to it. I would like to devote several evenings to a searching enquiry into the occult.'

He grinned and finished his drink. 'Young lady, you're more than I could stand. I'm not a genius. I'm a club owner with a modicum of intellect.'

'Intelligence is better!' She smiled disarmingly. 'You are a former intelligence agent, aren't you?'

'Young Nimmo?' he countered.

'Yes. Julius warned me somebody might try to get information from me under similar circumstances.'

'And . . . ?'

'It depends on whether or not we agree to have an affair.'

'If I just said yes?'

'I'd know if you were sincere or not.'

'And if the reply is no?'

'Tough luck, Bob is my answer.'

'I see . . . ' He studied her. Naked, she was a ravishing temptation. Dressed, she was about the same - mystery swathed in concealing material. He liked her forthrightness, her unjealous attitude. But would she always be an ungreen-eyed goddess ? That bothered him plenty.

'I won't change for the worse if that's what you're thinking,' she said softly.

'Can I be sure?'

'No!'

'All right!' His decision was made. 'Tell me what you know.'

She reclined on the bed, hand now content to fondle her glass instead of covering pubic glory. 'I wouldn't be positive but I believe that Julius Gold is not a Britisher. When we've made love he has spoken words which, frankly, sound Russian or Slavic to me.'

'That fits with my information,' Bob mentioned.

'You're a fool, Bob Thomson. You and this Colonel Hart of yours. You're living in the past. Julius - or whatever his real name is - doesn't. He gets around with kids. He speaks our language. He's willing to trip, or call a pig a pig. He knows where we tick and he activates the hormones we consider essential. But, and this is very important, he is one hundred percent brotherly. He doesn't talk about racial integration and ignore the fundamentals. I've seen him in bed with a coloured girl *and* a white girl. Both at the same time. I've seen him place his arms round a black shoulder and facially mean what he's saying. No crap. No counterfeit reactions.'

Bob refined the glasses. He had to hand it to this Gold character. He was an excellent agent. Russia seemed to spawn master-spies. Abel, for one. Blake in his way. MacLean and Burgess in another. Philby as a traitor de luxe.

'Dot, is Gold encouraging students to resort to violence?'

'Yes!' She accepted her drink, shook her head in thanks.

'And why does he confide in you?' This was the major mystery. Soviet agents did not normally permit themselves to leave an opening through which Western counter-intelligence could drive a wedge.

'He doesn't. I'm not stupid - even if I like a physical union.' Dot Clarke sat upright, her desirable breasts teasing his sight; her complete nudity a shadowy pleasure to be contemplated, filed away for some other strenuous day. 'I first met Julius when he visited L.S.E. There was an American there - I believe his name was Markam. He's since been ordered into custody pending deportation. Anyway, this Markam tried to seduce me - without success . . . ' and she laughed sarcastically.

'He gave me the impression of being a hot minute and nothing more. You know the American type - all mouth and rabbit-action!'

Bob grinned. He loved her description. What most Americans did not appreciate was that English girls happened to like their sex as much as the men. The nagging, stock-buying Yankee wife on her pedestal did not apply when it came down to brass tacks and Englishwomen. Reserve dammit - the London girl had more ummph between her toes than ten American beauties between their thighs.

'Markam,' Dot continued, 'refused to be discouraged. He wined, dined, almost bribed me to let him take my knickers down. Then, one night after he'd been to a meeting of militants, he asked if I'd be willing to meet Julius Gold. I said yes without knowing anything about his friend. That night, I slept with Julius. Three weeks later I moved into an apartment - er, flat - and became Julius's mistress.'

'You're not American,' Bob said suspiciously, 'Yet you use apartment.'

'Canadian,' she replied laughingly. 'Born in Toronto, Ontario. Married once and deserted within a year.'

'What the hell age are you?'

'Twenty next August 24th.'

'You start young over there, don't you?'

'I had permission,' she replied angrily.

'Whilst studying at college?'

'Naturally.'

'Any children?'

She laughed. 'Not when you take the Pill!'

'Thank God for man's ingenuity, eh?'

'I won't take it forever, Bob.' She eyed him seriously. 'Not only do I wish to avoid any medical problems but I happen to want a family. A daughter first, then a son. Two is ample. Two intelligent, happy children and a husband . . . not you, so relax,' and she giggled, 'but somebody my own age. Somebody who won't be an old, grouchy man when the kids need companionship.'

'There goes a wonderful love-affair,' he quipped.

'Not necessarily. We can still have the love but definitely nothing permanent.'

'And Julius?'

'The same,' she replied evenly. 'He's old - like you. No, maybe not your age, Bob. But too old for my family plans.'

'I've been told he's a teenager or in his early twenties.'

'The hell he is!' She sounded vehement. 'If anyone should know it's me. He gets puffed after the first hundred strokes. That's the advantage of being a slow-to-come girl. I can always separate the men from those virile boys. The young ones try to get it finished in double-quick time. The older ones struggle to make it last. But after forty-five minutes, age certainly tells in the grunts, gasps, pants per thrust. I'd venture to state that you and Julius were about the same age.'

'He's a little younger if my data is correct,' Bob confessed.

'Then you're in better sexual shape,' she laughed.

'Probably more practice,' he allowed generously.

'What is so important about Julius?' she asked, suddenly reflective.

'I think he's a Russian spy,' Bob told her. 'I believe he's trying to undermine our youth . . . '

'God, everybody is doing that,' Dot yelped.

'Yes, but is everybody encouraging teenagers to make bombs, start riots, injure the police?'

'Quite a few are,' she answered. 'There are West Indian and Nigerian agitators actively advocating violent overthrow of any British hospitality that doesn't fit their ideas of support. There are the Irish - building workers and IRA sympathisers like a Fifth Column *inside* the British economy. The Scots and Welsh have their nationalists demanding home rule. It's all a sign of our times, Bob. People use force to manufacture terror and get their way under dire threat.'

'True!' Bob admitted ruefully. 'But Julius isn't a special type. He's negative nationality. Take that name, for instance Gold - Yiddish if ever a name screamed Israel and wandering Jew. So what do we owe them? Nothing. Their men gunned down our boys like cannonfodder. The Stein group boasted how many Britishers they slaughtered. That should turn a few heads in the wrong direction for a starter. Not to mention an end to Israeli bond drives in the U.K. But our "friend" Julius insists on using a Yiddish name . . . why? I'll tell you, Dot. He figures nobody can be associated with Russia if he has a goldplated Jewish name. Anti-Semitism and colour-bars are the same thing today. Every man is a brother according to the principles of the young liberals. But are they? Do you consider Ho your Uncle? Do you want a Chink, a nigger, a Yid for a brother?'

She writhed on the bed, avoiding his direct gaze.

'Come on, Dot - do you?'

'Hell, no!'

'Then what's your problem?'

'I'm confused,' she complained.

'Shit! - as you youngsters would say. You know I'm right. Mankind isn't ready to accept colour and nationality as an equal yet. There are steps to be made - a united Europe first, an Afro-Asian agreement to stop slurring white inventiveness and superiority and, finally, harmonious acceptance of a federated global government that does, or does not include the Soviet-dominated areas. These are the steps. Nothing less. Nothing short of that will suffice. A world government that is positively separated from that ineffectual body called the United Nations. United be damned! Dis-united would be better. And, talking of that . . . why should the Organisation be ruled by a member from a dictatorship state like Burma? What a bloody Kremlin joke!'

'That's slander,' she accused hotly.

'Nope, it isn't. I'm entitled to my opinion. I'm voicing the thoughts of many global intellects. The U.N.O. should be ruled by a known democrat . . . and that means a person coming from one million percent democratic nation. Not a walled State like Burma. You can't tell me a man seeped in Burmese history isn't slanted. Nor that a majority of Afro-Asians believe their Secretary-General isn't sympathetic to their non-white, non-colonial cause.'

'I'd like another drink,' she replied simply. She rolled on her back, presented a voluptuous picture of curved buttocks and deeply-V-eed thighs. Reversed, of course.

As he attended to their glasses she gazed at him pensively. She liked what she could see; enjoyed his keen mind; wished he was younger and of that determinate age she knew her husband and children's father must belong.

'Bob,' she sat upright now, 'I'm having difficulty with your logic. Certain points you've made *sound* fine but when I have time to think them out you're all wet.'

'Like which ones?' He handed her a refill, sat watching her face. It was an education. He could almost see the gears grinding into action as she masticated his views. 'U Thant, for a start,' she replied after a long drink. 'You can't believe he would seriously take sides. Maybe Burma is a rotten nation shutting itself off from contact with the so-called Free World but that doesn't make him a louse playing games with the U.N.'

'All right,' he relented smilingly. 'I'm wrong on that score.'

'And others! You speak about humanity not being ready to accept coloured people into a white fold. The young are - and, by God, they count for a lot.'

'Next?' He was enjoying her rising ire. She actually believed what she said and he respected her opinions.

'All your assumptions are based on Establishment dictates. You think because you've been *ordered* to think. You try to argue but everything you say is colonial dogma. Why do you find students willing to stop lectures in order to protest about some evil or other? Not because they want to be anti-this or that. They know the system is wrong. Or needs readjusting. They're worried about the bloody mess your kind have got the world into and unless they - we - youth generally, do something the same old values will remain until a nuclear holocaust destroys us all.'

'Does a pacifist clobber the opposition?'

'Ah, the old debate!' She finished her drink, held the glass out demandingly. 'I'm going to get sloshed, Bob. So make it strong, eh?'

'How about some pot?'

She scowled angrily. 'You're a bloody bastard. Can't your side discuss anything without trying to accuse us of being drug-addicts and layabouts?'

'Sorry.' He meant it.

'I should hope so!' She moved, displaying more flesh than was necessary, smiling at his swift study of her possibilities. 'You're a randy bastard, too!'

'God, I'd be less than human if that thing didn't excite me!' His gaze pointedly showed which 'thing' he meant.

'Men!' She brushed aside her contempt, covered her nudity with a sheet. 'Perhaps we can get back to more intelligent conversation?'

'Go ahead!' He moved to replenish her drink.

'Look, Bob - Julius is a gold-plated slob,' and she grinned at her witticism. 'He's chasing rainbows trying to incite our crowd. We know where we're going and he doesn't. That's the major issue. He thinks we're stupid, ready to latch on to his schemes.'

'Some of you are.'

'Like always, man. There are people, and people. You've got the Amos Platt's and we've got morons willing to start an anarchist battle for what they consider freedom from authority. There are organisations in existence to correlate information from every nation in the world. Data relating to police behaviour; political weaknesses; student dissatisfaction with the running of universities. But the Julius Golds are always there, too. Men with messages to sell for souls. Men prompted by an East-West conflict that youth abhors. What Gold doesn't know is we've reached behind his Iron Curtain. Look at the liberal Soviet writers - all youngsters - convicted of crimes against the State. And how about some of their students, too? Sorry, Bob - your ideas of this youth revolution don't fit the facts. We're strong. We're determined. We're fed up with wars and military dictatorships. We want to be free - and that includes doing what comes naturally even if you old people don't agree that love-making, loud music and smoking hash is right. Let us find out for ourselves. We're not about to make fools of ourselves. We're interested in finding a new outlet for our energies, vitalities, artistic impressions. That's all.'

'What about these demos then?'

'Somebody has to protest,' she replied indignantly.

'Even if they bust a few heads, break windows, storm an Embassy?'

'Even that, Bob. You forget, Washington founded a nation by being rebellious and shooting Redcoats. We only throw stones.'

'Touché!' he grinned.

'Touch!' she replied, throwing back the sheet, revealing herself in all that silken, warm glory. Her eyes sparkled as she quipped: 'It hasn't lasted a month after all - so do more than feast your eyes, eh?'

CHAPTER TWELVE

FOR exactly a month, Tim Hart had played his role with Machiavellian skill. Not once had he erred in his judgement of L.S.E. moods. Yet, for all his consummate acting ability, he was still far from satisfied with the results he had obtained. He found himself more inclined to student views than ever and growing less enthusiastic for what his father and those Network Forty oldies called the *dénouement* of Julius Gold.

There existed a hard core of militants at L.S.E. with whom he could find no sympathy. Mostly, they were overseas students and some, in fact, who were neither students nor entitled to call themselves young. But to definitely declare that they were subjected to Gold's Soviet-based dictates was a horse of another shade. He had no proof. And his Network Seventy group *demanded* proof. As rightly they should!

Various aspects of the situation here, he thought, reminded him of a revolutionary council about to liberate the Bastille. Or shove cannonballs up an agitator's ass to chase the British out of New Orleans.

Every facet of British life was closely examined, broken down into its component parts and criticised with clear-headed logic. For him this did not make resultant protest undemocratic, not a tool of

Soviet-inspired disruptive tactics. He sympathised with those students coming from poor homes wanting to see a better deal for future generations. He liked to air his own views when an issue reached major proportions . . . the need for working men to go against employers and unions was his pet topic.

Then . . .

It was a Monday evening and the school was due to terminate its sessions for a bank holiday week-end. Word had circulated that a meeting was being held and that only those willing to spend their holiday in a Grosvenor Square protest march would be welcome.

'It'll be the same old story,' groused Ray McVey as he accompanied Tim down a corridor. 'The hard core will pack the hall, lock the doors and then we'll be all bloody accused of being a violent bunch of grant-taking bastards. I've seen it happen so often I'm sick of their fuckin' meetings!'

Tim shrugged. It wasn't for him to encourage liberal-minded people like McVey to attend. His image was hard-set - an out and out rebel.

'You'll get in,' McVey complained bitterly. 'You're their sort.'

'Shit! I'm no more entitled to attend than you.'

The Irish student grunted, waved at a friend, called: 'John come here.'

John Embling was tall, lean, gaunt almost. He had an insatiable lust for girls and his other love was protestation. Study came a sad third in his creed. Cold, quizzical eyes examined Tim as he waited for McVey to speak.

'You're a member of the inner hierarchy, John,' the Irisher stated not unkindly. 'Will our friend here be admitted tonight or won't he?'

'Everyone has a chance of getting in,' Embling growled.

'Oh, Lord - don't hand me that fuckin' lark. I'm your roommate, John. I won't be admitted, and that's for sure. Neither will Betty, Frank, Wallace, Glenn or Rosemary.'

John laughed deep down in his chest. 'That's your view.'

Changing the subject, McVey asked, 'What's the demo about this time, anyway?'

'Vietnam.'

'Can't we get something new to shout about?'

The tall youth tensed. 'Let's not have an argument *before* the meeting. Be there and you'll have every opportunity to say your piece.'

'You're kiddin', of course!' McVey snorted in disgust. 'You characters wouldn't let the Queen speak if she was against your tin gods.'

'What Queen? I'm anti-royalist!'

Tim felt the urge to smash a fist down Embling's throat. He hated these anarchistic bastards who decried everything that tradition held dear. Monarchy, for Tim, meant holding Scots, Irish, Welsh and English in a single unit. Without the Throne there would be no United Kingdom; no Commonwealth; no special relationship with America.

'Shit on you, too!' McVey snapped. To Tim he grinned. 'Let's leave happy bastard to his miseries. Come along . . . '

As he walked away, Tim felt Embling's gaze fastened on him like a burning torch - inquisitive, hostile, arrogant . . .

As McVey had said - the doors were closed immediately those hard-core adherents arrived. Banging, shouting, appeals did not make the audience lessen their determination to keep rival groups out. Essentially, the report of the meeting would read that a majority of students had attended and expressed their concern for those who had come too late to participate. It was the old formula. The communist method for safeguarding a minority vote.

Listening to vitriolic attacks on American policies in Vietnam, Cambodia, other South-East Asian territories, Tim wondered how the hell some of the lecturers present ever held their jobs. In a space of thirty minutes he heard a parade of blue-shirted, bespectacled teachers advocate total overthrow of the British educational system, exhort others to commit crimes against the community and deny those outside their legal right to voice dissention. No wonder, he thought, that so many students were being weened on violence when their guardians and mentors are set against peaceful solutions.

' . . . and Bannerjee has promised that his organisation will supply a hundred marchers if we can guarantee outside university support,' the speaker finished to tumultuous cheers.

Tim sat entranced. Bannerjee was a known agitator. His weekly paper - VOICE OF PEACE - contained more reference to brutality, pornography, sadism, savagery, Mansonism than any New York 'underground' sheet. Bannerjee had money - a useful attribute anywhere. He was a noted communist - regardless of his father's wealthy estates in India. As a holder of a 'foreign' passport it still was a mystery to Tim - and the majority of the British people - why the F.O. permitted him to stay in London. If Bannerjee had confessed his interest in this demo then it was certain to erupt into violence.

Everybody knew what Bannerjee's supporters expected - a punch-up and a chance to taunt the 'pigs'.

'Brothers - and Sisters . . . ' Tim concentrated on John Embling as the gaunt one took the dias. 'This afternoon I was accused of a heinous crime. I won't mention the name of the man who blasphemously told me he could not be admitted here tonight but I will say he was fuckin' lying!' He laughed as did his audience. 'However, my point is this - there are those who will accuse us - you and I - of deliberately using this hall, this union, to further our own ends. And that is a bloody lie! We are a democratic society. We loathe what is happening in the world - mostly thanks to American imperialism. Our friends in North Vietnam, China, Cuba, Albania know where we stand. We are solidly against any spread of war. Against the use of force to uphold tired, patronising regimes. Against corruption and the enslavement of the worker. We do not want to hear those old arguments against our new society. It is our right to deny all speakers of the Establishment the chance of expounding weary stereotyped dogma. We are free. We are the new generation. Our law is right. And to hell with those who oppress peasants and free-thinkers . . . '

The roar almost deafened Tim as he crouched lower in his seat. He had just heard the final argument against student power! From the mouth of a student!

'Brother Hart wishes to add something to what I have said,' Embling concluded after the accolade ended. There was a twisted smile on his gaunt face - a smile that warned Tim of suspicion; an attempt to throw him into a Lions den. 'Come on, Brother Hart. Up here . . . '

Tim walked to the platform with nerves ragged. Could he continue his masquerade? Would he have the gall to blast those institutions he held dear?

'Make it good!' Embling breathed as he went before the microphone.

Tim smiled reassurance. Grasping the metallic conveyor of dastardly information he gazed down at those vapid, open-mouthed beings ready to swallow each and every word from his lips provided it did not disagree with formulated opinions. At that moment, he admired those right-wing politicians addressing student bodies knowing, as he did, that any deviation from what was their creed could erupt into **a** personal vendetta ending in injury. It seemed a shame that education, democracy, tradition for free speech had deteriorated to this extreme.

'Maybe I'm out of order already,' Tim began, 'but it seems to me that Brother Embling has presented a case for further discussion.

'If I may . . . ' and he listened to their strained silence with heart hammering, knowing in advance he had better change his tactics, 'We are not engaging on a crusade not a pilgrimage. Crusaders attempt to gather support. Pilgrims could not care less if they are alone. We have other friends coming to rally round our flag but what we want is the general public expressing their belief in what we are doing. We are not pilgrims worshipping some mysterious deity. Our god is truth - war is evil!'

He got cheers for this and felt his tenseness evaporate slightly.

'If we have Bannerjee with us we are only encouraging those who are against us to point a finger and say they tried to make their demonstration violent. We don't want that! We want results. Good results for our cause. And we can't expect that if we let Bannerjee have his share of the parade.'

There were a few scattered supporters but the majority sat silent; hostile even.

'I'm totally committed to any project designed to eliminate war, or ugly scenes during a protest march. I do not like violence from the police nor can I abide it in our ranks. I beg of you - don't be foolish enough to have Bannerjee's mob rule thrust upon you. Be strong. Gather support and walk - not run. I can guarantee more results than the Bannerjees of this country can. Do as I ask and I'll arrange for television and newspaper coverage that is sympathetic to our cause.'

For six seconds the vast hall was quiet. Then, suddenly, as Embling rose to his feet and gestured for Tim to be dismissed, the audience erupted in a united roar of disapproval. He had failed!

That was Tim's thought as rough hands held him captive on the platform. Embling's face expressed the general attitude - traitor!

Holding his hands aloft, the gaunt Essex-born student asked, 'Do we accept this?'

'*NO!*' came the spontaneous roar.

'Do we refuse to acknowledge this man's membership?'

'*YEA!*'

Hands waving frantically for order, John Embling faced his 'mob' court and smiled. When the last voice had subsided into mumbling silence he spoke. 'Tim Hart, son of Colonel Brett Hart. A wartime master spy, commander of a unit which helped ruin much of Europe's heritage . . . '

'That's a bloody lie.' Tim yelled, feeling himself immediately restrained by rough, brutal hands.

'Ahhhhh!' Embling remarked pointedly. 'The spy's son denies his father's complicity in acts of wanton sabotage! Alright traitor - do you, or do you not, command a group calling itself Network Seventy?'

Tim shivered although it was blastingly hot in the hall.

'Well?'

'I do,' Tim admitted.

'And is this group not an off-shoot of your father's old department ?'

'Yes - and no!'

Roars of rejection filled the hall.

'Be specific,' Embling yelled.

'Yes, because we are sons or daughters of my father's group. No because we do not believe that their ways are ours.'

'What is the aim of this group of yours?'

Tim was well aware that Julius Gold had masterminded the situation, had brought him and Network Seventy into disrepute with L.S.E's student militants. All he could do was brazen it out.

Grabbing the mike, Tim hollered above the low rumble of those disinclined to have him present his argument. 'Network Seventy works for you - today's youth. It is for the right of peaceful protest, the right of expressing our opinions to society's authority. We do not believe, however, that all protests are valid. We think that Julius Gold is a Soviet agent trying to . . . '

The foot-stamping, shouting mob would not hear another word. Led by the ever-threatening Embling they effectively stopped Tim's speech.

From a corner of his eye, Tim saw two lecturers slip from the platform, quietly using a rear exit to escape involvement in what was about to happen. Tim knew instinctively . . .

And tried to find safety . . .

'My son is important to me, Inspector, but he is dust compared to what this man Gold is.'

John Trust tried to affect official nonchalance and failed. Few men could have faced Colonel Hart without blanching.

'The lad will be all right, sir,' Trust said.

Seated to one side of Trust, Bob Thomson smiled grimly. The old platitudes! Like hospital bulletins saying a patient was satisfactory after being mauled by a lion, it rankled in ordinary ears. Bob didn't trust - he chuckled at his thought - in Trust's declaration of Tim's welfare. The kid had taken one helluva beating and it was a bloody wonder he hadn't lost both his balls from one of those vicious kicks in the groin. He'd seen the bruises, the welts, the terrible evidence of playing a lone hand against forces most liberals thought were exuberant youthfulness.

'That's neither here nor there, Inspector,' the old man said. 'The question now is - have you apprehended this man Gold?'

'Not yet, sir.'

'Do you have jurisdiction?'

'That's being considered at the Yard, sir.'

'He's a spy. A Russian agent.'

'He happens to carry a Canadian passport and,according to Ottawa, it is perfectly in order, sir.'

Hart reclined in his wing-chair. James stood to one side controlling his desire to intrude. 'You've heard of agents using a dead man's passport before, haven't you, Inspector?'

Trust smiled. If only he had half the intelligence acumen this old bird had he'd feel qualified for his post. His only claim to fame came from a year spent in field intelligence - and that as a lowly sergeant who happened to speak fluent German. 'Colonel Hart, must I mention that you are retired from active service and that the Department of Defence no longer considers you an erstwhile member of its establishment?'

'You may, Inspector - and you'll get the same reply I always give Whitehall's snotty-nosed, old-maidish trash . . . I'm capable until I die. And that includes Clive Jenkins, too. Whitecollar workers, indeed! Neither he nor they ever accomplished a decent advancement for Britain. It was up to us, old boy. The men who risked their lives. Not those bloody-minded Civil Servants nor the petty Union clerks turned executives seeking self-adoration. The Britain I worship didn't get its Empire, its Commonwealth because it catered to unions, faceless men or a string of infantile regulations. It came from adventurers - Drake, Hawkins, Raleigh, Cabot, Clive, Rhodes, Livingstone. It came about through mishap, chance, opportunity. Not economic miracles and Monetary Fund purchases. I'm sorry, Inspector, I'm prejudiced. I believe that might tempered with true British justice is still right. That protest, demonstration and anti-White dogma is all wrong. I firmly go to my grave knowing that history will accord me more merits than any long-haired hippy or permissiveness. Gerald Nabarro has it right in his private member's bill - he deplores the pornographic society and those who would encourage these things.'

Bob Thomson smiled to himself. The colonel was really letting his hair down. He wouldn't blame Inspector Trust if he quoted section, paragraph of regulations showing that Network Forty had no valid reason to exist. Nor would he have felt it wrong had Hart been arrested under a breach of the peace proclamation.

Trust had an unenviable task to perform. He had been warned by his superiors what to expect - and what he must do.

'Colonel Hart, have you been directly responsible for setting up an illegal organisation known as Network Forty?'

'I have!' came the direct reply.

'And of encouraging your children to form another organisation known as Network Seventy?'

'Yes!'

'Then I must warn you, sir, that you have contravened the law and that . . . '

Bob shrugged, excused himself with a smile and went into the hall. He telephoned his lawyer, requested immediate assistance and replaced the phone knowing that here was the makings of a spectacular court case. And he was paying the shot . . .

CHAPTER THIRTEEN

'WHERE have all the bastards gone?'

Bob sank into his wing-chair, trying hard to concentrate on the television screen which competed for his attentions with a torrid kitchen-sink play that had neither beginning, middle or end. He was berating BBC for its 'almighty' attitude that what it presented was worthwhile whilst yelling about that 'other channel's trashiness'. For him, BBC didn't deserve the annual licence fee. Like in America and Canada where they had no fees whatsoever he wondered how BBC could survive if they had to compete on an equal basis with FREE television! It was his considered opinion that eighty per cent of the BBC's 'bright young men' would fall by the boards and seek new pornographic outlets for their perverted mentalities should the monopoly have to offer itself as a viable alternative to independent televised programming.

'To BBC?' he quipped.

She glowered at him. 'You're not with me, Bob.'

'Yes I am. More than you'll ever know.'

'Prove it!'

He switched off the television which caused him no pain. He switched off the standard lamp and left the room bathed in those subtle candle-glow fixtures his agent had assured him would seduce more females than a regiment of front-line troops.

'Oh, no!'

'Don't you like them?'

'Terrific - for a virgin!'

'And . . . ?'

'You know better than that, Bob Thomson. I'm no virgin!'

He rubbed his hands appreciatively.

'Rat!' she laughed. 'Please - be sensible.'

'Why?'

'You know why.' She walked the length of his lounge, paused by the french-windows overlooking the park. 'Why don't you make me think seduction instead of rejecting it?'

'You're in *that* mood?'

'Bob!'

He laughed, moved to her side. His hand rested lightly on her hip. 'I've forgotten what it's like to be young again,' he said.

'I'm not young. I'm experienced but I still enjoy being woo-ed.'

'The old way?'

'Is there any other?' she asked belligerently.

'The hippies have a way of saying "hi" and drop your knickers all in one breath.'

'I'm not a hippy, Bob.'

'You're pretty and young. Much younger than I should be fooling around with.'

'Do you consider age a barrier?'

'In certain ways.'

'You're crazy!' She smiled, removed her light-weight coat. 'Am I so terribly different from those women you seduce?'

'The equipment is the same,' he laughed.

'That's not what I meant, silly!' Her dress followed the coat and lay across a chair. In her half-slip, bra, stockings she looked like an ad for some sensually scented perfume.

'No more,' he commanded.

'No?' The slip came off next; then her stockings. In bra and panties with a suspender belt showing through black, transparent silk she looked like any whore's grandmother. All sex. All woman!

'Please . . . I'll regret this more than you!'

She tossed her brassiere over the chair next, then her panties. Lastly, she removed the suspender belt and stood naked for his admiration.

'Oh, God!'

'How do I compare with mother?'

Something snapped inside him. 'That's it, Wanda. Put it all on again!'

'I'm sorry,' she said simply.

'So am I. You're a wonderful girl - like Mai.'

Memories haunted him. 'Somehow I didn't think she'd ever marry.'

'Did you ask her?'

He crossed the room, helped himself to a very large Scotch. What had taken place all those crazy years ago was top-secret still. Especially from a daughter.

'If you don't answer me I'm going to demonstrate.'

He smiled, swung on her. She was reluctantly dressing, the reverse procedure more enticing than the original strip. Her lovely legs shimmering as light played on their firm roundness; shadows creating hell with his primitive urges and rippling back and forth over her exquisite skin. 'Thanks,' he said.

Their eyes clashed briefly. She was fully dressed now, feet pushing into her shoes. During the fast minutes as she completed her chore Bob had found himself verging on disaster. This was a girl any sane man would want for his wife. A girl to remind him of that other love way back in time . . .

When she spoke, the spell was shattered.

'I'm going home, Bob. I'm going to ask mother and tell her there's a man who has captivated me. I'm not pulling any punches. I shall inform her that the first attraction was physical, but . . . ' and her face flooded with poetic adoration, 'then I'll tell her I've fallen in love.'

'Wanda . . . you silly little . . . '

'Not now, Bob. Wait for me! It could be a year - two. I have plans.'

'Thanks for being honest.'

She laughed bitterly. 'I could have said all this after we made love, Bob.'

'There are times when it is better to wait,' was all he could reply.

They knew that British law did not encourage Biblical eye-for-an-eye justice. They also were fully aware of the penalties for those who placed themselves above that law. Yet, there existed compulsion. A most powerful emotion!

Nanette was their instrument - Karl and Brad her protectors. They didn't pussyfoot around. Nanette approached Julius Gold and reminded him of that night when his name had been Armand Pettu.

What they didn't realise was Stanley Edmond's desire to cast off his shackles. Perhaps if they had been less fervent, less bent on revenge they might have noticed the man's smiling face, his pathetic willingness to accompany Nanette to her flat. A flat rented for this express purpose!

Once inside the dismally furnished dwelling, the man relaxed - waiting with a patience born of years under a hammer. The girl's attempts to place him at ease, to promote a feeling of seduction, desire washed over him. He watched her begin the pantomime - an item discarded here, a joke there, clowning as she removed yet another article; and all the while conscious of her friends outside.

Finally, he could take it no longer.

'Don't prostitute yourself, girl,' he said softly. 'Bring them in!'

Nanette hesitated, feeling the atmosphere in that dreary room grow stale, uneventful. This wasn't what it was supposed to be. He should have panted and hurried to make love to her. He should not have known about the boys.

'You are a babe in arms compared to your mentors, girl. What is your name, anyway? Wanda? Gloria? Nanette?'

In her semi-undressed state she slumped dejectedly on the creaking, dirty divan. 'Nanette Aubin. But how did . . . ?'

'One of your cohorts warned me.'

'Joe Nimmo?'

'If you must know - yes!' He lit a cigarette with great care. 'And now you feel it is time to remove me from office, eh?'

Nanette stamped her foot. This man was infuriating. He did not have to appear so calm. He should have pleaded, begged, cajoled. Either he was a fool or else . . .

She narrowed her eyes, examined his open features.

'I'm not a devil nor do I have troops held in reserve, Nanette,' he smiled. 'It may sound weird to you but I'm glad we've reached this stage. You see, what happened to Tim Hart sickened me. I'm willing to cause any amount of economic distress, to encourage young people to revolt against their elders. But I'm not in favour of breeding a brand of fascist lout the likes of whom beat up your leader.'

'A fine time to decide that,' she scoffed.

'History records many men who have faced the truth of their situation during moments of peril. It is not being a coward to ask that you believe me. I've earned a savage reprisal for what I've done. That won't bother me. Nor would you venture so far as to kill me. It isn't your method.'

'I wish I could kill you, whatever your name really is.'

'Igor,' he laughed. 'You know, it sounds really wonderful calling myself Igor again!'

'Mon dieu!' Nanette hurried to the door, invited Karl and Brad inside. They seemed surprised to find her dressed; to see the Russian seated comfortably and smoking.

'He knows!' she said. 'And he's crawling . . .'

Fifteen thousand pounds bought an awful lot of privacy. For four weeks now the story had made front-page headlines in the Sunday newspaper with a three page spread inside. Igor had pulled no punches. He knew the power of hard cash in the West; knew, too, that privacy and security gave him more protection than a squad of Special Branch detectives.

From his Highland retreat, he dictated the weekly episodes dealing with his work as a Soviet master-spy engaged in the demoralisation of youth. But, throughout, there was an insistence that youth was right to rebel against corruption, depravity that swept its trash under clean carpets, the Bomb.

He proved - more than once - that he was not so much an instrument of violence as its slave.

Brett Hart threw his Sunday paper aside and frowned. He remembered those years spent fighting against the very thing the papers now glorified. Fifteen thousand pounds! He squirmed. The man was being treated like royalty - tax-free payment, a secluded home in the Highlands, a Special Branch detective to guard him. It didn't make sense . . .

'We've just had notification that no charges are being contemplated against Colonel Hart providing he gives an assurance that he will refrain from conducting a private espionage organisation in future.'

Bob Thomson read the letter for the third time. It didn't take much effort to know what the colonel would say. Hadn't he the proof that his networks had been successful? And this to set against Western intelligence sections who had been unable to unearth Igor?

Dialling a priority number, Bob waited for the call to be answered. A cigarette burned in an ashtray, a Teacher's in its glass looked refreshingly vital and he sipped that . . .

'Laurence? Bob Thomson here. I've a question . . . '

'Forget it,' came the metallic pleasant reply. 'Hart is safe!'

Bob grinned, had another sip. 'You're getting too smart for comfort these days,' he joked.

'Not smart. Just fed up with having the Minister rant and rave about that old reprobate Hart. Frankly, Bob - why don't you put the old so-and-so out to pasture?'

'You try it, son.'

'No thanks.' There was a pause during which Bob smoked his cigarette and listened to birds singing in the park outside his window. It was early Sunday morning and traffic hadn't yet built up to its thunderous roar. He wished it could always be the same - and knew it never would again. London had had it as far as birdsong and tranquillity were concerned. No number of motorways and ringways could alter the dead facade of this crowded city. It was transport, and to hell with the pedestrian all the way. Even home-owners counted for less than a litre of petrol fumes these days.

'What's your special problem, Bob?' came the voice.

'My solicitor has sent me a letter . . . '

'Forget that, too. The department is not going to press charges. And Hart doesn't have to promise a bloody thing. The Minister appreciates what he did but hates his interference.'

'When you're free be sure and visit the club, eh?'

'Bribery?' The chuckle warned him he was on safe ground.

'If you want to call it that.'

'Bob . . . '

'Yeah?'

'Maybe we can have a get-together with Hart?'

'Thinking the old master still knows a trick or two, eh?'

'Frankly - yes! We need men like him . . . and you.'

'When you've salved his ire let me hear. I'll arrange a meeting.'

'Will do. Roger and out!' The phone clicked into silence.

Mai Bedford sat before her dressing table and considered her image in the triple-mirror. The years had been extremely kind to her. She found it hard to associate with Martin Collins when her thoughts were on Bob, on Hart, and Department Seven. She was still Mai Bedford - single, attractive, in love with that ruthless, wealthy rascal Thomson.

Over her reflection she could see Wanda seated on the unmade bed. The girl worried her. She was a mother again; Mrs Collins to be precise!

'Has Bob said anything about his feelings for you, Wanda?' she asked softly.

'Not a bloody word,' the girl replied jokingly.

'And what makes you believe . . . '

'I'm your daughter, mum.'

Mai shook herself. This was silly. Wanda should not be mooning over a Bob Thomson. She was vital, young. He had aged - lost some of his sparkle, no doubt. 'He's old enough . . .'

'To be my father! I've heard that before somewhere,' Wanda laughed. She jumped to her feet, approached her mother. Hand on shoulder, Wanda gazed into the mirrored eyes, said: 'I love him, mum. Maybe I've inherited some of your feelings?'

Mai blinked back tears. 'If he agrees, Wanda - I won't stand in your way.' Suddenly, she knew what she had admitted. She still loved Bob - even after all these years! And Wanda knew, too.

'I'm sorry for you, mum,' the girl said and walked to the door.

Damn Hart and his networks! she thought and instantly had regrets. It was not the colonel's fault. What she and Bob had shared during those frightening months was a story he would never have detailed. Although there had not been mention of marriage, family, permanent love she had always felt that Bob needed just a little coaxing. He had not married. She had. Was the fault hers? Bobs? Hart's? Could she blame Wanda for emoting when she, herself, had always loved this man?

She had an idea. Slipping into her robe she went downstairs. Her son Tom sat with nose buried in a newspaper, scrambled eggs going cold on his plate. 'What,' she asked the boy, 'do you think about demonstrations as a means to an end?'

Tearing his attention from the latest cricket scores, Tom laughed. 'They're fab, mum. Why?'

'Would you like to start a demo of your own?'

He looked dubious. 'That depends on what it's all about.'

Mai smiled wistfully. 'I've got an old friend who seems set on making your sister his wife. I want . . . '

'WHAT?' The newspaper was forgotten suddenly as Tom shot to his feet.

'Sit down, son.' Mai took a chair opposite him, seeing his puzzled gaze trying to fathom what she had said. 'It's a long story and I think you should know the facts. But - basically, I want you to picket his club with placards saying "TOO OLD FOR YOUNG LOVE". Now . . . '

As she spoke, Mai wondered how Colonel Hart would appreciate her private joke - or was that sour-grapes? She didn't for a moment believe that Tom's efforts would deter Wanda or Bob. She just wanted him to know - a demo could mean more than a protest. It could also be a heart-felt truth . . .

THE END

TEENY

BOPPER IDOL

By Richard Allen

CHAPTER ONE

STEVE MORASH placed his copy of *WORLD POPS* on a table, lit a cigarette in thoughtful silence. Something bothered him and he couldn't quite place a mental finger on the trouble-spot. This worried him more. He swore aloud, reached for the tabloid again.

BOBBY SHARP OPENER

the headline said. Morash continued reading.

America's teenage sensation whose discs are currently topping the British charts arrives for the start of his U.K. tour this week. Next Saturday, he makes a London debut at the fabulous Discodrome. Julius Gerstein, latest fireball in the pop scene management stakes, announced details of the super night being offered the faithful. Naturally, top of the bill is wonder boy, Bobby Sharp. Also featured, however, are The Frogmen, Scrambled, Bacon and Rind, Anne Merrill, Rock Rolls.

For the event, Gerstein has hired a squad of security men with instructions to use whatever methods they feel necessary to protect his stars.

WORLD POPS *deplores this venture!*

We have already seen what happened when too zealous security arrangements were applied. Unfavourable newspaper comments did much to undermine the excellent handling of the concerts themselves. A repeat cannot be tolerated!

Fandom pays its money, expects a certain relationship between stars and people. Anything less stinks of high-handedness. Good sense must prevail and the security 'heavies' called off before a major disaster drops like a ton of sound on the heads of all those supposedly in tune with the fans.

'Those stupid bastards!' Steve Morash said aloud. His cigarette burned away in an ashtray, smoke wreathing his head in bluish coils. He flung the tabloid across his plush hotel suite, anger suffusing his rugged features.

As a top-notch publicity man he knew how readers could automatically latch onto a single wrong word, a bad sentence, a lousy tirade. And, in his opinion, *World Pops* had done none of them a favour publishing this trash.

Trash?

He got to his feet, walked across the thick carpet and gazed down on hurtling traffic flanking the gentle green of the park. His bird-eye view of clogged London reaching out like some terrible squid strangling all that was pathetically small and tranquil reminded him of New York. Not a pleasant memory, either.

Trash?

He thought hard about that. Not so much trash as an ill-timed, misplaced sentiment. Probably some editor trying to prove he could earn his salary.

Walking back from the window he hesitated beside a drinks' cabinet. *Why not?* he asked himself. He had never been a man to count the hours to the day's first noggin. Bourbon for breakfast did as much for him as bacon and eggs for the ordinary office-worker. He poured a drink, examined the label. *Hundred Pipers!* He sampled it. 'Not bad,' he told the amber liquid. A change from rye or sweetish American liquor.

Glass nursed against chest, Steve kicked the copy of *World Pops* further across the room. Bobby Sharp would do his tiny nut if he saw this!

Bobby Sharp!

'The little creep!' Steve hurled vocally at his unmade bed. He closed the bedroom door. Somehow the sight of disorder in a hotel annoyed him. If he got up around seven he expected a maid to be there, ready to straighten the mess. Sloppiness he did not tolerate. Neat packages appealed strongly.

He laughed bitterly. He remembered the start of that phobia. His detergent days, he liked to say. Pushing soapsuds down a community's throat. Using fast-talking girls to 'whisper' innuendoes about other powders, other biological cleaners. Causing doubts in wifely minds. Springing his product on the unsuspecting, susceptible, public. A hustler, that's what he'd been. A walk-the-line promotions expert. Sick to death of unsightly linens piled in kitchens where the dishes littered sink and draining board. Of women with heads wrapped in scarves and curlers jaggedly peeping from under turbaned protection.

God's, he'd loathed their untidiness then.

And now!

Thank goodness for Bobby Sharp . . .

Christ - what a conceited little bastard he was!

His discovery. His ever-so-charming-in-public monster!

What the hell did kids see in Bobby?

Certainly not a great voice!

Without the electronics Sharp fell very flat!

The telephone jangled its discordant brnnng-brnnng. He ignored it. The noise of a cleaner being used, the rattle of pass-keys came from outside his suite. About time!

He poured another *Hundred Pipers,* added *Canada Dry.* He could afford self-generosity. His ten percent cut of everything coming to Bobby Sharp gave him a handsome annual tax-deductible pay-packet. And he had expenses thrown in. Bobby paid for those!

Something had to be done about *World Pops.* He dare not let their 'challenge' go unanswered. It was too late to attack in the pages of their magazine. By the time he got into print the tour would have reached its crescendo.

No, he had to launch a front-page campaign on a national newspaper level.

He grinned, finished his second drink and poured a third. He was beginning to hit on all cylinders now. His mind raced.

Ignoring the pretty Spanish maids entering his suite, Steve Morash whipped out his little black book. The one carrying important names. Critics. Managers. Music-loving television personalities having their own chat shows. Radio deejays known to hero-worship pop stars. Columnists who'd play up a publicity gimmick for a ten quid backhander.

In less than an hour, Steve felt he had accomplished the 'impossible'. He had promises for coverage in three national newspapers. A mention on local radio. A chat show invitation. A columnist who, for £25 and dinner, would devote space for a 'personalized' opinion loaded with Steve Morash praise.

The maids had left and his suite looked reasonably tidy. Not perfect. Nothing like the way they did things back home, he thought.

He checked the time. The girls would be here soon! He called room service, laid on a luncheon. A wide choice of the best food available. Wines, too. Served in the suite at the precisely accurate moment. He believed in hitting on the beat.

He washed, freshed his face with the latest lotion advertised to attract female subjugation and prowled his rooms, like a man-hungry tiger suddenly deprived of its natural grubstake. Inactivity invariably got to him. He filled in lost minutes pouring another *Hundred Pipers* and let the satisfying glow permeate his system.

The world was a huge place, each corner presenting its own peculiar difficulties. In the States he could have contacted a few dozen people in the interval. Prominent men and women with outlets for his particular 'bent'. But not in London. His choice of contacts was severely limited.

The outlets drastically curtailed by the British way of life. Although changes were taking place, the staid, old-fashioned English holders of the media strings remained and a bustling, too fresh Yank had to wait in the queue. Had to bide his time. Had to fume and fret whilst the world of American ingenuity strolled by.

The experience taught him nothing!

He could no more change his personality than the 'man in the moon' could stop making cheese and beaming down love's seductive rays on an Earth which should, by now, have known that the silvery glow came from a 'dead' body and not an emotionally creative mysteriousness.

Padding back and forth across the carpet, Steve Morash had just about reached the end of his patience when the telephone rang. He grinned as he dropped the instrument back on its rest. Trust Jasmyn to be first, he thought - and got an extra glass ready. The host had to show he was on the ball . . .

Jasmyn Ragg entered Steve Morash's hotel suite and allowed the publicity man to kiss her. She withdrew fast when his hand settled too quickly on her curvacious bottom.

'Nix,' she hissed defensively.

Steve grinned, retreated to a safe distance. He tried, and therein ended the lesson. Jasmyn had a reject survival potential higher than any girl he had ever met. In a way, he didn't blame her. She possessed all the attributes supposed to make strong men weak and weak men drool. Blonde, eighteenish fresh, a figure direct from a Venus de Milo department store. Facially, she looked like a movie-star showing sensuality and childish naivety all in the same glance.

'I've selected my area,' Jasmyn said. 'I did some homework last night. I'll have Acton and Chiswick.'

Steve nodded. He, too, had spent the previous night sorting out London's various districts and comparing statistics compiled by other groups working the U.K. circuit. 'Think you can manage it in a few days?' he asked.

'Enough to spread the gospel,' Jasmyn smiled. She indicated the drinks' cabinet. 'Make mine neat!'

'Clear heads and all that shit,' Steve remarked.

'You've had a few,' the blonde girl acidly said.

'Name the poison . . . '

Without hesitation a drink fell from the girl's lips. 'Whisky, please.'

'Oh, the hard stuff,' Steve replied.

'So what?' She sounded exasperated.

'How about *Hundred Pipers. Scotch.*'

'With mix,' the girl said.

As Steve dropped ice into her glass he studied his top specialist. A Canadian by birth she had the classifications for a British tour. Acceptable where an American would not be. Attuned by an English mother and father to regard the entire British race as the supreme inhabitants of a globe long since divided into colour, racialist, nationalist segmentation. Attractive, younger looking than her eighteen years and, dressed in schoolgirl uniform, a natural for stirring up those still entitled to call themselves 'teeny boppers'. Old enough to entice a generation once removed from the crazy pop scene back into folds so 'kick-happy' that they got a second 'childhood' trying to please their exponent of the 'word'.

'Did you read *World Pops?*' Steve asked as he finished mixing her drink.

'Always do,' she replied, accepting her glass. 'Bottoms up . . . '

'When?' Steve laughed.

She castigated him with a withering look. 'Business,' she reminded.

Dropping the banter, Morash sank into a chair. He had an ability to separate his relaxations from the frenetic helter-skelter associated with 'selling' Bobby Sharp to a gullible public. Whatever ulterior plans he had for the gorgeous girl he shelved. Indefinitely. Totally in the search for publicity.

'What's your opinion of Becky Wilmott?' he asked.

Jasmyn shrugged, elected to sit at an angle to her 'boss'. She always placed boss in parenthesis because, essentially, she assumed she was working for Bobby Sharp. Not specifically Steve Morash. Bobby did not eye her limbs with lecherous intent. Steve did.

'Is that the best you can offer?'

Jasmyn frowned. 'For God's sake let me collect my thoughts.'

'Quick thinking . . . '

'Hell with that!' the blonde snapped. 'I'm not dealing with Sharp-ies.'

'Less of the Sharp-ies! Makes it sound like guys taking suckers for a run.'

'So?' Jasmyn smiled like a contented cow after the bull had been led away. 'Oh, hell - Becky's okay! She'll make her crowd eat Bobby and buy his discs.'

'Is that all?'

'What more can a gal do?'

Steve Morash sighed, lit a cigarette. Over his glass he surveyed the best operative he had available. Given a choice, he figured he would still plump for Jasmyn against all-comers. She had an in-born ability to catch a gang's mood. To estimate resistance and annihilate every opposition. For a *whispering campaign* she ruled supreme.

'Do we hit hard as usual?' Jasmyn asked.

'Harder! These people haven't had an indoctrination yet. It's up to you and Carole and Becky.'

'What about expenses?'

Steve brushed aside the obvious Jasmyn question. She - like him - loved her 'extras'. The tax-free incentive. 'Prove what you've spent and you'll get a bonus.'

'Not enough,' the girl replied. 'I can't make a dollar on that basis. Coffee and buns, taxis, gear . . . I want a hundred per!'

'Bucks?'

'What else?' The girl laughed, adjusted her skirt. 'A hundred pounds would buy a brewery stake. These kids don't lap it up like you!'

'Touche!' Steve Morash gestured and when he got a negative shake of the head helped himself to another drink. He prided himself on being able to carry his liquor. On tasting each and every glassful. On having an appreciation of the spirit.

The telephone jangled again. When he answered it was a respite. A joyous interlude. He found Jasmyn's intensity overpowering. And, too, his next arrival had not been known to curtly dismiss his initial approach.

'It's Carole,' he told his guest.

Jasmyn let the information slide over her head. She could not arouse much excitement for her rival. In this racket every man and every woman acted as an independent agent. Carole liked to think she had an 'in' that gave her special privileges. The way Steve fawned on her suggested more than a results sequence.

'Which territory will she *demand?'* Jasmyn asked, needling.

Steve riffled his dark hair with a nonchalant hand and grinned. 'How the hell do I know?' he countered.

'A prime area, I'll wager,' Jasmyn retorted. 'Okay - let's have a refill!' She motioned with her empty glass. 'I know how Miss Grab-all works . . . '

Steve Morash sat back, anticipating the arrival of luncheon. He had to admit his front-line troops had something the enemy could not match.

Class. And beauty. Brains and that indefinable something every kid in the world accepted - a mystique attached to believing.

'We'll slay 'em,' Steve offered as he toasted his team's gathering.

Jasmyn glared at her arch-rival, Carole. From a seat directly behind the protagonists, Becky watched the 'infighting', the thrust and parry verbal combat which could only lower each in her estimation.

'This country worships football players,' Carole said, indirectly brushing Jasmyn with her long-lashed gaze until it fastened like a leech on Steve. 'I've been introduced to Will Drumm. He's one of the heart-throbs, I hear . . . '

Becky, in her innocence, sighed. 'He is . . . he is!' she said.

'I've got him to accept an invitation for Bobby's Discodrome debut.'

Jasmyn scowled. 'What did you use as bait, darling?' she asked cattily.

'A seat,' came the cold reply.

'Crissakes,' Steve exploded. 'Forget the insults. Concentrate on what you're being paid to do!'

Carole tossed her raven-hair. Like Jasmyn she was eighteen, but a more adult version of womanhood. Leggy, busty, fully aware of men and what it took to make the other sex kow-tow to her every whim, she radiated sensuality. The type to have a coffee-bar crowd eat from her hand. 'I always act in Bobby's best interests,' she said.

Steve snorted, hid his derision in mixing drinks. His ten percent rose on the backs of fools like Carole. Sometimes on the shoulders of a girl like Becky. He liked his latest recruit. At seventeen, the redhead had visions of a singing career. Whereas the other two were strictly 'arousers', Becky wanted to learn the business from the inside out. Wanted to handle problems with authority should she ever make the star-rating.

'What do you expect us to do, Steve?' Becky asked.

Dispensing the drinks, Morash flowed forth his formula for success. 'Make calls on every school. Get into the coffee bar set. Visit bowling alleys, football grounds . . . '

Becky smiled. 'You're off-beam in England,' she said. 'We don't pay our soccer teams for a slave-driver season. Saturday games with, perhaps, a midweek fixture. That's the limit!'

Steve grimaced. 'So what? There are other sports. Other activities for young people!'

'I've got a wow,' Jasmyn announced triumphantly. 'A bunch of kids who want to be television stars!'

The publicity man eyed his best operative suspiciously. 'Where the blazes did you find that out? You're not supposed to start working until *after* this meeting!'

Jasmyn eyed her rivals for top honours with a jaundiced gaze. 'I went to Chiswick last evening. I got talking to a barman . . . '

'Chiswick?' Becky asked. 'Who gave her Chiswick?'

Steve avoided what could have been a girlish squabble. 'I worked it out and called Jasmyn. She agreed to start right away.'

'What do I get?' Carole asked.

'And me?' Becky requested.

Steve Morash wanted to blast each. He didn't. He knew how much Bobby Sharp's tour depended on these girls. How his fat percentage could he sliced by half if he didn't offer a satisfactory explanation. Allocate an acceptable territory. 'Soho for Carole. It's the London hub. Kids galore . . . '

'Dropouts and drug addicts,' Carole snarled. 'Not the type to attend concerts.'

'It happens to include some interesting areas,' Steve continued, searching his mind for alternative zones. 'Like Highbury, Islington and Paddington.'

Carole eyed him suspiciously. 'They're pretty scattered.'

'You've got expenses. Take a cab!'

'So where do I go?' Becky asked. 'The bloody East End, eh?' She sounded cheesed off.

'Bristol . . . '

Becky smiled. For once she had landed the prime target. Ever since she joined the 'Bobby Sharp road-show' she had been delegated the droppings. The waterfronts. The tenement areas. The wild, hard inviolate sections of every city Bobby toured. Mostly, she had argued, because she was English and her accent acceptable.

'Okay?' Steve asked.

'I accept, for once,' Becky replied.

'Right . . . ' Steve dropped his host attitude. 'Let's get this straight now! Bobby Sharp isn't a terrific hit here yet. But he will be. *If you do your job!* I want every kid in every part of Britain to have Bobby Sharp's name on his or - especially - her lips. Forget the guys. They follow what their gals say. Make the tender-stuff drool and you've got the whole mob. Shove Bobby at 'em hard! Sex, nice guy . . . You know that score!'

Becky got to her feet, postured. 'I'd never go to bed without first playing a Bobby Sharp record!'

'That's the ticket,' Steve enthused.

'God, how sickening!' Jasmyn frowned.

'Drop it!' Morash commanded. 'So you don't cotton to Bobby. Don't blow your cool letting it get across.'

'I shan't,' Jasmyn said. 'Far as I'm concerned there isn't a greater singer, a more charming rat than Bobby Sharp.' She pulled a face. *'The little bastard!'*

Steve's sentiments exactly. For his audience, though, he expressed sorrow. 'How can you say that?' he asked. 'Bobby's responsible for everything you make. For every cent in your bank account. For getting you free transportation round the world. For providing all your needs!'

Jasmyn Ragg tossed her eyes to the ceiling. 'Christ, save me,' she begged. 'Bobby's a selfish, arrogant, conceited so-and-so with ideas of grandeur. He can't sing. He doesn't read music. He isn't even funny.'

'He's a million dollars worth of talent,' Steve stressed.

'According to you!' Jasmyn added sarcastically.

Carole displayed her lovely legs, exchanged intimate glances with Morash and dismissed Becky's silent query with drooping eyelids.

'Bobby's fantastic,' she murmured. 'Take those other dime a dozen acts . . . '

'Names, please,' Jasmyn demanded.

'Doc Cureall . . . '

'Oh, Lord!' Jasmyn moaned. 'He's a gimmick. A thirty year-old posing as a baby-faced cradle-snatcher!'

'A hit,' Carole reminded.

'Yeah? I should be so smashing!' Jasmyn gestured with her glass. 'I'll have another, Steve-boy.'

Morash mumbled under his breath. His timing was slightly out. Luncheon could have been served ten minutes sooner than instructions. He didn't enjoy having his team bickering. Nor watch the way they fought for superiority.

'Bobby's got the fans with him,' Becky mentioned. She dared either of her companions to contradict, continued: 'Anyway, we've got to destroy the opposition. What does it matter who is the best? Bobby Sharp, for us, remains the greatest!'

'And don't I get paid to admit it,' Jasmyn growled.

CHAPTER TWO

BECKY WILMOTT suffered from an inferiority complex in the presence of Jasmyn and Carole. Her typically English up-bringing had not prepared her for the North American duo's publicity-dominated awareness. Nor for their deviousness. Both had progressed as far along the Steve Morash blazed path as any pair of eighteen year-olds could. And more than most would, dare.

Unlike her 'sisters in crime', Becky believed in talent getting the breaks.

Not Jasmyn!

Nor Carole!

Both girls held to the indoctrinated belief that anybody given enough push, enough newspaper coverage would reach the top. To prove their point they often quoted the case of Racquel Welch. A star whose career had been guaranteed even before her first picture appeared for critical approval or rejection. A star whose body and sultry face decorated newspaper column inches week by week in an all-out campaign designed to promote her far above talented, established actresses.

But Jasmyn had another idol. Not pop. Not from the Hollywood sound stages. And, not unexpectedly, a Canadian by birth if not by association.

Sister Aimee MacPherson!

The 'Four Square Gospel' *saint!*

An ex-salvationist whose antics made headlines, aroused speculation regarding her moral fibre but changed a sackcloth image into a multi-million dollar 'business'.

Father William Riker of Holy City fame once remarked: 'God winks his eye at any act we do if we take him in on the deal'. Sister Aimee Semple MacPherson had her special 'in' with the Almighty.

Carole, straight from the shoulder as always, did not cotton to Sister Aimee. She preferred Frank Sinatra's rise to fame. The 'bobby-soxer' era. The screaming *fans* paid to rocket a 'voice' into the all-time hit parade. 'He did what we're doing for Bobby Sharp,' she constantly declared. 'Make the bastards like the product even if they're tone deaf!'

Becky still believed talent had to come first. And no matter what Jasmyn or Carole said she would not - could not - let herself think differently.

Usually, she kept her thoughts to herself. Let the pair prattle and cajole and battle one against the other. She enjoyed listening. Getting pointers, she called it. The yarns they both told made her wonder how anyone ever got to reach the dizzy heights of stardom without a crooked publicity agent.

'I'm for Soho's evil square mile,' Carole said as they left Steve's ritzy hotel. 'Care to join me?'

Becky smiled offhandedly. 'Thanks - but no! I've sampled those unintelligent, depraved delights.'

'See what I meant?' Carole exploded.

Jasmyn grinned. With a half-inch to spare over her raven-haired opponent she felt a 'tall' woman's superiority. 'You've been saying how you could twist an alligator's tail and make him cry "Bobby" . . . Now, let's see what shakes *you* are with the hoods and junkies.'

Becky switched her gaze from Jasmyn to a glowering Carole. She felt better being out of this bickering. It did not arouse any side-taking in her. Indeed, if she had the right to make decisions she would gladly have dropped both 'whisperers' and started with a new bunch of girls.

'I suppose you've got it sown up?' Carole asked, viciousness showing through her pat expression. 'Been to bed with some half-pint yobbo who can influence the whole district!'

Becky stepped forward, effectively blocking the daggers' drawn glares from both girls. 'May I come with you, Jasmyn?' she asked, striving for innocence.

'You won't learn much,' Carole snapped and, tossing her raven head, strode off towards a taxi.

'That bitch!' Jasmyn shook her head, almost a copycat gesture. 'She couldn't teach Tiddles how to catch a mouse!' Taking Becky's arm, she lowered her voice, changed her entire attitude. 'There's a lot to learn, kiddo,' she said confidentially. 'We're supposed to be part of their scene. The locals, that is. We infiltrate and blow the popular poster brigade. We keep yakking and make 'em think they discovered Bobby. Get me?'

Becky knew the routine. Knock the opposition, keep 'whispering' Bobby Sharp . . . Bobby Sharp . . . Bobby Sharp. Until the suckers couldn't hear another name over their brainwashing.

'What made you decide on Acton and Chiswick?' Becky asked.

'A report by Simon Nelson . . . '

'Not *the* Simon Nelson?'

'The same,' Jasmyn laughed. 'Man, Steve loves to think he's the smartest P.R. in the game but he'd never hold a candle to Simon. There was a terrific, fantastic guy!'

'He died, didn't he?' Becky asked out of female curiosity.

114

'Yeah!' Jasmyn blinked back a dry tear, affecting unfelt sympathy. 'Drugs got him. LSD and a trip to the promised-land via a morgue.'

'That whole group went wild . . . '

The Canadian girl frowned. 'Trust the likes of you to grab that end,' she snapped. 'Don't you understand what makes an artist the tops? Can't you shove aside your petty morals and admit there are beautiful dreams in a peace pipe?'

'No, thanks,' Becky replied fast. 'I don't wear drugs. I don't accept that somebody is a better player or a better person for taking 'H' or 'C' or grass.'

Jasmyn shrugged non-interestedly. 'We all have our cross to carry,' she quoted wrongly. 'Anyway,' and she brightened. 'I'm going to have Bobby touted by a few thousand ravers and there isn't a better way to make the boss up the pay-packet. Is there?'

Becky withdrew a tissue from her Kleenex pack, blew her nose. She had discovered something very important. It paid to listen, to probe beneath the surface. It paid more dividends than being a stick-in-the-mud old-fashioned square-peg searching for a round hole that fitted. Jasmyn had been around. For three years. And what she didn't know about the seamy side of publicity wasn't worth knowing.

'Hell,' Jasmyn yelled, waving for another taxi. 'Let's get moving!' Waiting for Becky to join her inside the cab, she told the driver: 'Acton Town Hall, buster.' She settled back, grasping the passenger's strap. 'I adore these London cabs - don't you?'

The English girl wanted to blush. She felt for every American and Canadian who emoted insincerity. Why, she asked herself, do they have to do a conman act? Why couldn't they just say a London taxi was different and let it ride there? She hated fawning, dancing attendance on a race. Any race. But most especially her race.

Jasmyn pretended not to notice Becky's embarrassment. She watched London passing by the speeding taxi. For all its claims to fame she loathed the seamy, seedy, despondent streets that congregated outside those districts strictly set aside for those with money, or titles, or both. Here and there the city bustled, thrived, manufactured gaiety and opulence. But, mostly, its mish-mash areas reflected the miseries of ordinary working class people.

'You'll get a kick out of these jokers,' Jasmyn said as the taxi swung round Shepherd's Bush. 'Man, they're hooked on Bobby.'

'You're not!'

'You said it - I'm not!'

'Why?' Becky's childhood memories returned as they inched by the market. The bridge stood out like a dark blob. A time of terror in a five year-old's mind. A last recall of the father who thrashed her in public and drunkenly stepped in front of a lorry.

'He makes me sick to my stomach,' Jasmyn said. 'He thinks God made just him and the rest of us arrived on a garbage truck!'

'He makes the kids happy . . . '

'Christ, you don't actually believe that crap,' Jasmyn snorted. She twisted on her seat, fumbled with her bra strap through a flimsy dress. 'I'm getting bigger or else these damned things shrink faster,' she complained. She wagged a finger under Becky's nose. 'We're paid to make sure the kids love Bobby. Not to fall for the line Steve shoots.'

'How can you do your job if you don't believe in the end result?' Becky asked.

'Simple, gal . . . ' Jasmyn smiled, bent forward to peruse the Shepherd's Bush police station. 'I'm born greedy. Money talks and anybody willing to pay my price tag gets delivery of all services!' she roared at a private joke. 'That,' she explained later, 'does not include our Steve Morash in! I'd rather crawl into bed with a snake than let him touch me.'

The taxi gathered speed as the traffic ball-up round Shepherd's Bush eased a little. Becky sighed, gave her mind a rest. She had discovered a few more facts. Enough for this day. The mental storehouse was certainly getting packed to overflowing. Although she would not admit it to the likes of Jasmyn Ragg she appreciated the girl's frankness. She would remember everything when she decided to make her move into the glitter side of their business.

CHAPTER THREE

GLORIA DERRICK looked seventeen. Perhaps she belonged in that ruthless classification set up by some legal experts and social workers - worldly wise working class. Gloria wouldn't know about that. She did know she looked two years older than her actual fifteen, though. Men always wanted to date her and boys thought her *too* old for midteen frivolity.

In a handed-down dress and shoes supplied by the local Social Security office, Gloria wished to hell she could climb from the gutter her parents had created for her. Hope sprang eternal in her young heart. Hope called Johnny Holland. Her boyfriend. Another ambitious fifteen year-old.

Turning into Acton Lane, Gloria saw the taxi stop outside the Town Hall. She didn't pay much attention to the girls getting from it. Why should she? Her mind centred on Johnny and the Jolly Green Men . . .

She smiled and walked with head higher. She had picked that name. From a tin of peas. Not giants. Just ordinary blokes. Men. Or soon to be!

If only Johnny could get a break, she thought. He had talent. All the lads had talent. But how did they get somebody to listen? How to get on 'Opportunity Knocks' or any other television programme?

She arrived at the corner with a smell of bread being baked filtering through dreams of stage greatness. God, she was hungry! As usual, her mother had spent their money on her sherry. The damned house groaned under the accumulated weight of empty sherry bottles. Cheap stuff. Nothing grand like the ones they advertised on the 'box'.

She could hear the group's instruments now. She hurried. She recognized the number. Johnny would burst into song any minute . . .

Her hand hovered over the knocker. She waited - with infinite patience. Now . . . another bar and . . . Johnny!

'I saw her from Lookout Mountain.
A speck called Virginia . . .'

Her lack of education made the words lose some of their importance. She wasn't to know that the song's Virginia was a State and Lookout Mountain boasted of being a landmark from which seven American states could be seen on a clear day. It didn't matter much, anyway. The way Johnny sang it she just got all limp, all funny inside.

'Her shape could not be mistaken.
Not my Virginia . . .'

She leant against the door of Johnny's house and wanted to weep. Music had that strange effect on her. More so the songs Johnny sung.

'I sank into her wondrous depths
And knew the sweetness of her embrace.'

'Beautiful,' Gloria murmured softly to the wind. A rotten, dirt-swirling wind that blew down from the High Street. Carrying on its fume-laded invisible arms the germs, the stench, the decay of Acton.

'And others on Lookout Mountain watched
As Virginia made me her own!'

When the guitars ceased their strumming, Gloria knocked. Urgently. Ready to pour out her love. She didn't care if Mrs. Holland answered her impatient knocking. Mrs. Holland understood. More than any woman could.

'You, there.'

Gloria swung and stared at the two girls. She thought one looked familiar. Then, it came rushing back. Last night . . .

'Remember me?'

Gloria nodded, hearing footsteps coming to open the door behind her.

'Where is the gang?'

The door opened and a light hand brushed Gloria's shoulder.

'Hi, fella . . . '

Johnny Holland came to stand beside Gloria. He had the self-assurance of a young Rock Hudson. And the same type of features. Manhood waited to burst from his growing-older face. Eyes accustomed to seeing life in the raw watched Jasmyn and her companion with some suspicion. Dark brown eyes. Quizzical in their directness.

'You gave me the address,' Jasmyn told the young couple.

'Yeah - so what?' Johnny eased Gloria into the hall. Planting firm feet across the threshhold he blocked the Canadian's rush forward.

'Aw, come on,' Jasmyn smiled. 'We didn't finish our little chat, did we?'

'You did all the talking,' Johnny announced. 'About this Bobby Sharp.'

'The greatest,' Jasmyn breathed as if she meant it. Even Becky got the impression there couldn't be another pop star quite the equal of Bobby Sharp.

'He's okay,' Johnny allowed.

'Okay?' Jasmyn asked in awe. 'Okay? Man, he's way out. The tops! There isn't anybody better.'

'Johnny's better,' Gloria called from the hallway.

'Ah . . . ' Jasmyn tried the confidential approach. 'We know Johnny's terrific. Fabulous . . . '

We know? Johnny laughed. 'You haven't ever heard me!'

'I can spot a singer,' Jasmyn continued unabashed by the deliberate lie. 'It's got something to do with the chest. The way a mouth opens and shuts . . . '

Becky shut her ears. She hated the way the boy was taking in everything Jasmyn said. She knew what he wanted. Recognition of his talents. She sympathized. She wanted the self-same opportunity to get a spotlight turned on her. But nobody could gain from Jasmyn's sales talk. Nobody except Bobby Sharp.

Deaf to the words passing back and forth between the others, Becky studied Johnny Holland. He was much more handsome than Jasmyn had admitted. Tall, too. And those passionate, soulful brown eyes! Here was a kid with heart to give to a song. A male Piaff. She liked his hair style. Rounded so that the face seemed softer, less harsh than ones cowering under a skinhead severe cut. More in keeping with the gear than a suedehead growth would be.

' . . . "Roundheads" . . . '

Becky pulled herself up quickly, listened now.

'Roundheads, eh?' Jasmyn smiled. 'Apt, Johnny.'

The youth had had his wings clipped. Jasmyn's technique had overcome the initial suspicion, the almost frosty reception. That 'apt' remark got home.

'We're all ex-skinheads,' Johnny said, moving aside for Jasmyn to enter his house. 'We ain't no different except for the hair.' He motioned for Becky to join his new friend. 'Up the Rangers! Up Brentford!' He laughed easily. 'You support Rangers, miss?'

Jasmyn frowned, thrust Gloria into the background and came face to face with the Jolly Green Men. Each sported Johnny's hair style but there the similarity ended. Even their gear looked less acceptable.

'She wouldn't know which side is which on a football, Johnny,' Becky said. 'She's Canadian. They play ice hockey . . . '

'That's real brutal, ain't it?' The youth's eyes glittered. 'I saw a game on the telly once.'

'A blood sport,' Jasmyn said offhandedly. She quickly catalogued the room. Faded wallpaper, soapstone ornaments on the mantle, gilt-framed pictures of an Edwardian era on either side of a Woolworth mirror. One of those bought back in the days when *five-and-ten* meant value beyond belief. Furniture kept good simply by not allowing too many callers to sit on sofa or chairs. An empty fireplace. The trappings of modest incomes and a don't-throw-anything-away heritage. A junk dealer's paradise.

'I wish football let 'em slam each other,' Johnny sighed.

Becky shuddered. She had seen the violence that could erupt at a soccer game. And not on the pitch, either. In the stands. On the terraces. Outside the grounds. Between rival gangs of skinheads. Young hotheads seeking an outlet for their frustrations. Their desire to inflict pain on another person.

'Have you got a Bobby Sharp disc?' Jasmyn asked.

'Yeah - *one* single.'

Gloria smiled, brushed hair from her eyes. 'It's the number Johnny does best of all!'

Becky grinned. From the murderous glance Johnny gave his girlfriend she didn't but doubt if the kid copied the electronic Bobby's every note.

'Which one is that?' Jasmyn asked.

'Virginia's Love,' Gloria said.

'Ah, the ole Barber's hit!' Jasmyn clapped her hands. 'Wouldn't you kids like to go see Bobby Sharp's concert?'

Johnny shrugged. 'Yeah, I guess . . . '

'I'd like it,' Gloria said.

'I tell you how you could get free tickets . . . '

Johnny's face broke into a wide smile. 'That's for me! How?'

Jasmyn winked to Becky. Seating herself on the ancient sofa she ignored a broken spring jutting into her bottom. This was her break. What she got paid to do. A toe in Acton's teeny bopper door. A chance to boost Bobby's image . . .

CHAPTER FOUR

WAITING for an interviewer to appear, Steve Morash smoked and watched the camera-crews set up the studio. It always amazed him how many men the public-owned television network used for a relatively simple job like this. Money, to them, meant an increase in license fees or a government grant to cover tremendous outgoings.

'If they had to show a profit they'd cut down on manpower,' Steve thought.

A make-up girl darted forward, brushed his face with a 'pancake' pad, smiled and departed in search of another victim. A producer charged through tangled cables and had a hurried discussion with the director. Two camera teams ceased work and listened. Even the sound men and lighting experts halted and awaited an earth-shaking decision.

All that happened as far as Steve could see was a third camera moved into position for close-ups. A restless feeling permeated the studio now. Everybody stood twitching, glancing expectantly at the door.

God entered! And the studio began to hum again.

Steve scrutinized the man coming towards him. Tall, arrogant, distinguished looking. His suit had cost a packet, his make-up hours to cover a few skin blemishes. Carefully manicured hands held a pen and a script.

Dropping into a chair close to Steve, the man exhaled air with the sound of sheer exhaustion. Or exasperation. 'What a day,' he said in his carefully modulated voice. As yet he hadn't introduced himself nor acknowledged his crew.

'Same as any other, man,' Steve said.

'I'm Reginald Southworth.'

'Yeah, I recognized you.'

Southworth glanced at his script, frowned. 'I thought about five minutes should cover it,' he told his companion.

'Are we going out "live"?'

The television personality peered at Steve. 'Why?' he asked suspiciously.

'I like to know, is why. A recording can be edited. If we're hotting it up there's always the chance oath . . . '

'No swearing, please!' Southworth held up a hand in anguish. 'This is a clean show!' His eyes rolled. 'And we're on the air . . . *live* . . . in one minute!'

A stopwatch clicked somewhere behind Camera One. A voice shouted last second instructions. Another begged for 'quiet!'.

'I'll begin by asking about your position in the Sharp organization,' Southworth said.

'Sure, that's fine,' Steve nodded, relaxed.

'Remember - no commercials, no product mention.'

'How about the dates we play various cities?'

'Dates are allowable. You can say which theatre, too.'

Southworth took his signal from earphones, adjusted his tie and waited for the arm to give him a go-ahead.

Steve listened disinterestedly to the opening announcements. Not even a glancing reference to Bobby Sharp seemed to raise his enthusiasm. But, he enjoyed it. This getting Southworth all off-balance was precisely what he wanted. And when his turn came . . .

Southworth smiled generously. 'Mr Morash is a member of the Bobby Sharp entourage. What exactly is your position, *Steve?'*

'Suddenly it's Steve and smiles!' Morash thought.

Aloud, he grinned and said, 'You could call me the conductor of a very large bus, Reggie . . . ' He loved the way Southworth flinched but accepted the familiar. 'I'm the guy who calls out destinations and collects the money.'

'Ah,' Southworth said with an enormous smile for his audience. 'Ah, his manager. You must be very close to your client then?'

'We're like father and son. A happy family. I discovered Bobby, you know. A great talent. In my opinion, it had to be just a matter of time before he made the top on his own bat.'

'Coming from a publicist that is quite a statement,' the interviewer said.

'And true!' Steve lit a cigarette and leant back in his chair, completely relaxed and gushing now. 'Bobby Sharp sells himself. Watch him on stage - how he charms his audience and insists on singing what they want. You can't name me one single pop star who'd do that!'

'Some of the older stars did,' Southworth said, grabbing the bait.

'Sure they did and that's why the public remembers them. Perry and Andy and Frankie. Terrific performers all. Their success depended on a sympathetic understanding of what made an audience tick. Bobby Sharp's the same. He somehow gets right in there alongside his fans. Treats them like partners, not dollar . . . or pound . . . signs.'

Southworth seized the remark and wrung it dry. 'In his meteoric rise to stardom I suppose Bobby Sharp has made a small fortune?'

Steve Morash gave his highly-confidential smile. 'I've got news for you, Reggie - Bobby's made a whale of a fortune! He deserves it, though. He's the hardest worker I know in showbiz. And . . . ' Now Morash gestured with both hands as his features softened and tears almost sprang to his eyes. 'And,' he repeated, 'he doesn't keep it all, either. He's generous to a fault. His group are the highest paid. I'm taking home a bundle. All the staff receive fabulous gifts. But that isn't all . . . ' and Steve quickly overcame Southworth's attempted interruption. 'Bobby, Sharp never - never - broadcasts his philanthropic gestures. He even hates for me to mention how much he's given out to various charities, to dog and cat homes . . . the lad's a terrific animal-lover, you can guess . . . '

Southworth had the feeling he'd somewhere lost control of the interview. His intention had been to highlight the monetary aspects of pop and concentrate on the publicity machine that made it all possible. Now, he was being used to manufacture an image wearing a halo.

'I'm sure the British public will take Bobby Sharp to their collective heart,' Morash continued swiftly. 'He wanted to make this tour personally. To satisfy his many loyal fans in your great country . . . '

A cameraman groaned, got a blast from the producer. Southworth, too, wanted to groan. Why, he thought as he fumbled for appropriate words, did these Americans always have to drip emotional honey when they spoke about England, London, the British?

'Time's running out, Reginald!' a voice said in Southworth's earphone. *'Get one final question in!'*

'Mr Morash . . . er, Steve . . . ' Southworth smiled benignly in apology for daring to be formal. 'How many places will Bobby Sharp play on this tour?'

'More than is good for his physical well-being,' came the shock reply. 'We start off in London's Discodrome next Saturday and do a one-night stand in Manchester Sunday. From there we take in Leeds, Edinburgh and Cardiff. Bobby wanted to do an extra for the troops in Ulster but I refused to permit this. Can't have the boy creating a security risk, can I?'

Southworth was clearly relieved. He smiled weakly. 'Well, thanks for coming to see us, Steve. Best of luck to Bobby. I hope the tour will be a success.'

Steve laughed. 'No doubt about that, Reggie. We're almost booked solid - everywhere. So, if you haven't got your tickets yet, folks - hurry on down and make sure today. We wouldn't want any of you wonderful fans to miss seeing Bobby Sharp . . . would we, Reggie?'

The producer did a throat-cutting motion and Southworth suddenly exploded as the cameras 'died on the interview'. 'What the hell . . . !'

The producer stormed up, face red, eyes wild. 'I've a bloody good mind to drop this flamin' programme,' he yelled. 'I've never seen such an ineffectual interview!'

'Relax, guys,' Steve said, getting to his feet. 'We gave Bobby a plug and ain't that what it's all about?' He waved to the sullen cameramen, the other technicians. 'Swell job, boys,' he called and strolled nonchalantly off the set . . .

Johnny Holland switched on the television set. He felt his insides churning with excitement. Ambitious notions circulated through a head buzzing from the sheer cheek of Sharp's manager. He admired the bloke's performance, the way he got it across. But it had been naughty!

'Are you stayin' in?' his mother asked, drying hands on her apron.

'Naw,' Johnny answered offhandedly. 'I've got to see Gloria . . . '

Mrs Holland harrumped, turned into the kitchen. She didn't agree with *attachments* between boys and girls of school age. From what she'd heard about the permissive society they only encouraged children to do those things.

Johnny grinned. He knew how his mother felt. Knew his dad didn't give a damn. And that, in his book, meant a 'go-ahead'. He admired his old man more than most. Maybe being a clerk in a dreary factory wasn't the height of executive command but at least it was better than digging coal, heaving cargo or beating batter. It was a white-collar position. A step - a small step - in the right direction.

Leaving his house, Johnny collected two of his mates, Peter Acroyd and Bruce Barnes. 'Did you see the telly?' he asked them.

Peter nodded, hands thrust into pockets. 'Yeah - if only we had a bloke like that working for us!'

Bruce snorted. 'He's all mouth. Anyway, who needs a manager?'

Johnny jabbed his mate in the chest with a stiff finger. 'Every bleedin' act's got a manager and a publicity agent. How do you think the *Stones* and *Glencoe* got where they are? Not booking their own concerts. Not making the contracts.'

'Aww . . . ' Bruce suddenly grinned, kicked a stone off the pavement. 'Let's forget it! There's a game on today . . . ' He used both hands to tidy his 'Roundhead' hair-style as a slight breeze blew down Acton Lane. 'I feel in the mood to "do" a few Villa yobs!'

'I dunno,' Peter replied, glancing at the sky. 'Could rain by this evening.'

'You won't bloody melt,' Bruce scowled. He didn't want to miss the opportunity to get in a little aggro. It didn't seem right to spend most of their spare time in Johnny's front parlour. He enjoyed the music, the way the group moulded. But he missed his punch-ups and soccer.

'A change will do us all good,' Johnny said matter of factly. As leader he was entitled to make decisions. 'Anyway,' he announced mysteriously, 'I want to discuss an idea I've had.'

'What?' Peter asked.

Johnny shrugged, zipper his quilted hunting jacket. He'd paid a lot for the gear, believed it gave him class. 'Never mind now. I'll explain tonight . . . ' They entered the High Street. 'Hey, how's about getting old Charlie to show us the latest boots?'

Peter laughed, pointed at his new ones. 'Hawkins "Astronauts" with genuine Doe Marten's soles,' he boasted.

'That bleedin' Joe Hawkins,' Bruce growled.

Johnny raised an eyebrow. Trust Bruce to get off an his favourite gripe. Ever since they'd shared a copy of *Skinhead* their mob had tried to find a different approach to isolate them from the ordinary run of cultist sheep. They'd been 'suedes' before any other Hammersmith district gang. They'd scrawled 'Boot Boys - up the Rangers' on walls in Acton and Chiswick long before the Millwall yobbos got going in Underground tunnels. They'd even tried growing their hair long and disorderly. Only when their local barber suggested a 'rounded-off' style had they finally emerged from the herd into uniqueness. *Roundheads*. It had been Johnny's name. Like Cromwell's blokes. And the long-hairs, hippies, drop-outs were their enemies.

'I wonder if the shoe company used Joe Hawkins' name for their boots?' Johnny asked quietly . . .

CHAPTER FIVE

WITH Becky gone, Jasmyn Ragg got into the serious work of touting for Bobby Sharp. She did not give a damn how the younger girl made out in Bristol. The greed that constantly consumed her could not see co-operation between the Morash 'arousers'. It was, for her, a sales promotion campaign with each demonstrator getting a slice of the action depending on results. Personal results. And she could always prove her worth. Steve Morash had a way of checking. Clipboard guys at every concert or airport or hotel. Guys getting facts and figures.

Where do you live, doll?

How'd you get to hear about Bobby?

Dressed in her schoolgirl gear, Jasmyn entered the dismal cafe. With the Easter holidays closing every school she couldn't operate inside those nor get a small fracas started outside the gates. That one usually attracted a helluva lot of attention and, always, she won in any *mêlée*.

A couple of listless youngsters sat nursing cold coffees. Another shook his guts out to a Cat Stevens hit. The jukebox sound was deafening. Cup in saucer vibrating stuff. Down at the far end of the dingy, booth-lined greasy-spoon she spotted five kids wrapped in conversation. She headed for them, carefully detouring round 'dancing boy'.

'Hi, Frank,' she said and slumped into a seat beside a pimpled-faced youth. 'Buy me a Coke!'

The youth squinted at her, winked to his companions.

'I'm Larry,' he said, hand suddenly darting down to rest on her knee. 'But I'll buy a Coke. Okay?'

Jasmyn glared, delicately picked his hand off her leg. 'Drop dead!' she snapped. 'I thought you were Frank Bourne.'

One of the three girls at the table stared, asked: 'You're new 'round here, ain't cha?'

'Yes, and no,' Jasmyn replied sociably. 'I live with my aunt in Hanger Lane but Frank Bourne lives round the corner. Or so he told me last night . . . ' She left no doubts what she was supposed to have been doing by lifting her hands and shrugging as she rolled her eyes enthusiastically.

'There ain't no Frank comes in this caff,' the second youth remarked.

'Damn!' Jasmyn sighed, then, shaking a sad head, asked, 'Where can I get a ticket for Bobby Sharp's concert?'

'For wot?' a girl asked puzzledly.

'Bobby Sharp.' Expressing outright amazement, Jasmyn asked: 'Haven't you heard of Bobby Sharp?'

'He's a singer, ain't he?' the first boy replied.

'He's the greatest, man! So handsome and sexy . . . ' Wrapping arms about herself, Jasmyn did her acting nut. 'Gorrr! What a dish! Bobby Sharp!'

'I read where he's doin' a tour,' the 'in-the-know' youth said, anxious to make an impression. He liked this new girl. She had shape and the way she simulated passion got under his skin.

'Yeah,' Jasmyn breathed heavily.

'The Discodrome on Saturday night.'

Her face lengthened and she brushed, blonde hair from her eyes. 'But I haven't got a ticket . . . '

'You'll get in dead-easy,' the youth told her.

'That's what you think! It's all ticket. Anyway - everybody wants to hear Bobby Sharp!' Jasmyn sat in silence now. She furtively watched the reactions her campaign had on the five young faces. From the girls she got acceptance, a wishfulness suggestive of fandoms worst enemy a sexy-looking singer and no chance of ever kissing him.

The boys seemed uncertain, waiting for somebody to carry the ball to them.

'How much is a ticket?' the until now silent girl asked.

'Not much, I reckon. Frank - if that's his real name - said he could afford a pair and he was only earning a tenner a week!'

'Starvation wages,' the first boy said. 'I take home nineteen.' He glanced at his mate, then the girls. 'If Tom'd come we could make it . .'

126

He hesitated. The warmth of Jasmyn's thigh suddenly brushed him. Provocatively. 'Tom an' Jerry,' he laughed. His knee dug against Jasmyn's. 'You could go with me then?'

'Tom and Jerry?' Jasmyn tried to sound enthusiastic. 'Are you kiddin'?'

'Naw,' a girl frowned. The way she gazed at Jasmyn's conquest it was obvious she wanted to book him for her escort. 'Jerry's a nice bloke but bloody slow - if you know what I mean?'

'I'm not,' the youth said, a hand under the table proving he was slightly faster than an express train.

Jasmyn decided she'd done enough here. She deliberately studied her wristwatch. 'I'd like to go with you all,' she said plaintively. 'I honestly would but . . . I've got to shop for my aunt. Look . . . ' and she rubbed her thigh back and forth under the youth's fondling palm. 'Is it a deal we get tickets for Saturday night?'

'Man, it's on,' the boy answered readily.

'Okay!' Jasmyn squeezed his hand, got to her feet. 'I'll meet you here tonight. If you've got the tickets for Bobby Sharp I'll let you take me . . . and she paused pregnantly, 'out!'

The youth was still sweating on her promise when Jasmyn left the cafe. The gospel according to St Morash had just been preached to the Actonites. From that small beginning the 'word' would spread like wildfire. Jealousy alone would get the girls talking. Hope surely one of the boys!

She had another seven hours to plug, plug, plug the name. BOBBY SHARP, in caps. A routine grown so normal it had become a bore. If it hadn't been for the travel, the money, the feeling offered by close proximity to showbiz she'd have kicked over the traces long ago.

'To hell with it,' she muttered, annoying an old woman staggering along under a shopping burden. *Give a year, and I'll quit - and count my loot!* she thought. *'None of this housewife bit for me! I'll have a maid, car, a guy paying alimony once I ditch him!'*

She walked with a jauntier step. It was an old dream to hustle through a marriage, take the sucker to a divorce court and live off his monthly payments until she wearied of divorcee status or had bled the sucker white.

Bobby Sharp and the job were like tentative toddles by a babe rarin' to run, let alone walk. And run she would one day. Soon.

Becky Wilmott allowed herself exactly one hour to get acclimatized. Starting at the bus depot, she entered Bristol's city centre, skirted the floating harbour and climbed the incline to the cathedral. Directly across from where she stood momentarily enjoying the sights she had the Council House and College Green. She made mental notes of the wonderful places she would some day visit when time did not press so demandingly. Continuing up Park Street she reached the university. Street signs gave directions for the zoo and Clifton suspension bridge.

Reluctantly, she turned and descended the hill. The university crowd didn't count. They were too old already, too involved in politics and the Underground heavies. Anyway, Bobby Sharp wasn't noted for capturing fans above the ripe old age of eighteen.

Moving down a side street, Becky wondered how it must have looked way back when the dwellings were brand new. Probably homes for wealthy merchants or retired sea captains, she thought.

A man in a small corner shop gave her the information she wanted. She posed as a saleswoman flogging teenage gear. The type to appeal to schoolgirls and the working classes. Armed with a district and best wishes, she took a bus and alighted near Bristol Rovers' Eastville ground. Until that moment she had been a member of a team. Now, she was alone. Success or failure rested in her ability to cajole Bristol's teeny boppers. Bobby Sharp had to go over big here or else . . .

CHAPTER SIX

TRUE to her promise, Jasmyn Ragg turned up at the cafe and met the youth. He looked different dressed in a suit, white shirt and tie. She hated the way his disappointment smashed at her. Why couldn't people have stones where hearts were? she thought. How much better for individuals like herself to verify that Bobby Sharp concert tickets had been purchased before letting him down on 'their date'.

'Sorry, love.' she said, affecting sincerity and a hasty arm squeeze. 'I can't make it tonight. *My aunt* . . .' She avoided a more detailed excuse, leaving the aunt hanging in mid-air like some ogre. 'But,' and she brightened for him, 'I'll be here Saturday night. Count on that!'

'I worked it so Jerry takes Flo,' the youth said with a listless voice. It wasn't so much that he had big plans for tonight. It was the way his mates would rib him. He knew the bastards were happily watching from somewhere close. Ready to jeer if the girl didn't show. Ready, when she left so quickly, to accuse him of not 'having it!'

'That's terrific . . . ' Jasmyn pushed against him, kissed his dry lips. A sisterly kiss. Hurried. Retreating to escape arms that almost immediately wanted to encircle her. 'Not here,' she smiled. 'Saturday - after the show! I promise.'

The youth seemed anxious to believe her. 'Can I walk with you a while?' he asked, glancing round to see if his mates were anywhere in sight.

Jasmyn frowned. She didn't want to get trapped but . . . 'Okay. Just to the main road!' She took off at speed, hoping to hell he would believe her rush and not drag out their parting.

Skilfully, the youth manoeuvred her across the busy Uxbridge Road, got several heavy lorries and a coach-load of tourists between him and the cafe. Then, grinning, he patted her bottom. 'I'll leave you here. See you Saturday okay?'

Jasmyn figured he had a valid reason for darting round a corner. She suspected it had something to do with her failure to accompany him. Not that it mattered! She didn't give a damn about the youth. Her mission had been completed the moment he purchased tickets. And, he'd go alone. Saturday night was not allocated to him or any of the teeny boppers . . .

Walking alone now, Jasmyn got to detest the Uxbridge Road district. Dirt and an air of slow decay permeated the region. Factories and a high immigrant population overcrowding small family style dwellings had done their equal best to destroy what must have been, in her opinion, a decently pleasant pre-1939 working class area.

She quickened her step. A few more calls and she'd call it a night. Already, the skies were darkening for day's end. Or rain. If only she could get a mob in one spot she could work on them. She did not consider the possibility of failure. Her super confidence in her abilities was the keynote of successful 'arousing'.

A light-hearted mood suddenly prevailed. She hummed *I've got you under my skin* as, mentally, she flung mudballs at an imaginary poster of Bobby Sharp's face . . .

Johnny Holland hummed a number to himself, too. His gaze wandered over Loftus Road, picking out fuzz and club stewards with equal ease. He speculated on the possibilities of getting away with a punch-up. From the number of blue-coats it appeared that the club had strengthened its crowd control force tonight. Of course, one had to anticipate this. Aston Villa supporters had a reputation. Just every bit as much as Queen's Park Rangers fans had at home. And away.

Gloria tugged at his sleeve. 'Don't get clobbered,' she pleaded.

'I won't. Fact is, I'm not sure we're going to have an aggro,' Johnny told her.

Bruce glared at the pair jostling through a terrace throng next to him. He couldn't complain about Gloria. She fought every bit as ferociously as the rest but she did have this fault. A once-in-a-while withholding. A backing off from real violence. 'Crissakes, that's why we came,' he moaned.

Johnny patted his shoulder, let the other shove ahead. Peter Acroyd had barged through struggling supporters to join them. 'I told you I had an idea buzzing round in me head, didn't I?'

Bruce nodded over his shoulder, kicked an ankle. When an irate man swung with blazing eyes Bruce sneered into his face, dared: 'Want to make it a scrap, mate?'

The man quickly lost his ire. 'Er . . . aw, hell!' He shuffled sideways, mumbling under his breath yet afraid to voice his pain.

Peter grinned, added insult to injury by swiping the bloke with an elbow aimed at the stomach. His steady stare added another dare.

Johnny pulled Peter away. He didn't honestly know yet if aggro was on the cards. His slowly maturing scheme had not planted deep roots. Not shown signs of bearing edible fruit. Until it did, doubts clouded his thinking.

'Whatscha got in mind, Johnny?' Bruce asked with mounting impatience.

They formed a small huddle against a crash barrier. The players were on the field kicking the balls around, limbering up under the referee's official gaze. Gloria glued her body hard against Johnny's side. Bruce and Peter formed the front rank, the remaining members of the 'Jolly Green Men' taking secondary place in their rear.

'If we get a chance we'll clobber Villa's skins,' Johnny said softly. 'But only when I say so!' He fixed each of his gang with a leadership in challenge stare. When they passed his order by he smiled grimly. 'I've got good reasons, mates. We could blow some minds next Saturday.'

Gloria tensed, head tilted to gaze into her dream-man's face. Peter felt a tingle of excitement race through him. Even Bruce seemed on the verge of apologetic encouragement. Mike, Bill, Walter beamed acceptance.

'Don't ask me to explain it in detail,' Johnny said, shattering their curiosity. 'I will - tomorrow!'

'What if we don't agree?' Bruce asked, slightly annoyed.

'We've lost nothing!'

' 'ceptin' aggro,' Bruce mentioned with sullenness.

'Jeeze, nobody ain't said we're not going to kick shit out of Villa's skins, have they?' Johnny asked.

'No-o-o,' Bruce admitted.

'Then let's get down behind their goal!' Johnny grabbed Gloria's hand, pulled her in his wake.

Darkening skies overhead went unnoticed in the floodlight glare. The ref had called both captains to the centre circle, tossing coin in his hand. The smiles shared between the threesome were the normal friendly ones handed out free, gratis and at no cost prior to every match. What happened once the game started was another matter. Another picture.

Johnny Holland slammed two Villa supporters aside, opened a wedge for his gang to pour through. Funny, he thought, how the best laid plans go for a burton when the game is about to start! The crowd's seething infected him.

But not nearly as much as it hit Bruce . . .

Jasmyn Ragg entered a pub. She felt in desperate need of a drink. Five lousy coffees dispensed by uncaring scruff behind cafe counters had not satisfied her desire for a fluid, liquid throat. She felt pleased with her efforts, though. Bobby Sharp had gained a popularity he did not deserve.

'Rum and Coke,' she told the barman. *'Captain Morgan's . . .'*

Filling in time, she studied the pub's inhabitants. Mostly ordinary with a smattering of pretentious looking types. One man in particular caught her attention.

'Anythin' else, miss?' the barman asked with a thickly sliced Irish accent.

'Yeah - change from this,' she quipped, laying a fiver on the counter. Now was definitely not the moment to invite trouble. Especially North versus South Irish trouble. There was enough of that going on in Ireland. In Ulster. By rights, if her father had had his way and she had been a son instead of a distaff daughter she (or was that 'he'?) would have been in the forefront of the battle to preserve a loyal Ulster within the United Kingdom. Always depending, naturally, on a son being less greedy and less inclined to pursue personal ambitions, when the 'great call' sounded throughout the world to keep Ulster from surrendering one inch of its territory.

She wanted to giggle, out of character. She could remember how it had been in Toronto. Her dad had been an Orange big-wig. A true-blue die-hard Ulsterman. And then . . . The day of celebration. July the Twelfth. Orangeman's Day. The parade which halted all Toronto traffic. And at the head of the parade - a Red Indian carrying a raised umbrella to ward off strong sunshine. And, in the carriage lauding the Grand Master - an Italian. An Italian Protestant, no less. An Italian Protestant Orangeman. Like his Redskin brother. Lord, how her dad had crawled into his shell and almost died!

Jasmyn stifled her desire to laugh and concentrated on the one man in the pub who interested her. She was not out for a conquest. Just testing her ability to make him respond.

God, he's a handsome devil, she thought.

The man smiled, nodded an unspoken invitation to join him. She felt foolish in her 'working garb' - her near schoolish gear. She wished to hell she had on a sparkling dress like the one the Queen wore to the film command Performance. What an outfit that had been! Encrusted with gems. Real gems, too. A smack-in-the-eye creation when those Hollywood starlets were striving to outshine British royalty. What a laugh! Not once in a million years would anyone get the upper hand over *her* Queen. *Canada's Queen!*

Mixing *Coke* with her *Captain Morgan's*, she sent a message - subtle, no more than a small smile, an inclination of the head, a drooped eyelid.

'That's an interesting concoction,' the man remarked as he took a stool next to hers. 'What's its name?'

Jasmyn lifted her head, stared into his icy blue eyes. A tremble shook her entire frame. 'A normal enough drink in Canada,' she said deliberately.

'Oh, you're a Canuck?'

'All the way from Ontario's pastureland,' she joked.

'I've been in Toronto and Montreal,' he said easily.

'Never mind Montreal,' she humorously frowned. 'Stick to God's country - Ontario and Toronto!'

'CKFH - 1430 on your dial,' he joked. 'Or maybe - The Golden Nugget Tavern at Bloor and Yonge?'

'All you can eat from noon till one ack emma!' she replied, laughingly. 'With jazz and Dixieland music thrown in for free!'

Memories flooded back, wishes filled with returning. Jasmyn had heard the old saying: 'It's great to get away from Toronto but so goddamned nice to come home again!' She believed it. She really believed it!

'I'm Mark Rowe,' the man said, extending a hand.

'And you are . . . ?'

'Jasmyn Ragg.'

'On a quickie visit?'

'On business,' she replied too fast.

His eyebrows raised. He stared at her outfit. 'You can't be older than . . . ' He hesitated.

'Don't tell me you're one of those?' Jasmyn asked with heavy heart.

'One of those?' Mark seemed puzzled.

'Schoolgirl fetish!'

'God, no!' He withdrew a gold cigarette case from a pocket, opened it gingerly and offered its contents. 'I'm positively certain you're much older than that. Have one?'

Jasmyn accepted. A menthol brand she liked. Normally, she smoked a Canadian brand but they didn't have a British sale. Not one outlet she had discovered. But these *Everest* had a peculiar smoothness, a real menthol coolness she found satisfying.

'How old are you really?' Mark asked, applying a light to her cigarette.

'Old enough.' She winked.

'Single?'

'Definitely! And you?'

'Same carefree status . . . *Jasmyn!*' He emphasised the christian name. 'Well, cheers.' He raised his glass, sank the contents in one swallow.

Taking her time, Jasmyn finished hers, left the empty glass like an accusing finger on the bartop. When he reached for it, smilingly moved it forward, she knew he had been hooked. Wondered if she honestly wanted an affair right then. It was one thing proving to herself she could attract any man of her choosing. Another to be gluttonous. Desiring more than distant worship.

'Care to change your brand?' Mark asked. 'You haven't lived until you've sampled our Scotch.'

She held her laughter deep inside. Apparently he had the idea she'd just climbed off an *Air Canada* plane. Was as yet totally unacclimatized. *So, okay. Let him have his fun. My pleasure to fool the masses.* 'You name it, Mark,' she smiled encouragement.

Beckoning the Irish barman, her escort ordered: 'Your *special* bottle, Pat - *Hundred Pipers,* for the lady from Canada.'

The Irishman sulked, glared at Jasmyn. 'Sounds more like from Belfast,' he snapped.

'My dad came from there so watch it, buster,' Jasmyn growled. This was her first experience of having a slight family trace of dialect brought to her attention. She had never been called out back home. But then, Toronto had so many Ulster people it was sometimes difficult to tell whether or not a man, or woman, belonged as a native or through prolonged residence.

Pat retreated to his bottles, disgruntled. Mark seriously studied his companion. The sudden antagonism shown to the Irishman did not quite go with a facial gentility, an aura radiating composure. 'Do you carry that torch?' he asked anxiously.

'What torch?'

'The Irish one!'

Jasmyn laughed aloud. 'Christ - no!'

'I'm glad!' Mark breathed easier. 'There's nothing worse than civil war. Especially in this district. Half the population here is Catholic Irish. Rebels to you.'

'I'm Canadian,' she reminded him. 'Part this, part that but essentially, free from involvement. I won't start a fracas. I promise, Mark!' There, she'd satisfied him. The 'Mark' bit worked wonders.

Pat returned and sullenly deposited their drinks directly in front of Mark. He avoided Jasmyn with a frosty deliberateness that stank of provocation.

Mark Rowe jumped in fast. He could sense Jasmyn's tensing. Her silent rebuttal. And he didn't enjoy the Irishman's attempt to stir up trouble. 'Anything else, Jasmyn?' he asked.

'A *Canada Dry* . . . '

Pat stood mute, motionless.

'You heard the lady . . . ' Mark bristled now.

Pat tossed his black head. 'And you, *sir?'* He made it clear what breed of dog he gave to Mark.

'The same!' came the sharp reply.

When Pat moved away, Mark grunted. 'A fine bloody thing when we can't expect civility in our own country,' he remarked.

'Forget him,' Jasmyn advised. 'What line of business are you in?'

The two *Canada Dry* splits arrived. Mark paid the exact amount, let Pat wander off sulking more than ever. No tip meant indifferent service for the next round. It showed plainly.

'I've got a small estate office,' Mark said to Jasmyn, his gaze following Pat with more than a trifle of animosity. 'Four doors down the road. Nothing much but it keeps me solvent.' He smiled.

'Real estate,' Jasmyn corrected.

'Not in England,' Mark re-corrected. 'When I was in Toronto I took a job with a firm on Queen Street East. I found it so terribly difficult to fit in.'

'No wonder,' Jasmyn laughed. She poured her *Canada Dry* into the large *Hundred Pipers*. A sudden thought struck. She asked, 'Isn't this going to cause disharmony when you use the pub after I've gone?'

'Pat isn't a regular,' Mark told her. 'He works for C.A.V. during the day. I don't normally drop in after hours.' He looked pensive. 'You talk about business as if this visit is . . . '

Jasmyn interrupted. 'It is! I'm one of Bobby Sharp's publicity brigade.'

'Bobby Sharp?' Mark appeared lost in a darkness of ignorance.

'Teeny bopper idol. The hottest showbiz property since Sinatra's bobby-soxers screamed him into a multi-million dollar fortune!'

'Oh!' Mark's expression showed he did not follow the chart ratings.

'Supposing we finish these drinks and let me make one more stopover?'

Mark cocked his head in query.

'I'm a working gal,' Jasmyn smiled. 'I just thought you'd like to take me back to my hotel, wait for me to change and then . . . Well,' she palms-up gestured, 'do the town!'

Mark beamed. 'That's a terrific notion. I'm game - but when does this "stopover" end?'

Jasmyn glanced at a clock ticking away behind the bar. Allowing for ten minutes publicans usually gave themselves she reckoned it was 9:30. She didn't know the clock had ceased recording hours or minutes five years previously. It ticked. But did not shift its immobile hands. Electricity was a marvellous invention!

'I could arouse a few saps in another half-an-hour,' she said.

'Arouse? Saps?'

Jasmyn laughed. 'I'll explain after we dine. And wine.'

Mark glowed. This was his type of woman. Direct. None of the English hedging. None of the socialite leaving it to the 'master'. 'Agreed! Name a time and place . . . ' he said.

It was exactly 8:07. Villa fans were cockahoop. Their team had scored first. Even with a dramatic scrambled equalizer coming less than ninety seconds later, glorious Villa had shot ahead again with a spectacular solo goal by McMahon.

Johnny Holland cursed. His 'Roundheads' itched for action.

'Christ, listen to 'em!' Bruce howled.

The Villa skins roared their lungs out.

Peter champed at his bit, enforced by Johnny's indecisiveness. 'Bastards!' he snarled. 'Can't we have a bloody go?'

The Rangers got the ball in midfield. Thomas slipped his tackle, sent a looping cross into the area. Villa rushed back, crowded their goalmouth.

'Easy . . . Easy . . . Easy . . . ' the Rangers fans chanted.

Bowles latched onto the bobbing ball, killed its bounce and neatly sliced a banana into the net to one side of a wrong-way 'keeper.

'Two all!' Bruce roared.

'ONE - TWO - THREE - FOUR . . . ' the home supporters roared.

'Look at 'em!' Peter yelled doing a shuffling dance. His finger had a section of Villa scarves in aim.

Johnny felt the excitement cancel out his reserve. He wanted to smash some Villa heads.

'Johnny . . . ' Bruce pleaded.

'Screw it!' Johnny charged down the terrace, closely followed by his 'Roundheads'. His new 'Astronaut' boots caught a screaming Villa skin in the bollocks. His fist lashed into another's face.

Bruce Barnes gave one lung-bursting shout and took an enormous leap, both feet close together and aimed at his target. His body hurtled through the air, held on course by other bodies forming a small, arrow-shaped tunnel down which he catapulted.

Peter Acroyd shuddered. He didn't appreciate Bruce's form of aggro. He liked getting his opponent at close range, bettering him by skill. This shooting arrow tactic where boots smashed a bloke into submission - and, not to mention, hospital - had never appealed. He saw Bruce's heavily soled boots slam into the Villa skin's groin. Heard the agonized groan. The *cluoop* as the senseless youth hit the terrace; screams tearing from those frothing lips.

'I got one!' Gloria screeched. Her fingernails raked the youth's face. Her knee finding his unprotected groin.

Johnny belted the guy, kicking sideways to ward off a flanking attack. 'Hit hard - retreat!' he shouted above the crowd's throbbing.

Peter smashed his fist into a Villa's face, kneed another from his path and belted Bruce's latest victim to clear a passageway. He'd seen the fuzz charging into the terraces. Noted stewards battling struggling innocent supporters to get close enough to recognize faces. He didn't want to be forever banned from Rangers' grounds. He lowered his head. Yelled: 'The grass are coming!' and slammed Bruce in the ribs to make his mate aware of the situation.

'Let's fuck off,' Johnny growled to Gloria. He grabbed Mike's sweater. 'Tell 'em to get out!'

Gloria shook all over. She loved the excitement, these aggravations. But she wanted Johnny and his mates to get the hell out of Loftus Road grounds. For her, the most important thing was a singing career. *Johnny and the Jolly Green Men.* A real scene. Not unlike the hormone stimulated flow brought about by aggro, or sex . . .

CHAPTER SEVEN

SEEN from the aircraft, Bristol's approaches looked like some crazy patchwork of turned soil, grazing, housing development belonging to a Midwest community striving for international status. But when the aircraft banked and gave an oblique vista of Bristol, the city, the similarity vanished.

Bobby Sharp sighed, gazed through the porthole-type window. His first impression drastically altered. This was no smalltime town. It appeared as a thriving metropolis.

A port. A senior citizen in the places to visit league.

'Do we have the usual arrival?' he asked his personal secretary.

Lloyd Morgan consulted his diary. According to Steve Morash's calculations their British touchdown should be a riot. 'We do!' he said simply.

'Key me in,' Bobby demanded imperiously.

'After landing we have a limousine standing by. You walk toward that but you duck behind the aircraft's tail and get into one of the escort cars.'

'How big? What make?'

Lloyd stifled his desire to clip Bobby's wings. He hated the bastard. Loathed Steve Morash for tempting him. If it hadn't been for the forty thousand dollars a year salary he'd have opened an emergency chute and slid Bobby Sharp down into shark-infested depths.

'I'm not exactly sure,' Lloyd answered eventually.

Bobby reached for his airsick bag. Landing always gave his stomach a toss. In the air he felt fine. On take-off it was invariably touch and go. Mostly just touch. But landing . . . Mostly go! Into the bag . . .

He could feel the plane bank now. If he had been looking from the porthole window he would have seen the runway widen, lengthen, suddenly vanish.

God, he couldn't take these final approaches!

'FASTEN YOUR SEATBELT' . . .

'NO SMOKING' . . .

The illuminated notices scared him. Like warnings before they trundled the coffin out and laid the pathetic corpse to rest!

'You okay?' Lloyd asked.

'Yeah . . . ' Bobby gurgled, lowered his head and brought the bag up smartly.

Lloyd smiled to himself. 'Hope he vomits his bloody gut out,' he thought. 'Wouldn't it be fantastic if he hit my home-town looking like Satan whitewashed!' Fifteen years in the States hadn't lessened his attachment for Bristol. *Good old Bristol!* The striking clock of Christ Church of St Ewen. The Georgian splendour of Orchard Street. Quay Head, by The Centre. Corn Street and the historic Nails. Where the ancient saying 'Pay down on the Nails' originated.

Suddenly, Lloyd felt himself a Bristolian again. His sojourn in America meant less than a sand grain sifting through a timer. What did the years count when compared to heritage, he pondered.

A pocket claimed air from under the plane and it dropped several feet. Up front, the pilot made the necessary corrections, kept his craft perfectly on course.

Bobby Sharp didn't know this!

Nor did he care!

He let fly . . .

The plane taxied to its appointed bay. Bobby Sharp straightened, closed his airsick bag and wiped his mouth with a monogrammed handkerchief. Face pale, eyes watery, body still trembling he asked: 'Now what?'

'We wait,' Lloyd said.

Some of the clinging vines Bobby kept round him for kicks and that old showbiz desire to feel important came forward, clustered like weeds about the flower.

'Gee, ain't it terrific - we're here,' one said.

'Yeah, man - fantastic,' another agreed.

'They're really packin' 'em in outside, Bobby,' a third trilled.

Lloyd peered from a window. Like always, Morash had performed miracles. Bristol airport bad never been so crowded. Screaming teeny boppers crawled from out of every doorway, over the observation areas, the restaurant bar.

A make-up girl squeezed through Bobby's yes-men and took over Lloyd's seat. Deft hands worked on the star's face. When she finished all traces of landing sickness had vanished.

'Okay, okay,' the teeny bopper's idol snapped, rising. 'Let's get this show on the road!' A mirror held aloft by the girl showed his Brylcreem bounce just perfectly casual, his cheeks bronzed, eyes bright and aglow.

'Five minutes more,' Lloyd mentioned.

'Why the hell we gotta wait?' Bobby asked with mounting anger.

'For the cars to get into position.'

'These British kids ain't gonna kill me,' the star growled, pushing past his cohorts. 'I'm fed up being ordered to do this and that. It's about time everybody realised who rates in this outfit.'

A stewardess patiently guarded the exit, hand on door, smile plastered on her pretty features. Being in the presence of 'greatness' did not give her palpitations like it had when she first joined the airline. She'd flown with some super stars since. With heads of state and, once, royalty. To her, Bobby Sharp came way down the list of those entitled to get her respect and dancing attendance.

'Okay - let's go,' Bobby told her.

'Sorry, sir,' she replied unmoved. 'I've got instructions not to open the door until control gives me clearance.'

Swinging, eyes blazing, Bobby fixed Lloyd with his exploding ire. 'Goddammit, Morgan - get this bitch out of my way!'

A few of his cronies glared at the secretary, at the stewardess. They knew which side their bread was buttered. Who lavished cash and gifts on them.

Lloyd shrugged, gently reminded, 'We agreed to abide by the airline's rules when we hired this plane. If anything happened to the aircraft we'd be held responsible and I don't believe you'd like Steve shelling out next year's take to pay for repairs.'

For a moment it looked like Bobby Sharp had lost his voice. Strange sounds came from his throat and his skin darkened as rage consumed him. Contracts and agreements meant absolutely nothing to him. He had no business sense. No idea of what made the world tick outside his own limited sphere. The sudden shooting to the heights of teeny bopper worship had left him a helpless cripple in anything even remotely approaching commerce. He knew this and felt all the worse for being reminded by Lloyd Morgan.

'Your cars have arrived, Mr Sharp,' the captain's voice said from a loud-speaker.

Bobby cooled down slightly. The sooner he got off the plane now the better he would enjoy life. He wanted to taste the adulation of his fans. Hear their screams. Feel their hands tear at his clothes.

The stewardess swung the exit door open, smile no longer lingering on her face. She wouldn't forget the 'bitch' remark. Although she had been hired along with the plane she fully intended to make a request to get back on scheduled flights. She didn't want the displeasure of flying back to the States with Sharp.

Brushing past her, Bobby stepped into sunshine.

His arms raised, his charm reached out to embrace his many fans.

'What a damned turncoat,' the stewardess thought.

Lloyd Morgan smiled, whispered, 'Sorry, miss.'

The girl shrugged off Bobby's ignorance. 'Forget it,' she replied. 'We're used to dealing with bums!'

Becky Wilmott stood way back from the screaming, pushing teeny boppers and let them surge against crush-barriers in a demented effort to come into close personal contact with their idol. She felt reasonably satisfied at the turnout. Time had not been on her side, she'd found. The Bristol kids hadn't reacted with the same fervour as those in London. Probably, she had told herself, because they did not suffer from over-publicity.

A security man joined her, shaking his head in wonderment. 'Look at 'em,' he groaned. 'A bunch of passion-starved schoolgirls! There must be all of a thousand . . . '

Even as he spoke a new wave hit the airport. Yelling, displaying huge banners Becky had supplied the previous evening. Banners calling for 'BOBBY SHARP - WE LOVE YOU. STAY IN ENGLAND FOREVER!'

'Bloody marvellous how they get the youngsters worked up,' the security man said and hurriedly trotted to join his mates forming a ring round the American entourage.

For Becky the marvel was that she had managed to arouse so much enthusiasm. Steve, too, had somehow worked another miracle. She noted - pleasurably - BBC and ITV television crews covering the event.

As Bobby Sharp stepped onto the tarmac a howl went up from his fans. Arms raised like an ancient hero about to approach Mount Olympus, the singer beamed at 'the faithful', blew kisses with triumphant ease.

'Ohhhhh!

'Bobby, darlin' . . . '

Joyful tears mixed with frenzied hair pulling. Even now it was becoming painfully obvious that the security force could not contain the mob for long. Far down the field a couple of planes waited patiently for control clearance to taxi towards the unloading aprons. The cars drawn up close to the huge jet with its freshly-painted BOBBY SHARP SPECIAL emblazoned down its fuselage belched fumes as the drivers fumed to get away.

And all the while Bobby Sharp did what his teeny bopper fans wanted - he smiled, waved, pranced like some ballet dancer.

Suddenly, the security cordon broke. Fans rushed into the gap and, in seconds, frantic girls were tearing the clothes from a now frightened, running, idol.

Becky's heart thudded as alarm bells sounded inside her head. She watched the security crew beat back the girls, reform ranks and hustle a scared singer into his car. She sighed when, with three girls flinging themselves across the bonnet, the limousine managed to make an undignified exit. And as a door opened and a man came out to chase the delightedly screaming girls off.

Only when the last car careened from Bristol's airport precincts did Becky breathe easily again. The arrival had been beyond her wildest dreams. A success to rank with those landings and take-offs according more accomplished, more internationally famous stars.

CHAPTER EIGHT

MARK ROWE climbed across Jasmyn's sleeping body and went to the bathroom. Standing in the doorway he glanced back at the girl, a smile touching his firm mouth. She looked even more desirable sleeping, bedclothes slightly rumpled and one side of her totally exposed.

Forcing himself to concentrate on the day ahead and not the night just passed into uninhibited history, he whistled softly, ran water into the tub.

Jasmyn opened one eye, then the other. She lay quite still for a minute, memory returning with a smugly satisfying glow. She listened lazily to Mark's morning preparations. Somehow the idea of sharing this intimacy every waking day did not disturb her. Providing, that was, marriage did not go hand-in-sex with the experience.

When Mark came back she studied his athletic nakedness unashamedly. Modesty belonged in television drama shows. The permissive society did not shun nudity between lovers. Nor even close friends, it appeared.

'Seen enough?' Mark asked, grinning.

'I suppose!' She yawned, tossed the bedclothes aside. Getting to her feet she stretched, scratched and sighed. 'Where's the coffee?'

'In the cafe across the street.'

'God, don't you have anything here?' She was fully awake now.

'A bottle . . . ' he suggested.

'I'll have a shot!' She looked round the bedroom. Her clothes and his lay in disorder on floor and chairs. A stocking dangled from a standard lamp. 'We sure didn't waste any time,' she said without a blush.

'Pour me one, too,' Mark requested, sorting out his underwear from hers. Something rankled him, gave him second thoughts about her. He didn't mind brazenness and immodesty. But he did not wear early morning hints of that nature. It was bad enough trying to keep his mind on business - and he had a few deals nearing completion that demanded his attention right after a snatched breakfast. 'There's hot water if you want a bath,' he told her.

She smiled, raced her palms deliberately down her bursting breasts, down her hips, over her flanks and buttocks. The pose, she knew, was provocative. Designed to seduce. To complete her conquest.

'I'm not a sex maniac,' Mark snorted and gestured towards the bottle.

Jasmyn's eyes narrowed dangerously.

'If you're going to have a drink for God's sake take it,' he snapped.

The girl planted both feet firmly on the floor, legs apart, hands on hips. 'Look at me,' she commanded.

Mark stared, unable to keep his gaze on her face. Seeing every pleasurable indentation, swelling, curve.

'Well?' she asked.

'Well what?'

'Don't you want to?'

He shrugged, climbed into his trousers. 'Tonight,' he said.

'What's wrong with now?'

'I've got work scheduled.'

'You bastard!' she spat.

He grinned, tucked his shirt inside the trousers.

'If you don't . . . ' she began to threaten.

'I'll have to find another screw for this evening, eh?' He didn't appear dismayed.

Jasmyn growled deep in her throat, flung herself into the bathroom. Slamming the door she leant against it, breasts heaving as she tried to recover her composure. It had been a long time since any man denied her what she craved. 'The bastard!' she sobbed in anger. 'The hell with him . . . ' She turned the tap viciously, heard water cascade into the tub. 'The rotten bastard!' she moaned and stepped into the tepid mixture . . .

Steve Morash spread the daily newspapers over his hotel suite floor and stood back to estimate the publicity value of splash headlines and pictures. Three papers had given Bobby Sharp's arrival decent coverage. Two more included a picture on their front pages with a smaller account of the Bristol airport disruption. One didn't even mention Bobby. Another put the item on a centre-page spread.

BRISTOL GOES WILD FOR LATEST TEENY BOPPER IDOL said one of the tabloids.

SHARP HITS HIGH NOTE said a right of centre conservative edition.

BOBBY IS THEIR DARLING captioned a picture of the singer being mobbed.

TEENY BOPPERS FLATTEN SHARP some smart writer claimed inside an ultra-society column.

For the most part, the text gave Bobby Sharp a welcome, gratis publicity in the form of disc mentions and plugged his tour by date and location. An editorial went so far as to examine the teeny bopper craze and favourably compare today's youth with those stage-door 'johnnies' who chased luscious dancers in Edwardian days. 'Now the boot is on the idol's foot,' the item continued. 'Men - and in many instances, young boys - are pursued for their sex appeal by hordes of ravishing-bent girls straight from the classroom . . . '

Steve sat back, smoked nervously. His anticipated telephone call had not yet come. Why? he wondered. It wasn't like Bobby to disappoint him. Nor to miss an opportunity to blast the guy who'd made it all possible.

'The ungrateful bastard!' Steve snarled aloud.

Grabbing the phone he left word with the reception desk to admit Jasmyn Ragg, Carole Latham and Becky Wilmott. To anybody else he was 'out'. Next, he contacted the hotel's switchboard. The only call he wanted put through was from Bobby Sharp. *Yes - the Bobby Sharp!* He was grinning when he hung up on the operator. He figured her for seventeen and a pop fanatic. Her exhaled 'OHIIII!' at the mention of Bobby's name tagged her for a concert seat.

Pouring a *Hundred Pipers,* Steve relaxed. The big moment had to arrive soon. He didn't like it when Bobby failed to jump through expected hoops. And he was damned if he'd make the first gesture. The first contact.

The telephone jangled discordantly. He waited for six rings then - 'Hiya, Bobby - have a nice flight?'

Heavy breathing filled Morash's ear.

'Bobby - is that you, kiddo?' Steve frowned as he waited . . . And waited.

Suddenly, sound exploded in Steve's ear. 'You lousy sonofabitch! You no-good fink bastard! You percentage creep . . . '

'Ya loves me, eh?' Steve said.

'Meaning?' Bobby's voice dripped acid, antagonism.

'Nothing, kid!' Steve felt it wise not to mention Bobby's best kept secret. His addiction to the comics. His daily battle with plot in the Dick Tracey, L'il Abner, Terry and the Pirates strips.

'Why ain't you here with me?' Bobby asked, all hurt sounding now.

'I should stick my neck out and get the pants ripped offa me?' Steve joked.

'Listen, kid, you're doin' swell. You rate, man. In the newspapers. On television. With the fans.'

'I didn't like for us to land at Bristol,' Bobby complained. 'Man, that was small. Why didn't you make it London?'

144

Steve finished his *Hundred Pipers* and poured another. The taste helped him get rid of the sourness Bobby was spreading like peanut butter.

'I asked . . . '

'Yeah, I was thinking why not,' Steve laughed. 'Can't we ever have an understanding you remember? I warned you what to expect. I told you London was out - too big, too important, too many stars coming and going like crazy.'

'So I'm the superstar . . . '

Christ, how conceited can this creep get? Steve thought.

'I'm the cat these chicks want to have eat 'em up!'

If they ever knew they'd toss your ass down a drain! Steve told his protégé silently.

Aloud, he tried to sound friendly, fear-allaying. 'Bobby, you're a Yank. These kids are British - used to screaming their damn-fool heads off for some British group.'

'I ain't a group, man . . . '

'You ain't more'n a name on the charts here.' Steve interrupted viciously. 'A goddam picture on an album cover - flip side at that!'

'You a fickin' lousy publicity agent,' Bobby lamented.

Steve grinned, mock-bowed to the telephone held at arm's length and sipped his Scotch.

'And this joint ain't good enough!' Bobby's voice had the dregs of no-fame hangover.

I've got to put him where he belongs, Steve thought. *Smack the bastard down to my size.*

'I didn't sleep a wink . . . '

Steve growled: 'You slept like a log! You slept so much you couldn't even get out of bed to ring me . . . '

'I've been awake for hours,' Bobby bluffed.

'Doing what?'

'Reading the newspapers!'

'Okay - what did *The Express* say?'

'Er . . . can't recall off the cuff but it wasn't bad!'

'And *The Mirror*?'

'The usual . . . '

'Ahh, what about *The Times*?' Steve made his voice glow in praise-worthiness.

'Fabulous, Steve!'

'You liar! *The Times* didn't rate you for a single line mention!'

Glorious silence filled Steve's ear. He enjoyed every costing minute and let Bobby have the benefit of his displeasure by gurgling happily on his drink. When he finished it he laid the telephone down - making sure Bobby knew the treatment he was getting - and replenished his glass. Only then did he bother to pick up the phone and ask: 'Had enough?'

'You're drinking already?'

Steve grinned, supped loudly into the mouthpiece. 'Goddamned right! Want to boot my ass off the team?'

'Don't tempt me,' Bobby warned. 'I could snap my fingers and a thousand publicity men would come arunnin'.'

'Yeah? Try it, punk! I've got an airtight contract. Solid, man. Solid! You're my boy come what may. Hell or high water. Rain or shine. Sink or swim.'

'I was underage when I signed,' Bobby bleated.

'Not when you initiated a rider last year, pal . . . '

'I did what?' The disbelief came across strong.

Steve set his glass on a side-table. This was his big moment. The day he had waited for through countless insults and tantrums and displays of grandeur. 'You signed a form in *your* lawyer's office last year giving me all rights, all managerial responsibilities, all the agreed terms of the original contract your parents accepted on your behalf as guardians . . . '

'Trickery!' Bobby screamed.

'Sure, pal - trickery! Like shit! You had that shyster check every clause, every loophole. You signed on his say-so. Now you're stuck. Like always, kiddo!'

'It ain't legal in England,' Bobby said after a pause, seeking one little out for his salvation.

'It's valid everywhere in the goddam world you sing,' Steve replied. Suddenly, Steve burst out laughing. 'Think of it, kid - you're famous. You're the tops on every chart. You're being hounded by schoolgirls more'n you ever dreamed possible in that little no-account Hicksville community you came from and you're bitchin' about rights? You've got rights, man. Rights to molest and rape and seduce. If the newspaper hawks don't tie your tail to their headlines and holler BOBBY SHARP FATHERS TEENY BOPPER CHILD. How about it, *pal*?'

Bobby relented. His voice softened. A respectful son now addressing a knowledgeable father approach. 'You win, Steve-boy. What's on the agenda?'

'A smash in the nose for you, son . . . ' Steve supped as gurgles non-alcoholic came across the wire. 'A kick in the ass! A big screw-off . . .'

'Steve . . . ' The plaintive call was sweet music.

'Get lost, Bobby!' Steve dangled the telephone then, face screwing into a compassionate series of wrinkles, lifted it again. 'Sorry, kiddo - you've had a rough ride. I'll make it soft saddles next tour, I promise.'

Listening to Bobby praise this and that, and knowing every word came from a mind devoid of honesty, incapable of separating truth from fiction, flooded with greedy deviousness. Steve wanted to throw-up. He didn't. Only because he could counter everything Bobby said. With more deviousness, more dishonesty, more fiction.

' . . . so don't walk out on me, Steve. I need you.'

'And I need you, Bobby-boy.'

'You do?'

Steve shook his head sadly. It was pathetic how the guy got so sentimental. He never would if their circumstances switched. 'You know I do,' he said, fingers crossed.

'So what comes next?'

'Stay put!' Steve commanded, in charge of affairs again. (As if he had ever been cashiered!) 'I've got a gimmick going for us.'

'What is it?' Bobby had enthusiasm back.

'Better you don't cotton too quickly, kid. Surprise and genuine embarrassment will make us headlines.'

'Whatever you've cooked up is fine with me, Steve.'

'Okay . . . Okay, call it Father's Day! Send me a gift. Or something suitable. Like a bottle of Scotch.'

'Which brand?'

Steve shrugged off a desire to get right back to the slanging match. This kid was too much for him. Far too much. A swelled-head, a big-mouth, a rotten performer. Yet, he had to be a sucker, too!

'A case of *Hundred Pipers,*' he said off-hand.

'Done . . . ' Bobby's voice faded in a metallic click.

The goddam fool'll do it! Steve thought. He slammed the telephone on its rest, grinned then. *What the hell,* he mused. *I can use a case of this beautiful stuff!*

'Where are those bitches?' Steve asked his mirror when he went to the toilet. Bobby's anticipated tirade had already vanished from his mind. He was way out on a limb now.

Drying his hands he returned to the comfortable suite lounge. He wished to hell that his next visitor was Sir Lew Grade. That's what he needed - one of those showbiz moguls taking an interest in his *product*. A star-studded Transatlantic extravaganza featuring the teeny bopper idol, Bobby Sharp.

Dreams . . .

Only dreams . . .

CHAPTER NINE

THRUSTING his latest 'Replica' model into its hiding place, Johnny Holland felt ten foot taller in his dream-saddle. He had finally reached the day when he could strip his Frontier .45 Colt and re-assemble it intact. Without having recourse to the instructions issued by the Japanese model makers.

'I should sing Country and Western,' he thought aloud.

'What did you say, Johnny?' his mother asked, entering the room.

'Nothing . . . ' He glanced guiltily at his hiding place.

'Come now, lad . . . ' His mother puffed pillows on his bed. 'You said somethin' - admit it?'

Johnny grinned, placed an arm round her shoulder. 'I said I could sing Country and Western if you and dad had an ear for it.'

'Go on with you!' Mrs Holland stomped from the room, face not unsympathetic to her son's latest notion. She wished he could find some recognition. Anything to stop his group doing 'their thing' - as Johnny called it - in their front parlour.

Johnny patted the pillows. Little did his mother know how hard the middle pillow had become. He had his Colt 'Frontier' and his Mauser 1896 model which Winston Churchill once carried as a sidearm.

Not that he would ever use them for anything else other than private showing or to acquaint himself with weight and handling of a weapon he could never hope to own legitimately. It was like a detective thriller reader, a second-hand kick.

'Johnny and the Jolly Green Men' . . .

He had to make their group known to the public. Had to bring his singing abilities to the notice of those who offered the contracts.

Taking the morning newspaper and spreading it across an old Victorian worktable he used to compose his group's numbers on, Johnny studied the timetable for Bobby Sharp's Saturday night concert. What struck him forcibly was the comment about television 'sticking its neck

148

into the pop cauldron' by presenting a live broadcast interview featuring several stars of stage, screen and radio against the backdrop of the teeny bopper concert. This was, according to the columnist, an unprecedented invasion of the 'take your choice what happens next' brand of instantaneous mayhem. A trip down frightening viewing lane. An open invitation for those addicted to permissiveness to exhibit the worst features of pop's already strained image.

Johnny loved the idea!

He saw visions . . .

When he carefully folded the newspaper and placed it inside his middle pillow alongside the Colt 'Frontier' and Mauser the germs had begun to infect his mind.

'It's our only chance,' he said aloud.

A clock chimed. He glanced at the marble one on his mantle and pulled a face. The damned thing hadn't worked since his grandmother died. Probably before that. It said the same hour, same minutes after every second of every day. A useless monstrosity he often wanted to flog to the junk shop down in Chiswick. Only the tag 'heirloom' stopped him from making a few extra quid.

He could see from his window the woman next door standing at her gate chatting away with old Mrs Walker from the bakery. He scowled. He didn't like either and any idea of leaving before they finished their gossip was out of the question. Every time he met the old biddies they gave him what for and decried his attempts to make good.

All they could say was 'Roundheads! What a load of rubbish!'

Roundheads . . .

He didn't think his group counted as rubbish. No more than skinheads or suedes or smooths. They were one and the same with a different hair style. That was their only difference. They enjoyed aggro, gear, football, reggae, birds.

Birds . . .

He grinned and sat on the bed, watching through his curtains as the pair outside got heads closer together. Some poor bitch was really getting burnt ears the way they talked.

Birds . . .

Gloria was one helluva bird! A looker and more than willing to engage in all the Roundhead activities. She could fight and everything else.

God, why don't they get back to housework?

He wanted to burst from his house and shout obscenities at the gossiping women. He wanted to shock them. And couldn't. He had to

149

stay aloof. Remain cool. Trust that his mother could mollify both when it came to complaints about his Jolly Green Men's 'sound'.

He liked the title for their group. His first nomination had been the 'Preventy Men' - taken from a fake parchment map of 'Smuggler's Devon' given him by a schoolmate. But when 'Jolly Green Men' had been suggested by Gloria he'd jumped onto her bandwagon. They shared a 'thing'. An association of minds. A mutual harbouring of feeling.

Jesus, if they don't get away from that gate . . .

He came off the bed, prowled back and forth round his room. He wanted to leave the house. He hated being coshed by a pair of do-nothing bitches.

He thought next about school. He loathed it. Next to fuzz he detested schoolteachers. Young simpering birds more interested in getting screwed by bearded wonders fresh out of teachers' colleges than in giving education to their charges. Stupid bits who didn't know a damned thing about geography, history, maths or anything. Filling in for older women who found that new standards and new methods were less effective than the school boards cared to contemplate. Older women tired of fighting a trend towards liberalization.

Maybe I'm unique, Johnny thought. *Maybe I don't fit. Maybe I want to learn and reach greater heights than the authorities want me to reach.*

He thought about Peter and Bruce. Both semi-literates. Both uncaring. Sound was their gospel. Sound and aggro. When it came to a quiz programme on the goggle-box they were lost in the first simple question. Like - 'New York is the largest city in New York State, but what is the capital?' Or - 'The lion is known as king of the jungle but which bird is called king of the air?'

His mind automatically answered both queries. Albany and the eagle.

Mrs Walker waved and moved away. His neighbour stayed at her gate for a few more moments. No doubt waiting for another gossip to saunter by! Then, seeing none, she retreated indoors.

Johnny shot from his room, out the street door and was at the corner before the neighbour came puffing into her path hoping for another round of chatter . . .

Carole Latham reviewed her campaign in Soho without enthusiasm. She had discovered from the first uneventful moment that the nut she was expected to crack refused to yield to any pressure applied. The inhabitants of London's depraved 'square mile' didn't cotton easily to suggestion. Not unless it happened to fit with their drug, strip, porno, drinking way of life.

She'd found the area dismal. Lacking the colour some American magazines liked to play into top features. The people, too, lacked life with a capital 'L'. They went about their humdrum tasks with a listlessness and counterfeitness that shocked and amazed. Jaded was her word for them. Beyond hope. Beyond redemption. Outside understanding.

She remembered most the number of guys who'd tried to seduce her. Creeps for the most part. Kids still sporting their acne and pimples. Kids sold on 'grass' or the mind-blowing 'H'. Kids drifting aimlessly through Soho's narrow streets, back alleys. Kids used by crime's overlords. Kids flogging body and soul for the elusive kick, the great dream.

Paddington was little better. The Irish there wanted showbands from Dublin. Or condoms to take back to the Republic. By the gross at discount prices! Or an easy piece to satisfy labouring appetites. Or the home for illegitimate bastards spawned *en masse* amid the flats and rooms of the overcrowded area. So much for their Church!

Notting Hill had been worst of all. She didn't wear coloureds grabbing for a white girl. She didn't wear it at all. Nor could she begin to understand their soul music, their loud-mouthed insistence they were British. Their hatred for anything American. Their cat-calls and hoots as derision followed her down what had once been a decent street of decent homes, now a slum.

She'd had the rough end of the stick!

Thanks to that bitch Jasmyn!

And where did Becky get off with Bristol and television coverage?

Entering Steve Morash's hotel she had a head of steam all ready to explode. She was early. Deliberately. What she had to say was meant for Steve's ears alone. Not to suffer Jasmyn's cattiness nor Becky's silent condemnation.

In a large mirror to one side of the foyer she caught her reflection. She smiled a little. The image gave her hope again. Not many girls or women could compete against her when she made up her mind to dress for 'the kill'. And she had dressed that morning. Killer togs, she called her gear.

The elevator man gave her the eye of approval as he positioned himself for the best view. Carole liked it. As the man lapped up her creamy skin she glowed. She didn't even mind the mental strip, the rape he performed between floors. She knew she was good. What the lads called 'hot stuff'.

Steve opened the door of his suite, glared. 'What's this?' he asked, blocking her entrance. 'You're early.'

Carole brushed him aside, walked across to the large window overlooking the nearby park and then - slowly, using every wile in her book - turned with the light catching her raven hair, outlining her superb figure, glinting off nyloned long legs between sexy-kinky black leather boots and a provocatively short cowgirl fringed skirt. The small jacket in calfskin, the satin blouse straining across her breasts and the mini-Stetson set back on her hair all combined to create an impression of Texas Sue about to entertain the saloon crowd.

'Okay, okay - so you've got it!' Steve snarled and helped himself to a cigarette. 'I've seen this game played to its conclusion many times. Let's not ass around, Carole. We've got important business to discuss.'

'Like a better deal for me, eh?' she exploded.

Steve Morash grinned suddenly. 'You're a randy bitch,' he muttered.

'So what? You don't seem to care!'

'I do, kiddo - I do!' He got to his feet, went to the liquor cabinet, eyebrows raised in silent query.

'A stiff jolt,' Carole replied.

As he poured the drinks, Steve felt warmth get closer . . . closer. He didn't have to turn to know that Carole was now standing by his elbow, breathing down his neck, her subtle perfume teasing like hell. *Watch it, son*, he thought. *She's after you and the reason ain't your sex appeal!* Setting the *Hundred Pipers* bottle back inside the cabinet he added *Canada Dry* to his drink, asked as if unaware of her nearness, 'Mix?'

Her hand reached over his arm, took the glass. 'No, thanks,' her voice whispered in his ear. 'I enjoy it better straight . . .'

He waited until the sound of her swishing across the suite signalled an all clear. Then, he swung and confronted her delightfully displayed legs crossed as she occupied a seat directly facing him. 'Let's cut out the "I-can-get-it-wholesale" routine,' he snapped. 'I'm not in the market for buying cheap so down to business, eh?'

Carole smiled, lifted her glass in mocking toast. 'Mud in your goddamned eye, Steve,' she said and tossed back the drink. She felt encouraged by his desire to reject that which she sensed he wanted most. She had always been of the opinion Steve liked her enough to form an alliance outside working associations.

Steve swore mentally. This bitch had his number alright. She knew the excitement coursing through his arteries. There existed between them a sort of suspended orgy that would, eventually, happen yet, for the present, had to be kept in abeyance.

'Screw you for giving me Soho *et al* as a territory,' Carole said.

'No dice?'

The girl gestured with her empty glass for a refill. 'None! Oh, I got a few coffee bar addicts steamed up but nothing spectacular.'

Steve took her glass, poured a smaller drink. He didn't want Carole getting antagonistic when Jasmyn and Becky arrived. He had enough on his particular plate without turning his suite into a female battleground.

'I caught the arrival on television,' Carole remarked acidly.

'Not bad, eh?' Steve handed her the second drink.

'Not good, either.'

'Sour grapes!' Steve snapped. 'If you'd handled the assignment you'd have raved. And no comments . . . ' His hand silenced her retort. 'I'm getting fed up with this rivalry between you and Jasmyn. I've got an organization to run, not a jealousy bureau. You're paid over the odds for what you do and I expect results. Just results. No snide remarks. No disruptions of meetings. Understand?'

Carole shrugged and sipped her drink this time. She recognized the danger signals. Steve seldom flashed his eyes when a pretty girl offered her all. When he did it meant but one thing - watch out!

'I said do you understand?' Steve repeated.

'Yeah . . . yeah! *I get the message. Crissakes, must you rant and rage to protect Jasmyn . . . ? '

Steve bristled. 'I don't protect anybody, and that's gospel! Jasmyn happens to get results. Like you do. Like all the staff has to or else . . . I'm not in this racket to play favourites, Carole. I'm in for loot. Bread. The long green with the short future. Cabbage. Moolah. Nothing else!'

'Don't give me a lecture,' Carole sighed.

'God, what the hell has gotten into you?'

The girl shifted uncomfortably in her chair. All her bright ideas flew out the window. Steve wasn't in a receptive mood. Far from it. He had something pressing on his mind, she reckoned. Her gear didn't attract him. Her obvious charms seemed to run off his eyeballs like water from a duck's back. It had been a mistake coming here so early.

'Look, let's forget this,' Steve cautioned. 'Suppose we enjoy a quiet drink and chinwag about subjects far removed from Bobby Sharp and work?'

Carole nodded, smiled distantly. *Maybe* . . . she thought. 'I'm sorry, Steve,' she told the man. 'I wanted to impress upon you how dissatisfied I felt . . . '

'That's kaput!' he said. 'Go freshen that drink. You need spiritual strength.' He laughed at his quip, watched her get from the chair and walk to the liquor cabinet. He couldn't help but notice the way her buttocks moved, the shapeliness of her legs.

Hands shaking slightly, Carole sensed his new-found desire fixed on her figure. If only he would make one pass, she mused. One oblique reference to her sensuality. One hint at his fascination for her shape. But he didn't.

Instead, the smouldering continued as flames awaited blowing into dancing life.

'How's your hotel?' he asked.

'Fine.' Carole's voice sounded dead, almost as if talking was an effort she didn't wish to make.

'Aw, come on - buck up.' Steve grinned, tossed a cigarette to the girl.

'Do I have something to shout about?' Carole caught his lighter, returned it with her smoke going.

'You ain't dead so that's a starter.'

'Christ, cut out this idle chatter.' Carole got to her feet as anger flushed her face. Some of her drink splashed over her skirt and she glared at the offending spots. 'Now look what you've made me do!' she accused.

Steve whipped a handkerchief out, came to her and brushed lightly at the moisture. He could feel the firmness of thigh under the material, the desirable curvature. His hand came away like she was on fire. His eyes narrowed, focused on her agitated breasts, her heavy breathing.

'You don't have to stop, you know,' she said with a slight husk.

'I goddamned do!' He moved away. 'The others will be here soon!'

'So, there's time for something - isn't there?'

Steve Morash sighed, forced his face into a smile. 'Yeah, there could be - but there won't. Sorry, Carole - that's how the cookie crumbles!' Deliberately, he walked to the suite door, flung it open. 'Safety first,' he muttered and headed for the bedroom. And a clean handkerchief.

CHAPTER TEN

JULIUS GERSTEIN had only recently entered the pop arena but already his impact had reached tycoon proportions. Making money came easily to Julius. His family had always been engaged in commerce and the rag trade especially. It had been totally predictable that he should, in one form or another, enter showbiz. Where else could one create an enormous market for clothes made in his factory?

Unlike many adventurous individuals catering to pop's screaming thousands, Julius considered them bloody nuisances. Garbage with money to pay into his enterprises. Yobbos and the like. He didn't give a damn if they ever enjoyed an act or got their money's worth. Fact was, he couldn't even stand the sound of their music.

Bobby Sharp, according to Julius, was an investment. A huge investment. The amount he was having to pay for just one appearance almost broke his heart. But he knew the returns would justify the out-goings. Providing, that was, Bobby made his appearance. The contract negotiated by Steve Morash had one clause which gave Julius Gerstein nightmares.

Bobby Sharp would get paid a specific sum come what may once he arrived in England.

There was no out for Julius if Bobby failed to walk onstage Saturday night. He could not keep the money paid by the teeny boppers for their tickets yet Sharp would have his slice regardless.

The more Julius thought about the crazy contract the more he realised he'd been conned by a smarter promotion's man. He could remember well the way Steve Morash had covered the inclusion of the disastrous clause. 'No sweat, Julius,' Steve had said laughingly. 'Bobby ain't ever missed a performance in his life but we've got to consider he's never been in England before. I don't know how your kids react yet. I've heard they can cause a helluva lotta bother for hotels and halls, though. We'll stick this in anyway. You know the score - expenses to cover hiring his personal plane and the like . . . '

They'd switched fast to security arrangements with Steve agreeing to pay for airport protection and getting his star to the concert. Only after some insistence had Julius managed to get a split on the cost of providing a twenty-four hours a day guard at Bobby's quarters. With a cast-iron promise that nobody, not newspapers nor radio nor television, would know the exact location of Bobby's British hotel.

'The bleedin' liar,' Julius growled for perhaps the tenth time. Slamming a fist against his other cupped palm he swung away from his ornate desk and prowled round the room. It was from this office that he controlled his evergrowing empire. High in a towering block with views of the City from the three large windows, Julius often considered himself one of the elite whose job it was to monopolize growth ventures.

'The bleedin' liar,' he growled again. Standing before a recently acquired oil painting of himself he thought about the telephone call he'd received from an agitated security guard stationed at Bobby Sharp's motel. 'The bleedin' liar!' Scowling, he pushed his thick dark hair from his broad forehead and considered the possibilities of reaching Morash and landing this latest baby in his lap. He had an idea he'd get a cool reception. Lacking proof of Morash's complicity in what was obviously a publicity plot he hadn't a leg to stand on if it boiled down to angry words.

'I'll show the bastard!' he said to the picture. 'I'll give those little blighters something to think about!'

He hurried back to his desk, thumbed through an address book. When he found the name he sought he suddenly smiled. A mean, hungry smile that could only mean trouble for somebody else. If *World Pop* could accuse him of employing 'heavies' for the concert then, by God, they'd have something else to yap about when he finished this chore . . .

From the dual carriageway directly across from the motel, Johnny Holland watched the teeny bopper crowds collect. He'd been one of the first to arrive but not one of those stupid enough to try getting past the nine big guards forming a human barrier between the entrance posts.

Like the others, Johnny had been tipped off. Unlike the rest he knew why. *Publicity!* The kind to create headlines. And sell another hundred thousand discs.

Johnny was glad Gloria hadn't come along with him. The way the screaming teeny boppers were surging forward in close-packed waves somebody had to get hurt. And knowing how Gloria loved to be in the thick of things she could have been the one to suffer most.

He didn't mind being an observer. Patience would have its rewards. Sooner or later the gathering crowds would overcome the security screen and sweep through the motel. When they did, Johnny Holland would sneak inside and do what his native cunning told him was the right way to get his break in showbiz.

Oh, yes - he had it all down pat. Planned to take into account every possibility. Or so he hoped.

A bus arrived at the stop almost outside the motel. Like Amazon warriors charging into battle, schoolgirls leapt from the vehicle and joined the milling throng joined in mortal combat with the security men. The noise was deafening now, drowning the sounds of traffic belting by.

Shrill screams rent the air, each a plaintive cry for 'Bobby' . . .

Inside the motel, Bobby Sharp and his entourage kept in contact with Steve Morash's London hotel. This was to be a major highlight in their campaign. A chance for newsmen and television to get into the act. All agreements concerning secrecy went by the boards once the teeny boppers discovered Bobby's motel hideaway. Or so it had been planned.

Bobby peered from his window, careful not to move the curtains. The last thing he wanted was for the fans to reach him. It was enough that they should catch a hasty glimpse as he whisked off to another prearranged rendezvous. One that *would* remain secret.

'They ain't gonna hold 'em,' he yelled to Lloyd Morgan. 'Sonofabitch, tell Steve we've got to run for it.'

Lloyd grinned, spoke into the phone as the 'bleaters' joined their 'hero' in hysterical antics by the window. 'Steve,' Lloyd said, 'we've got a problem here. Bobby insists we leave immediately.'

'Nothing doing,' Morash's voice roared in Morgan's ear. 'You've got to stick it out until the photographers arrive.' Morgan held the phone away from his head. 'We stay,' he told Bobby Sharp.

'The hell I do!' Bobby marched to the phone, grabbed it from Morgan. Any of his teeny bopper fans seeing him then would have had second thoughts about the public charm so successfully exploited by the machine. 'You there, Morash?' he snarled.

'I'm here, Bobby . . . '

'Get offa my back, man. I ain't gonna have my skin torn for any picture-man.'

'Take it easy, kiddo,' Steve's soothing tone said. 'You've got guys out there who'll protect you . . . '

'You're jokin' . . . ' Bobby darted a glance at the window.

'Those goddam dames are murderin' the guards.'

'Are they *inside* the motel yet?'

'Naw - but nearly,' Bobby admitted.

'Well, kiddo - hold out. Please. We've got all the media rushing to cover this thing . . . '

'Not good enough, man. You shoulda had them ready.'

'Christ, can't you understand a contract?'

'Yeah . . . yeah! I've heard that bull . . . '

From the other side of Sharp, Lloyd Morgan caught sight of a dark van drawing up outside the motel. Standing on tip-toe he could make out blue-uniformed men pouring from the van and driving a relentless wedge into the screaming teeny boppers.

He saw a truncheon raised . . .

'Give me the bloody phone,' Lloyd snarled and seized it from Bobby's grasp. 'Steve,' he bellowed down the instrument, 'have you gone crazy? What's the big idea sending us a bunch of thugs?'

Silence came from the earpiece. Heavy, agonizing silence.

'Lemme see,' Bobby grunted, pushing his yes-men aside.

'Steve - how's about an answer?' Morgan asked.

Johnny Holland couldn't believe his eyes. He'd been on the point of crossing the dual carriageway to put his plan into operation when the vanload of security men arrived. Now, he watched in utter amazement as the newcomers used force to drive the terrified girls back from the motel's entrance.

From the age of ten Johnny had fought to achieve recognition. His passage through fads had taken him into vicious situations fraught with personal danger. He'd never felt fear gnawing at his innards nor had he shirked a fight. As a skinhead he'd loved aggro. He and his mates had been terrace terrors the equal of any older gang from South London. When he became a suede he'd shown some of the local disco owners what a determined character he could be. And, with his latest style - Roundhead - he had kept to those traditions started by the original skins.

But in all his aggro days he had never seen anything like the savagery of Bobby Sharp's security team. He'd fought against other blokes. Sometimes birds if they happened to get into a battle but never willingly. This, across the street, was just a shambles. Big blokes using fists and truncheons against a bunch of frightened girls.

Hatred for the 'heavies' made him fidget. He searched the crowds across the street. If only he could find a few blokes he'd bloody well show the goons what it meant to get a boot in the balls! He cursed. The three kids he spotted couldn't fight their way out of a paper-bag let alone join him in an aggro. Little guys probably brought there by a big sister.

Hell, he thought angrily, *why don't the fuzz come and help?*

Lloyd Morgan slammed the telephone down on the table and rushed to the door. Flinging it open he raced past parked cars and grabbed a security guard by the arm. 'What the hell's going on?' he demanded.

The guard turned startled eyes on him. 'Christ, I don't know. They aren't ours, mate.'

Pushing past the man, Lloyd confronted one of the newcomers. 'Okay, buster,' he snarled. 'Let's have your explanations . . . '

The man was a giant. Thick armed, barrel-chester, flattened nose in an ugly face. A product of some East End slum. A thug for hire.

'Who sent you?' Lloyd asked.

'What's it matter to you, mate?' the man growled.

'A great deal. I'm in charge of operations here.'

'Yeah?' The giant grinned. 'That's wot you thinks.' He placed a hand on Morgan's chest, pushed him back with tremendous power. 'You git into the motel, mate. I'll have the guy see ya.'

Lloyd opened his mouth to argue, thought better of it and swung on his heels. This was the final straw. He'd come home to England, been given a brief glimpse of his native Bristol, witnessed yet another Bobby Sharp tantrum and had Steve Morash refuse to answer a vital query. *Okay*, he thought, *okay. Damn 'em all. I quit. Like I should have ages ago. I wash my hands of Sharp and Morash. I sacrifice more dough per week than some suckers earn in a year. But I don't care. I honestly don't care.*

He felt better already. Ready to face Bobby and those scared little hangers-on. God, he loathed them . . .

CHAPTER ELEVEN

MUSIC, KIDS AND MY FUTURE

by Bobby Sharp

Yesterday, shortly after I arrived in England, I was asked a question. 'Do you see yourself as a sex symbol?' an agitated reporter shouted from a crowd.

I said then what I say now. I'd be lying if I didn't believe I possess sexual powers to make an audience react in the emotional way they do. After all, most of my fans are young girls. Decent kids who happen to enjoy my music and, more especially, me.

Steve Morash set the evening paper down and smiled. It had taken him more than four sweating hours to write what Bobby was supposed to have said. Four hours spent dragging out every emotional outburst an editor could permit under a famous name.

And for what?

He frowned then. Yeah, for what? For Julius Gerstein's hired goons to blow the whole show. His eyes lit on the second evening paper. On the accusing words

TEENY BOPPERS BOPPED

And on the text

Has the pop world lost its money-mad mind?

Today, against defenseless girls, the heavy mob brought a new meaning to the word security. Posing as security agents supposedly protecting teeny bopper idol, Bobby Sharp from over-zealous fans, these men battered happy schoolgirls into submission and turned an exuberant occasion into a disgusting, brutal episode to forever blacken the name of pop music.

As if this wasn't enough, a picture showed just what the extent of the security mob's mayhem meant to passers-by. A woman with hand to mouth and obviously shocked stood in the forefront with truncheons being used in the background against panic-stricken girls.

Steve could imagine how the national dailies would handle the story. Especially the pair the youngsters seemed to read. He mentally shuddered to think how Bobby would behave. He decided to be there first thing in the morning. Bobby had successfully sneaked into his new accommodation. One nobody except the organization knew about.

Julius Gerstein . . .

The name trickling through Steve's mind brought an angry flush to his features. If he could get his hands round the bastard's throat he'd have squeezed every ounce of breath from that profiteering body. He'd met all kinds of managers, promoters, exhibitors. But none the equal of Gerstein. Of course, he had never been in contact with a rag-trade merchant before. It was a unique situation in London that a man branched out to this extent. And all because he wanted to peddle a few more clothes. Sickening! Disastrous from his point of view, too.

He felt weary, in need of relaxation. He'd been working ever since breakfast. Some people would laugh at his idea of work but more would admit that using the brain and keeping abreast of changing events so that each gave of its best for the cause could tire a man more than actual physical labour.

Pouring a *Hundred Pipers* he lit a cigarette, studied the park through his window. Young people walked in it, an older couple seated on a bench apparently enjoying the sights and sounds of this slice of heaven within the always bustling metropolis. He envied them. The young and the old. Not that he would give up his 'career'. He liked the constant battle, the putting one across others. But he did miss those far-off days when he, too, tossed aside the cares and woes of the daily strife and simply sat on a bench and soaked in life's tranquillity.

Those had been the days . . .

New York. Summer. Not much in the way of muggings then. Central Park still a blissful spot for those seeking an out from the buck-chasing torment. Oh, sure - the park had always attracted drop-outs and bums. He remembered an old businessman who'd tried to coax him back to a beat-up apartment for 'booze and buggery'. Christ, he could still feel the shock travelling along his forearm after he'd knocked the bastard cold. What a punch that had been! A haymaker fit for knocking a heavyweight champion on his ass.

Boxing brought back a few memories, too. When he was a teenager, fresh into the world of commerce. Ninth Avenue. The rag-trade area. Trundling a goddam wagon round the streets, sweating under the load. Clothes. Coats. Dresses. Sweaters. The like. And him a product of the West Side. Tough, ready to leap at every opportunity to make an illegal dollar. He'd been hard then. Real tough. Able to smash to a pulp anybody daring to cross him. And he'd made his killing. A whole rack of expensive gear sold for a lightning two hundred to a fink who squealed on him the next morning. Man, did he have trouble with the cops on that caper. Lucky for him the sonofabitch fink stank in the eyes of the precinct captain. Word against word and the cops letting him off with a warning. Yeah, he'd been a hellion alright . . .

The telephone ringing shattered his reverie.

It was Carole. With a proposition - a visit to a disco, dinner and drinks. The hint of more to come drifted after he'd agreed to meet her. Nothing brassy. Just a suggestion. A hormone exciting tone in her voice and a subtle *'they make wonderful coffee in my hotel, Steve. We could sample that, too - eh?'*

He took a fresh *Hundred Pipers* into the bathroom, sampled it as he showered and shaved again. He had a thing about close-shaves before meeting a date. No woman had ever been able to complain that his whiskers hurt her delicate skin. Nowhere. No-time.

Wilf Russell, folded the floor plan of Julius Gerstein's 'Discodrome' and glanced at his director, Ed Cronin. 'Well, what do you think?' he asked.

'It's dodgey, Wilf. We could be letting ourselves in for trouble doing this "live" . . . '

Lighting a cigar, an affectation rather than a love for the exquisite flavour, Wilf Russell settled back in his plush office chair and stretched long legs. He had the appearance of a youngish graduate from Oxford and his tweed suit supported this impression. Collar length sandy hair and a weak face partially shielded by horn-rim spectacles did not encourage confidence in some of those with whom he came into contact yet he could proudly point to a success rate in television's jungle that was sound, if unspectacular.

Watching the deliberate posture, Ed Cronin wanted to laugh. But didn't. He knew this coverage could shoot them both into the upstairs 'heavens' of the company. If it went off as scheduled they'd have the bigwigs eating from their hands. If it flopped - and that was always something to be considered - they'd be on a breadline.

Ed had been around television for many, many years. First as a helper carrying heavy equipment for an outdoors camera crew. Then as a cameraman and, finally, a junior director. His only big break had been two years previously. A missed golden chance. A programme taken off the air before being seen due to a poetical pressure and a changing outlook by the top men.

At forty, Ed didn't enjoy taking orders from any youthful go-getter, but he hid his feelings and worked as closely with Wilf as circumstances permitted.

'I've fought to do the show, Ed. I've really fought. Believe you me, there have been problems to overcome. You know the score.'

Cronin nodded in agreement. Policy did not include live pop coverage. Neither network allowed it. But this wasn't really a pop concert getting the live spotlight. Wilf specialized in personalities. In semi-documentaries. In interviews with stars, authors, politicians, people in the news. His idea of having the Bobby Sharp concert as background for an investigation into pop as a profit-making *controlled* racket had finally won approval. But reserved approval

Not wholehearted support for the idea.

'Do you think we'll get a high audience rating?' Ed asked.

'We should. We've done our bit to make the programme topical and some of the Dee-Jays have plugged it gratis.' Wilf smiled grimly. 'Of course, those who will appear have been our best publicity assets.'

Ed grinned, lit a cigarette. 'I wonder what they'll say when they discover we're pulling a fast one?'

'Are we?' Wilf frowned, adjusted his spectacles. 'It wouldn't surprise me if they'd been whispering together and pulled one on us. I spoke to Dexter Bradshaw yesterday and he hinted something extra-special was in the wind.'

'That's what I'd expect from Bradshaw,' Ed snapped. 'He gets my wick with his smarm and silver-tongue. It's one show I never listen to now . . . '

'Ah, hell . . . ' Russell ground his cigar in a huge ashtray. 'Let's kick the coverage around some. Can we be sure the kids won't upset arrangements?'

'Pretty sure,' Cronin replied. 'Gerstein has guaranteed security at every camera position. And he's even making arrangements for wire screens to be erected.'

Wilf looked puzzled. 'Now why would he go to that expense if he can guarantee protection for the equipment?' He drummed slender fingers on his desk, thoughtfully opening the floor plan again after a decent interval. 'Look, can we alter the One and Two camera locations?' he finally asked.

Bending over the blueprint, Ed Cronin got the first butterflies in his stomach. He would have many more in the following days. 'Why?' he asked as nerves started acting up on his old ulcer.

Wilf Russell shook his head. 'I don't know for sure but something worries me about these sites. Something worries me about these sites. They're too exposed. Too involved with the teeny boppers for comfort.'

Now he had uneasy qualms!

CHAPTER TWELVE

JOHNNY HOLLAND had nothing much on his mind as he walked along the Uxbridge Road. He had a meeting with Peter Acroyd and Bruce Barnes in an hour but until then he felt free to do as the fancy took him. Almost as if a telepathic communication had suddenly been sent through the air directly into his head he jerked round and froze.

Now, he had something to do!

He relaxed. He could handle this situation alone. Jackie Campbell had no reputation as a great fighter. In fact, Jackie was a soft touch. Easy black meat.

What a bloody name for a wog, Johnny thought. He wondered how many coloureds went about with British names.

Slowly, savouring the fear rolling round in those big dark eyes, he approached the other. The few people in the vicinity would not bother to rush to a spade's rescue. Old biddies out doing their small shopping, an unemployed middle-aged man who looked like he couldn't lift a pintpot never mind fight, a few kids playing a game.

'Hi, Jackie,' Johnny said easily.

'No . . . ' The coloured youth backed away until his spine was pressed against a wall.

'Don't be afraid,' Johnny laughed softly. 'I ain't going to hurt you - much!' His fists bunched. Excitement flowed down his legs into his boots. He felt the urge to kick but held it in reserve. He wanted to draw this confrontation out to its most enjoyable finale.

'Lemme alone!' the other squealed.

'Aw, is de big bad whitey scaring Sambo . . . ' Johnny loved his impression of a Minstrel. He even wanted to sing a few bars from Stephen Foster.

'Fuck you!' The black youngster found courage from somewhere deep inside and jumped forward, small fists swinging.

Johnny ducked, brought his boot up. He heard air whoosh from Jackie's lungs, saw pain flash across the ebony face. His fists drummed relentlessly now - smashing the coloured youth upright when all he wanted to do was double and clutch his injured groin.

'Leave 'im alone, you rotten little beggar!' a voice shouted at close range.

Johnny glanced over his shoulder. One of the old biddies came charging forward, handbag swinging, ancient features contorted in rage. In a few seconds she would be on him.

Aiming one final kick at the coloured youth's abdomen, Johnny turned and fled. Laughing and gesturing at the woman who now bent over the collapsed Jackie.

He felt terrific. He'd wanted to do that spade for a long time. He knew it would stir up the others belonging to Jackie's mob. Hoped they'd come into his territory and try to revenge the beating.

Slowing to a walk, Johnny whistled gaily. A bit of aggro never hurt, he reckoned. Providing, of course, it did not interfere with his ambitions as a potential pop star. He wanted that more than anything. To see his name topping a bill. To hear television announcers say 'Johnny Holland' with some kind of reverence. To have articles written about him in all the fan magazines. To have managers and big promoters chasing after him, waving contracts worth thousands of pounds under his nose.

If he reached those heights he would give up being a Roundhead. He wouldn't be able to keep his aggravations out of publicity's glare then. He'd have to change. Drastically. Have to get a new image. Not a change of hairstyle, though. That would stay. He'd be the first Roundhead to make headlines since Cromwell knocked those proper Charlies all over England.

He liked that!

Maybe he'd get a new name for the backing group. 'Johnny Holland and the Knockers' . . . And when some twit interviewer asked why 'Knockers' he'd tell him, 'cause we're Roundheads, mate. We knock those longhaired gits off their bleedin' high horses!'

He chuckled and day-dreamed as he continued into the High Street. It did a bloke good having something like this to keep his mind occupied on a do-nothing day . . .

Steve Morash perched on the corner of Bobby Sharp's bed and waited for the explosions that must follow the idol's perusal of the morning headlines. Outside the bedroom he could hear excited twitterings from Bobby's yes-men. He hated those bastards but he allowed them to tag along if only to swell his star's ego.

He knew that Lloyd Morgan's decision to quit yesterday had been directly influenced by Gerstein's unorthodox handling of their security problem but he sensed that the hangers-on had contributed quite a lot to the break-up.

'Okay, Steve - have *your* say,' Bobby snapped. The crumpled papers lay in a discarded heap on the floor now. The face framed by fluffed pillows drawn, hard, even vicious.

'Before you get uptight, let me remind you about our relationship,' Steve said softly, striving to lower the temperature before they reached a slanging match.

'Scrub that bullshit,' the youth snarled. 'You're strictly a manager-cum-P.R. I owe you sweet nothin'.'

'Okay, if it's drag 'em out and clobber the bastards then I'm ready!' Steve got off the bed, squared his shoulders and grim-faced readied himself for a real verbal battle.

'You betcha that's the ticket!' Bobby jumped from the bed, caught his toes in a blanket and almost landed on his ass. He growled, flung the offending cover at the wall, sending a vase smashing to the floor. Water and flowers formed a coloured pool by the table. 'Goddam way they make beds in this lousy country . . . '

Steve smiled slightly. He liked seeing the so-smart Bobby take a pratfall.

'Let's get a few items in perspective,' Bobby raged. Using his fingers he ticked off the items one by one. 'First - when the hell do I get to see the sights? Two - there ain't no dames in my life. Three - I've a mind to get pissed . . . '

'You do and I'll break your neck!'

For a moment a tinge of fear shone in Sharp's eyes. Then, blusteringly, he countered Morash's quiet threat. 'Lay a goddamned finger on me and I'll have your hide, Steve. I'll opt out from under the contract. I'll get you thrown into the hoosegow . . . '

'I could ruin you, Bobby. I could gimmick your microphone. I'll make you a laughing stock!'

Bobby Sharp froze. He believed Steve now. Although they came equipped with several replacement mikes Steve had the sway with everyone concerned to carry out his threat. More than anything else, this pointing finger frightened him into near submission.

'You wouldn't toss your percentage down the drain,' he bluffed.

'You're a fish in a pond, Bobby,' Steve said. 'A very small fish in a very big pond. If I wanted, I could go looking for another no-talent bastard in the ocean and build him up so high you'd wonder what the hell had suddenly smacked you in your no-voice guts. Do I make myself clear?'

Quickly, with a cunning born of desperation, Bobby changed tactics. He forced a smile, tried the magic charm. 'Ah, shit, Steve - what's the sense in us kickin' hell outta each other! Come on, pal - shake?'

Steve accepted fast. He usually did. His percentage stake demanded it. He always had the satisfaction though, of knowing he'd pegged the bastard down another egotistical notch.

'How's about dames?' Bobby asked slyly.

'I'll have the gals come over!'

'Those pigs?'

A memory of Carole's naked flesh shot across Steve's mind. He thrust it aside. Gulped down a bitter comment pill. 'Look, kiddo - we've got one paternity caper held in abeyance until we hit the States again. Let's not knock 'em up in every foreign nation, too.'

'I didn't lay the bitch,' Bobby shouted. 'That randy Carl did!'

Steve believed him. He knew Carl Ritter's reputation. If he got a chance he'd hire them another drummer. He didn't wear getting underage stuff drunk and implanting the idea she'd been implanted by *the* Bobby Sharp. 'Okay, we'll have our day in court,' Steve mollified. 'But let me supply the screws, eh?'

Bobby nodded eagerly. 'Sooner the better, Steve.'

The little punk, Steve thought. *Making a pimp out of me next!*

'Can we do anything about these newspapers?' Bobby asked.

'Nothing!'

'They've murdered me,' the star wailed.

'They murdered the security mob - not you,' Steve reminded.

'I'm sufferin' . . . '

'You're always suffering.'

'I want compensation from Gerstein . . . '

'Christ, listen to him!' Steve moaned. 'You want? You? Hell's bells, kiddo - since when could you read and comprehend a contract? Since when did you start making decisions how to knock the Press or play it cosy to the vest? Tell me, kiddo. I'm interested to know!'

'Aw, shit!' Bobby hauled off his pyjamas. He wore garish Chinese dragon patterns in outlandish crimsons and greens and blues all mixed into a nightmarish colour fantasy. Naked, he scratched his testicles, oblivious of the other occupant of the room. 'Sonofabitch of an itch,' he moaned. 'I swear I got crabs . . . '

Steve laughed aloud. 'No hope, kiddo,' he chortled. 'Crabs maketh the man and you've a few to go before you claim that title!'

Muttering to himself, Bobby Sharp entered his private bathroom. He wished to hell he could decipher Morash's remarks. *A few to go?* What did the bastard mean, years? Or dames?

Johnny Holland finished his coffee and sat back against the hard partition of the booth. Usually, he detested coming into Frank's cafe but Peter had a cousin who worked in the joint and they somehow managed to get three cups for the price of one.

'You're a cool bastard,' Bruce said, swilling the dregs of his cup over the table. He grinned, wiped the mess with his palm and smeared the residue down his greasy Levis. He didn't give a hoot about washing them. He had a mother with a penchant for cleanliness. Once she spotted the mess she'd have the trousers into a washing machine and consider it an honour to see her son walk from their house looking all fresh and clean.

'We'll have the spades after us,' Peter Acroyd remarked.

'Scared?' Johnny asked.

'Me? Scared of bleedin' wogs? You must be jokin'.'

'They've got some bloody big nignogs,' Bruce reminded.

'And they all go to the dogs or Social Security,' Johnny laughed. Nothing could undermine his sensation of greatness. It wasn't a brilliant success by any means. Jackie Campbell had been soft. A bloke their smallest, least offensive member could have done. But he'd been the one. In daylight. Out in the open. In their territory, too. 'Hell, they've got to think this one out. Get around to using their brainless minds. When they come after me we'll take 'em. No doubts.'

Peter shrugged and beckoned his cousin for further coffees. He didn't stop to count the cost. He realised the poor sap ran scared of them. Wanted to get into the Roundheads but didn't rate a vote. Chicken, that's what he was. Born chicken. Afraid to say no when it meant he put money in the till for what Peter and his mates drank.

'You worked out how we cash in on Bobby Sharp's publicity?' Bruce asked.

Johnny beamed. This was really his day. He'd whipped a oncer his mother had hidden in a vase and forgotten about. He'd done Jackie Campbell. Now . . .

'Have you read the papers yet?' he asked his mates.

They both nodded. He didn't have to go into which section of the papers they'd scanned. Sports pages first. Music next. Maybe the comics and, perhaps, a fast glance at headlines. Television a must.

'They're going ahead with the programme from the Discodrome,' Johnny said.

'So what?' Peter asked, gee-ing his cousin by a cup rattling signal.

'We're going on telly,' Johnny announced.

Peter dropped his cup. It clattered to the table. Frank, the proprietor, glared but shrugged off any damage as a deduction in Peter's cousin's wages.

Bruce gasped, bent forward. His eyes glinted like a hopheads.

'The way I see it,' Johnny continued as if neither of them had shown the slightest reaction. 'This programme goes out live. If we can grab the microphones for even three minutes some producer will sit up and take notice.'

'The fuzz will an' that's certain,' Peter said.

'Jesus,' Bruce breathed, 'how can we . . . ?'

Johnny held up a hand, silenced his companions' desire to infiltrate his genius. 'I've got it worked out,' he said with proud leadership command. 'We storm the stage, take their instruments, which will be lying around in the background, and go straight into *"Virginia's Love".'*

'Bloody marvellous,' Peter scoffed. 'Wot about their security men?'

'How many tickets did that bird give us?' Johnny asked quietly.

'Ten!'

'And I bought six more . . . '

'You did?' Bruce seemed puzzled. He couldn't understand anybody spending money when they had all the tickets they needed.

'For a reason - and you guys are going to chip in, too. I'm getting every Roundhead to that concert . . .'

Peter suddenly caught the drift. 'We got a mob, eh?'

Johnny nodded excitedly. Now they were melding. 'By the time Bobby Sharp gets on stage we'll have their security arrangements sorted out.'

Bruce interrupted eagerly. 'And we'll be on the telly before anybody knows?'

'Bloody right,' Peter rasped, glaring as his cousin carried their delayed coffees across to their booth.

CHAPTER THIRTEEN

ONE dream more than any other hounded Bobby Sharp. In it, he was an artist. A great painter. A master of his craft. A man able to depict the undraped female form in all its subtle beauty, in its naturalness. He often saw the result of his artistic efforts - a reconstruction of an ancient Roman orgy in which all the men wore togas and all the women were stark naked. Full frontal nude. Sensual. Seductive. Shimmering flesh tones highlighting those darker regions that drove men crazy.

And, just before awakening, the dream would shift through multi-coloured patterns until the women were nothing more than fat-bellied strippers from some tumbledown joint in some decrepit section of any teeming city. Floozies. Has-beens. Fat whores. Cheap tarts.

Bobby never spoke of his dream. But he worried about it. Suddenly, he came face to face with the reality behind the dream . . .

Steve Morash hadn't been joking when he'd said he'd bring the dames to the hotel. There they were. Jasmyn, Carole, Becky. His 'pigs'. Girls who'd sell their soul for a slice of the Bobby Sharp action. Touts. 'Arousers'.

Glancing round the suite, Bobby had to admit that Steve's organization counted for one helluva lot. Booze flowed freely. The babes acted like they enjoyed being man-handled. Especially that bitch Jasmyn. God, didn't she go for the orgy routine!

'Take your choice - Jasmyn or Carole,' Steve's voice said in his ear.

'Nuts!' Bobby rasped. 'I'm for Becky. She's pure. Sweet, undefiled.'

'Nothing doing, kiddo,' Steve replied, grabbing the idol's arm and wheeling him from the scene. 'Becky's out. O-U-T! Get me?'

'Why?'

'Seventeen is why, man!'

'Big enough is old enough according to my daddy,' Bobby slobbered.

'Not here!' Steve steered the singer through his yes-men trying on their antics. 'You leave anything under eighteen strictly for the rapists. If you don't . . . '

'Whom should I take then?' Bobby growled. 'Jasmyn who hates my guts or that cheap bitch Carole who'd let any guy lay her providing he had a bankroll to pay for accidents?'

Steve saw red. He wanted to bust Bobby on the snoot but *Mr Percentage* took over and squashed the urge.

'Come on,' Bobby snarled. 'Let's be honest with one another! Which bitch? Jasmyn or your little bedmate, Carole?'

Steve stiffened. 'My bedmate?'

'Yeah, man. Yours. I saw the way she looked at you when I ordered her to take her clothes off. God, wasn't it a scream . . . '

Steve's fist lashed out. At the vital split-second he veered off course and let the blow whistle over Bobby's shoulder. His face mirrored his frustration. He couldn't knowingly damage the personality that gave them both a fortune. A highway to untold wealth.

Bobby sneered. Brushing aside the ineffectual fist he leered. 'Stupid bastard! That's what you are - a stupid bastard. A sucker for a hunk of hair, a roll in the hay. A bustin' out all over for a hot screw!'

'One more word like that and I'll really slam you into hell,' Steve warned.

'Ah,' Bobby shouted triumphantly. 'Ah, then you are taken in by the bitch!'

'You little creep,' Steve raged. 'You pathetic little nothing! You don't have the first inkling of what makes a man and woman click. What is a fore-runner of true romance for you counts as an invitation to lay.'

'You know what I'm gonna do, punk? I'm gonna go an' prove what a cheap little tart she is. I'm gonna take her and make her perform in front of everybody. That's what I'm gonna do, *pal!'*

Steve balanced on tip-toe. Every muscle in his body yearned to put every last effort into a once-for-a-lifetime kayoe right on Bobby's button. And he didn't toss the punch. He got a better idea. One from the publicity agent's book. One which said if the girl was willing then she was what the antagonist said she had to be. He dropped to a flat-footed stance, glowered. 'Okay, kiddo. Okay, go ahead. See if you're top dog. See if you can make her . . . '

Carole loved the party. She adored the booze flowing, the way Bobby and Steve chased her as if they were in competition for her every smile, her every attention. More than this, she enjoyed the pushing aside of Jasmyn's quite prominent presence. It didn't count that Jasmyn hated Bobby from the word 'go'. That was a secret kept by the entourage. It was just how Bobby treated her. The courteous smile, the infrequent drink handed around. The eye darting from Jasmyn onto herself. The sudden flush expressing desire. Urgency. Suggestion.

'Watch it,' Steve whispered as he helped himself to a snack from the buffet laid on. 'The bastard's out to make you his latest momma.'

Carole waved to Bobby across the crowded room. 'Get lost, lover,' she hissed.

'You're not going to let him . . . '

'If he grabs me and rips my clothes off he can do it right in front of these creeps,' Carole husked.

'I thought we had a thing,' Steve reminded.

'Honey . . . ' and she swung to face him. 'Let's make it clear. I'm me. You're you. We had a little break from monotony. That's the limit. But Bobby . . . ' and she sighed. 'Man, I'd let him flay me alive for just an hour in his bed!'

Steve shook his head in regret. He'd picked a loser. He had to salve his wager somehow. And he elected Jasmyn to be his aide. Grinning, patting Carole's bottom, he moved away and headed directly for the no-like-no-see-no-intimacy member of their troupe.

'Don't tell me I'm suddenly in demand,' Jasmyn gritted when Steve stood next to her. She held a drink in one hand, an *hors d'oeuvre* in the other. Her attire was somewhat disarranged. Her hair in absolute disorder.

'You're not,' Steve grinned. 'But I'm not going to have Carole steal your thunder!'

The blonde bounced her breasts, shook her hips and simpered. 'That's my boy! Tell me how to spike her guns.'

'You're a better judge of that, Jasmyn. If you can't shake an ass . . . '

Jasmyn deposited the hors d'oeuvres, the glass on a nearby table. Flouncing her hair she straightened with breasts thrusting against the flimsy material of her crumpled dress. Eyes glassily reflecting her semi-inebriated condition she managed a stance of heroic proportions. 'I'll give 'em something to talk about for years,' she announced. 'Watch me . . . ' She cocked her head, listened. Then, hearing nothing conducive, enquired, 'Can't we have decent music for my revelation?'

Steve gripped her arm. Sweat poured from his forehead. 'Wait a second. Don't move until you hear the beat . . . '

He hurried across the room, found the record-player. He quickly searched labels until one attracted his attention. This he placed on the player, set the pick-up arm and moved away. The hell with Bobby! The hell with Carole! This was something to remember . . .

172

What a choice, Jasmyn thought as the music blasted into action. Every fibre of her being reacted with compulsive yearnings. She knew the tune. Knew its connotation. Knew the movie from which it came. And the routine.

That was important!

The routine!

The strip . . .

The bumps and grinds . . .

Those little nuances to make a man take notice. Make him quiver. Make him . . .

Blonde hair streaming, she gyrated across the floor. Like magic the yes-men separated, formed a wall-hugging square. Even Bobby dropped Carole's arm. Fastened his lascivious eyes on her. Drooled.

Yes - drooled!

She could see that!

And it inspired her to supreme heights . . .

God, that music . . .

She whirled, frenetically. An Injun doing a devil's dance. Casting off the shackles belonging to the white man. The garments . . .

Those covering garments . . .

Things to make her believe nudity was a shame. A crime. An indecency.

Away went stockings . . .

And suspender belt . . .

And dress . . .

Hair tumbled, wrapping round her now . . .

Hands mysteriously pandering to those whims rampant in the sweat-stinking room. Yearning hands. Seeking, hands. Up and down flesh hands. Moving . . .

Caressing within inches . . .

Moving over curves, down into crevices . . .

Brassiere, too . . .

Panties next . . .

Nude - glorious nudity. Unashamedly naked . . .

Cavorting . . .

Exhibiting . . .

Suggesting . . .

Begging . . .

Cajoling . . .

A frenzy rising to its crescendo as she roared into the majestic finale . . .

Kicks . . .

Bumps . . .

Grinds . . .

Rotating, shaking, jerking, doing her nut for a wildly appreciative audience . . .

Exploding into one final gyration . . .

One last leap . . .

Propelling her across the room . . .

Straight at Bobby Sharp . . .

Into open arms . . .

Onto receptive lips . . .

Hearing rasping entreaties, the degradation to culminate the dance - and the slam of door! The togetherness. The ultimate shame . . .

Steve Morash breathed again. He saw Carole standing alone. White faced. Trembling. Angry. Across the room, Becky hid her face in her hands.

Suddenly, he felt like a bastard!

CHAPTER FOURTEEN

BY four in the afternoon, fans already formed long queues outside Julius Gerstein's Discodrome. Bobby Sharp was the major attraction but some of those willing to risk inclement weather voted for their personal favourites. Groups like The Frogmen, Scrambled, Bacon and Rind. Or for individual artists like Anne Merrill and Rock Rolls.

All though, shared the opinion that Bobby Sharp's bill-topping appearance had made them purchase tickets.

Wilf Russell's hand-held cameramen roved the growing crowd, taping interviews for eventual relay on the 'live' telecast.

Steve Morash's hired reporters roamed the lines, chatting up the dolly-birds, getting copy - and dates - for the morning's columns. Not Monday's. But the Sunday specialized extra-read comments. The dates being a personal affair between dolly and newshawk.

From his Rolls-Royce parked on the opposite side of the street, Julius Gerstein eyed the activities as his calculator mind clicked into high gear. *'Thanks,'* he mused, *'to my foresight, Sharp is still packing them in!'* Not one regret nor one single sympathy for the victims of his ordered security assault touched a purse-string.

Becky Wilmott tried to look like any ordinary passerby as she strolled along the pavement opposite the Discodrome. She didn't have to be here. Her job had finished the night previously. In a coffee bar. After the record shop bit.

But she had to see the results.

Had to believe it was all possible.

That the party for Bobby Sharp had not been the end-all of showbiz's involvement in frenetic publicity. In the lies, the worse-than-Nazi-propagandaism. She had to believe there were those who came to hear. To see. To applaud for applause's sake alone.

Some of those in the queue looked familiar. She couldn't be sure. She thought a girl's face was one she'd looked at in Bristol. Another from Battersea - one of last night's recruits. A pre-party convert.

She wondered how many tickets were still available. She knew the girls had been chanting the story since early in the week - *sold out.* The last she'd heard was there were as many as five hundred seats available. Open for last minute rushes.

She thought about Jasmyn and Carole. Jasmyn with the one person on God's sacred earth she hated. Carole in Steve's bed. A second choice mating. And how she had avoided those ever-groping hands. Those lecherous whispers. Those yes-mening innuendos.

Was it worthwhile?

Did stardom's rating bring any joy?

Was hitting the spotlight so important?

She walked slowly, still fascinated by the queues. In her heart she knew - it was always worth the torments. Always important. Always joyous to be queen of the pops . . .

Even king - like Bobby Sharp!

'I want those kids checked before they get in,' Julius Gerstein hollered. 'I don't give a fuck if the Press screams. I want 'em frisked!'

Steve Morash stood back, scowling. They had another two hours to opening. He hoped Julius would cool off by then. If not, he could have to stick his nose in - welcome or not.

'We can't shake down a whole audience, Mister Gerstein,' a uniformed man said. His face spoke volumes. Utter contempt for the boss, agreement if pressed hard enough.

'You can bleedin' do whatever I want,' Julius commanded. He stomped on an innocent ant, ground its broken body to fluid beneath a savage heel. 'It's my Discodrome. I don't have insurance to cover a bloody riot.'

The security man shrugged. 'Sorry, sir,' he said with as much tact as he could muster. 'We're paid to provide a service - not a police job!'

Julius scowled, wagged a finger and advanced. 'I'm paying for this operation . . . Do I or don't I get what I'm bloody paying for?'

'You do, sir!' The man stood his ground. Ever dubiously.

'Then?' Julius asked.

'Can I check with my office?'

'Christ - no!'

'But. . . ' the man said.

'But shit,' Julius stormed. 'You do what I want or else . . . ' He flung his short body at a door, slammed it open, made a grandstand exit.

Steve Morash came into the picture then. He went to the puzzled security man, said: 'I'm Mr Gerstein's partner in this enterprise. Do your best. Try to sort out the trouble-makers from the legitimate fans. That's all we ask!'

The man suddenly smiled. 'We can do that, sir. It's just . . . '

Steve nodded with an embracing smile. 'I get the picture, buddy. Play it cool, eh? We've had enough bad publicity . . . '

The man nodded sagely. 'You certainly have had, sir.'

'Then you're agreeable?'

'Right on the job, sir,' the security man replied, saluting.

Steve thanked his precious gods for their deliverance. If all the security goons were as malleable as this one, Bobby should have a trouble-free concert. He thought about the television coverage. The dollar value of an American star making it big . . . B-I-G . . . in the U.K. Like Jack Jones. Or David Cassidy. Or Jimmy Osmond. Even film stars like Robert Vaughn. Blurbs to take back home and shove up the anti when an agent tried to pull the old 'he isn't internationally accepted' routine.

Leaving the security boys to sort out their contradictory instructions, Steve took a tour of the Discodrome. He had to admire Gerstein's ingenuity. The place had everything necessary for pop success. Acoustics. Stage bigger than any legitimate theatre. Lighting complexes to beat Hollywood at its celluloid best. Dressing rooms any star would accept. Offices fit for kings - never mind press, television, visiting managerial staff. Electronic gadgetry on a par with the most recent advances as required by the record companies. Scenery designed to slot in with every mood, every whim of an irascible designer.

It has cost a packet to make this joint.

It had also taken some guts to invest the money on the premise that those packing the seats would someday buy gear made by Julius Gerstein, and not a hot competitor.

Steve got a little jealous under the collar and, then, tightened up. He remembered a clause in their contract. The one which gave exclusive rights to Julius Gerstein Holdings to reproduce every costume worn by Bobby Sharp during his performance, or performances, within the United Kingdom.

Shaking his head, Steve had to admit that covered a lot of ground and gave Julius a lot of opportunities to double his profits from tonight's show . . .

Bobby Sharp smiled for the clicking shutters of the Press and freelance photographers in the lobby of his hotel. All secrecy had been dropped now. This was *THE* day. His debut. His comet-like sortie across British heavens.

Exuding all the charm he could muster, Bobby posed for every picture. He didn't quibble. Nor did he object when a demanding freelance begged for 'just one more, Bobby' and 'another, Bobby' and 'this way, Bobby'. He gave his all. Mr Personality Plus. Everybody's teenage idol.

He even ventured a personal opinion when asked if he had enjoyed London. He said: 'Fantastic. The greatest city in the world.' Which pleased the Press, his yes-men and the hotel management. And got him going inside. He'd seen nothing of London's bright lights. Nothing except a few passing street standards from a closed-in limousine squeezed between a pair of gay crumbs who gave him a giggle and a 'yes, Bobby' whenever he asked a simple question or sought to know where the hell he was.

'What did you think of Bristol, Bobby?' a newshawk asked.

'Terrific city,' came the stereo reply.

'And the way *your* boys manhandled *our* girls?' another unscheduled enquiry asked.

Putting every ounce of heart into his reply, Bobby said: 'That wasn't any of my doing, pal. Those goons were hired by *your* Julius Gerstein. Ask him what he had in mind. Frankly, I love all my fans. Every last one of 'em. I wouldn't hurt any. Not even to battin' 'em with a wilting daffodil . . . ' He smiled tenderly as if a guy with his sweet nature could ever hurt a bumble bee let alone a female type girl.

The same reporter didn't appear satisfied. He asked another question. 'Have you demanded that Gerstein's heavy mob be off-duty during the concert?'

Bobby glared momentarily, remembered the clicking shutters and forced his public smile back on his public made features. 'I've voiced my disapproval of everything smelling of force,' he said. 'In fact . . . ' and a brainwave hit him smack in the speaking chords, 'I've instructed my agent, Steve Morash, to cancel the engagement if Mr Gerstein does not offer an apology to my fans and restrain his men for the show.' He beamed into twenty clicking cameras.

Steve Morash heard the news from Julius Gerstein. Prior to Bobby's arrival at the Discodrome. In an office which was a smaller version of the tower-block edifice from where Gerstein controlled his empire.

'I'm bleedin' fed-up with this creep,' Julius growled.

'I'm paying out big money and what does he do to me? I'll tell you,' and he waved his hand imperiously when Steve tried to speak. 'He's crucifying me, that's what! He's talking from a mouth too big for his trousers.'

'Simmer down,' Morash said. 'Let's have the beef.'

'He wants me to apologize for hurting his bloody fans. He wants me to restrain my men tonight. Jesus Christ, am I the bogey man or something?'

Steve felt a cold hand pressing on his spine. The hand of fate. Trust Bobby to lay the cat amongst the pigeons. The little bastard hadn't any sense. Give him an audience - especially from the Press - and he'd undo every bright idea Steve ever put into operation.

'Forget it, Gerstein. I'll handle this situation.'

Julius came to his feet, face screwed into an unhappy dramatization of a man facing the gallows. 'You should be so lucky,' he bleated. 'He's put me on the spot, not you. He's said I'll apologize or else . . . '

'Or else what?'

'No concert!'

Something snapped inside Steve. 'He'll sing!' he promised tightly. *'And* he'll do more'n that. *He'll make those apologies.* In person. From the stage. In your name, of course,' he added, watching Gerstein's face to see if the penny dropped fast.

It did, like a thunder-bolt.'

'Not in my name, Morash. I don't retract anything for anybody.'

'Then give me one assurance,' Steve pleaded. 'Tell your boys to soft pedal the kids tonight. Tell 'em to play it so cool they'll freeze to death.'

Julius glared. A man of substance didn't enjoy being placed in a position of countermanding orders. Yet, if by going along with Morash he could remain aloof, freed from the necessity of being classified an ogre, he could afford one minor concession. He nodded, not committing himself to more than silent agreement.

Steve sighed. He felt he had won a partial victory. Everything now hinged on how Bobby reacted.

CHAPTER FIFTEEN

JULIUS GERSTEIN had no understanding of how fandom looked upon its pop idols. He could not begin to comprehend the emotional attachment young girls had for their favourite stars. Nor did he realise that members of a specific group were recognizable at a distance just from the way shoulders sloped, or hips revolved when walking, or from a peculiar hair style.

He did not believe the association between performer and fan was every bit as 'intimate' as that shared by man and wife.

And so, the best laid plans of mice and men went astray as it so often did that Saturday evening.

It was a major human error!

Such a trifling thing . . .

The elaborate plan to get the stars *inside* the Discodrome without being seen failed. Julius had laid on a huge van, weightless scenery he intended to use for a future production of a hippy play. He had hired coveralls and cloth caps- and a variety of other clothing.

The idea was for the groups and, especially, Bobby Sharp's entourage to pose as scenery erectors and walk into the Discodrome carrying the light materials as if they didn't count in the scheme of things.

A terrific notion!

But one doomed to failure simply because Bobby Sharp's mentality could not accept the necessity of wearing street clothes under his coveralls!

The van arrived on time. Parked outside the stage door.

A few teeny boppers watched its arrival and the first exodus suspiciously. But when all they saw was a bunch of ordinarily-clad youths carrying painted backdrops into the theatre they lost interest.

Except one!

Aileen Stevenson . . .

Nottingham seemed a long way away to her that Saturday evening. And it was. Weary hours of hitchhiking away. A hungry distance calculated in the amount she had eaten since leaving home after a hurried breakfast. She didn't mind, though. She had a ticket. A few quid left of her savings. Bobby Sharp's performance still to come.

At fifteen, Aileen dreamed of being kissed by her idol. Ever since she first looked at his picture in a pop magazine she had been crazy for Bobby. She'd bought every record of his supplied to an avid British market. She'd saved, scrimped and sweated to make this Mecca-trip from the moment she'd heard Bobby was due to make a British tour. She had tickets for every one of his one-night stands.

Nobody knew more about the public-image Bobby Sharp than Aileen Stevenson!

She'd even sent an international reply coupon costing £3 to the States for copies of the 'Bobby Sharp Fandine Mag'. A glossy production showing every costume Bobby wore on stage, his home in California, his backing group in 'relaxed' mood, his cars, his parents enjoying retirement provided for by an adoring son.

What Aileen didn't know was that Steve Morash had masterminded the entire magazine. Was the culprit responsible for projecting an entirely false image. Bobby didn't send his parents a single dime. He didn't own a lush Los Angeles home. He didn't entertain his group for relaxing weekends.

Bobby had a house. Outside 'Frisco. With high walls, servants and seven vicious dogs to keep intruders off his property. His parents were practically *persona non grata*. They lived on a meagre income and reflected glory. And the backing group, in Bobby's opinion, could starve or feast depending on how much they were willing to knuckle under his tantrum-dictatorial thumb. That was the real Bobby Sharp. The super-inflated ego masquerading as a nice guy. A charming young man. Everybody's friend.

Aileen didn't know this!

The way she felt about Bobby Sharp it is doubtful if she could have cared!

She loved her idol with every fibre of her young being. She worshipped him from afar. Wished she could worship him from a distance of a few inches.

When she saw a colourful backdrop carried by two youths come from the van her heart almost stopped beating. Her eyes popped. Her mouth went dry.

'Bobby,' she croaked.

Suddenly, her feet flew. Her arms reached out. Her hair streamed. Her voice found strength.

'Bobby . . . Bobby!' she screamed.

Her voice carried. Down the alley to the fans waiting expectantly for the arrival of their heroes. Down to the stage door.

Steve Morash hung around the stage door entrance waiting for Bobby. He had a few 'debts' to settle with his discovery. A few hard-hitting home truths to hammer into that egotistical head.

He felt pleased with the smoothness of Gerstein's operation. Bacon and Rind had gotten inside the Discodrome without any problems. Anne Merrill, Rock Rolls and The Frogmen, too. It wouldn't be long before Scrambled, Bobby and his backing group made it.

Then . . .

'Bobby . . . Bobby!'

The scream shattered Steve's composure. He hurtled forward, brushing aside a startled security guard. Dashing outside. In time to see the young girl fling herself on Bobby Sharp. In time to see the teeny bopper's idol plant a sensual kiss on his fan's lips.

'The bastard! The stupid bastard!' Steve voiced his sentiments even as he pulled the girl away. Pushing her to one side, he saw the screaming hordes rushing down the alley. Shouted: 'Inside . . . Christ, move 'em!'

His foot found its target and he propelled Bobby inside the stage door with a toe up his ass. He grabbed Scrambled's lead singer, hurled him in the same direction. 'Forget the stuff,' he roared, desperate now. The mob was less than twenty feet away. Coming strong. Yelling their heads off. 'MOVE!!'

Scrambled scrambled to obey. They had no inclination to get caught up in a frenzied battle to evade their fans. Bobby's group, too, had the stage door objective uppermost in mind. They streamed from the van, rushed to gain a relative safe haven.

Steve felt himself swept off his feet, carried on the tide until he slammed against the van's side. He fought to extricate himself from the screaming, tearing, delirious mob. It didn't matter now if they recognized anybody or not. Everyone belonging to the van had a fan value regardless of age, sex, status.

Even as the weight of girls ripping at him rubbered his knees, Steve could see thick-shouldered security men bursting from the stage door. He wanted to yell for them to go back. To stay out of this. He couldn't. Eager lips clamped on his, hands snaking inside his jacket to embrace him.

'God,' he thought, *'is this what it's like being a teeny bopper idol!'*

Rough hands hauled the girl from him, hoisted him to his feet. 'You okay, mate?'

Steve nodded, hearing the screams echo down the alley. Mingled now with the gruffer shouts of Gerstein's heavy mob. With the agonized yelps as young girls once again felt the superior weight of hard fists on their flesh.

'Stop 'em!' Steve called. 'Don't let 'em ruin it here!'

The man holding him grunted.

Steve tore away, flung himself at another security goon drawing a truncheon. 'Not that! Goddamit to hell, have some feeling, man!'

A girl sobbed at Steve's feet, clung to his legs. Blood smeared across her pretty face.

'Christ - leave 'em alone!'

Steve's voice roared above the general sound level. Security men halted in their tracks. Girls with tears on their cheeks backed off in fright.

'Get the hell inside,' Steve roared again.

One by one the security guards retreated to the stage door. Some even looked ashamed. Most, though, had those grim East End features stating they didn't give a damn who got hurt so long as they obeyed orders. And got paid for their mayhemous conduct.

'Lock the door,' Steve said, safe now inside the Discodrome. He glanced down at his clothes. Ruined. Torn. Filthy. 'Christ,' he muttered and turned away . . .

CHAPTER SIXTEEN

FROM his control room enclave Wilf Russell watched the build-up of air time. He liked Ed Cronin's choice of camera angles. The way those being interviewed were framed against the live performers on stage. The subtle switching of shots - long, medium, close up. Ed's imaginative mixing between speaker and an obvious reference to an act. The flashing cut to audience doing its demented nut.

He had the signal. Forty seconds. Thirty. Twenty. The guests shared his nervousness. They could not afford a goof either. Each man or woman knew he or she was putting a neck on innovation's chopping block. Setting a trend. Going against all predictable proof. The pundits had long said live television of a pop scene meant a lost career.

Ten seconds left . . .

Sweat coated Wilf's palms. Carefully wiping each on his tweeds he lit a fresh cigar, tried to look at ease. His spectacles steamed up next. He removed them, frantically used a clean handkerchief. Replacing them he got the count-off . . .

Four . . .

Three . . .

Two . . .

One . . .

The floor director's finger swung across to Alan Foxx.

An artificial wide lit the interviewer's face.

'Welcome to Discodrome, London's latest meeting ground for all pop fans . . .'

Wilf felt the tension evaporate. Now they were underway he felt immeasurably better. Until the programme finished he would be too busy following the direction, the questions to get uptight.

Alan Foxx, too, sensed relief. He had only recently gone before the cameras. Always, prior to Wilf's request for him to cover this momentous event, he had sheltered behind radio's unseen barricades. A voice cajoling. Not a face and body being left wide-open for every form of acting criticism.

' . . . and our first guest tonight is none other than your old mate, disc-jockey Perry Grogan . . .'

Cronin gave a thumbs-up signal to Wilf. His monitor showed success looming large on their combined horizon . . .

'What about this, Perry?' Foxx asked.

Grogan brandished a cigar, an affectation like Russell's. In his velvet suit and floral cravat he looked like any young man about town. The only trouble being he belonged to an age group more middle than youthful. 'Fantastic, Alan. Unbelievable.'

Cronin crawled inside. He couldn't stand Grogan. The man was nothing less than an idiot. A big-headed nobody who'd been groomed for stardom because his daughter had the misfortune to marry one of the director's bastard sons.

'I believe you visited Houston, Texas. Their famous Astrodrome. How does this compare, Perry?' Alan Foxx had an easy-flowing manner that usually put his guests right into the act. A shared experience.

With Grogan, however, there could be but one spotlight. The one on Grogan. The man had such an inflated ego it was a wonder any small screen managed to carry a picture of his entire head. 'No comparison, Alan,' Grogan rumbled. 'One's an outdoor arena with a gigantic roof. This . . . this . . . ' and the cigar waved majestically, 'is a mere concert hall. An acoustically contrived, stereophonically manipulated Hell's cavern. Frankly, I don't know how those kids can stand the abuse their ears are put to.'

Alan Foxx frowned; caught his monitor and, realising the camera was lingering on him, suddenly grinned. 'That's being rather hard on Julius Gerstein,' he said.

'Julius can handle criticism,' Grogan announced righteously. 'He hasn't done so badly avoiding it over the incident at Sharp's motel, has he?'

Wilf Russell wanted to vomit. He'd warned each guest not to bring that controversial issue into the discussion. Trust bloody Grogan to bust the show wide-open before it got half-warm.'

Alan Foxx shrugged. 'Have you listened to the *sound* out there yet, Perry?' he asked, tactfully avoiding getting drawn into the pro's and con's of security abuses.

'Not me!' Grogan made the statement as if his word just had to be the final one on any topic. 'I refuse to be deafened.'

'I have and I must say it was rather surprising. I expected to be blasted but the effect is stimulating. Soothing almost,' Foxx said, cutting his radio comrade dead. He didn't like the other any more than Cronin.

Grogan scowled. He knew what was happening and didn't enjoy being pegged down. 'You should see a doctor, Alan. You've got wax in your ears!' He guffawed loudly, rolling in his seat.

'Jeeze,' Wilf moaned in the control box. 'He's sending me back to the cutting room . . . '

The Frogmen finished their number, took their well earned applause. Throwing kisses to the screaming girls jumping up and down in the front rows, the group backed off stage.

'It's a terrific audience,' the lead singer told Anne Merrill.

'Not many boys, though,' the Scots lassie said.

'Hell, you can't have it both ways,' the Frogman laughed. His hands formed the outline of a shapely girl. Bulging over breasts and bottom. 'That's what I like.'

Anne smiled, prepared to go on stage. In her kilt and carrying a guitar she did not radiate the natural sex appeal that belonged to her in ordinary street clothes. Nor did the nymphomaniac streak in her make-up show. Her co-performers knew her penchant. Her agent did, too. But never the fans.

'Get 'em going, Anne,' the Frogman chuckled.

She twisted round, glared at him, quipped: 'And coming . . . ' Then, tossing her kilt, she vanished through the hanging velvet curtains . . .

Sound surged at her from the huge hall. It was a two-edged sword. Shooting at those seated out front. Coming like arrows off the domed walls back to stage centre.

She waved, walked directly to the microphone. She didn't use backing. Nor did she believe in warm-up preliminaries. Her business was putting a song across. And that's what she did. Straight. No frills. No seeking adoration. Just a singer letting go with everything she had. Which happened to be a considerable talent!

Seated in the fire-glow security of his lounge, Charles Treffry kept his gaze glued to the colour television screen. It was his responsibility for giving permission for this programme. His alone. As head of broadcasting for the network he could so simply have scribbled 'NO' across the suggestion presented by Wilf Russell. He hadn't. Now, he calmed the doubts that had mounted during the past weeks. So far, so good. Outside of Grogan's *faux pas* which Foxx had successfully covered, the programme welded beautifully. Blended intelligent discussion with background action and brought the youngsters into their scene without subjecting them to strictures and editorial cutting.

The disturbances feared for by M.P.s and others closely associated with television broadcasting, had not materialized. Maybe they would not. He sincerely hoped not anyway. If live coverage was to come into its own this show for the first time going out live had to be the justification. Had to be the precedent.

Foxx was interviewing the *Daily Globe's* music critic now . . .

'Is this typical of what actually happens at a pop concert?' Alan Foxx asked.

Harry Jones crossed his legs, carefully straightened his trouser creases, nodded a craggy head. 'About normal, Alan. Of course, let me admit that I don't often attend pop. I'm more at home in the opera or ballet.'

'But you do have a keen interest in open-house tours, I believe,' Alan insisted.

Jones grinned. 'I like that. Yes, I do. Open-house, in case the listeners don't know, is my coining for any occasion like this one. As distinct from a selective audience invited to attend the British debut of some famed American artist. A critics night, I call that.'

Foxx shuffled papers on his lap without glancing at them. A natural rapport between the men had been established for the viewing public. Alan could play it off the top of his head now. 'What about Anne Merrill? Isn't she an under-rated singer?'

'Very much so. I admire her simple style. And her voice . . . ' Jones kissed his fingertips, blew the kiss camerawards. 'Fabulous.'

'Do you have any records you would call strictly pop?' Jones nodded quickly. 'Quite a few, Alan. I've even got one featuring you . . . '

Foxx laughed, held his hand up. 'Not that oldie. Not that, please!'

'You were a mean guitar player, Alan.'

'Mean is right,' Foxx laughed delightedly. 'So mean I didn't play half the notes . . . '

Charles Treffrey had to smile. He could remember the suggestion arriving on his desk. The one name that held his hand from tossing out Wilf's idea had been Alan Foxx. He respected the disc-jockey. Respected his wholesome approach to a balanced choice of music. And the manner in which he treated listeners who wrote in with requests.

Not many dee-jays spent their own money hiring a private secretary whose sole duty was keeping a running correspondence with fans going.

If this show rated the term 'hit' he would see to it that Foxx got a regular network slot. A talk-show. A late night publicity boosted challenge to those other programmes put out by the rival network. He might even let Wilf Russell and Ed Cronin in on the act . . .

CHAPTER SEVENTEEN

JOHNNY HOLLAND nudged Peter Acroyd in the ribs. 'Pass the word along. Get ready!' His gaze never left the stage. Never seemed to wander from Scrambled doing their act.

Down their row the 'Jolly Green Men' and spare Roundheads bent forward expectantly. They'd all been waiting for an order. For some upper-echelon remark relating to the forthcoming assault, not just a comment about this or that performance.

Gloria Derrick sighed, shifted until her thigh was plastered against Johnny's. 'Can't I . . . ?' she started to ask.

'No! Bleedin' hell, must I go through this again!' Johnny tore his eyes from Scrambled's energetic number. 'I've told you - this is for the blokes. Just the blokes!' He glanced down at her thigh. 'And quit that, too! I'm not interested.'

Peter whispered against the sound bursting from the walls: 'They're set, Johnny. Say when . . . and how!'

Johnny viewed the front facing security men. They appeared to have the stage effectively blocked off from the screaming, jumping, hand clapping teeny boppers. Other guards along the Discodrome's curved walls carried whistles - warning devices to alert a stand-by force, no doubt.

He had paid attention to how the guards worked back and forth along the stage forecourt. Watched how they moved in groups to head off sections of the audience showing signs of erupting into unmanageable mobs.

'When Bobby Sharp starts singing there's gonna be some movement,' he said over the music's blare. He paused waiting for those nearest to get their heads closer. 'I want us to move with the girls. Right down front. To the left of centre . . . '

Bruce Barnes studied the situation. 'Christ, Johnny that's the spot they're really guarding!'

Johnny nodded eagerly. 'Yeah - and that's their weakest link. Look . . .' His finger jabbed air. 'See the way those girls have a wedge in there?'

A group of schoolgirls all wearing the same uniform formed an arrowhead near the place. They didn't seem bent on rushing the performers. Just swooning every time one of the group gyrated his hips or tossed long hair in their direction.

'Well,' Johnny continued as if this was a military operation and he the general in command. Which, in a sense, he was! 'Well,' again, 'those blokes ain't going to be worried. They've got their lot in hand. But when the bloody Discodrome explodes they'll spread.'

Bruce grinned. 'Yeah, they will - won't they!'

'I want you guys to cover us.' Johnny told his Roundheads. 'Give 'em the boot! Start an aggro . . . ' He rubbed his palms down his trousers. 'They're big but big balls make a lovely target!'

The Roundheads laughed.

The Jolly Green Men laughed.

Only Gloria Derrick didn't laugh.

She didn't want to knock Johnny's plan but she wondered if the security heavy mob would let a bunch of kids wearing boots get near enough to inflict damage.

Steve Morash fondled Carole Latham's bottom and whispered, 'We'll leave here right after the show.'

'I've promised Bobby I'll go back with him!'

Steve glared, dropped his hand from her flesh. 'You what?'

'Jasmyn doesn't want a repeat,' Carole murmured. 'I volunteered.'

'You crazy bitch! Didn't we have it off good?'

'Yeah, sure - but it's Bobby I really want.'

'There's no understanding taste,' Steve growled and left the girl standing in the wings. Any respect he had for Carole vanished in a twinkling. He didn't rate Bobby as an equal in the love-making department. In fact, he didn't rate Bobby for more than a temporary meal-ticket.

Already, Steve was wrestling with the deployment of his 'arousers' for the next tour stop. Becky deserved a prime territory for her efforts. Jasmyn and Carole always did an excellent job but his current mood gave Jasmyn the advantage of 'soft' regions.

He halted, caught sight of Bobby emerging from his three-star dressing room. The teeny bopper idol's gaudy costume brought back memories of triumph. And tribulation. Triumph in the States. Tribulation when that goddamned fan had spotted the outfit showing from under Bobby's coverall on his stage door arrival.

God, he could kill the little bastard for that!

Bobby strutted towards Steve, cocky to the last. Sequins glistened on his gear, the mauves and purples royally declaring this was the King of teeny boppers.

'You're next,' Steve grated.

'Man, ain't you late tellin' me?'

Steve's fist formed, unclenched. 'Wipe that smug smile off your face before I smash you!'

'You know,' and Bobby's stiffened finger jabbed relentlessly at Steve's chest, 'when we get back home I'm gonna hire Murder Incorporated to erase you, man.'

'They'd kill you for free,' Steve shot back. His arm brushed Bobby's away. 'What's this I hear about you and Carole? Wasn't Jasmyn enough?'

'That bitch!' Bobby spat. 'She hates me. She's gotta get her ass kicked from my scene!'

Steve smiled mysteriously. 'Didn't she wear your kookie tricks?'

A stagehand came rushing up. 'You're call, Mister Sharp. His gaze fastened worshipfully on Bobby's face. A face that changed from undisguised hate for his agent to charm for the man.

'I'll be there directly . . . '

The stagehand darted away.

Steve mimicked Bobby's personality role. From normal to assumed. 'Christ, ain't we wonderful,' he lisped.

'Get offa my back, man,' the idol yelled.

'Is that what Jasmyn said?'

Bobby glared. He detested his deviationist tactics spoken aloud where sympathetic souls could overhear. He wanted the image of a typical, decent young American to remain inviolate.

'You bastard!' Steve hissed.

'It takes one to know one,' Bobby said after a pause. Striding off, he wondered if his comeback had been original. When he decided it wasn't his temper rose. Enough to slam past his backing group without the customary smile, the encouraging word, the star's willingness to admit, in privacy, that he owed them a debt of gratitude.

'Christ, who the hell . . . '

Josh Getz, drummer, placed a hand on Carl Tucson's shoulder. 'Let the bastard rot in hell,' he growled. 'We get paid.'

Carl shrugged off the soothing hand. 'One day,' he threatened.

'One day,' Josh grinned, 'we'll be tops of the pops. On the "Lucky Strike Hit Parade" . . . '

'I smoke Camels,' Carl replied and, smiling away his ire, followed Bobby on stage.

The scream ripped through Discodrome. *'BOBBY . . . BOBBY . . . BOBBY . . . '*

'Ohhhhh!'

'Arooooo!'

'Bobby - don't ever leave me!'

'Kiss me, Bobby . . . '

'My darling . . . '

Johnny Holland witnessed the scene as one who wanted the adoration for himself. The last girl had almost fainted when she cried 'My darling . . . '

His gaze centred on Bobby Sharp. On the uniform . . .

The uniform . . .

'Jesus - I got it!'

Peter and Bruce danced out of Johnny's way.

'I got the bloody bloke's number!' Johnny shouted.

Peter shrugged as Bruce tried to figure out what was wrong. They were supposed to rush the stage. Now . . .

'Look at his gear,' Johnny yelled above the deafening roar for the star of this and any other show. 'Look at it!'

Peter looked.

Bruce looked.

Gloria, Mike, Bill, Walter, Ted, George, Frank, Ian, Sam, Jim, Victor, Larry, Bob all looked.

'A bleedin' load of sparklers,' Peter said.

Gloria squinted, tried to catch what Johnny had caught. She knew enough to recognize the signs. There had to be something about that outfit . . .

'I see it!' Gloria screamed. She did a little jig. 'I bloody see it!'

Johnny grinned triumphantly.

'The name,' Gloria chanted. 'Bobby Sharp and . . . ' She shielded her eyes from the fifteen spots focusing on the star. 'And . . . *I got it!'*

'L-O-V-E!' Johnny said.

'LOVE,' Gloria repeated.

Johnny grunted, drew Peter and Bruce into his tight circle of confidants. 'He's got bleedin' L-O-V-E stitched in fuckin' sequins onto his gear!'

The Roundheads squinted, narrowed their eyes, tried to see what their leader had seen. Some did. Some didn't. The Sharp regalia had been designed by experts. By men paid a fantastic sum to transmit a message that registered in the subsconscious. Not the conscious. Men determined to circumvent government decrees. Men beyond the fringe of commercialism's decency. Men recruited by an astute Steve Morash to *implant* a LOVE relationship even if the by-product of that same commercialism happened to be a detestable little bastard!

'Now what?' Bruce asked, shattered by Johnny's discovery.

'We wait,' Johnny snapped. 'We wait for the last number. OUR NUMBER . . .' He chuckled.

Gloria looked down at the wedge which had broken under security pressure. 'They've beat us, Johnny,' she wailed.

'Like shit,' Johnny hollered. He pointed at the right of stage area which now supported screaming teeny boppers doing their nut for Bobby. 'You stir 'em up. Get 'em ravin' like hell.'

Gloria welcomed a chance to show her worth. She kicked, battered, clawed her way past bouncing, happy fans. She understood. A strain here. A strain there. And the security boys would be hard put to offer solidified resistance to Johnny's determined attack . . .

Alan Foxx still did not feel in any way, shape or form that the reception for Bobby Sharp had progressed beyond live television's capabilities to handle. In the obviously hysterical reaction to Bobby's appearance on stage he found a new dimension. A new format. His guest at that crucial moment was none other than fandom's greatest exponent of the publicity barb. The ever-effervescent and ever controversial Arthur Kyle. He of the frock coat, the opera-topper, the cape and cane.

'You have been linked with many causes and many changes in the pop scene. You're an exponent of self-expression. Can you honestly state that this . . .' and Alan generously covered the background shots with a magnanimous wave, 'is typical of today's youth. That this is a teeny bopper world gone stark, raving crazy?'

Kyle adjusted his monocle, presented his silver-headed cane for viewing dissension and tilted his topper. A shock of golden hair tumbled forth. 'I say this is what young people want,' he pontificated. 'Bobby Sharp is just an example of liberation. Sexual liberation. Parliament talks about free contraceptives for the poor, the deprived. Who is more deprived than today's younger girls? They need a legislation aimed to encourage adolescent awareness . . .'

Alan Foxx's face showed where he stood on Kyle's issue. 'You misunderstood my question, Arthur.'

'I didn't, you know,' the man replied. 'I'm taking this golden opportunity to bring home to every parent the need for daughters to have The Pill, to have . . . '

Foxx rebelled. Drastically. 'I'm a parent, sir . . .' he interrupted sharply. 'I wouldn't want my daughter to be on the Pill at age fourteen. Or fifteen. Not even at sixteen.'

'Why not?' Kyle cut in quickly. 'She would be subhuman if she didn't have an awakening of sexual desire. Like those girls out there. They're opting for Bobby Sharp because he represents the best choice for the release of masturbatory . . . '

Alan Foxx coughed, erased the final innuendo. His voice, when it rose above Kyle's, sounded strained. 'Thanks, Arthur. You've been an invaluable help in understanding this phenomenon . . . or should that be phenomena?'

The phenomenon exploded in Alan Foxx's eyes. In Wilf Russell's eyes. In Charles Treffry's eyes. In some four million viewers' eyes.

Suddenly, as if catapulted from top-secret rocket installations, Johnny and his men charged. Broke through the security-veneer. Gained the stage.

A frantic signal reached Alan Foxx and he swung to catch the spreading disease . . .

Johnny sensed the magic of being in front of an audience. On stage. He charged forward, sent Bobby Sharp flying as he grabbed the mike. He swung, saw his 'Jolly Green Men' take care of their instrumental opposites. He glowed. This was it . . .

Alan Foxx wanted to cut his throat. All their careful planning. All their taking into account of the endless probabilities. All Gerstein's self-praising security precautions. All blown. Gone for a burton.

Phyllis Shankley almost threw a fit. Her eyes popped and she forgot that the monitor carried the scene. She wheeled on her chair, stared through the plate-glass window separating the television discussion from the Discodrome's continuous activities. 'My God,' she gasped. 'It's a happening . . . A real honest-to-goodness happening!'

And, for once, the ever-cool, ever-right columnist whose judgements on topics ranging from 'what shall I do with my too sexy boyfriend now he's got another girl?' to the sublime 'have I the right to demand a three night week?' suddenly found herself exposed for the inconsequential twit she always had been. When she pointed, panted and said: 'Jesus, Murphy, they can't do this to me!' she covered the subject admirably.

Johnny Holland clutched his hard-won mike. He ignored Bobby Sharp screaming at him from the stage forecourt. He didn't count the bodies strewn across the raised dias. All he saw were his men - the Jolly Green Men - giving him the high-sign.

'Go, Johnny!'

A wave.

A nod.

And the music blasted . . .

'This is JOHNNY HOLLAND AND THE JOLLY GREEN MEN,' he told the frenzied audience, his voice strong - getting to them over the shouts and roars of the security heavies. 'And now - *Virginia's Love!'* Grinning, he swung on his 'men'. 'Let's go, gang . . .'

Wilf Russell's hand moved to terminate the transmission. Hesitated. *This kid's got something,* he thought as the 'new' sound rose sweepingly to fill the Discodrome. His eyes tore away from the frightening spectacle of Bobby Sharp struggling to climb back on-stage as a pair of youths clung to him, doing their best to prevent him reaching his goal.

'Kill it, Wilf! For God's sake - kill it!'

Reluctantly, Wilf's hand moved again. As producer he could prolong the moment of Johnny Holland's triumph. But . . .

The monitor screen blanked out . . .

'Christ, now what?'

Wilf flicked fingers across his control console. The voice belonged to Ed Cronin. But the urgency belonged to the network. To Charles Treffry. To those various boards responsible for the codes of broadcasting standards.

'Wilf . . . can you hear me?'

Wilf thought about Johnny Holland. If he ever got another opportunity to produce a television show he'd bring that determined young man on . . .

CHAPTER EIGHTEEN

STEVE MORASH moaned, pushed Carole back onto her side of the bed and swung his legs to the floor. Naked, he padded to the door of his suite. He didn't imagine many people would be strolling along the corridors this early in the morning. Didn't care, either. He opened the door, lifted the bundle of newspapers he had on daily order.

Back by the window, Carole's sleeping form nothing more than an outline under the bedclothes, Steve lit a cigarette and began searching through the nationals.

ACTON GROUP TAKE OVER
TEENY BOPPER SHOW

Steve smiled, blew smoke from his nostrils. Headlines first. Text later. He could pretty well write what each paper had to say. Or he thought he could . . .

TEENY BOPPER SENSATION

He had to admit it was a sensational display of initiative. An admirable trait in one so young . . .

JOLLY GREEN MEN OUTSMART HEAVY MOB

Now there was a clever splash headline . . .

SHARP FALLS FLAT AS HOLLAND MARCHES ON

Steve frowned, started reading the comment under this glaring invite. Within seconds, he was getting that old 'detergent feeling' washing through his system.

Last night, amid scenes more reminiscent of a battlefield than a pop concert, a British sensation emerged triumphant from the shambles of an American teeny bopper idol's fall from grace . . .

Steve felt ice form on his spine. Mental ice. *Was this the break he'd been waiting for ever since Bobby started acting like a god?* he asked himself.

. . . and surely it will not be long before Johnny Holland reaches chart-topping, heart-stopping fame. The lad from Acton has the voice, the guts and the musical inspiration to find success. We wish him well!

Steve hurried through the other papers now. Each, he discovered, formed the same opinion. This kid - this cheeky, loveable kid from London - had the writers eating from his dare-devil hands.

'That's it then,' Steve muttered and got to his feet.

'That's what?' a sleepy Carole asked, pushing her head above the covers.

'I've got me a new boy - if I'm lucky,' Steve laughed. He slapped his naked thigh. 'By God, have I ever got me a new boy. . .'

Carole yawned, snuggled down into the bed again. She didn't have to energize her brains at this ungodly hour. If Steve wanted to talk in riddles then let him - but she wasn't about to listen. Nor get excited.

Ignoring the girl, Steve hustled into the bathroom. Today would bring him joy. Today, he'd tell Bobby Sharp where he got off. And Johnny Holland where he got on the musical bandwagon! He had it figured already. He knew exactly what kind of publicity campaign to run. How to approach the record companies. How to get them jumping through his hoops for Johnny's signature.

Across the City from his tower-block refuge, Julius Gerstein reckoned the cost of signing Johnny Holland. He had spent most of the night calculating his profit from Discodrome's fiasco. Well, fiasco in one manner of speaking but certainly not in hard pounds-pence.

Would the kid let him act as his manager?

That worried him! He'd read the papers. Seen what Johnny had to say about the use of 'heavies'.

The hell with it!

He didn't have to believe everything they said in newspapers. He could outsmart a kid. But . . .

He turned cold. What if Steve Morash had the same notion? What if the American P.R. man had already jumped his gun? He could imagine that bastard charming the innocent kid and warning him to beware of people like Julius Gerstein. .

Johnny Holland enjoyed his breakfast. He had one newspaper to read. One only. And he couldn't take his eyes off the column written by his favourite television critic.

. . . left a sour taste in Wilf Russell's mouth. The inadvisability of presenting pop 'live' came home to roost with a vengeance. However, one startling fact shone through the disastrous event. Johnny Holland. This young man will certainly cause a few teeny bopper hearts to flutter this morning. To agents and disc productions managers I say - act fast. Johnny Holland isn't going to be in the wilderness for much longer.'

Johnny smiled. By studying the tactics employed to promote Bobby Sharp he could tell the columnist a few things. He wasn't going to be rushed into any contract. They could come and go. He'd listen and only when all their offers were in would he and his Roundhead mates make a decision.

And that was a guarantee!

THE END

GLAM

By Richard Allen

CHAPTER ONE

BRILLIANT sunshine spread like a carpet across Trafalgar Square, shimmering on the water in the Mountains. Wheeling pigeons banked, swooped in for a landing. Tourists, cameras at the ready, waited expectantly. As always, no photographic record of London would ever be complete without that family snapshot showing mum or dad or the kids feeding a pigeon.

Coming from Canada House and crossing the square, Doc MacMaster felt hope flood his being. Entering The Strand, he glanced at passing girls with just the right amount of reserve mingled with middle-aged interest. He didn't pause, though. The appointment made for him meant more than any frivolous fancy.

He wondered what the outcome of his meeting would be. The fact that Reginald Whitaker thought enough of the proposal to set up an informal Board discussion surely meant a more than fifty percent chance of success!

Automatically, Doc studied the people he approached. Did they look like the types to roar their lungs out at a hockey game . . . He smiled absently. He'd have to watch that! *Ice hockey in Britain.* Not at all like back home in good old Toronto where hockey ruled supreme at Maple Leaf Gardens. Or in Montreal at the Forum.

God, he hoped the deal went through. Not just because he had an investment stake, either. He wanted these people to get enjoyment from a terrific sport . . .

A newspaper seller held aloft a copy of the *Standard*. Back page headlines showed just what he was up against, in London anyway.

WEST HAM DEFY SLUMP

In the six weeks he'd devoted to reading every British paper, he'd come to a conclusion about soccer. It had a helluva grip. Especially for the emotional young.

Glancing at his watch he reckoned he had time to grab a quick coffee and scan the headlines. He bought a paper, popped into one of the many small joints serving snacks.

And, five minutes later . . .

'Hey, mister . . . '

Doc swung, newspaper almost falling from his hand. He saw the counterhand coming round to menace him.

'ow's about payin', mister?'

Doc suddenly grinned. 'Sorry, mac,' he laughed. 'I was lost in something else.' He handed over a fifty pence piece, waved aside an attempt at giving change. 'Keep it . . . this place's been lucky for me!' He walked from the cafe, head high, step lighter even than before.

Now he had a second string to his bow. A better arrow with which to penetrate the starchy British attitude towards innovation. A new scene. An idea to link an assured money maker with an enthusiastic intangible.

The girls looked somehow prettier, more inclined to return his flirty gaze. He'd known for a year or more he had entered 'that dangerous age' when the younger birds made his hormones emote stronger than ever before. When the thought of an assignation got him steamed-up. When it took an awful lot of will-power to refrain from getting involved.

'To hell with being careful,' he mused and almost winked at a cheeky-bottomed seventeen year-old whipping her ass back and forth to attract attention.

But, for the moment at least, he remained aloof from temptation. First the meeting. Next a quick telephone call and, lastly, another discussion. Only after all had been accomplished dare he let his passions run riot.

In Fleet Street now, he hurried. Time was growing far too short for comfort. He must not be late. He knew exactly where the *'Cheshire Cheese'* was and went straight to the bar. Newspaper reporters and others associated with the majestic weight of the Press congregated, loudly voicing opinions contrary to those they expressed for general consumption.

Doc smiled to himself. *And so the hypocritical world kept turning!*

Five minutes left. He ordered a *Seagram's V. 0.* with *American Dry*, listened to an argument over the merits of E.E.C. membership. As a Canadian he deplored British entry into Europe. As a sportsman trying to flog ice hockey to a tightly-knit European community he had to admit, privately of course, that the Common Market gave him an excellent opportunity to exploit what was now regarded as a game long overdue for expansion.

Finishing his drink he went upstairs, soaking in the ancient atmosphere. The sawdust. The family-style eating arrangements. An aroma of first-rate cooking drifted from room to room.

When he saw Reginald Whitaker rise to his feet and come forward with hand outstretched, distinguished features relaxed into a genuine smile, Doc MacMaster erased an oldstanding notion from his mind.

Englishmen were not the formal, stand-offish bastards they liked the world to believe!

Flushed with excitement, Doc arrived back at his hotel and hurriedly scribbled a cable . . .

WHITAKER IN AGREEMENT. REQUIRE FINALISED DOCUMENTS WITHIN WEEK. TERMS TO INCLUDE DUAL CONSTRUCTION AND - REPEAT AND - MULTI-PURPOSE PAVILION ALOE HOLD FESTIVALS, CONCERTS, ETC. OUR PERCENTAGE THIS THIRTY. SITE AVAILABLE. HAVE GIVEN WORD. QUERY YOUR ACCEPTANCE.

Only when a hotel porter ambled away with the cable did Doc lean back and sigh. His stomach felt bloated. He normally didn't eat such a massive midday meal but what they'd offered at the *'Cheshire Cheese'* had been too taste-teasing to refuse.

His expectations of an acceptable deal involving Whitaker and his Board had always been subject to him having to make the concessions. But, by God, he'd won every point. Had conceded absolutely nothing of the original scheme. All he'd done was to slip in a suggestion - one born in the snack bar - and let them carry him along their enthusiastic path. He got to his feet, opened his bag. Taking a bottle of *V. O.* from it he helped himself to a generous drink. He felt he deserved it. Drinking was, for him, in moderation, a pleasure. Like his occasional cigar. Or a visit from his grandchildren. Frowning, he pushed away a mental picture of his ex-wife. It didn't do, in Doc's book, to dally with the past. Not even the pleasantries associated with a marriage that had lasted some eighteen years.

Taking the clipping he'd torn from his newspaper before meeting Whitaker, Doc read it again. He wanted to be word-perfect when he spoke to Steve Morash. *So much depended on his ability to con the American con-expert!*

Finishing drink and reading simultaneously, Doc drew his telephone close and called the operator. He guessed which hotel Steve would use and asked for it. As he waited patiently, he tried to remember how Steve looked. It helped, Doc reckoned, to have a picture of the other prominent when conversing over a distance. All he could recall was a handsome bastard with a way of charming everybody within earshot. A casual, but neatly expensive dresser. A guy known to attract females like flypaper did pestiferous insects. A quick-thinker. An ideas salesman. A publicity machine combined inside one skeleton.

A voice spoke in his ear. 'Steve Morash here.'

Doc tensed. So far, so good. He had batted one-hundred percent. And providing he didn't goof it up he could hit a home run . . .

Setting his telephone on its rest, Steve Morash grinned. Lady Luck still rode on his shoulder, he thought. What he'd been told in 'strictest confidence' gave him a terrific feeling of elation. Good enough to call for a drink. He walked to the liquor cabinet that came with his hotel suite, opened it and poured *Hundred Pipers* into a Waterford crystal glass. *Only the best for Morash!* Adding *Canada Dry* he sipped the Scotch, nodded his satisfaction. A man in his elite position deserved the best at all times!

So Doc MacMaster had clinched a deal involving one of Britain's largest sporting goods manufacturers . . .

A deal guaranteed to spring yet another surprise on the pop world, too.

And he - Steve Morash - had been invited to get in on the ground floor!

He liked it. More, he thoroughly enjoyed the prospect of rubbing Julius Gerstein's nose in the dirt. He hadn't forgotten Gerstein's mind-blowing act after Johnny Holland disrupted the Discodrome debut featuring America's chart topping teeny bopper idol, Bobby Sharp. Nor had he forgotten kicking Bobby's ass out of this same hotel suite and signing Johnny to an exclusive ten-year contract. Now Doc was offering the golden opportunity to himself as an integral part of the British scene. Oh, he loved it!

And, what was more, he knew Johnny Holland would go overboard for the proposition.

Idly, he kicked approaches round in his head. How best to present a *fait accompli* that Johnny would figure had been his suggestion from the beginning. How to swing the 'Jolly Green Men' behind him if there should be a slight hitch. How to offer something for Gloria Derrick, knowing she had Johnny's ear, too.

A mental light flared into brilliance. What cartoonists portrayed within balloons as an 'idea'. He grabbed the phone, got a line and dialled. What better man to fill-in his lack of sporting knowledge than a sporting columnist. One he could trust to keep his mouth shut! Not that he intended dropping hints. Oh, no! Not Steve Morash whose right hand seldom knew which pocket the left dipped into. But he had to get information. The type a knowing individual could obtain from the proper authorities if only he knew who they were.

Even as he waited for the columnist to answer, Steve was way ahead planning the next move. That's the way he operated. Like a chess player, everything had to be calculated so far in advance the current move got hidden in the overall pattern.

CHAPTER TWO

GEORGE ARMSTRONG got the ball across. The little winger had played his heart out as usual but in these dying minutes of a vital game his efforts seemed doomed to bring the much needed Arsenal point.

'What the hell are we doin' here, Johnny?' Peter Acroyd asked in a disgruntled tone of voice.

Johnny Holland opened his mouth to reply, snapped it shut quickly. The action down on the pitch rose to breath-sapping excitement. A goalmouth mix-up and . . .

'OOOOHHHHHHHH!' the Highbury crowd gasped.

And no wonder! Jennings pulled off a fantastic save from a Mike England header that almost became a record-book own goal.

'Footballer of the year!' Bruce snarled.

Johnny relaxed as the game died a little now. He didn't share Bruce's hatred for the team. Nor did he reckon Peter's lack of interest in any match that did not include Rangers or Brentford. He knew, basically, what was eating his mates. No aggro . . . That had to be the reason.

He pulled them close to him, whispered in a lull of crowd support: 'Watch it - those bloody newsmen are waiting for us to give 'em a story!' His gaze swept the eager photogs, the scribble-happy reporters.

'Screw 'em!' Peter said.

Johnny didn't argue. His mates would heed *the word*. In the old days, when they'd been a bunch of Roundheads trying for glory and showbiz fame, he'd been their leader. Now, with success tucked under their collective belt, he definitely was leader - right down to how they should think, act, carry out ordinary things.

Anyway, he liked this treatment they were receiving. Seats in the directors' box, spectators watching them and trying to figure out how important they were in football circles.

If only they really knew!

Steve had said they should change their image. Make an impression. Create an interest. Build fans where none had existed prior to *that night* . . .

God, he remembered that alright!

Bobby Sharp could have slit their throats for what they'd done to his first British show. And he hadn't been the only one, either. Julius Gerstein, for all his smiles and attempts to sign them, had proved himself a right East End rag-trade swine. Once Johnny decided to accept Steve Morash's offer, Gerstein had come out where his viciousness, his snide snipings could be anticipated.

The only bloke who'd been half-way decent about their grabbing viewing time and making headlines had been Mr Russell. He'd admitted how much they'd cost him personally. But he'd also admired their spirit, their pluck. He'd even gone so far as to claim some credit for getting them into the public eye.

'The ref's ready to blow,' Bruce remarked.

Johnny glanced at his new watch. A *Bulova*. Just like Steve wore. He'd bought a pair when he signed the contract to appear before a Coventry audience as a professional entertainer. One for him, the second for Gloria. 'About half a minute,' he remarked, trusting to the timekeeping guarantee.

Exactly thirty seconds later the final whistle blew.

'Rangers could have taken 'em both and won,' Peter said.

Johnny smiled benignly at an Arsenal bigwig. Nodded to a Spurs front-office supremo. 'Don't show your colours,' he hissed. 'Let 'em think this is the greatest thrill we've ever had . . .'

Peter Acroyd wiped disgust from his face, beamed. Bruce Barnes softened his disgust with a drawn result and tried to follow Johnny's example.

Five seats further away, Gloria Derrick got to her feet and made muttered excuses for going to Johnny's side. 'What the hell do we do next?' she asked, lost in this protocol demanding world they'd entered.

'Wait until some bastard invites us to have tea,' Johnny replied. 'Or until our car arrives.' He made the last sound like the best idea.

'I could do with a beer,' Peter said.

'You're too young,' Johnny told him.

'The sh . . .'

'Too young!' Johnny repeated firmly.

Peter scowled, moved into the background. He loathed the public image that said kids his age couldn't - mustn't drink alcoholic beverages.

Christ, his old man had allowed him to sup mild and bitter since he'd been ten. And if his father thought it right then why should some blue-nosed bastards make him wait another year?

'I don't see what's so special about this kind of life, Johnny,' Gloria complained. She missed the feeling of being closest to Johnny when the gang went somewhere together. She'd been forced to sit miles away from him during the game, just so she'd be odd-girl-out in a foursome of boresome plum-in-the-mouth bitches educated at some elite school or other. Prim little dears who wouldn't hurt a fly unless it was open.

'We've got to play it cool,' Johnny said, glancing round to make sure he wasn't being 'quoted'. 'I'm not sure what Steve has in mind, Glo.' He used their extra-special term of endearment to mollify her. 'He's a hot man when it comes to publicity . . . !'

'Yeah - terrific!' Gloria remarked acidly. 'He sets up this match and doesn't even come with us. What's he doin', eh? Drinking or having it off with some bird?'

Johnny laughed easily. 'Are you jealous?'

'Me - jealous of him?' Gloria sounded like she could reach the moon on the heat generated by Johnny's improper suggestion. 'I don't see any bloke 'ceptin' you.'

'What time is it?'

Gloria pulled back a sloppy sleeve, glanced at her new *Bulova*. She started to tell him the time and paused in mid-data. 'It's almost . . . ' She smiled, caught his inference. 'I love the watch, Johnny,' she finished lamely.

He smiled, placed an arm round her waist. 'And I love that outfit!'

'Do you?'

In all the years they'd been mates, Johnny couldn't recall Gloria ever looking so desirable. Not desirable in a sensual way. Just sweetly, attractively, well-dressed desirable. Like a film star viewed from afar and garbed in some fantastic creation to heighten her appeal.

'I bought it on Steve's advice,' Gloria said, posing naturally.

Johnny inclined his head, made a mental note to congratulate Steve. The Empire-line suited Gloria. The hair style especially. Not so severe as Peggy Lee now wore. But pulled back and heaped high to show off her pert face to advantage. He wondered how much the dress had cost. Knowing Steve and the places he frequented, it would come off expenses in the region of a hundred quid.

'The hell with cost,' he said aloud.

'What?' Gloria asked, frowning.

Johnny grinned, pecked at her cheek. 'Nothing, Glo . . . Did he have your face made-up by a beauty salon, too?'

The girl brightened. 'Yes,' she breathed ecstatically.

'Man, you should have seen the girls who attended to me!'

'Old or young?'

'You bastard!' Gloria kicked him lightly on the shin. 'If I ever catch you . . .'

'You won't,' Johnny assured. 'Steve had a long talk with me. Strange birds are out. It's you an' me . . .'

Steve Morash basked in televised glory. His idea had hit another publicity high-spot. The national news gave, as usual, Saturday afternoon's sporting coverage. And included a shot of Johnny Holland attending the Arsenal-Spurs match. Brief though the passing crowd scene was and the mention even briefer, it did establish Johnny as a 'soccer buff'. Or so the man from WORLD POPS had mentioned over drinks. An additional few thousand had been another credit, given freely by the same reporter.

Alone now, Steve searched himself for some meaning to this endless pursuit of publicity. It would not have been so bad if he - Steve Morash - got the spotlight. But he didn't. Always the fame and the adulation went to somebody else. Like Bobby Sharp or Johnny Holland. Never Steve Morash. Never the man who really counted.

He shrugged off a momentary complex.

His talent lay in gaining publicity, in promoting for another human being. He couldn't sing. Not a goddam note. He couldn't fake twanging a guitar. The only instrument he knew how to operate so that music came from it was a stereo - and, as any fool realised, a recording of some sort or another was required to make even that innocuous instrument work.

'Shit!' he said to the ceiling. 'Christ!' he said to the floor, swinging his feet off the bed and sitting bent over, head in cupped hands.

He felt in desperate need of company. Female company. He didn't want to be surrounded by babbling pop youngsters. Nor with those whose jobs depended on how many quotes they got about this or that groups' off-beat interests in birds, drugs or booze. He deplored those sickening parasites who infected the wounds of pop. Who fed on the shattered remains of weakened flesh.

Why don't they recognise that stars are people? he asked himself. *Ordinary people like me.* Guys and dolls with kinks. With appetites more healthy than those who glory in tearing them apart for one small mistake.

Shaking off his mood he poured yet another *Hundred Pipers*. He needed a bracer. A face-the-human-race-Scotch courage.

He grinned, spoke to his mirrored reflection. 'That'll hit the Dutch hard!' He toasted his image. 'To us, pal. To the sonofabitch who made us a little and to the Limey bastard who'll make us more!'

Hand poised for the second toast he frowned into the silvered-backed glass. 'Sorry,' he said and his eyes meant it. 'I've got to kick this Limey bit. It ain't right. *It ain't right!* Goddammit . . .' and he swung from the mirror now, pacing to the window overlooking the park. 'I've got to admit - *I like the English . . .*'

And, for just a fleeting second in time's lifespan, Steve Morash uttered a sentiment he honestly meant.

Jasmyn Ragg flung her coat across a chair and kicked shoes under it. Tomorrow she would be nineteen. A year older. No wiser and certainly not suffering from the 'sweet sixteen and never been kissed' kick. She'd been kissed. And more. She'd been everything pleasurable. But none of her varied experiences had touched bone. Touched the tendrils of her emotional seat.

She giggled, lit a cigarette. Maybe some of the guys she let play around could have aroused maternal instincts within her. She couldn't be sure any more. She didn't wish involvements. Didn't want marriage unless it was to a wealthy guy who'd pay alimony when she divorced him.

God, I'm greedy! she thought.

And then, she ground her cigarette into an ashtray. 'I'm going to celebrate,' she told the offending butt. 'I'm going to fling off the restraints. Let my goddamned hair down. Find a guy who'll wine, dine and please me. And then he'll pay handsomely for it, too . . .'

Which guy? a small voice asked silently inside.

Jasmyn removed her street dress, followed it with brassiere and panties. She let her long blonde hair fall loose. She rolled her stockings down each leg, then she postured before a mirror. What she saw she liked. A figure to make other girls blush with envy. An immodesty to make a stripper wink jealously.

Laughter ripped from her open mouth. 'Steve Morash,' she said aloud. 'He needs something to occupy his mind . . .' She paused, smiled seductively. 'And his hands!' she finished.

The idea of sharing Steve's bed did not appeal and she went back to sorting through a list of available men. She reached a grand total of one. Steve again. There had to be somebody else and, so, she recounted. Her votes fell in Mark Rowe's corner but she'd definitely finished with him. Most definitely. But there wasn't another man in her life. She couldn't count Johnny Holland although the kid interested her. She'd been directly responsible for bringing him his golden opportunity but, even so, that could not wipe out the sad fact he was underage. For her, anyway. She didn't wear cradle-snatching.

Then . . .

She remembered Steve's telephone conversation with her earlier in the day. *Doc MacMaster!* Why not? He was Canadian. Torontonian, too. They'd have lots to talk about. The Maple Leafs. Hockey and baseball versions. Politics. Comparisons to make. That was usually an all-embracing subject when compatriots were together.

Doc MacMaster!

She remembered him when, as a young girl, she'd watched television and listened to Foster Hewitt get all up-tight as the Leafs came roarin' in for a goal. And there was Doc - right in the centre of her screen. The best forward Canada ever produced. Including the Rocket, Ted Kennedy and Jean Belliveau. She didn't count Lindsay and Howe. They'd gone 'over' to play for Detroit.

Wouldn't it be fantastic if she landed Doc?

Jesus, she thought quickly, her mother would blow her stack if she had the slightest inkling. Mum had always doted on Doc MacMaster. Called him the sexiest thing on a pair of skates. More than one family row had started with mum's 'don't dare interrupt me when I'm watching the Doc' routine. Meals, visits, neighbours in for a coffee and talk, all went out the window of good intentions as a daffy female drooled over a televised personality.

She didn't drool. She just happened to have a more mercenary turn of mind than her mother. She enjoyed being with *great men*. *Distinguished* personalities. *Known brands*, as she preferred to call socialites and the famous. But that didn't include drooling. They were all the same full-length on a bed. Or almost so!

Before turning on her bath-water she telephoned Steve. Where could she locate Doc MacMaster, she asked. Steve's hinted crudities didn't stop her from repeating the question. She'd long ago reached the age when a man's innuendoes fell from her like water from a duck's spine.

She did, though, listen hard to Steve's final bit of advice. 'Don't you goddamned spoil what we've got cookin', Jasmyn,' he warned. 'Don't let Doc know we're linked. Not even by association. If you do . . . '

'Steve, I swear I won't divulge anything,' she said.

'Believe me, Jasmyn, when I say I'll make sure you're booted out of Britain if you do!'

Memory of work permits rushed in on her. Steve had accepted responsibility for her. Had guaranteed her job did not encroach on those positions a Britisher could fill. He had her in a corner with deportation round the bend.

'Okay, kid - have fun. Remember Doc's older than me so don't wear him out too much . . . !'

Jasmyn hung up, furious. She wouldn't go against Steve but she'd sure as hell make him eat that last crudity. She sure as hell would - if circumstances permitted . . .

Her hand was still shaking in fury when she dialled the Doc's hotel number. She had it figured. A friend of Steve Morash's. Her mother a fan. Her, too. And would Doc give her the honour of celebrating a birthday - one Torontonian to another . . .

Doc MacMaster cradled his telephone and smiled distantly. He was an old softie. It sure gave him a thrill hearing his grandchildren begging him to come home soon. He loved those youngsters. First thing he'd done on reaching London proper was to mail off a pair of 'Guides to London Town' and two models of Beefeaters. Airmail, yet. To keep a promise made at Malton Airport . . .

If only, he thought, *they'd been old enough when I was making headlines and capturing credits galore playing for the real Leafs!* He didn't go for the current team. Toronto wasn't the same when the Leafs failed to make the Stanley Cup playoffs. What a shame! What a goddamned cryin' shame!

He let his mind roam back to the 'old days'. *Hockey night in Canada - and the Leafs at the Gardens presented by Esso.* 'Happy motoring' - and Foster Hewitt doing the commentary.

God, maybe he could get the commercial channel here carrying the hockey!

The only problem was sponsorship. Britain hadn't developed enough yet to let sponsors put out shows. They depended on the creeps in the backroom presenting nudity, four-letter filth and everything a left-wing doctrinated group thought funny. Especially the 'government' channel. The one getting the cream of licence fees. Not like in Canada or the States where nobody paid a television fee. Where the government didn't ask for one. Where every network made money on its viewing rating and its general appeal and not on the basis of who knows whom and what little clique was presently guiding opinion.

Doc shrugged and helped himself to the first drink in four hours' tedium. He couldn't remember the tough years of depression but he knew how Seagram's had placed their ads. Bread, butter and roof first. Then, only if the money held out for a luxury - *V.O. in moderation.* He felt a company putting essentials before their product deserved his affluent support now.

Not that he, personally, had starved. Some guys had been compelled to work on road-building projects. Living in camps. Getting food and a meagre ration of roll-your-own tobacco per week. And five bucks sent back to keep the wife and kids. Just that. Until well after the war against Germany had started.

But not him!

Thankfully, his father had been a hockey player. Been able to support his kids and give them enough vitamins to grow into hockey players, too. Big kids. Hard kids. Nice kids . . .

When the telephone rang Doc grabbed it.

He listened to Jasmyn Ragg's plea, heard her infectious laughter come down the telephone wires into his ears when she admitted to deception. She was just nineteen. Tomorrow. And if she had to celebrate she wanted to share her far from home joy with Doc MacMaster.

Doc smirked in the unseen sanctuary of his room. He visualised how this Jasmyn Ragg looked. Recalled those pretty English girls walking The Strand, Charing Cross Road, Leicester Square, Fleet Street, Regent Street.

'A few drinks and that's it,' he said.

'No dinner?'

Doc laughed. 'Who pays?'

'If you insist - Dutch treat . . .'

'I don't insist. Where are you staying?' Even as he asked Doc knew he'd been suckered. And yet - he didn't care. He liked the voice pouring an address into his ear. He liked being famous again. One of the hockey greats again. *And they talk about 'ham' actors . . .*

CHAPTER THREE

THE floor of Julius Gerstein's office looked like a hurricane had swept through the room and deposited fashion drawings haphazardly across the plush carpet. Seated on his desk, legs dangling, Gerstein surveyed the disorder with a critical eye. He didn't see anything wrong with the way his tower block office looked. Quite the contrary. This was business and if making money meant disruption then he willingly suffered it.

Whatever else Julius was, he knew about clothing. Especially men's clothing. He possessed an uncanny ability to predict what men within the 15 to 30 age group would be wearing nine months in advance. He had the necessary insight, a flair for colour and the essential feel of cloth to keep him a jump ahead off his nearest rivals.

For Sammy Ric seated in a chair with pencil poised over a notebook, Julian was the greatest living expert on mod gear.

'We'll go for broke on these designs by Kemble,' Julius said. 'Have Ruth re-draw each showing the blokes wearing platforms . . . ' He wrinkled his nose, pointed at another batch of impressions. 'Bloody rubbish those! It's a waste of time doing business with Kirkham. Tell 'em I said so!'

Sammy nodded, made notes.

'When did Baxter say he'd show us his work?'

Sammy rifled pages, read: 'Tuesday afternoon'.

'Too late.' Gerstein snapped. 'Telephone him. I can't let it slide. I've got to have his preliminary shirt sketches this afternoon.' He swung his legs off the desk, kicked a drawing he disliked. 'Wait . . . ' He pulled his lower lip, thought fast. 'Change that. Only the casuals. I'm going to buy from Sovereign. They'll deliver on time.'

Sammy glanced up with admiration gleaming in his red edged eyes. This type of instant decision was what made Julius the great man leading the field, not a follower.

'Okay . . . okay, that's all!'

Getting quickly to his feet, Sammy slipped notebook and pencil into a pocket and gathered up the drawings. Without hesitation he left 'the presence' - thankfully aware that Gerstein's parting 'This afternoon!' meant he once again could act the role of sales manager.

Alone now, Julius switched his thoughts from the rag trade to showbiz. Its interests in both kept him busy. Made him a very wealthy man. Gave him power.

Punching a button on his inter-office speaker he spoke softly, firmly. 'Get me the Discodrome. I want Anka Shippe . . .'

Waiting for his secretary to connect him, Gerstein scowled at a newspaper on his ornate desk. Some of the print had smeared and was almost unreadable but the essentials were still clear.

'Johnny Holland signs new recording contract for Dolphin,' it said. *'Now, for the first time, enjoy the sound that knocked television off the air . . .'*

The body of the advertisement listed eight numbers. All available, it remarked, at department stores everywhere in the United Kingdom.

Two columns separated this from a write-up purporting to 'disclose' what made Johnny Holland the greatest thing on the pop scene.

The telephone interrupted Julius's furious thoughts. He grabbed the instrument, barked, 'Shippe?'

A voice like yesterday's bent wind lisped a reply. 'Yiss? Anka Shippe here.'

'Gerstein. Bring Narcissus to my office at five this afternoon.'

Shippe sounded alarmed. 'Is something wrong, Mister Gerstein?'

'I'll explain then. Be here sharpish . . .' Julius dropped the phone on its rest, smiled grimly. What he had in store for Johnny 'Bastard' Holland would shake the foundations of showbiz. He still hadn't forgotten, nor forgiven, the Acton kid for blowing a fabulous deal. The sudden appearance of Holland's 'Jolly Green Men' had blacked out Russell's television coverage of a Discodrome show and lost Gerstein a fortune.

By five p.m. Julius Gerstein had settled on a new line of casual shirts, seen the first drawing displaying platform soles and arranged for a consignment of cloth to get samples made up. His earlier mood had slightly evaporated but he was far from facing the world with a carefree expression. There was still the nasty taste of Johnny Holland in his mouth.

When the office door opened and Anka Shippe entered, Julius wanted to laugh. He didn't. Although the forty-year old singer had long since gone over the top, he had a following. Limited, admittedly. But large enough for Gerstein to collect a sizeable hunk of change every year as his percentage.

Anka stepped aside, waited fearfully as Narcissus followed him into the room.

'Take seats,' Gerstein commanded. 'Shut that door.' He hid another laugh. He knew how Narcissus dressed on stage but he hadn't honestly expected the other to roam London's streets in the same gear.

Anka took the lead, advanced timidly towards the desk. His orange slacks fell over buckled shoes, clashing violently with a green velvet jacket cut to show a trim figure. A face like a very buck-toothed rabbit's chinlessly wrinkled above a crimson shirt and gay floral tie.

Narcissus moved faster, with more assurance. He had the strut of stardom, the classical features of a Greek god, the height to still wear unfashionable drainpipe trousers. Except that his trousers shimmered, twinkled as ruby sequins dazzled on the silvery material. His frilled shirt hung open almost to his hairy stomach and the blue shadow round his eyes sparkled under the weight of golden stars glued there.

'Wotcher, mate,' Narcissus said with a deep voice that did not, somehow, go with the gear. Nor his face.

Ignoring the greeting, Julius got right down to facts. 'I've got a problem on my hands. I want it removed. I don't care how you go about it but I will not tolerate failure.'

Anka seemed to relax. Narcissus frowned, leant forward. Hair flowed over his eyes sheltering whatever thoughts lay behind their narrowed blueness.

'I'll guarantee top-billings for you both at three special shows in Discodrome,' Julius continued. 'I'll also arrange for a tour - headlined by Johnny Holland . . . !'

Anka Shippe giggled. 'And the Jolly Green Men . . . '

Gerstein frosted the aged songster. 'This isn't funny, Shippe. I don't have to explain what Holland did. How he got to the top. I will say, though, he isn't going to get away with a bloody thing.'

Narcissus brushed hair from his eyes and sat erect. When he smiled it reminded Julius of a girl. A pretty young girl expressing delight. 'You wants 'im done,' he said with a thick Birmingham accent.

Gerstein shook his head viciously in the negative. 'Not done the way you mean,' he corrected. 'I want him ruined. I want the little bleeder to suffer. To be toppled in disgrace.'

Anka sniffled. Long manicured fingers twitched on his orange lap. 'How do we . . . ?'

Julius Gerstein came to his feet, face black with rage. Leaning on his desk, bending forward, he snarled, 'Don't ask me. Don't tell me. Get results. You've got friends in the *business* . . . ' and he emphasised business with emotional nastiness, avoiding Narcissus as he did so.

'Ring them in. Make it a helluva party lined up against this Holland bastard. Okay?'

Narcissus got to his feet now, too. He didn't like the 'business' crack but he accepted it as he usually did disparaging remarks thrown by those who could advance his career. 'Leave 'im to us, mate,' he boomed. 'You'll 'ave the bleeder's 'ead on a platter.'

Gerstein smiled, let his rage simmer as he fixed Anka Shippe with a stare. He couldn't for the life of him grasp what made this ineffectual man a hit in so many quarters distantly removed from those clubs catering for 'specific' entertainment. 'You take orders from Narcissus,' he warned. 'I'll get started on the arrangements. You'll hear through the usual channels about a tour and dates.'

Walking to the office door, Narcissus hesitated. Turning, he splayed his arms with palms upwards. 'Do we give 'is mates the treatment, too?' he asked.

'The whole rotten bunch!'

Anka shuddered, let Narcissus drag him from the room. It was patently obvious how little the aged man wanted this assignment. How eager the 'glam boy' was to get cracking.

Alone again, Julius Gerstein frowned and went to the window from which he could gaze across the City. The view seemed to flow power through his being.

'The bloody types I've got to deal with,' he said aloud. 'Shippe's a weakling but Narcissus is a weed. Stronger than anybody'd think . . . '

In his digs, Narcissus went over every pop magazine he could find under the bed. He believed in keeping a year's issues handy. One never knew when information relating to another performer came in handy. Like this time . . .

He unearthed a picture of himself, drooled over it. Ever since childhood he had been mesmerised by his own image. He could remember posing in front of mirrors, gazing on his face with narcissistic delight. When he'd gone into showbiz the easiest thing he had ever done was select a stage name. *Narcissus* came straight from his heart.

He smiled to himself, tore the picture from the mag. There it was right across the glossy print - NARCISSUS. A better name than William Frederick Gibbons in his estimation.

God, what a laugh that would have been!

Willi . . . Or Freddy . . . And the Gibbons - a chattering monkey with long arms. Not for him. Not any more!

It was bad enough having a Brummagem accent without letting people get at him by name. Bad, too, being what he was!

He shrugged in a girlish fashion. He'd been 'one of those' as far back as he cared to retreat in life. But he'd never been a sissy. He could lick any three blokes in a street brawl. Had often come home with blackened eyes, bleeding nose, cut lip. And always in the knowledge the others fared worse than him.

'They don't seem 'ellbent on attacking us nowadays,' he said aloud, thinking about Anka Shippe, Tankard and some others he personally knew in the business. Maybe it was because the law had been changed to make it legal. Or because people were more educated to recognise a little of this, a little of that in themselves.

At twenty-five he'd had his share of setbacks and comebacks. Fighting against depressions and sarcastic bastards who'd done their damnedest to boot him out of Equity. Out of the pubs. Out of clubs. And then out of pop. But he'd shown them all. He hadn't battled as a kid for nothing. His tooth-and-nail rise to stardom had been accomplished by sheer guts. Plus letting them slap both cheeks as he applied more and more make-up.

Man, he really loved that scene!

Most other entertainers reckoned he was 'putting it on' for a gimmick. They didn't know he actually *wanted* to express his feelings in this manner. Those who knew didn't worry, either. If Anka had any guts he'd have done the same. But he didn't.

'That's not nice,' Narcissus said, staring down at an old photograph of his mate. 'You can't 'elp bein' soft, darling . . . '

The slam of a door somewhere in the house brought him back to the chore he had to do for Julius Gerstein. Angrily, he thumbed through the magazines, building a head of steam against Johnny Holland and his gang. It didn't matter what the publicity boys said - he suspected that Johnny had been mentioned sometime in some publication. Nobody shot to fame like that overnight. Not in his book, anyway. All he wanted was one small clue. One finger to point at his enemy. To start talk going the rounds. To weaken the oppositions very, very strong position.

And so, he kept looking. Searching. Growing more annoyed at every minute spent thumbing pages . . .

CHAPTER FOUR

JOHNNY HOLLAND knew there was something important in the wind when Steve invited him back to the hotel. Usually, after a strenuous recording session, Steve paid off the professional musicians who did the hard work and insisted Johnny and the lads went straight home. Not today.

'Listen to what I've got to say first, Johnny,' Steve said when they got comfortably settled in the luxurious suite. 'When you've heard me out you can criticise or agree with my finding - but not until. Okay?'

Johnny nodded. 'Fine with me, Steve.'

Lighting a cigarette, drawing his drink closer, Steve smiled. He didn't offer one of either to Johnny although he suspected his star indulged. Some things he prided himself on and one was never willingly to corrupt a minor. In this day and age that covered a lot of territory the kids considered old-fashioned guff but, nevertheless, Steve stuck to his guns.

'Right, Johnny - I've got a friend who is currently in London organising a hockey league . . . ' He saw Johnny's puzzlement and grinned. 'Ice hockey. The game they play in Canada and the States.'

'Oh!' Johnny said. He didn't know anything about the sport although what he'd seen of it on the telly looked exciting.

'This guy,' Steve continued, 'is an old-time professional player-turned-manager-turned-arena-owner. That doesn't mean anything to you but when I say he's loaded and got important connections I'm not kidding . . . '

Johnny smiled faintly. He wished Steve would swear more in his company. He knew the man did when he thought the 'Jolly Green Men' weren't around. He hated being treated like a young kid who wasn't supposed to see evil, speak evil, hear evil.

'Anyway,' Steve said, blowing smoke from his nostrils, 'Doc MacMaster - my friend - came to me with an idea. He has a solid promise for the construction of a new ice-palace *providing* he also builds a pavilion for putting on pop shows and the like. And that's where you and I come into this. Doc believes - and I agree - that ice hockey won't really catch on in England unless some famous personality gets the kids to take an interest. Which is my way of saying you, Johnny.'

As Steve got to his feet and went across the room to freshen his drink, Johnny let his thoughts run riot. He couldn't yet figure out what he was supposed to do but if there was a new place for pop shows and he had an 'in' then that suited him.

Returning with a new *Hundred Pipers,* Steve settled into his chair and said: 'I know how much you like soccer, kid. You and your pals. But I'm asking a big favour. Forget the Saturday games. Forget everything you've ever enjoyed and get to like ice hockey. I want you there, in the arena, every night the team plays. I want you yelling your goddam head off as if this sport is the only one in the world worth seeing.'

'Hell - no!' Johnny yelped. 'Me mates would do me if I asked them that!'

Steve sighed. 'What is more important to you, Johnny. Soccer or staying the teeny bopper idol?'

'Both!' came the instant reply.

'And money? Where does money come?'

'With the other two,' Johnny smiled.

'I can guarantee to double your annual take, kid . . . '

Johnny's eyes widened and his heart thudded.

'Doc MacMaster's a generous guy. He doesn't know from nothing about showbiz. He does understand money, though. How much a hockey player can make in a year. How much a percentage of the house is. And Doc's had a few sessions with me calculating to the bare bone the maximum he can afford to offer us *if* we go along on the deal!'

'How much?' Johnny asked.

'Five hundred pounds for every appearance at the hockey games. Two thousand per one-night stand!'

'For each of us?' Johnny asked in disbelief.

'For you, buddy-boy. You're the star. We scale down figures from here on for the group . . . '

'No, thanks,' Johnny said firmly. 'We get a fee and we split even.'

Steve looked exasperated. 'It just doesn't work like that, Johnny. All top singers take the largest cut. The backing boys know this and they're goddam glad to tag along for the ride.'

'We're different, Steve.'

'You are at the moment,' Morash explained patiently. 'It can't continue, though. Look at it this way - supposing something happened to your voice and singing was suddenly out of the question. The public wouldn't accept you as an ordinary guitar player. They'd stop buying records. They'd stop coming to shows. *But they wouldn't quit listening to your group!* That's the big difference, Johnny. A group can continue without the star and a star can keep plugging along without the same group. But a star without a voice is nobody. You could be the world's greatest musician but once the fans have accepted you as just a singer they won't allow you to change.'

'Blimey, I never thought of it like this,' Johnny said. 'Christ, I've been a stupid bastard.'

Steve shuddered mentally. All his worrying about language and Johnny gave a mouthful to prove what others had said - there ain't no pure-white angels in pop.

'Okay, Steve - have it your way,' Johnny announced, trying for the big star image.

'Including the ice hockey deal?'

'Ahhh . . . '

'Money, kid,' Steve teased.

'Lemme talk to me mates?'

'I must have a decision by tomorrow morning.'

'I promise,' Johnny said. He laughed. 'They ain't going to like missing football aggro . . . ' He coughed behind a hand to erase his last word.

Steve didn't bat an eyelid. He'd heard and filed 'aggro' away for future reference. But, for the moment . . . 'Explain about the cash,' he said. 'That should make them putty for you to mould.'

'What will they get, Steve?'

'Fifty each for the games. Two for a performance.' Steve watched closely for a reaction. He'd upped Doc's offer by fifty quid but he figured he could convince the hockey man of the wisdom of this.

'It's less'n . . . ' Johnny started to argue.

'Their split now?' Steve smiled. 'I agree. But it's bonce . . . ' He liked that. An English saying he'd heard used. One just right for this occasion.

Johnny couldn't quite decide. He didn't want to work out the mathematics. He'd always been a dope with figures. 'I guess it is, Steve,' he finally admitted. 'I'll tell 'em anyway and let you know first thing in the morning. . . '

Doc MacMaster nursed his pint and listened to Jasmyn enthuse about the pub with a fixed smile on his face. He had to admire the girl's effervescence, her natural beauty. He felt real proud seated opposite her knowing that some of the young guys there kept making eyes at her, furtively winked behind his back.

'They've got fabulous turns every night here,' she said.

'You know the kind - drag and the like.'

Doc squirmed. He hated drag acts. Loathed any man who wasn't a complete man. He didn't mention this, though. He was enjoying the pleasurable company. The unspoken, unconfirmed end of the evening's companionship.

'They've got a group called Tavern who're going on television next week . . .'

The pub was crowded. More people were obviously waiting for the acts than had come just to drink. Frantic bartenders tried to cope with orders which, in Doc's opinion, were far from the norm. He'd been sympathetic when he'd gone to order. A pint for himself and a *Babycham* for Jasmyn.

'Do you come often to watch this?' Doc asked.

'I've been just twice. Why?'

'I wondered, that's all . . .'

Jasmyn wagged a finger across the table. 'You're trying to discover what type of girl I am. Well, for your information, I enjoy drag acts. I like camp humour, too. But this doesn't mean I have to like the guys, does it?'

Doc grinned, took a long drink. He found the taste peculiar. Not bad. Strange, rather. There was definitely a helluva lot more body in a British beer than anything brewed in North America. 'I reckon not, Jasmyn' he replied. 'I find it difficult sorting out the boys and girls these days. All that make up . . .'

Jasmyn shrugged. 'I don't dig them all.'

'Whom do you dig?' Doc asked, interested now from a financial angle.

'Johnny Holland and the "Jolly Green Men", David Cassidy, Rick Springfield, Slade, Marc Bolan, Rod Stewart.' Jasmyn sat back, glass now empty. She could sense Doc's fumbling for something to say. She knew the man was lost in her pop world. Probably the only singers he could name were Bing Crosby, Perry Como and Andy Williams. Or, maybe, some of the old Country and Western stars of yesteryear. Cowboys like Roy Rogers, Gene Autry, Hank Snow, and the still top Nashville man, Tennessee Ernie Ford.

'I'll get another drink,' Doc said with a small laugh. An admission he didn't follow her scene.

'If we're staying for the show you'd better make that a couple each. Long drinks, too,' Jasmyn mentioned. 'You'll never get near the bar once the Tavern start their antics.'

'Good idea,' Doc said and pushed into the seven deep crowd.

218

Alone, Jasmyn cooled a guy's immediate approach. As he moved towards her she hissed: 'Get lost!' and glared coldly. Another youth with long dark hair got the same treatment when he winked suggestively. Although she was pleased to be the main attraction in her neighbourhood she still reserved her acceptance of any man for those with the bread to entertain her royally. Like Doc had done by taking her to *The Contented Sole.* She'd heard of the place but never visited it. Now she had, she'd be back again and again. Nowhere in the world had she ever been given such generous portions of fish for a main course. And what fish! Perfectly prepared, delightfully served. And the atmosphere . . . Sawdust, Edwardian clothes, and old, old music with the customers encouraged to join in and sing. Friendly, too. And so reasonably priced. She knew it was a tourist 'must' but that didn't take away from becoming a 'regular'.

She glanced down at her stomach to see if it bulged. She'd eaten so much she swore she had gained several extra pounds.

Doc returned, caught her glance. 'Pregnant,' he asked with a wide smile.

'I could be,' she laughed. 'God, I'm full . . .'

Doc indicated the beers. Four pint pots. 'They won't lessen the stretched feeling of your skin.'

Jasmyn pulled a woeful face. 'Thank goodness I don't have to wear a girdle. It would kill me.'

Doc expressed interest with raised eyebrows. 'No girdle? You amaze me. I believed all young things wore those these days.'

'Nonsense, sir!' Jasmyn raced her hands down her sides. 'All me. Well,' and she rolled her eyes provocatively, 'nearly all. A few items aren't . . . ' Her eyes twinkled mischievously. 'And don't ask me what *they* are!'

'I wouldn't dare. Not here!'

'Let's drink, eh?' Jasmyn wanted to leave him guessing. The more a man pondered before arriving at the homestead front door late at night the better chance a girl had of sending him packing minus what he'd started out to get. Or, if she decided to let him come indoors and make like an Olympics athlete, the wondering would serve to stimulate.

As Doc raised his pint a blast of music heralded 'Tavern' . . .

'My God!' Doc almost dropped his glass.

Tavern looked like, spoke like, acted like a bunch of frivolous schoolgirls. They wore gym-tunics, tennis shoes, black stockings, wide floral ties drooped down white blouses. Each had a school 'hat' balanced on long untidy hair. Each sported his/her own brand of make-up. All smiled with lipsticked lips. They even sang like girls, too.

'Christ - I don't believe it!'

Jasmyn giggled hysterically as she watched Doc's features pass through a series of bewildered expressions. She wondered what he'd say if he ever saw Narcissus . . .

'They're not . . . ?'

Jasmyn nodded. 'Sure they are. So what?'

Shaking his head sadly, Doc tried to watch the highkicking antics of Tavern as knickers came into sight. The worse they got the more inclined the man was to make excuses and take Jasmyn to another pub.

'You're not enjoying yourself,' Jasmyn mentioned.

'Are you?'

'Yeah!'

'Okay, that's fine. I don't mind, providing you . . . ' He stopped speaking. It was impossible to hear a single word now. What with the blasting sound coming from Tavern and the roars of encouragement from the crowd he reckoned it better to save breath and concentrate on his beer. One thought, however, raced through his head - he was past this generation. Way past. The gap of generations had widened remarkably in a few years.

CHAPTER FIVE

Pop 73 magazine said it . . .

ROD . . . from soccer to stage and stardom.

Rod Stewart's unique gravel-lined voice can do justice to practically anything, from the Mick Jagger-Keith Richard song 'Street Fighting Man' to the beautiful 'Man Of Constant Sorrow'. But ask the man himself how he feels about being a star and he simply says, 'I'm conscious of what I am, but I don't think I'm a super star'. Well, that might be his opinion but there are millions of fans the world over who would not agree.

Born in London on January 10, 1945, Rod Stewart started playing the guitar at an early age, although he cannot exactly remember when. He was also good at soccer and during high school played in the same team as Ray Davies, leader of the Kinks. Rod so excelled at his front line wing position that he was chosen for the Schoolboy International team and represented England in international matches.

Johnny set the magazine down. He enjoyed reading the snippets about pop stars even although he now got the opportunity to meet most of them in the flesh. For him, Rod Stewart represented something more than a great talent. Rod had been a football hero and that, as any Roundhead would agree, added to his greatness as an entertainer.

I wish I'd been a football star, he thought.

He had a lot on his plate at the moment and he washed his mind clean of speculations. He wanted some new music. Words to sing. Beautiful words like those in, say, *Snowbird*. It wasn't enough to resurrect 'oldies' and do another bloke's bit. A star had to have special songs, written exclusively for him.

Steve had done his share of searching. And, too, there were always the pluggers flogging this or that 'fantastic number' which usually meant something less than satisfactory going for a helluva fee. He wasn't taking into account the legitimate music publishing houses now. Ones able to win the Queen's award for industry and the like. But even they didn't seem to have exactly what he wanted.

He remembered seeing the Glenn Miller Story on telly. How Jimmy Stewart had searched for a 'sound'. And how, when he found it, the Miller magic gave birth to a cult.

That's what he wished he could find. A sound. A very special touch exclusive to Johnny Holland. A type of song, maybe, he alone sung. Something, anything, to set him apart from those other teeny bopper idols. It wasn't enough any more to be screamed at and adored by girls just slightly younger than himself. He wanted the whole world to sing his praises. From nine to ninety.

Funny, he mused, *how I'm changing. How I'm thinking of me - Johnny Holland - and not Johnny and the 'Jolly Green Men'*. He blamed Steve Morash for this. For the ice hockey deal that gave him top rating against the group.

God, the blokes had been furious about the deal!

No matter how he tried to explain the situation they'd refused to agree with Steve. As Peter had put it: 'I ain't bleedin' giving up football aggro for any bloody Canadian. And certainly not for ice hockey - jeeze, we couldn't belt a bloke in an arena like they've got!'

Johnny hadn't pushed them. Instead, he'd set up a meeting with Steve. Let their manager-agent swing 'em!

He wished to hell he could go out and enjoy himself. He had a yen for the old days when Acton meant action. Not this hibernation. Afraid to get caught up in a bunch of hysterical fans.

Steve had suggested he buy a house somewhere on the outskirts of London. Even deep in Surrey's stockbroker belt. He could afford it. All the guys could if they really wanted to get away from home. Steve had the authority to spend for them, to make parents listen.

Would he like living so far away from this area, though?

A section of his mind roared 'yes'. Another brought memories to the fore, coaxed him to say 'no'.

All the pop mags told how soon the big hit stars headed for the countryside and very decidedly went for rambling, ancient mansions. Steve had talked about tax reliefs and future investments. He didn't understand a bloody thing about finance although he recognised the need to do something drastic, and fast, about paying so much tax.

His earnings already showed huge slices going for nothing. Money he wanted to spend on himself, not immigrants getting social security. That's what he thought. If only the government would ask a bloke what he wanted done with the bread they snatched, most taxpayers would feel better, he figured. But they didn't. They grabbed and they lashed it out on keeping a bunch of foreigners in the country even although many Britishers were against them.

Christ, if I had my way . . .

Suddenly, Johnny smiled.

He had it by the short and curlies!

He'd been searching for a sound. Now - he had a gimmick.

One the Roundheads would cheerfully go along with, even if it did mean having to accept the ice hockey deal!

The more he pondered how to present the idea the better he liked it. He wasn't yet precisely certain of the tone. Nor how Steve would get it across to the Press.

The Press . . .

He laughed and slapped his thigh. Those reporters he'd met would turn on him like snarling wolves when they discovered what a strong racialist he was - but to hell with them, and their newspapers. Every bit of adverse publicity would build a fantastic following. He'd be hated by a lot of entertainers and he didn't give a damn. The main aim was fandom's acceptance and he figured he knew Roundheads, skinheads, boot boys and all their ilk enough to start counting record sales by the million. No matter what the Government or Opposition thought, Johnny was sure he had caught the basic need of his generation. And a lot of oldsters too.

Steve Morash almost flipped his cool when Johnny excitedly explained his gimmick. He listened in silence. He had to, Johnny ran off at the mouth like a fire-engine unable to stop for traffic lights until it reached the conflagration.

At last, Johnny sat back and grinned. 'Well, Steve - how about that, eh?'

'You honestly expect me to agree?' Steve asked in dismay.

'Sure! Don't you?' Johnny seemed puzzled by Steve's lack of enthusiastic support.

'It's insane. You'd be committing showbiz suicide. Can't you get it into your head - what you did or thought before hitting the charts doesn't count anymore?'

Johnny slammed a fist down on a coffee table. His eyes blazed. 'I'm not interested in what people think. Not the ones you're worried about. I'm all for making bread, man. For selling discs. For getting my fans to attend every show . . . '

'Yeah - terrific!' Steve interrupted. 'You'll be the fittest discard in the history of pops . . . '

'You are too weak,' Johnny said suspiciously.

'I don't love anybody. I don't hate anybody. I'm only interested in me. *You* if you insist on specifics. But what happens to you, Johnny, also happens to me. I make out okay on a percentage and a few expense account fiddles . . . ' Steve had to chuckle at his temerity. With Bobby Sharp he could never have admitted coining an extra quid from the expense-sheet.   With   Johnny   the   kid   expected   his agent-cum-manager-cum-friend to slice a few hundred off the top here and there. Johnny had a mercenary soul, a native cunning which said everybody nicked a little.

'So?' Johnny asked.

'So I'm not prepared to let you ruin a promising career,' Steve answered, the chuckle dead now.

'Look,' Johnny insisted. 'Look - they won't know who to blame. If we get some bloke to say he's responsible for the words I'm not to blame for singing 'em, am I?'

'The lyrics matter,' Steve said slowly, trying desperately to make himself understood. 'But it's the singer who gets the credit or the blame if they drop a clanger. Think about it, Johnny. How many stars are noted for the songs they make famous? How many are hit when somebody raises the roof like if the BBC banned a disc because it was not in the public interest to broadcast racial or obscene material!'

'I hate the way they've come over and . . . '

'Stop being so hung up,' Steve grinned.

Johnny took little notice. 'I want to give this a try, Steve,' he said forcefully.

Morash shrugged. It went against his grain to have one of his clients dictate policy but. . . 'Johnny, if we give it a whirl once and get adverse results will you listen to reason and drop the silly notion?' he asked.

'Yeah, Steve. All I want is a chance to prove I'm right.'

'Okay, kid,' Steve whispered almost. 'I'm found us a guy who can write goddam good lyrics. I've read some of his efforts. I've also got another musician in my sights. I'll arrange for them, to meet you - with me along as chaperon . . . '

He saw Johnny's inclined head, the quizzical gaze and explained: 'Making sure you don't go overboard on the racialist thing.'

CHAPTER SIX

NARCISSUS had it made. *Trust Julius Gerstein to arrange a behind-the-scenes coup de grace,* he thought happily. Johnny Holland on the same bill with Tavern, Anka Shippe and himself. He wondered how the hell Gerstein had pulled the strings. Steve Morash was an astute agent-manager and not one to fall into line when Julius whistled. There had to be a third party sympathetic to his boss. Or else, a promoter who owed Julius a helluva big favour. Maybe even money.

Contrary to expectations, Johnny Holland had come from nowhere to grab the spotlight at Discodrome's fiasco on television.

'At least Tavern are going to slaughter the bastard,' Narcissus said aloud. When he heard his own voice he glanced round, smiled grimly. He still hadn't quite got used to having dressing room privacy. Not that he gave a hoot in blazes who happened to be around when he changed or made up. Modesty had never been one of his vices.

Tavern . . .

They'd been his stroke of genius. His frontline troops. The ones to cause aggravation as he got to work backstage, so to speak.

Especially Lonnie McGovern. The Irishman had a way of causing trouble and appealing to the spectators as if he was the blameless innocent. Usually the ruse worked. Not many showbiz personalities believed what a newspaper columnist had once claimed . . . 'McGovern is the nastiest individual in a group dedicated to disharmony in the business'.

Anybody who reckoned his kind were pushovers had another thing coming once they saw McGovern in action. He could remember one occasion . . .

They'd been jostled and pushed getting to the wings. It had been in the early days - a mixture of camp and legit stars putting on a charity performance for homeless families of four or more kids. McGovern had been drinking, too. A bad thing before a show in Narcissus's opinion but a scene carried to extremes by the entire Tavern group.

Then The Aussies had come barging forward. Big, hefty blokes. Brash to boot. Giving their time free, gratis. Feeling like they were headliners. Which they were, in an unbilled way.

McGovern had taken exception, voiced a few insults.

One Aussie had sneered, made remarks about the school girl outfit the Irishman wore. Laughingly quipped about 'not dating dames who used too much lipstick'.

McGovern hadn't even given a warning of his intentions. His fist closed, swung, landed like a steam-hammer on the Aussie's jaw. And then, before the other Aussies could act, McGovern's pointed shoes went to work. His fists swinging like windmills in a follow-up attack.

When the big men from Down Under recovered they took terrible revenge. But they went on stage minus their tenor. As they did for their next two performances . . .

Narcissus was grieved and had a few private thoughts for Holland's destiny.

He applied blue shadow to his eyes, got out the box with the golden stars. One by one, meticulously arranging each, he adhered the stars. He gazed into the rectangular mirror.

A tremor raced through him, his hand actually shook as he used a brush to apply lipstick, curving his mouth into a desirable blow. A dab of powder removed the last traces of manhood - a very faint beard shadow. He really would have to shave minutes before each show, he mused. He didn't like the daily growth but short of suffering untold agonies there was nothing he could do about it. He didn't fancy the cure - skin grafts from his arse onto his cheeks and chin. Okay for those RAF blokes during the war that was supposed to save humanity from its dictatorship enemies. But not for him. He wasn't any bleedin' fighter-plane hero. Not even a bomber crew conscript.

He could hear music blasting away outside the droning room. He had five minutes before his appearance. Quickly now, he got into his strides - metallic silver, sequinned galore. He slipped on the shocking pink shirt with the almost Elizabethan frilled front, the monstrously hanging, laced cuffs. Three buttons done left most of his hairy torso displayed - one concession to those who sometimes rejected too much drag gear. Next, a golden, tartan vest - the tartan divisions formed by smaller sequins.

A loud knock on the door startled him. He lifted a leg, tied his platform shoes one by one. The door opened, McGovern entered.

'Don't do that, dear,' Narcissus growled.

Nervous, ducks?' the Irishman asked with a smile.

'Bleeding right, mate.'

"You're on . . . '

Narcissus postured. 'ows it look?'

'Fabulous, bhoyo! A beautiful doll in a t'in glass cage!'

Narcissus tossed his head, rolled his eyes, 'You're only sayin' that 'cause it's true,' he quipped and went to the door.

'You seen the bill fer Torbay?'

'Yeah!' Narcissus breathed heavily, barely able to hide his thudding heart noise. 'Ain't it bleedin' marvellous?'

'I'll do the little . . . ' McGovern held up a hard fist which, somehow, seemed incongruous when taken against his schoolgirl gear. He hadn't yet put his wig on and unkempt hair added to the incongruity.

'Make sure you do, mate,' Narcissus snapped. 'Look - get the others after this show and I'll stand drinks.'

'Get you, ducks,' the Irisher chortled, 'Lashin' out.'

Narcissus frowned. His reputation for being tight hurt deeply. He wasn't free with his cash, he knew. But neither did he stint when entertaining 'friends'.

'Ah, Jezu . . . Go on! Don't miss your cue . . . '

Shrugging and tossing his head, Narcissus strode off towards the stage front. *Sometimes*, he thought, *I detest that bloke's crudity. So anti-social. So typically country Irish. Pigs in the parlour type. Loutish. Yet, a battler and part of a rave group.* A man to keep in with even if doing so brought him - Narcissus - into disrepute with Anka and their really close pals.

Steve Morash studied the bill for Torbay's first of the season pop concerts. He was far from happy about the acts sharing the spotlight with Johnny Holland. He felt inclined to withdraw his boys from the show. Only the presence of what he termed legitimate performers made him reconsider.

He didn't like Anka Shippe. Nor Narcissus. He definitely deplored Tavern's presence. He'd heard about them from Jasmyn Ragg, even ventured to catch their act. And gone away disgusted. He didn't object to their drag but he did feel the songs they sang were particularly obscene. Too suggestive. Beyond the limits of decency. He hated to contemplate what their mentality was like.

Norris Drumm had, in his estimation, committed a gigantic *faux pas* promoting a show so unbalanced. It was positively loaded with midnight characters.

No doubt, though, the new Torbay hall would be packed to overflowing. And not just with teeny bopper fans there to scream for Johnny Holland. There'd be the Narcissus lovers. The Tavern yobbos out for cheap kicks. The Shippe oldies grinning toothlessly as the old fag went through his ancient routine in his high-pitched, sickening voice.

Did he honestly dare let Johnny come into contact with the group?

He didn't know. And decided to test opinions . . . Jasmyn and Becky Wilmott would have ideas. After all, they worked to promote Johnny on every show. They whipped up support and got to hear what the coffee bar youngsters had to say. They, more than he, knew the score!

The hired car slowly toured the Farnham area, its driver making no attempt to speed. He had his instructions. *Show the guys every property on this list.* Mr. Morash had been very adamant. 'No matter what they say don't you take orders from anybody but me! Arrangements have been made. They get shown over each house!'

Johnny didn't mind. Peter didn't, either. Only Bruce seemed disgruntled, bored, ready to return to his beloved Acton.

'If I see another bleedin' house I'll scream,' Bruce snarled.

'Don't you want to better yourself?' Johnny asked sarcastically. 'Man, I could really go for having one of these . . . '

'Me, too,' Peter quickly said. 'I liked that big red-brick pad. Christ, wasn't that swimmin' pool huge?'

'Go drown yourself in it then,' Bruce snapped.

227

'What a grouch!' Johnny smiled, nudging Peter. 'If he didn't have a bloody penny he'd gripe like mad. I've heard him sayin' about wealthy landlords and how he'd buy a swell place . . . '

'Talk!' Bruce replied. 'Blokes talk like that.'

'You meant it, you bastard,' Peter rubbed in.

Bruce turned, faced his mates. A strange expression filled his face, darkened his eyes into molten pools. 'Maybe I did but, man, the more I see of this countryside the more I miss bloody London. There's somethin' 'bout the Big Smoke . . . '

'You've said it,' Johnny sympathized, understanding how it could be. 'But we've got loot. We've got a chance to escape from one-up-one-down. So what if we miss our old mates? Jesus, we can't stick there all our lives.'

'I can and will,' Bruce affirmed.

'Not me!' Peter retorted just as firmly. 'I want a big house and servants. I want a gardener and a chauffeur.'

'Hey, you haven't won the bleedin' pools,' Johnny told him.

'Nearly as good,' Peter grinned.

The car swung off the road, turned into a long driveway. Trees breathed in the slight breeze, waving leafy branches across the tunnel-like entrance. Just visible now, as the car slowly rounded a gentle bend, was the largest home they'd yet seen. A Georgian mansion with at least ten windows split by a portico-ed door. A solid, imposing construction fronted by green lawns and tended flower-beds.

'Oh, God!' Johnny gasped.

'Crikey . . . ' Bruce exclaimed.

'Too bloody huge,' Peter said, mind still enraptured by the visions of the red-brick house.

'There must be fifteen bedrooms,' Johnny muttered.

'You could house the whole bleedin' street in that,' Bruce ventured.

The car came to a halt outside the front entrance. Out to one side of the house were garages for six cars. A stable block. An enormous greenhouse. Outbuildings for the gardener and his equipment. A walled kitchen garden nestled behind these, its brown earth and growing plants just visible through a pseudo Norman-arched doorway.

'Oh, Lord - it's . . . It's something!' Johnny said, sold on the property already.

'It's a palace,' Peter agreed.

'A bloody barn of a pad,' Bruce said to dampen their enthusiasm.

A man appeared at the front door, smiles wreathing his salesman's features. He came towards the car.

'Don't let 'im flog it to you, mate,' Bruce warned.

'Depends on the price, don't it?' Johnny remarked and quickly got from the car. He could feel the atmosphere 'attacking' him. It was with difficulty he contained his bubbling desire to rush indoors and marvel at the splendour he suspected was sheltering behind those facade walls.

'The son's gone,' Bruce lamented.

'Yeah . . . ' Peter decided. He'd have the red-brick house. But he wanted to view this one too just to have a comparison, just to satisfy himself he had made the right choice . . .

CHAPTER SEVEN

PETER ACROYD slammed from his home, spat at a blowing piece of dirty paper. A scowl darkened his features, fists formed on his hands and his knuckles whitened. 'Bloody people!' he snarled. Bashing hated heads would have made him feel better.

What the bleedin' hell does my old man know about anything? he asked himself. The rage inside rolled into a volcano of torrid emotions. He viciously kicked a stone. Watched it streak straight for a dog, just narrowly missing the creature.

He reached Johnny's abode. Standing outside, wondering if he should knock or keep walking along the street until he found an outlet for his bitter frustrations, Peter saw a movement behind the front room curtains. They parted and Johnny's hand beckoned him in.

'What's wrong?' Johnny asked as he opened the door to admit his mate.

'My old man,' Peter snapped, thrusting past into the hall. 'The bleeder won't let me buy my house . . . '

'Christ - why not?'

'Says I'd be wasting my lolly. Says I only wants it 'cause all the bastards in showbiz have to get big expensive pads to attract birds and have drug parties.' Peter's face broke, tears formed in both eyes. 'Jesus, Johnny - I've got to have that bloody house! It's my money. I can afford it, you said.'

Although he felt for his mate, Johnny's upbringing did not permit of such outward displays of emotion as placing an arm round a shoulder or offering token commiserations. All he said was: 'Steve'll know how to handle the bastard. Leave it to him.'

Peter nodded half-heartedly. 'What about you? Did you tell your people?'

Johnny grinned, putting the screws on Peter's dilemma. 'Yeah. Dad's delighted. Says he wouldn't come between me and this chance.'

'Christ, you're lucky!' Peter dropped into a saggy chair, heard the old springs groan complainingly. 'I'd like to round up the boys an' get an aggro going!'

Johnny's eyes narrowed. 'Quit talking like that.'

'Like what?' Peter asked defensively.

'Aggro, is what. We don't make that scene now, man.'

'You don't but I bleedin' do,' came the harsh reply. 'Don't you even miss the odd punch up?'

'Yeah,' Johnny admitted sadly.

'Then come on - let's go start one down in Chiswick.'

'If we're caught . . . '

Peter laughed. 'So the fuzz take us into court and we get fined. We've got the bread for fines. And nobody ain't gonna bother. After all,' and his face contorted into a cunning mask, 'you're going to sing the *Aggro Addict* number tomorrow, ain't you?'

Johnny nodded thoughtfully.

'Well, then,' Peter encouraged, 'an aggro today'd be the thing, man. Give the song some bloody feelin' I say.'

The bottled up inside desires to unleash ex-skinhead violence on some unsuspecting immigrant sent Johnny Holland racing for the front door. Racing down the Lane into Chiswick. Racing to undo all that Steve Morash's crash course of instruction had achieved.

Almost . . .

But not quite!

'I want to, Peter,' he said slowly. 'I want to get me boots out and put on a pair of braces again. But I can't. We can't. None of us . . . '

'Shit on that,' Peter yelled, jumping to his feet. 'I'll wager Bruce and the others won't be chicken! You've grown away from us Johnny. The blokes don't speak about aggro anymore 'cause you're against it. But they want a real punch-up. They've got to stay as they were. Me, too.'

Johnny fretted and fumed. His every instinct urged him to go along with Peter's craziness. To kick over the traces of Steve's insistence he avoid, like a dozen plagues, anything smelling of violence. Of Roundhead tactics.

'You're yellow,' Peter accused.

'That bleedin' does it!' Johnny growled. 'Come on! I'll show you.'

Steve Morash had the driver's report and the telephoned enquiries from two estate agents regarding deposits and legal representation. Now, with contracts spread on a table, Steve checked them carefully. He wanted to be absolutely sure of his rights, of the small print standing - in legal terms - of the parents. Regardless of what the lawyers had written into each separate contract, Steve wanted to have the Hollands and Acroyds verify their agreement to the pending purchases.

He didn't anticipate trouble. Even if there were dissentions he figured himself capable of fast-talking the boys into new homes. The investment angle alone must weigh heavily with people whose entire lives had been spent in working class semi-security.

Satisfied the contracts were in order, that he could use as a last resort - his power-of-attorney granted by the boys' folks, he got to his feet and slipped into a sports jacket. But first . . .

He took another look at the pictures of a 'cottage' down in Hampshire. *Cottage* . . . He grinned. Trust the English to call a six-bedroomed, three reception rooms residence within an acre of land a mere cottage. Back home in the States this would have rated a real estate agents tag of 'sumptuous dwelling. Country estate. Palatial, spacious. Larger than a house . . . '

His eyes lit on the price. £37,500.

He didn't need to hesitate. His share of the most recent recording contract gave him the down-payment. His percentage from estimated earnings for the next two years would pay off a mortgage. And he could live on what he made by padding expenses.

Living in hotels was past history for Steve Morash now. According to the solicitors for the seller, he could have vacant possession within three weeks. Always providing, they'd added, he paid the required £15,000 immediately.

That was a laugh!

In a way it was ridiculous. Pop stars making more than Cabinet ministers. More than the Prime Minister. More than some industrialists responsible for keeping huge organizations going; thousands of men employed. Even managers and agents salting away fortunes quite a few tycoons would have considered well within their range.

He could certainly afford fifteen thousand.

And he had the letter to mail agreeing terms, asking particulars for the exchange of deeds and deposit. He also had typed letters notifying Johnny's and Peter's agents they wished to go ahead on the deals for their respective houses. All those required were the counter signatures of the parents.

His intention was to mail all three from Acton. After he'd reached there by a devious route which would take in some London sights he'd been too busy to sightsee as yet. A drive through the park, into South Kensington, past Earl's Court and the Olympia, through Hammersmith.

Anyway, he wanted to have a better idea of where his 'clients' came from, what kind of surroundings they had known during the formative years. The night he'd gone to talk their parents into signing contracts had been dark, and his mind far removed from taking in the scenery. Well, it was daylight and he'd soak in atmosphere . . .

As he walked past Turnham Green station, Johnny hummed the music of *Aggro Addict* to himself. *What a hit it should be*, he thought. *A real skinhead rave!*

Scattered words flitted through his mind between comments from his mates . . .

'This is the story of a skinhead youth,
Who like a hero fought;
He looked for aggro everywhere
And every danger sought . . . '

Peter Acroyd started laughing. 'Christ, I just thought of a joke . . . '

Bruce frowned. 'You watch telly too much, mate,' he said.

Johnny tried to catch the next lines of the song, found them slipping away. His only worry about the lyrics was their ballad tone. Personally, he approved of the writer's attempt to make the skinhead cult appear as a 'knight-in-shining-armour' grouping of blokes sharing common notions - but would skinheads accept this? He hoped so.

'I don't get all my jokes from the telly,' Peter complained.

'From the grave, then,' Mick chortled, cutting in for the first time. 'Jesus, they're so old . . . '

Johnny closed his ears. He had to fix the words in his conscious mind . . .

'The eyes were staring from their sockets,
The mouth it ghastly grinned,
And there was a gash across the brow,
The scalp was nearly skinned!'

'Look!' Bruce yelled.

Johnny gave up. It was an impossibility to concentrate with the gang doing their collective nuts over one pathetic Asian youngster.

'Where there's one there's got to be another,' Peter remarked.

The Roundheads formed a close-knit defensive unit - walking the pavement like an army patrol in Ulster; ever alert, ready for trouble.

A dog darted from a smallish front garden, yelping and leaping. A toddler followed its pleasure romp. A woman raced from the house, grabbed her child, carried it back indoors. The dog, deprived of company, came towards the strangers - ears flattened suspiciously.

'Git away!' Mick roared.

The dog inched backwards. Tail down now.

'Grrr!' Bruce yelled, stamping his foot. As the dog turned and bolted into its house Bruce roared with laughter. 'Flea-bitten coward,' he chuckled.

'Where's the aggro?' Peter asked.

Johnny prayed they wouldn't come across any. He wanted to get back to learning the words of his song. Didn't wish to get caught up in an aggro that could make headlines. And that's what it could be. They'd reached the main road now. The police station wasn't far away. A Catholic church stood on the opposite side and he could see a priest talking to some of his faithful on the steps. All things against a daylight punch-up!

'Well, well,' Bruce sighed, pointing.

The man was in his thirties, casually dressed and walking slowly towards them. His greased black hair alone stamped him as a person from the Far East. His dark skin completed the picture.

'A very nice bloke,' Peter yawned mockingly, dusting off his knuckles on his trousers. 'A Pakki, so help me!'

A cab drew into the kerb, a man got from it. Paying off the driver he started walking. Suddenly, he broke into a run. His arms waved, his voice thunderous as he called: 'Hold it, Johnny . . . don't!!'

Johnny heard the voice and swung. His heart slowed to a decent beat. The others, too, hesitated and turned to face the newcomer.

'If you lot were goin' to do what I think you were it's a goddamned good job I arrived in time,' Steve Morash snarled. 'Christ Almighty, can't you get it through your thick heads this is out?'

The Pakistani came level with the group, glanced at Steve gesturing wildly and smiled. Shaking his head, blissfully unaware of how close he had come to a beating, he continued unmolested.

Peter glared after the immigrant. Bruce fidgeted. Mick and the rest shuffled their feet resentfully. Only Johnny seemed relieved.

'I'm not going to lecture,' Morash said. 'I'm here on business. *Your* business! Have any of you mentioned buying properties to your parents?'

Johnny nodded eagerly. 'Yeah - it's okay for me.'

'Me old man won't hear of it,' Peter growled, the aggravation now directed towards his father.

'None of us wants to move,' Bruce said, getting a cue from his other Roundhead-Jolly Green Men mates.

Steve didn't mention the fact he already knew there were but two of his clients willing to take the first, important step away from the area which could hold them forever down. Instead, he withdrew the letters he wanted signed from his pocket and grinned. 'We'll see how long your father holds out against me, Peter,' he remarked.

'You won't be wantin' us along, Mister Morash,' Mick said fast. 'We'll just shove off . . . '

'You won't!' Steve barked. 'You're not getting out of my sight until we get things straight between us . . . '

'Ah, hell,' Mick exploded. 'I don't have to be treated like a bleedin' kid.'

'Would you rather I released you from showbiz then?' Steve asked. 'I'm willing. You see, boys - I don't handle creeps. I don't stick my neck into any noose for any thug bastard!'

Johnny grinned. Morash had to be boiling inside to swear. It was going to be an interesting get-together. One packed with endless possibilities. One destined to keep them as a group or bust him into the clear as a solo star. 'We can talk at my house,' he suggested much to Mick's disgust.

'Right! Let's go . . . ' Steve waved them ahead, pausing long enough for Mick to fall docilely into line . . .

CHAPTER EIGHT

BECKY WILMOTT waited for Johnny Holland to appear on stage as trip-hammers exploded inside her head. She sincerely wished him every success although she worried about the song he intended to sing. She thought, my God, why hadn't Steve put his foot down hard and forbidden this! Looking round at the audience jam-packing the large hall she doubted if they would appreciate a skinhead battle-cry. They'd done their nuts for Narcissus. Bacon and Rind had nearly lifted the roof. Even aged Anka Shippe had met with moderate success.

But Aggro Addict . . . She didn't think it would receive applause!

On the other side of the restless fans, Jasmyn Ragg sat motionless, ears wide-open. Steve hadn't sounded happy but his orders to memorize every comment expressed about Johnny's performance had to be obeyed. A lot depended on what she and Becky overheard. A helluva lot!

The ice hockey deal, for one.

And those mansions Johnny and Peter had gone out on a limb to get. One more act and then.

Becky caught Jasmyn's gaze, smiled faintly. Across the distance of the hall the tension they felt seemed to jump like an electric arc, sparked both into nervous activity.

Backstage, there was more than tension. A current like an atomic generator going berserk flowed through the several performers waiting in the wings.

Coming from their dressing rooms, Johnny Holland and his backing group sensed the unusual build-up. It was impossible not to notice the stone-eyes fixed on them, the unsmiling stepping back to let them through. Even the electricians and stage hands appeared less inclined to partake of the normal well-wishes.

'Somethin's wrong,' Bruce muttered.

Johnny's gaze swung to Tavern. An old familiar crawling down his spine reminded him of pre-aggro moments on the terraces. 'Unhook your guitar,' he whispered.

Like soldiers fixing bayonets the Jolly Green Men quickly switched their instruments from across shoulders into left hands.

Lonnie McGovern noted the preparedness and frowned. He enjoyed getting in a telling first blow before his enemy was even remotely aware of a forthcoming assault. He studied Johnny Holland. About his size and build. Younger and certainly not in his judgement a fist-fighter. But sturdy and quite capable of taking good care of himself in a brawl.

'Do we wait or let 'em have it before they go on?' Ian Donaldson asked.

Johnny drew level with Lonnie.

'Make one bleedin' move and I'll turn you over,' the teeny bopper idol said softly.

McGovern hesitated, fist by his side. He didn't care for the glint in his opponent's eyes. Nor the deadly threat. Another thing that got him was the way the backing group had silently paired off with his Tavern mates. As if each had a mission and maiming the outcome.

'Well?' Johnny hissed.

McGovern forced a grin, unclenched his fist.

'Get the hell back,' Johnny snapped, feeling cocky.

'Yeah - sure!' McGovern half turned away.

Johnny relaxed, certain he had won the verbal conflict.

McGovern wheeled like a snake about to strike. His fist formed, shot out . . . bounced off a guitar as Peter Acroyd stuck his instrument between the contestants.

Johnny growled deep in his throat, his foot slamming under the guitar's bulbous end straight into McGovern's groin. He didn't hear the injured Irishman's anguished scream. A blast of sound from on-stage drowned all but the yelled word Peter let rip . . .

'AGGRO!'

Tavern didn't stand a chance. The annihilation of their foremost fighter left them wide open for the Roundheads' concerted attack. Peter's guitar slashed round, knocking Ian Donaldson off-balance. Set him up for a vicious kick. Bruce, too, acted fast. His guitar jabbed into a cosmeticised face, knee following into the pit of the defenseless stomach.

An electrician shuddered, dropped his gaze to the floor. He couldn't stand the sight of this slaughter. It reminded him of France - of watching freed P.O.W.'s take revenge on their German masters.

Johnny smiled grimly, waited patiently for McGovern to struggle to his feet. It gave him a high degree of satisfaction to let the other come erect before unleashing fists and feet in a savage display of skinhead brutality.

'Jesus Murphy,' McGovern gasped, sinking to his knees, hands clutching injured parts. Blood spurted from a broken nose, spilling down his schoolgirl's tunic.

'Okay,' Johnny yelled. Grinned when he realised the music had stopped and his voice could be heard like a foghorn blasting a warning across the entire Channel. 'Okay,' he repeated softer. 'Let's get out there . . .'

Further back in the wings, Narcissus scowled. He hadn't anticipated this outcome. His plans would have to undergo drastic re-thinking. And, too, excuses would have to be prepared for Julius Gerstein. He didn't doubt for one second that a full report of the action would arrive on Gerstein's desk by the next morning . . .

For the second time the chorus ripped into the stunned audience . . .

'I'm a skinhead boot boy,
A hard man to beat . . .
A real aggro addict,

The toughest down our street!'

Becky curled up inside. The frenetic screams from those who liked the tag 'teeny boppers' had dropped away to a semi-silent ripple. It was as if each member of the huge crowd was hanging on every blood-splattered word. Unable to do more than listen.

He's killed his act, Becky thought.

Throwing arms into the air, Johnny let the final guitar twangs signal the end of his number. He could sense the audience reaction, got creepy crawlies on his spine. *Maybe Steve had been right all along!* Like lightning, he made his decision. 'Play *Cling to me . . .*' he told the group. 'And make it fast!'

Smiling widely, he went to the edge of the stage apron, ready to give his all in a desperate effort to erase his previous number from their minds . . .

'JOHNNY . . . OH, JOHNNY!'

Becky sat upright.

Jasmyn wailed. It took more than one voice to signal acceptance.

'OHHHH!'

'AGAIN, JOHNNY . . . *AGGRO ADDICT* AGAIN!'

As if the teeny boppers had been suddenly shaken from slumber the hall erupted. Screaming, leaping, crying girls yelled, clapped, pleaded for another chorus.

Becky slowly relaxed. *By God - he'd done it!*

Jasmyn smiled, unable to believe that the improbable had become the truly possible. She didn't wear the number as a song but if the fans wanted Johnny's choice then, by all that was in her to promote him, that's what they'd get. Johnny held his hand aloft to silence the first bars of 'Cling to me'. Behind him, their fears no longer evident, the Jolly Green Men basked in the glory that was specifically Johnny Holland's.

CHAPTER NINE

NELSON HAMPSHIRE'S column in the 'Mercury' had always been acclaimed as the foremost commentary on the pop scene. Read nationally, it got into more homes than any six of the leading magazines covering the antics, releases and gossip of those involved in entertaining youth.

The morning after the tune burst upon the pop world as a song to be reckoned with, Nelson Hampshire had this to say . . .

'In five inglorious minutes, Johnny Holland accomplished what ex-skinhead mates failed to do in five years of terrace terrorism.'

Spreading his 'Mercury', Steve Morash settled back with a much-needed *Hundred Pipers* and soaked in Hampshire's vitriolic criticism.

'It is my opinion that this song should be brought to the attention of the Race Relations Board and anyone daring to sing it slapped down with a legal injunction.

'We have seen, in varying degrees, gimmickry taken to extremes by those unable to win fans by legitimate talents but never- and I repeat, never - have I witnessed such total disregard for . . .'

Steve finished his drink fast. His head swam. His eyes no longer able to separate the words as visions of impending disaster zoomed into focus. God damn, Johnny! So, okay. The audience had gone wild for the number. Had kept Johnny on stage fifteen minutes longer than scheduled. Had made him sing it four times before they'd had a bellyful.

But an audience captivated by the personality didn't count when it came to getting a recording company to undertake making a disc. Or fans scattered far and wide to buying the product.

Compelling himself to read the final paragraph, Steve shuddered.

'We can do without Johnny Holland and his skinhead songs. We don't want our children tainted by a bigot's blatant begging to attack a minority group. For myself, I shall refuse to publicise this artist until he sees the folly of his vicious ways'.

The telephone rang. Steve tossed the newspaper on his bed, reluctantly lifted the receiver . . .

Three minutes later, pouring another *Hundred Pipers,* Steve considered the day from his hotel suite window. Warm and sunny. Mellow and fantastic.

Funny, he thought, *how one man's meat is another's poison!*

Contrary to Nelson Hampshire's expectations, Johnny's recording company wanted to cash in on his adverse publicity immediately. The executive who'd called believed they had a golden disc on their hands. 'We had the boys there yesterday,' he'd said. 'It's terrific. A live performance. We think the second rendition comes across best. The teeny boppers don't let up for a bloody second . . .'

First, though . . . Steve left the view, went to his wardrobe. He had an important appointment with an estate agent. About his cottage. His mood was more conducive now than it had been reading the 'Mercury'. Once he moved in he would be within twenty miles of Johnny's home, twelve from Peter Acroyd. He smiled walking to the suite door. It had been a satisfying battle with old man Acroyd. The labourer hadn't given in easily - but he had eventually. No matter what happened to change the man's mind now he had committed himself in writing. By signature. Relieving Steve of the necessity of taking the affair to law.

Doc MacMaster gently set his newspaper on an empty chair and concentrated on his breakfast. Nelson Hampshire's column upset him. The edge was off his hunger. He toyed with the eggs and bacon, barely tasted the one slice of toast he ate. He didn't know what to do. Wished he could fathom Reginald Whitaker's reaction in advance of their meeting that afternoon.

So much had hinged on this Johnny Holland kid. Now . . .

Personally, he deplored racial antagonism. While he did not go all the way in advocating a complete mingling of black and white he did, nevertheless, stress the necessity of peoples working and living in harmony. He believed that men who could play a game - any game - in sportsmanlike brotherhood should be able to carry this mutual admiration into life's daily stream.

Basically, though, he realised the undercurrent of emotions rampant in present day Britain. The mass loathing of a hard core youth element for those from coloured overseas communities.

He had a tough decision to make. Whitaker would, no doubt, want explanations. Dare he link their rink success with Holland's apparent anti-social, anti-race attitudes? Or could he come right out and say he believed that this kid could draw in a huge following?

And where did Whitaker stand?

Ah, there was the rub!

He wished like blazes he had another day before the meeting took place. A day in which to evaluate the impact of Holland's lyrics.

A sudden thought hit hard!

Jasmyn Ragg . . .

She would know! If anybody in London knew what was happening behind the scenes it was the Canadian girl. And, he figured, she owed him one favour.

Yes, he could contact her. Not Steve Morash. The American publicity-genius wouldn't give away a goddamned thing. But Jasmyn would hint. That's all he needed. A hint.

Julius Gerstein smiled broadly and carefully folded his copy of the 'Mercury'. He loved Nelson Hampshire's comments. It did him good starting off another day knowing that Holland was under the cosh. And he had an idea how to capitalize on the columnist's suggestion about the Race Relations Board, too.

He had acquaintances up and down the country. Blokes who couldn't refuse to carry out his 'orders'. Men utterly dependent on his supplies. Men with skeletons galore in their dark, dirty cupboards.

He jabbed his intercom. 'Come in, Miss Glass.'

The office door opened almost immediately. He had his secretary trained to obey at the snap of a finger. She understood what would happen if he ever decided she was getting too old to 'jump' to his every command.

The woman was in her late fifties, greying. She wore severe clothes, had a prissy mouth and cold eyes sheltering behind rimless glasses.

She sat facing his desk, pencil poised over her steno's notebook. She didn't speak. She had long ago discovered Gerstein's disinterest in anything the 'paid help' had to say off the cuff.

'This is a general letter to Maury Collier, Bert Lewis, David Green, Aaron Gull. No duplicates. Each re-typed as personal correspondence.'

Gerstein padded back and forth behind his ornate desk. He wanted the letter to hit without leaving him open for a comeback should a copy fall into the wrong hands.

'As you know,' he said with clipped precision, 'I have interests in Discodrome and several entertainers. Unfortunately, at the moment, we have an element in show business which is doing nothing to help me in my quest to clean up this side of my investments.

'Nelson Hampshire, columnist for the "Mercury", has seen fit to take exception to one performer. A certain Johnny Holland. I agree fully with Hampshire's writings. I believe the matter should be brought to the attention of the appropriate authorities.

'Frankly, I wish it was possible for me to intervene personally. Anything I say, however, would be misconstrued.

'There is another aspect to be taken into account. Complaints from various sections of the country must constitute a general opinion opposed to Holland's racialist policies.

'Trusting you understand the situation. A spontaneous reaction will assist my campaign to gather momentum . . . '

Julius slumped into his chair, a smile touching his lips. It wouldn't matter whose hands got hold of these letters. 'His campaign' he could explain to any barrister was strictly a reference to his desire to make showbiz a cleaner, safer place for youth.

'That's all, Miss Glass,' he snapped. 'Finish each in the customary way.' His gaze was already fastening on a trade journal as the woman got to her feet, dismissed with the usual curtness.

CHAPTER TEN

EXACTLY three weeks from Johnny's first rendition of the new song the charts showed it topping all rivals by an astonishingly clear margin. Record sales continued to soar, and all Johnny reckoned, because a dee-jay had unwittingly played the disc at a peak listening hour. An error which the radio authorities had been unable to rectify.

Reports from various clubs and groups returning from tours confirmed the popularity of Johnny's big hit.

Only radio now ignored the existence of it - a totally anticipated reaction.

It was said that the Race Relations Board had been *inundated* with letters bitterly attacking the song and its singer. Whether or not there was any truth in this it was impossible to say. No word had yet come from the Board itself. No action had been taken officially.

Certain M.P.'s tried to make headlines deploring 'this ill-advised trend', castigating 'those who will do anything in their nefarious search for fame, fortune and fans'.

But, at soccer games, the true impact of the number reached its climax. The terraces at several famous grounds echoed to the strains of youthful voices raised in eager harmony as *'I'm a skinhead boot boy, a hard man to beat . . . '* ripped across the pitch.

For Johnny Holland the greatest tribute came one evening when he re-visited Acton. The coffee bar he had frequented blasted the tune from its jukebox as he walked by the open door. That, in his book, was fame. In his home neighbourhood. Played by old mates.

He could afford to smile, keep on walking, towards the Town Hall. Royalties and performing rights never ceased to amaze him when Steve Morash brought the latest reports round to his new house. His only regret was his failure to convince his parents that they should move in with him.

If only his mother would weaken in her resolve not to get too far away from her 'friends' . . .

Friends, indeed!

Gossips. Catty bitches who smiled to one's face and scathingly blasted when the back was turned. Bingo addicts without one scrap of intelligence in their 'eye's down' and 'doctor's orders' heads. Gin-biddies. Stout-stuffers.

As he knocked at his former front door, Johnny got an excellent example of the types his mother thought were friends. The old dear three doors away . . . Peeping through her curtains. Then, excitedly dashing to the gate as if she was expecting her loafer son to appear by magic. Eyes wide, thin lips working overtime to get as many questions answered before he escaped to the sanctuary of his parents' front room.

'Johnny,' she panted. 'My, it's wonderful seein' you again. How are you . . . ?'

Johnny frowned. 'What the heck does it matter!' he snapped, deliberately turning his back to her. Wishing to hell he'd kept a key.

He heard the woman's snort of derision, whistled his new hit to antagonise her further. And he was sure it did. Hadn't her daughter lived with an immigrant for six months until she got pregnant and the man kicked her out!

Hurry up, mum . . .

'They're out,' the woman called, voice packed with venom. 'Won't you come in and have a cuppa?'

Walking to the kerb, Johnny gazed up at his old home. Only after a lengthy pause did he face the woman. 'I don't drink tea with anybody who isn't me mate,' he said evenly, and smiling satisfaction at the hurt and anger in her eyes, strode off towards the High Street.

He felt like a king chastising a particularly nasty courtier. Fame gave a bloke the chance to do these things. Money made him powerful, beyond reproach. It certainly was a lovely way to live. A real scene now.

Writing for WORLD POPS, Steve Morash asked a very interesting question: 'How can those pretending to present a true picture of the top pops justify their exclusion of a number which, by every criterion, is selling more discs than the next two hits?'

He also answered an old-standing question concerning his position in the Holland-chain. 'I try to think of myself as the voice of Johnny Holland. It's my job to let people know when Johnny will be at a definite place at a specific time. When he will sing. At what concert. When he is leaving a city or arriving in a town. What he eats for breakfast, lunch or dinner. What he wears. How his new home is shaping up. That's about it.'

The thing that pleased Steve most about the issue of WORLD POPS his article appeared in was their editorial comment concerning presentations of pop music on radio and television.

'It is not enough to play the music of a number whose words are rejected by a minority of listeners or viewers. Lyrics make a song more often in pops than the actual sound. A singer makes a hit. The combination of both are vital to faithfully reproduce a chart-topper. Take heed, producers. *World Pops* will campaign relentlessly for the right of every singer, group or whatever to put over his or their hit in the way the recording company thought fit to market the disc.'

All it needed next, Steve thought happily, was for Nelson Hampshire to eat his words and give Johnny's song a plug!

Walking to the french-windows of his study, Steve gazed down the length of lawn that ended in a small, private frontage stream. Trees stirred lazily in an even lazier wind. Flowers waved their colourful heads as if to acknowledge their 'master-in-the-window'.

Owning such a place gave him a sense of not only belonging but having roots in England's fertile soil. He'd spent thousands attending auctions, getting the perfect blend of furniture and ornaments to match the oak beams, the cottagey atmosphere. Rugs to highlight low-ceilinged rooms and a gardener to create beauty from a long-forgotten wilderness.

Johnny Holland, also, had been spending like crazy. His mansion required five times the amount of furniture, rugs, bric-a-brac. Fortunately, Johnny hadn't gone shopping alone. Nor even just with Steve. He'd hired an interior decorator and issued orders: 'Make this something right out of *Homes & Gardens!*' The woman had done that. Transformed a barn-like void into a home any lord would be proud to call his.

Peter, on the other hand, had problems. His father had insisted on *seeing to everything.* Which meant cheap, shoddy goods from a chainstore furniture retailer, thin carpets from a 'bent' dealer in Ealing and hideous council-house brass souvenirs, a la Brighton, on display in prominent places.

Steve felt sorry for Peter. The kid tried but his father killed the growing spirit, the urge to improve. It was the cloth-cap image never wanting to better itself which had held back so many areas of the country.

'You can't get enough of it, eh?'

Steve slowly moved aside, allowed Becky Wilmott to join him. The perfume of her matched his mood, served to overwhelm the rose scent.

'I never thought any house could be so wonderful,' the girl allowed. 'If this is what stardom can buy then I want to be tops of the pops!' She meant it, her voice so sincere it caught the man off-guard.

'You didn't know?' she asked as puzzlement bounced off her face.

'No, I didn't, Becky.'

The redhead smiled wistfully. 'I guess eighteen is pretty old to make the parade,' she said.

Steve stiffened, relaxed within a split-second. He grinned next. 'God, you had me worried for a moment,' he laughed. 'I was way back in the days when Californians used to quote a legal saying - eighteen'll get you twenty!'

Becky frowned. 'What's that mean?'

'Simply,' the man replied, still chuckling, 'that eighteen was too young to take to bed!'

'And twenty meant the number of years you paid for the pleasure?' Becky asked, eyes twinkling now.

'So correct it hurts,' Steve commented.

'Not in England. I consented. I've got a birth certificate to prove I'm the age to say yes,' and she giggled with an arm round his shoulder, 'I take the Pill to let me enjoy everything an experienced man like you can teach me.'

'You're incorrigible, Becky!'

'Damned right,' she answered.

'Listen, kid . . . '

'Not that, Steve. The Pill - *remember!*'

He shrugged, moved away from her sensuousness, her heady aroma. 'Crissakes, be serious. This is strictly manager to client stuff.'

Becky's heart beat faster. She wondered how her soft breast could contain the feverish activity.

'If you've got any talent I can . . . '

'I want an honest appraisal, Steve.'

'You won't get a snow-job. That I guarantee.'

'I'm not Johnny Holland. I don't want to be racialist and I don't want to appeal to one section of the community.'

Steve nodded agreement, returned to his desk - a Queen Anne antique which had cost him £750 at auction. A radio in the background played early afternoon music. As it faded an announcer said: 'I hope you enjoyed *New World* and some Rooftop singing . . . ' Every room in the house had its 'Hacker' *Helmsman* portable - in Steve's opinion the best produced in the U.K.

'Are you really going to give me a trial?' Becky asked.

Steve smiled provocatively.

'God, get your eyeballs up above my navel,' Becky quipped.

'Yes, I'll arrange a recording session. You let me know which number you'd like to sing and I can find musicians to do the accompaniment.'

Becky forgot herself in the excitement flooding her showbiz orientated mind. She perched on a corner of the Queen Anne desk, raised one leg and held its knee in her clasped hands. Her skirt fell away, flowed to reveal her luscious thighs, her skimpy panties.

'You keep teasing me and I won't talk about a pop career,' Steve hinted.

Becky adjusted her clothing, glared at him. 'Steve, please . . . '

'Okay. Now, what's your type of number?'

'Sweet. Sentimental. Swingy.'

Steve visibly shuddered. 'God, save me from that!'

'You're not interested then?'

'I am, Becky. I definitely am. I was only jokin'. Listen to me carefully now. A lot of old music is coming back, jazzed up a bit, mind you. But it's basically old. The Alice Faye songs . . . '

'The who?' Becky showed her ignorance.

'Alice Faye. A movie star favourite back during the war years. Blonde, beautiful and what a singer!'

'Never heard of her,' Becky admitted ungraciously.

'Be that as it may,' Steve grimaced. 'I fancy you doing some of her material. "Rose of Washington Square", "All Alone By The Telephone", "Alexander's Ragtime Band". I reckon we can get sheet music for 'em all. Can you read music, by the way?'

'Reasonably,' Becky said. She pulled a face. 'Can't we get decent new music written?'

'Not for a sampler, kid.'

'Alright. But pity you if those songs ain't what the recording companies want!'

Steve made a mental note to verify this with his contacts. The initial cost of hiring professionals and recording studios would be substantial. He didn't want to toss his dough down the drain of lost opportunity any more than Becky would want to have a rejection slapped on her style.

'Okay, that's that,' he grinned, hand automatically landing on her thigh. 'Now . . . '

'Not in the afternoon, Steve,' she said.

'Why not?' he asked.

'Well . . . ' She was stuck.

'See?' His hand moved upwards.

'Haven't you got things to do for Johnny?'

He laughed, lifted her skirt and placed his hand on her softly warm flesh. 'I've got a thing to do,' he said suggestively. 'It's taking care of you . . . '

Becky sighed. The price of fame kept soaring . . . Like his hand!

'Let's get upstairs,' Steve rasped.

A Scottish voice came from *Woman's Hour* reading a short story. 'Then her eyes dropped . . . '

Becky's eyes dropped demurely. 'Must you be so crude?' she asked.

Steve grinned, came to his feet. 'After what happened last night?'

Becky sighed again, relented. She walked at his side through the study, out into the hall. She loved this old cottage. Somehow, she imagined, it had been a haven for reprobates and a succession of mistresses. Everything 'reeked' of this . . .

Maybe that's why I'm jelly in his quivering hands, she thought as he prodded her ahead of him climbing the rickety stairs . . .

CHAPTER ELEVEN

FOR Jasmyn Ragg and Becky Wilmott the one-night stand in Manchester presented no problems. Two hundred frenzied teeny boppers queued all night to make sure of their tickets for the 'Johnny Holland spectacular' that threatened to overflow the city's latest 'stereophonic auditorium'.

Advance warning of a brand new Holland number added to the excitement generated in pop circles. In every classroom the topic most discussed was 'Johnny's song'. Would it be another skinhead battle-cry? Or a rousing football terracer? *(Terracer* - a word coined by columnist Martin Mann in the 'Globe & Mail' when he handled the ultra delicate subject of songs they sing behind the nets.)

Becky could have told her coffee bar acquaintances. Jasmyn could have repeated the lyrics when she 'aroused' her disco fanatics.

A SPAGHETTI RING IS ALL YOU'RE GETTING . . .

Even Steve had wrinkled his nose at *that* title!

Peter had suggested an approach to a canning company for the free plug.

Bruce hadn't been enthusiastic although he admitted he liked the 'ring' . . .

Johnny had only said, 'Ouch!'

What they all agreed was that the song had possibilities and no racialist overtones. It gave Johnny a chance to get back into Nelson Hampshire's good books. An opportunity to appeal to mums, not their trendy daughters.

What nobody knew in advance was that Johnny intended to introduce yet another controversial number. One his 'group' knew only as music. An instrumental number. Their 'solo'. He'd worked long hours with his lyricist on the words. Tried to get a title and could only call it POEMS.

But what poems!

He'd spent weary hours trying to get the right accent for each 'poem' - the London one he didn't have to mimic but those supposedly from Birmingham, Newcastle, Bristol, Glasgow, Cardiff, Liverpool and Southampton had to be studied. Studied hard, too.

He had a problem on his hands when they were about to go on-stage, he knew. The group wanted to do a 'solo' spot. He'd promised. But he felt sure he could out-talk Peter, Bruce and Mick when it boiled down to doing it his way or not at all.

Creaking, near-senile Barry Dodd the lyricist hadn't been too pleased when Johnny informed him that the 'poems' would be publicised as being authentic examples of the skinhead culture and anonymous contributions sent to one Johnny Holland free, gratis and for nothing. He'd wanted a credit. But a hundred quid soon made him see 'the light'.

Johnny had learned the 'racket' fast!

Money gave him *carte blanche*.

Plus, of course, a private contract between Barry and himself for a split royalty. That had been a clincher! Johnny didn't give a damn nowadays. Steve could rant and rave all he wanted. But, essentially, the teeny boppers were screaming for what Johnny gave them. Not what some manager-cum-agent-cum-friend decreed.

A woman appeared in the doorway, outlined against a hall that contained more footage than his parents entire ground floor. A hall that boasted fifteen oils and a pair of Dutch marquetry tables with Italian marble torcherie holding sprayed floral arrangements. A hall bare of carpets or rugs, its beautiful ancient wooden boards polished to shimmering perfection.

'Excuse me, sir,' the woman said with servile insincerity. 'Will you be wanting the staff during the next few days?'

Johnny tried to assume the 'master role'. He felt he lacked the maturity, the ability to 'command' servants an owner of such a splendid residence should have, and it came through in his reply-question answer. 'Er . . . do we need them?'

The woman smiled faintly. 'Not if you're going away, sir.'

'I leave it to you then, Mrs Bedford.'

The woman nodded absently. 'We have prepared a simple meal for tonight, sir. Roast lamb.'

'Terrific!'

The woman stared at Johnny, inclined her head and, after some slight hesitation, nodded with more than a little compassion. 'Yes, sir. Cook says she'll be ready to serve about seven-thirty . . . if that's your wish, sir?'

Screw Steve and his servants! Johnny thought angrily. *I always feel inferior. I don't really know how to behave in these surroundings but -*

'Terrific,' he said again, which covered a multitude of sins.

The woman backed out of the room, softly closed the double-doors behind her.

'I've got to have Gloria here,' Johnny said aloud. 'It's time I got married . . .'

The word sent explosions through his system. Much as he liked - maybe he loved - Gloria, he didn't honestly want to get married. He didn't have the drawback most teenagers faced when they rushed into matrimony. His profession could never be classed as secure but the money already accruing to his account meant he could splurge, get spliced and not have to worry for the coming year. More, if he handled his affairs properly. But that wasn't enough for getting hitched to one woman. He wasn't old enough to forego all the pleasures an adolescent should experience in the 'so called' formative years.

To blazes with the canons, the do-gooders, the female magistrates who pontificated on juvenile problems, the women politicians who knew better than those who had to live within an environmental slum.

If he wanted to marry Gloria then, by Christ, he would! But he didn't . . .

He liked her as his 'soul-mate'. His sidekick. His bird. Nothing more!

Not yet, anyway!

Another year, or two. When he had 'established' himself as one of those undying acts. A Tommy Steele. A Frankie Vaughan. The Arthur Askey of the pop world. A Frank Sinatra covering many generations.

He liked to regard himself as a bloke who'd be around for as long as he wished to entertain. His dream was to fade out in a blaze of glorious publicity with a song equally as good as Sinatra's farewell -'I did it my way!'

And he fully intended to do it his special way!

To hell with the blue-nosed bastards who went crying to the Press, the Race Relations Board, the Church.

To blazes with those who didn't want the great big British public to hear what the nation as a whole thought.

To the devil with politicians willing to sell white British rights down the river for a few hundred thousand coloured votes.

He - Johnny Holland - had the power to bring the message right into the homes, coffee bars, discos and concert halls where it could be digested.

He didn't think of himself as a crusader. He hadn't the humanity for that. But he did believe in Britishers first. Immigrants and people of a different skin tone belonged, he thought, elsewhere. Not as citizens with special rights. Not able to get holidays in the lands of their birth paid for by the highly tolerant English, Scottish, Welsh taxpayer. And then to be re-admitted when they'd gloatingly lorded it over their island-in-the-sun kin.

His heart hardened more as the thoughts rushed willy-nilly through his brain.

He had to have a song composed about this injustice! One to make every immigrant lover sit up and squeal . . .

One the sportsman 'Kop' couldn't fail to take up and sing!

Just for a fraction of time, Johnny Holland approached greatness. His special kind of greatness. A patriotic hysteria those who had opened the doors of immigration could never know. A frenzy akin to total self-destruction in a desire to right so many wrongs forced upon his fellow-Englishmen.

Yet, for all the wrong reasons!

Without realising how close he had come to being 'the chosen one', Johnny let his violent nature take control. Let cultism dictate where a clear head, a positive policy could have welded historic mention.

And the greatness dissolved in brutality! In thuggery!

In gutter-uttering . . .

POEMS . . .

The stuff criticism was made from. The material to undo everything his young, dedicated - in a way - heart cried out to bring to the attention of his elders. Youth's frustration. Youth's torment. Youth's inadequate expression.

(And why? Because youth got left-wing education that kept it down. Kept it within controllable limits . . .)

Johnny didn't know!

None of *them* did!

And those who knew smiled in the knowledge that *an aim* had destroyed an English ability to contest the alien challenge . . .

Julius Gerstein knew what it was all about. Profit. Gear for the sheep who followed his directions. Percentages from the artists who obeyed instructions and didn't take a wrong step.

It had always been a big giggle for Julius when he heard about youth's rebellion against 'standardised' clothing. When the Establishment - albeit those who had the most to gain from pulling wool over blind eyes - complained about this new breed of youngster who didn't heed fashion dictates.

Like hell they didn't!

Youth, bluffed to its last penny, was a stupid sheep docilely treading the Gerstein path.

Take the skinhead cult . . .

Braces made by one of his concerns. Union shirts bought on the cheap and flogged at treble the cost. Boots quickly purchased from a bankrupt merchandiser and put on 'special' with a one-hundred-fifty percent mark-up. Sold out in two days, too. Levis - with dirt rubbed in - peddled at thirty per over the odds. '

Or tanktops . . . old gear brought out of mothballs and upped by £3 per unit.

And now, Johnny Holland T-shirts. Tatty stock hurriedly sent to a silk-screener and put on display with a huge imprint of Johnny's face and the chorus of *Aggro Addict* beneath.

To safeguard himself, Julius had made a deal through Steve Morash. A minimum royalty for Johnny's appearance at the open-air concert to be staged in the Midlands the following month.

Profit . . .

Money to grant him more power!

Squeezing the maximum for the minimum.

So far, his plans had met with a temporary set-back. Johnny Holland still rode the wave's crest. Still stayed out of reach.

But not for much longer.

The Midlands concert would see the curtain rung down on the Holland legend . . .

He had Narcissus's guarantee. Tavern's apologies for not 'doing' the bastard when they had the golden shot. Anka's promise to 'arrange' something extra-special.

Julius didn't go much on Shippe's promise. He doubted if a wet lettuce could topple Johnny Holland and his Roundheads . . .

CHAPTER TWELVE

DOC MACMASTER read the 'Standard' report of the latest soccer violence with misgivings. Such happenings were unknown in Canada and he felt, tempers flared and emotions boiled every bit as much over an ice hockey contest as they did for a football match. But why the violence? The senseless destruction of railways carriages? The uncivilised muggings and window-smashings?

This latest bout of indiscriminate savagery had no tangible attachment. The so-called fans supposedly going to support their team had not been 'robbed' by a negligent referee. They'd won. Handsomely. Yet they still felt it necessary to celebrate by creating a mayhemious path from ground to home town.

If this was the pattern of today's youth could he risk letting an acknowledged leader of cultism become the symbol of ice hockey thrills?

Could he put an entire venture in jeopardy because he bad spontaneously tossed in pop to consolidate a deal which might have been otherwise threatened . . .?

The answer had to be in the negative! Definitely so!

He sat down and composed a letter to Whitaker. A cable to his American partners . . .

'Much as I regret,' the letter began. And ended with, ' . . . and contrary to expectations I must stress, again, the necessity of withdrawing my offer to S. Morash for Johnny Holland's services.

'If, by this, you deem it unwise to participate in a joint venture linking an ice rink with a concert pavilion then I repeat my responsibility for expenses already incurred.

'My love of hockey is such that I cannot, in any way or shape or form, bring the sport into disrepute. I would rather opt out of all negotiations and leave final agreements to those whom I have represented and those with whom I entered into preliminary speculations.

'I remain,

'Sirs,

'Your obedient servant,

To his North American partners, Doc sent the following cable. Short. To the point.

AM BACKING OUT. TEENAGE VIOLENCE AGAINST ALL I HAVE TRIED TO ENCOURAGE IN YOUTH. CANNOT VISUALISE HOCKEY SUCCESS HERE ON SPORTSMANSHIP LINES. SORRY. WHITAKER GIVEN SAME REASONS.

Tears stung the great man's eyes as he carefully folded the letter and placed it in an envelope. More tears fell as he telephoned for a bellhop to collect an overnight cable.

Failure didn't rest lightly on those powerful shoulders. Neither did the admission that the English could not separate their sport from a post-war tendency towards kicking the underdog where it hurt most.

He wondered where he'd gone wrong. How he could have mistaken youthful exuberance for the viciousness that seemed to penetrate every level of society. And it wasn't just with those called juveniles, either. The entire population appeared ready to accept horrible crimes as part and parcel of modern day life. He thought about the handling of desperate criminals. The way so many so-called responsible persons wanted to mollycoddle the villain. Suspended sentences. A mere few years inside for child molestation. One or two more for rape and murder.

And, what was most astonishing to him, the high and mighty attitude of elected Members of Parliament spouting about their moral duties when they rejected hanging as a deterrent when they should, in reality, have followed the dictates of their constituents.

Something stank when the voter got nudged into the shadows of his representative once the results were announced . . .

Johnny Holland received word from Steve Morash. It didn't unduly upset him. He had never been in favour of ice hockey and although he stood to lose quite a tax-free sum he didn't honestly give a damn. More to the point, he would feel better with the blokes now. They'd frosted his balls on the deal.

Not that they'd been able to bite too much into his bread. Steve had conned them all into a new contract. One giving them secondary status. A backing group status.

Like Steve, Johnny knew about Jasmyn's affair and he wondered how she'd take the latest news. He didn't worry if she sat down and bawled. That was her business. His was taking care of Number One - Mr John Holland. But he wanted Jasmyn on his team. Becky, too. They'd earned their keep more than once during the rough patch after his controversial number hit the stores.

Ice hockey . . .

The more he thought about MacMaster's rejection on grounds of association with undesirable types the more he wanted to give the Canadian the works. British style. It would serve him right if he got the arena going and then had to suffer Johnny Holland's presence as a paid-up seat holder . . .

God, that would be a giggle. And the blokes would go for it. Maybe even a little aggro . . .

Jasmyn lay naked in Doc's arms. A faint light glowed in the lounge, casting deep shadows across their bodies as it filtered through the partially open bedroom door. She didn't find it unusual for a man to have light seeping into the refuge shared with one he professed to adore. To love eternally.

'Don't underestimate Johnny,' Jasmyn said. 'If he ever gets the notion you've cut him cold he might decide to make things rugged for you at the rink.'

Doc smiled, kissed her right breast. He liked the way she arched to his mouth. The immediate reaction of her nipple to his suctioning lips.

'Don't be greedy,' Jasmyn said without much resistance.

Doc withdrew his head, leant on an elbow gazing down at her svelte nudity. The age differential didn't matter when they were like this. Nor did he consider her young enough to be his daughter. She was old enough, big enough, wise enough. She'd gone along with him. Unforced. Able to cut out at any stage of the game.

'A penny for 'em . . . '

Doc smiled distantly. 'Nothing,' he muttered.

'Thinking about a wife can have disastrous results,' Jasmyn said.

The man jerked away, face frozen into an unhumorous smile. Suddenly, he *did* think about his ex-wife. His grandchildren. *And this mere strip of a girl.*

'Aaw . . . '

Doc got off the bed, slipped into his pyjama bottoms. 'Sorry, Jasmyn - you shouldn't have mentioned her.'

Jasmyn cursed silently. Trust her to say the wrong thing at the wrong time. She'd been so sure she had him snared. Wealthy. Famous. Old. The kind of guy she'd hankered after. The sort to agree to a separation when a marriage broke down. The kindly figure who'd legally offer grounds for divorce and shell out a fairly hefty alimony.

'I think you'd best dress and go home,' Doc said.

'Yeah, I reckon so . . . ' Jasmyn hid her disappointment. This was but one battle. She would fight several more before she triumphed. Until then, she figured an acceptance of defeat rated a smile . . .

Becky Wilmott trembled as nerves got the better of her equilibrium. She had dreamed about this moment so long she couldn't quite place the reality where it belonged - in Steve's capable hands.

'You okay?'

The girl nodded, unable to speak.

'The hell you are,' Steve grinned. Taking her hand he squeezed it reassuringly. 'The mike ain't gonna take a bite out of your mouth.'

'Oh, Lord . . . '

'Easy girl . . . '

Becky stiffened her body, repeated several times, *'I must not give in to stage-fright.'*

'Okay now?'

She nodded, still too tense to sing.

'Can I safely get the guys ready?'

'I think so, Steve.'

'Honey,' and he gripped her forearm with fingers that almost bruised. Hurt like hell. 'This is it. The big one. Your chance. Ready?'

Becky took one more deep breath. Exhaled leisurely. 'I'm ready, Steve.' As he smilingly started to walk away she reached out, caught his swinging arm. His eyes came to meet hers. 'Thanks,' she said with deep sincerity.

'I'll be sayin' that once you've recorded,' he said by way of encouragement.

Becky understood. She felt so much on the ball thanks to his low-key handling of her attack. Somehow his very presence gave her the boost her natural nervousness needed to overcome a complete breakdown.

Steve had done her proud. Not only had he supplied nine professional musicians but he had also seen fit to add a singing group whose voices most people would have recognized for the number of unheralded appearances they made in television jingles.

As she waited for Steve's signal she studied her lyrics. Doubts still tormented her. Would a record company accept such a strange ballad? Would they figure it too old fashioned for today's market? Would some long-haired semi-executive brush aside his locks and throw a fit when he heard her version of 'The Hermit of Warkworth?'

Speaking softly, she murmured the words . . .

'It happened on a summer's day,
Led by fragrant breeze,
I wandered forth to take the air
Among the greenwood trees.'

Becky smiled to herself. It was so ancient it could practically be called Biblical. But that was, according to Steve, its major charm. 'After all, kid,' he'd told her, 'there's a trend to gospel type songs. Maybe we haven't gone that far back but we're nearly there!'

'Then climbing up his rocky stairs,
He scales the cliff so high,
And calls aloud and waves his light
To guide the stranger's eye.'

Steve grinned, patted her back. 'Fantastic, Becky,' he said easily.

'Will it sell?' she asked.

'No reason why not,' he replied. 'The music sounds just perfect.'

'I'm not worried about the music,' Becky remarked.

'Remember, this is one number in a sampler offering a wide selection. You've got some terrific material. Old standards, a few near-misses and the 'Hermit'. You can't miss, honey . . . '

'*If* I do I'll be your house-guest forever and ever. I'll become a lady hermit . . . !'

Steve laughed. 'That'd be fantastic if only I believed you meant it!' He winked suggestively, fondled her bottom.

Without knowing why, Steve had gotten through to her reserves of strength. Becky knew exactly what had happened. What they'd shared during the past week hadn't been a fleeting affair in her heart. Her mind. It had been an introduction to something more lasting. A permanent relationship. An eighteen year old's knight in shining armour charging into a mass of foes to rescue the fair maiden, a dream come true. Although she operated in a world peopled by hard nuts, bearded wonders, grotty little bastards and the vicious vultures hovering above all, she didn't belong to them. She was Becky Wilmott - aloof from the rat-race. A nice girl trying to compete. A dreamer at rock-bottom. A maiden in need . . . And Steve had satisfied that need. Opened a whole universe to her eyes.

'Ready?' Steve asked, withdrawing a little when he saw the depth of her emotional involvement.

'I'm ready, Steve . . . '

Christ, he thought, *I've sold her a bill of goods she can't shake off.*

'If I fluff a line . . . ?'

Steve pointed at the smiling, patient musicians. 'They'll forgive and keep on playing. We run through regardless. This first take is experimental. Relax. Take it in your stride. I'll signal when we're set to record the master.'

Becky's swinging hips going to the microphone showed he'd convinced her. It was a dirty trick but one he felt necessary considering her tension. Actually, they'd record from the first bar. Perfection on a sampler wasn't the criterion of recording company success. The essential was getting her voice across. Showing she could handle a song. A style.

'Good luck, kid,' he murmured and gave a thumb's up to the control boys . . .

CHAPTER THIRTEEN

IN his heart-of-secret-hearts, Johnny Holland had ambitions to remain in show business the rest of his life. When he grew older, was married, had children, he hoped to support them all on an income derived from record sales. He liked to think he would still be a name in the game when he hit his forties. A name like Andy Williams. A great like Perry Como. Popular as Des O'Connor. Making 'comebacks' like Donald Peers. Have a dedicated following like Frank Sinatra. Be spoken about in reverence as Bing Crosby was even today. Have a matured voice like 'iron lungs' Vaughan Monroe.

Far be it for him to hazard a guess as to the type of music they would be listening to in twenty years time, but he reckoned that Country & Western would be around. Strong as ever. The standby for a steady income.

He enjoyed the 'folk' singers. If he had to make a decision even now on a career-long style he would almost certainly have jabbed a finger on C&W as the lasting image.

The gimmick he currently used which had brought him instant popularity didn't necessarily have to remain. Indeed, the sooner he dropped it the better. Getting typed as *the skinhead singer* could only hurt his ambitions. But, for the while, he enjoyed his fame. The adverse criticisms. The hue-and-cry by blue-nosed do-gooders.

It was Johnny's desire to cash in on his *Aggro Addict* number for the next year. No longer. If he succeeded in getting into the charts five times with controversial songs he would be satisfied. *Poems* was already creeping up the table. At number fifteen it had jumped ten places in one week. Not bad going for an unplugged song.

Looking over his engagements for the coming month, Johnny noted the names Narcissus, Shippe, and Tavern reappearing with monotonous regularity. Since his brush with Lonnie McGovern of Tavern he'd been ever aware of their shared billings. Even Steve had remarked about it. But did Steve really scan the advance lists?

'I've got to have this sorted out,' Johnny said aloud to a bronze figure of Shakespeare. Since getting the statue he'd taken to addressing it as he did his mates. He'd been forced to read one of Shakespeare's plays in school and had hated every line. But that didn't stop him from sharing a sort of camaraderie with the playwright's dominant talent. There were a lot of things Johnny didn't understand. Ballet. Opera. Classical music. Yet he respected each. In an uncultured, off-hand way.

Waiting for Steve to answer his telephone, Johnny got around to thinking about his loneliness. The house was far too big for one bloke. Much as he appreciated having it and being surrounded by fine possessions he couldn't quite get used to wandering for hours without meeting people he knew, without bumping into a situation demanding an aggressive nature. Everything here was so placid. So bloody tranquil he often wished he'd hired a few bruisers to supply him with aggro.

God, he really missed the gang fights, football punch-ups, his mates deliberately antagonising some stupid black bastard. He knew he'd have

257

grown out of all this one day. In his twenties. Like most skinheads did when they got engaged, or married. But that wasn't yet. Gloria and he were far from getting down to the nitty-gritty of sharing the house, lives on a permanent basis.

Frankly, he wasn't even so bloody sure Gloria would be the one woman in his life!

Over the past few months they'd grown apart.

He suspected the change was more on her side than his. Gloria loved to believe she was responsible for his success. When he'd made the grade - and not Sir Lew's - she had retreated into a semiconscious shell and didn't bother to effervesce as she had once.

Steve didn't answer his ringing telephone.

Johnny swore, slammed his instrument down with a bang. It seemed he remembered something about Becky Wilmott having a recording session in London today. And Steve being there to arrange details.

Becky . . .

Now there was a girl he could go for. A real smasher. Nice and yet . . . Steve was her man! They all knew that. Bruce had even made up a poem about the pair. Trust bleedin' Bruce to sink to the depths . . .

'Up Queen's Park!' he shouted at Shakespeare.

The statue didn't reply. Like Steve!

'What bleedin' team did you support?' Johnny asked, bending over the bronze and glaring at the bearded face. 'Millwall? Arsenal?' Memory returned. A schoolteacher mentioning that Shakespeare had been born in the Midlands. Or thereabouts. Where the hell . . . ? Stratford. That's it! 'A bloody Coventry supporter, eh?'

Johnny felt right proud. Geography had been another weak subject. He didn't care much for distance separating places providing he figured they were within an area.

'Up the Sky Blues!'

Satisfied he'd made Shakespeare's day, Johnny walked through the open french-windows and strolled in his gardens.

An old man glanced up from the greenhouse direction and quickly dropped his head again. One run-in with the 'young master' had been more than enough for the head gardener. He preferred to deal with people who knew a calcifuge plant from a weed. *Master Holland's* last attempt to name a flower had rather shocked him. He'd never heard anyone calling a De Caen poppy anemone a forget-me-not and expecting not to be challenged.

Johnny grinned and carefully avoided the gardener. He'd set the old boy back fifty years with his non-knowledge of flowers and plants.

He'd deliberately insisted he knew what he'd been talking about but the man's lack of humour had somehow caused a rift between them.

What the hell! Johnny thought. *I don't have to worry. He's my employee. I can fire him if he gets on my wick!*

I won't, though . . .

Gardeners were hard to come by. Especially here. There were so many wealthy people with huge estates, monstrously large gardens. Men like old Dodds could find employment overnight. Maybe even at higher wages than Johnny was paying.

No, he had to suffer this stay-away-from-me attitude and watch his garden take shape. Beautiful shape, admittedly. Like a park shaded by gigantic trees. Something for the snooty neighbours to envy.

He'd heard the gossip. About that guttersnipe pop star who moved into the Creech residence! Lowering the tone of the area. Giving it a rotten name. Probably holds drug orgies and sex parties. What does a mere lad want a sizeable home like that for? Don't invite him to any of the local functions. He'd shame the likes of us!

Just thinking about what he'd overheard when going to the village post office or visiting the record bar made Johnny furious. He should teach the bastards a lesson . . .

He laughed aloud and old Dodds glanced up.

Johnny waved generously.

The gardener nodded back, quickly got on with his chores.

Walking down the long, sweeping, curving driveway, Johnny marvelled at the number of acres surrounding the main house. If he had planning permission he could construct an estate in the grounds to house a few hundred people. Not that he wished this upon himself. He'd seen what estate kids did to destroy landscapes, telephone kiosks, interiors. There'd been a time when he, too, indulged his passions in such activities. Not now. He'd grown away from childish vandalism.

At the main entrance, Johnny stood and studied the gates. There had been a sign there once. A house name. An occupier's name. He tried to picture how a wooden plaque would look, decided against this in favour of wrought iron painted white. That would make it stand out against the black metal gate.

God, how his neighbours would hate his guts! Imagine the first person driving past catching sight of the new sign!!

AGGRO ADDICT, it would read.

And his letters . . .

Mr J. Holland,

'Aggro Addict',

Windthrope Lane . . .

Christ, a real giggle. Especially if his postman happened to be one of those stuck-up squares one finds in the posher parts of London.

A giggle . . .

Worth spending a few quid on the sign . . .

GLAMS ARE HERE TO STAY

World Pops justified its position as the leading magazine covering *the* scene. It's five-page article dealing with the 'glams' of pops carried several four-colour pics of the up and coming glitter boys. Narcissus got a page to himself, a picture to make any young girl's bosom heave ecstatically. It showed him wearing his make-up, frilly shirt, silver sequinned trousers, platform soles. 'Stars in my eyes' ran the caption and those golden stars certainly came out bright and clear.

'Some years ago,' the article read, 'a singer like Narcissus would have been laughed off any stage in the country. Not now. *Glams* are here to stay. Witness the ever-increasing number of pop lads doing their thing in a variety of outfits bordering on the demented, the super-spangled, the exotic.

'Of course, this is not a novelty in the animal-bird kingdom. Many spectacular species are known for their male fashion displays while the unadorned distaff hides her bushel under a nearby plant . . . '

Julius Gerstein threw the glossy mag aside in disgust. He read it because he was intimately involved in the scene. Not because he believed a bloody word it said; not because he found its contents entertaining even.

Narcissus . . .

The bloke he'd come to learn to detest!

For once, Gerstein didn't rate profitability above a desire to rid himself of an objectionable character. The ex-Birmingham 'song-bird' - through his failure to take care of Johnny Holland - had assumed the role of a major thorn in Julius's side. And when a Gerstein hated, watch out!

Data filtering through to Julius showed how far Johnny had come in the last six months. From nobody to teeny bopper idol. Bobby Sharp's proposed second British tour had been called off and it was no secret in pop circles why Johnny's image would not be dented and any American trying to outshine him would only suffer from a comparison.

The latest item of news fed into Gerstein's ear had brought a flush to his cheeks. Holland had had the audacity to call his country mansion

Aggro Addict after his first major disc success. A recording which, now, had earned a golden disc. And *Poems* wasn't far behind, either.

It really bugged Julius knowing that Steve Morash had this kid under contract for ten years!

Glancing at his diamond-studded wristwatch, Gerstein scowled. He wasn't in the mood for a conference. He had problems enough with his rag-trade affairs. Late deliveries. Samples which didn't appeal now he'd seen them on a live model. Cloth shipments held in abeyance at strike-bound docks. Always bloody strikes! If it wasn't the flamin' dockers it was the railways. Or the transport drivers. Or some other union disrupting decent businesses.

Jabbing his desk intercom he roared: 'Are they here, Miss Glass?'

'Yes, sir . . . '

'Okay, let's get it over with!' He silenced the connection. He was always careful to do this. He knew a competitor whose ideas had been pinched due to carelessly leaving an intercom switch open. It wouldn't happen with him!

The office door opened and in walked Narcissus, Shippe, McGovern and Blaine. Watching them find chairs and offer half-hearted smiles, Julius studied the man Blaine. He had few reasons for ever meeting the broad-shouldered, balding Scouse. Taking the man at percentage value he had no valid reason for doing more than pass a few telephoned words with the other. Ten or twenty quid per year didn't make for a Gerstein enthusiasm and a wish to waste valuable time discussing future prospects or forthcoming penny-ante engagements. Pub singing, club crawling between stints as a Soho stripclub doorman tout did not make for big-time agent-client relationships.

But Blaine had one talent which Gerstein felt he could use to advantage.

Blaine had been a professional boxer once. A man with seamy connections. In police circles, Tom Blaine held the key to several protection racket mysteries - if he ever got around to squealing.

'I'm busy so I won't take up your time,' Julius said quickly. 'We all know what is on the agenda. Johnny Holland! You, Narcissus . . . ' and the menacing finger pointed directly at the 'glam-boy', 'You've tried and failed. You, Shippe . . . ' and the finger moved swiftly to probe Anka's fragile mentality. 'You haven't come up with a bloody idea let alone tried to cripple the bastard.'

Anka's high-pitched voice sallied forth. 'I can't resort to violence. I'm not built for that!'

'Agreed!' Gerstein smiled grimly. 'McGovern . . . '

The Irishman uncrossed his legs, frowned. 'I'm me own worst enemy, sur,' he said.

'Drink!' Julius sarcastically commented.

'That an' a likin' fer humanity . . . '

'Irish lies!' Gerstein snapped. 'Don't blarney me, McGovern.'

'Never, sur . . . '

'You're pissed,' Julius scorned and immediately wiped the booze-hound from his plans. 'Blaine . . . '

Tom Blaine sat forward. Not a muscle moved on his impassive face. Only the snake-like eyes showed he was even paying attention.

'How many heavies can you get for a job in the Midlands?'

Blaine cocked his head inquisitively. 'What for?'

'I want the Holland outdoor concert broken apart.'

'I could raise ten, maybe twenty guys . . . '

Julius nodded thoughtfully. 'I have the honour to supply security guards for the show. I'll use my own men.'

Blaine smiled frostily. 'The ones you hire for Discodrome?'

'Yeah - why?'

'Me mates,' Blaine admitted.

'I realise that,' Julius said. 'They'll have orders to make it look good but they won't seriously hinder what you've got to do.'

'If I know the mob they'll help,' Blaine replied.

'Over my dead body!' Julius bent forward, forearms resting on his desk, eyes intent. 'I want it to look good. I want them to appear as if they're fighting your crowd off.'

'I get the picture,' Blaine said. 'A fake kayo.'

'A dive,' Gerstein mentioned. 'Like you took against Sykes.'

Blaine's features contorted into a hideous mask. 'Nobody accuses me . . . ' he started to growl.

'I'm saying you made a dive, Blaine. And I should bloody know,' Julius stormed. 'I was the bloke whose money you took!'

Anka Shippe gasped, squirmed as if trying to shelter inside the chair's wood.

McGovern smiled. This was a juicy piece of gossip.

Narcissus waited, not a flickered false-eyelash betraying his inner heat.

Blaine sat back, dejected. Beaten by a harder punch than Sykes had supposedly landed for the regional championship.

'I don't often swear,' Gerstein explained with a triumphant smile. 'I apologise.' He didn't mean it but the habit came of long standing. 'Now - can you handle this?'

Blaine nodded, not daring to trust his voice.

'How much?' Julius asked.

'About twenty per man?'

'Fifteen!' Julius never accepted a price.

'I don't . . . ' Blaine tried to argue.

'Fifteen or nothing!'

Blaine acknowledged defeat. 'Fifteen - in advance.'

Julius hated paying before results but he understood the type of man he was buying. He counted off £150, pushed it across his desk. 'That's for ten blokes. If you hire more I'll settle after the concert.'

Blaine shrugged. 'I'll do what I can.'

Turning next to Narcissus, Gerstein asked, 'And you're ready for back-stage action?'

The 'glam-boy' nodded.

'I won't go into details but, essentially, they're the same as before. Get him off-balance. Make him nervous. Anything to make him blow his cool when Blaine's men start rioting.'

'It won't flop, mate,' Narcissus said with an overconfidence he truly didn't feel.

'It had better not,' Julius Gerstein snarled. His right arm lifted, brushed them away as a lazy loafer would shoo-off an annoying fly. For him, the conference had ended.

CHAPTER FOURTEEN

FACE-OFF, an authoritative magazine dealing with global ice hockey, carried an exclusive interview with Doc MacMaster.

'Britain's entry into a new-Euro-league hangs in the balance,' Doc was reported as saying. 'For a while we - my North American partners and the City syndicate here - believed we had a solution to make our proposition viable. Unfortunately, this idea has now been proved to be questionable. Not only does hockey seem likely to lose but also show business generally.'

Face-off's editor, himself an old time hockey great, had more to say on the subject. In a footnote to the interview, Cy Young stated:

'It is to be regretted that those earning fantastic sums from a minimum of effort can throw an exciting sport like ice hockey into the doldrums again.

'I make no bones about which star I refer to - one currently enjoying fanatical following for his racialistic songs.

'But let the microphone-clingers and glitter maniacs beware. The day could come when ice hockey takes its rightful place in the minds and attentions of our youth. When it does, the millions now available for those who grow fat on outrageous records will cease to flow.'

Seated in his office, surrounded by the clatter of typewriters and eager reporters shouting for a copy boy, Cy Young grimly replaced his telephone. He had anticipated Steve Morash's call. Expected the rantings. The accusations. The threats of legal action.

He didn't give a damn!

He loved ice hockey. Loved it as much as he did his chosen land. Eleven years in England had him wondering at times if he was still a Canadian or a Britisher. Both parents had come from the 'Old Country'. Both had taught him to believe the links between Canucks and English were too strong for any force, any dark shadow, any petty dictatorship, any irritating happening to sever.

What a load of horse manure that had turned out to be!

A sell-out in the interests of 'Ted Heath for Euro president' had put paid to beliefs spawned in building a nation from timbered hinterlands, against all the odds.

God he loathed 'Toothy Ted' - prime mover of everything the people *didn't* want, *couldn't* accept, *refused* to confirm in local elections. And yet, the man stayed aloof. Determined to put personal whims through regardless. Without consultation. Without the promised majority decision. Broken promises. Broken again. Afraid to ask the electorate what they thought. Shrugging off every anguished price-rise scream with a morning-cloudiness-head-above-the-fog mysteriousness that only incensed those who had so trusted. So believed.

Cy never stopped to count the cost when he got mad!

Speaking one's mind came easy.

Like telling Steve Morash to drop dead. Get lost. Sue. Bring on his teeny bopper idols and make a show out of a shambles!

'I shouldn't be running a publication in England,' he said aloud. And grinned guiltily as he quick-glanced at his companions. Nobody heard. Nobody noticed. He smiled down at his hands resting on a pile of fresh copy.

His mind raced in top-gear. He still had the Canadian way, of shouting emotions and letting the devil take care of his own. He hadn't discovered - and didn't want to - how to control his 'in print' attacks on those things he felt deeply for, or against.

He'd been crazy enough to send free copies of the current *Face-off* to Steve and that little creep Johnny Holland. With a compliment slip. And the additional written remark on each: THANKS FOR SLAMMING A DOOR IN DOC'S FACE!

And he was wild enough to write an article for publication in one of the better Sunday papers. An article condemning those who capitalized on political promises, those who made fortunes from youth's desire to find an outlet and, especially, those who 'shamed' the oldest standing contract of all in an English deal - breaking a gentleman's word to abide by hands shaken in agreement.

The motto behind his desk said it all for those who would criticise his blistering attack . . .

SPEAK YOUR MIND - YOU *COULD* BE GODDAMNED RIGHT! IF YOU'RE WRONG - WELL, ISN'T EVERYBODY ONCE?

Another motto stayed in his head. One he kept to himself. One some of his closest friends suspected but which they didn't venture to mention . . .

'If you're an outsider don't open your mouth until you've paid tax for five years. Then, by God, holler your head off . . . you're one of 'em now, boy!

Steve Morash sizzled as he replaced his telephone. He hadn't a leg to stand on with Cy Young - and he knew it. Johnny had nailed him to a sacrificial cross. A T-shaped altar dedicated to aggro and racialism. *Christ*, he thought, *couldn't the little swine have listened to me? Didn't he know that this wasn't putting on the ritz for a few days. Instant glory. Fleeting kisses from Lady Luck's wham-bang passing throughness.*

Music was a food - and foodstuffs never should be poisoned!

As a publicist without scruples he admired Cy's stick-to-the-old-guns determination to blast them. He loathed getting shot down by another North American - let it ride by telling himself there wasn't much love shared between the 49th divided peoples. That undefended frontier was a lot of nonsense dreamed up by democrats trying to salve something from the fact that no American army had ever been able to defeat the rugged, unyielding Canucks.

Steve grinned and helped himself to a slice of toast. He'd have to watch this. Englishmen didn't go for Yanks tearing Canadian 'colonials' off a strip. Most of all, Canucks didn't go for it! He'd heard about the World War Two episodes when more American blood was shed behind some British dancehalls than ever on Europe's battlefields. Blood that slid off hard Canadian fists.

Jesus, hadn't a pair of Mounties tamed Sitting Bull when the entire Seventh Cavalry failed to revenge Custer!

Logic got to him then. *Face-off* wasn't a large circulation general magazine. Its buffs didn't contribute much to Johnny's - and his - fortunes. The fear, though, was that somebody else on the pop side would read Cy's 'notes' and take up the standard for a crusade aimed at knocking Holland off his throne.

Somebody like Julius Gerstein!

Steve hadn't been exactly idle these past few weeks and it hadn't come as much of a shock to learn, from a reliable source, that Julius guided Narcissus, Tavern and the 'old queen', Shippe.

Finishing a coffee, Steve frowningly considered the Midland concert. All Gerstein's boys were due there. As would be Johnny and more top-liners than at any other event for the whole year. Also present, Steve knew, would be the Julius 'security mob'. He doubted the wisdom of this. Not many writers about pop liked those boys. He'd bet the newspapers would have a full brigade of photogs on hand just watching, and waiting, for the first sign of 'security' brutality. Which, in his estimation, meant the possibility of dissident groups coming out in force to capitalize on the additional publicity they could gain for their cause. Or causes!

'Ah, hell . . . ' Steve jumped to his feet, anxiety filling him. Somehow, somewhere he had to find a countersecurity group to keep Gerstein's hoodlums in check. Even if he forked out a bundle personally he intended Johnny's stint to go ahead without interruption. Without incident.

It wasn't any use getting in touch with the promoters. They were in cahoots with Julius. That he knew for sure. And he doubted if other managers or agents would take kindly to a suggestion they all stick together and opt out unless more satisfactory arrangements could be guaranteed.

Speaking to his mirrored image, Steve slantedly grinned, asked, 'Could I get a score of British Bobbys to assist me?'

CHAPTER FIFTEEN

FOR the past few years farmer Richard Thurlow had fought a losing battle against inflation, the lack of farm-labour and a Common Market encroachment that now threatened to eliminate him altogether. Unlike many other farmers situated in parts of the country still considered rural his two hundred acres lay smack within the rough rectangle bordered by Birmingham, Coventry, Warwick and Worcester. A highly industrialised region. Too close for comfort. And certainly near enough the highly-paid car factory jobs to entice young men off the land.

Gazing at his dilapidated outbuildings and the farmhouse roof which was urgently in need of immediate repair, Thurlow consoled himself with the singular thought that he had done right in leasing his land to *that pop chap*. He knew the whole village was against him. Knew the police did not look upon him as a friend any more.

Even their local newspaper had campaigned to have the 'festival' cancelled and the 'tranquillity of our tiny plot preserved'.

What tranquillity? Thurlow asked himself.

Transporters rumbled past on a trunk road bordering his farm. Cars roared round bends meant to be negotiated at a mere thirty. An accident black-spot, the police had often claimed. Planes came down low overhead, preparing to land more executives with bulging briefcases containing expansion plans and an end to yet more farming land.

There's no tranquillity, no hope left here! he mused bitterly.

Out in the fields, men were already at work putting up latrines, tents. A ten-foot high fence boxed-in his property. Signs had been posted at various road junctions announcing directions to the 'festival'. Posts carrying loud-speakers rose like shameful beacons from the four corners of the central 'arena'. An area dominated by the massive platform - covered - on which the groups and solo artists would perform.

Looking at the several caravans for the entertainers to change in, Thurlow began to wonder if money was as important as he had felt when first approached. He liked the idea of getting ten thousand pounds for doing nothing. *'A hard bargain, man,'* the promoter had said, not seemingly put out by paying such a terrific sum for space alone.

His eyes switched to the farmhouse and swine pens, the barns where his small herd would shelter. It looked like a scene from a war film. Barricades to protect him from the 'peaceful, music-loving fans'. His wife and daughters warned to stay indoors during the concert. He, too, *advised* to remain well away from the 'enthusiastic gathering'.

A police car rolled into view, cruised and departed without so much as a wave in his direction.

It hurt him!

Everybody else did whatever they thought fitting to make hay whilst the sun shone. But not for him - or so it would seem. He was a lonely man now. Unable to visit the pub.

Unwanted at markets. Not invited to attend auctions by their several local estate agents and farming brokers.

He just hoped everything would go off as mentioned by that promoter. *Smooth, man, nothin' to worry about!*

The 'arousers' were out in full force. Jasmyn in Birmingham, Becky in Coventry. But the other outfits had their armies in the field, too. Poster putter-uppers, salesmen flogging records cashing in on the advance newspaper publicity, dropouts making a few quid circulating the discos and clubs, agents touting for their stars to make personal appearance on radio or at supermarket openings. All the jazz associated with a major pop scene.

And Johnny Holland's 'special troops' - his Roundheads getting in touch with skinhead mobs!

Unknown to Steve Morash, Johnny had decided to spend a few hundred making sure his supporters would be at the festival. His real fans. Not the teeny bopper element who had shot him to fame. But the terrace terrors who bought his current 'hate' discs.

Reports reaching Johnny suggested there could be a fantastic aggro at the festival. Hairies and their ilk were already seeking shelter within the concert zone.

'Bleedin' shame we gotta be on stage,' Peter said as they drove North from their stockbroker belt homes. 'I'm getting rusty as a farm gate . . .'

Johnny laughed, gazed at the London build-up. He had grown so accustomed now to being surrounded by trees, lawns, flower-beds and birds - feathered variety - that The Big Smoke's tightly clustered houses and the filth of streets inhabited by those who didn't give a damn how they existed made him feel sick. He couldn't understand why Bruce and the others insisted on staying in Acton. In Chiswick. In a neighbourhood guaranteed to choke ambition and talent.

'I'd love to put the boot in again,' Peter said.

Johnny didn't reply. He wanted to feel the old thrills raging inside him. Wanted to smash a few immigrants; to have a go on the terraces. But he had more of a desire to get far away from temptations. To succeed in showbiz. To prove that he could do it unaided.

'What if we get involved?' Peter asked.

'See we don't!' Johnny ordered.

'I bleedin' can't hold back the blokes . . . '

Johnny frowned. The others had a fleet of cars laid on. To take them into Birmingham to their hotel. Steve had seen to that end of the arrangements.

'You know 'ow Bruce can get . . . '

Dressed in his finest gear, Johnny Holland shrugged off Peter's wail. Since occupying the mansion he had come to regard himself as a swell. A man-about-town. Somebody. A voice the kids listened to and obeyed. Yet, deep down, he was still the same Johnny who'd booted the hell out of enemy fans on the terraces. God, he'd loved Enoch's bit in the paper about Pakistanis being aliens. Not entitled to vote. Not even to be here if the brass ever admitted it.

They were making good time now as the driver weaved through heavy Willesden traffic.

Johnny indicated a smallish, slightly built Pakistani standing on the kerb, scared to venture forth onto the zebra crossing as cars whistled past non-stop. 'Him!' he said triumphantly. 'A song about a crazy driver who collects points for frightening the hell out of pedestrians.'

Johnny then presented his rather elaborate score system for 'knock downs' which varied from five to ten depending on the kind of nationality one happened to collide with. It was an extraordinary vicious calculation - macabre in the extreme and one that would hardly help the British in their efforts to retain relationships with the Commonwealth - or for that matter, with the Americans.

Peter stared again, his eyeballs rolling. 'You can't,' he muttered. 'Jesus, Johnny - the fuzz would 'ave you.'

But Johnny wasn't listening. His mind had retreated into a composer-lyricist world apart from their journey, the interruptions.

Peter Acroyd shuddered, settled back into a corner of the limousine they'd hired. He worried about Johnny's desire to get them a stinking name with the other groups. Much as he detested Pakkis and their Asian mates he didn't go for singing about it. A punch-up now and then relieved his emotions.

'Anyway, wot's this alien bit?' Peter asked, jogging his companion's arm.

Tearing himself from a flow of unrhyming phrases, Johnny shook off the residueous satisfaction. 'Eh?' he asked.

'Pakkis ain't foreigners . . . Are they?'

'We've been told they're immigrants and that's good enough for me!'

Peter sat up straight and took an interest. He was far from being a great brain. His political acumen lacked cohesion.

But he believed he knew enough. He'd read the newspapers and though many advocated tolerance toward immigration he fell for only those views which he wanted to believe. It was easy for him because he had an inbuilt hatred which was hard to fathom; perhaps his views had been manufactured by the wrong guidance to such an extent that they overwhelmed all the arguments - no matter how humane and sensible they might be - to the contrary.

He wanted to spray walls with slogans with little thought that the defacing of buildings would in itself be an eye-sore which would defeat the whole point of his argument. It was something that even the British might deplore more than the entry of unfortunate immigrants and, if it got out of hand, drive them (the British) to foreign climes.

Nonetheless, the use of aerosol paint was, he thought, the real answer to immigration. He obviously hadn't heard about those early pre-war days when GO HOME YANKS had little or no affect - nor justification after they had taken part in such horrendous hostilities.

'Bloody hell,' Peter said, sure now of his ground. 'It couldn't be done. The fuzz are always near there and they've got security blokes on guard, too.'

'I could do it if I bleedin' wanted to,' Johnny snapped.

'Then you do it, mate . . . ' Peter laughed. 'Steve'll bail you out!'

Driving with the utmost care, aware of his responsibilities, the hired chauffeur listened to the rantings of his two passengers and wondered how the blazes these kids ever got to earn such fabulous sums for doing what he - and a lot of others - had done for nothing during the Thirties and the War. None of them, in his opinion, had the stuff the pub entertainers had had way back when . . .

And this drivel about painting a name everywhere! Well, the only time his lot ever scribbled anything on a wall was in some filthy toilet and always clean compared to the muck the graffiti specialists scrawled today.

Mind you, he mused, he agreed with their Enoch for Prime Minister bit. No other man had ever been able to call himself a true-blue Tory and get the dockers and market porters out in sympathy with his aims. People didn't think of Mr Powell as this or that party member. He was an Englishman speaking his mind. Saying what the majority believed wholeheartedly. No wogs. No Common Market. Britain for the British and to hell with what the world thought as long as our blokes made out.

He'd been a driver for five years now. But only because he'd been turfed out of his job by a Yank firm who'd come in and decided their

British workers were a bunch of union layabouts and not able to carry out simple mass-production jobs.

And what's happened to the product since? he asked himself. *Down the bleedin' drain. The Yank parent company had a global market and the British slobs got the dole . . .*

He heard Johnny say: 'Half our bleedin' profession are bent . . . '

For once, the driver forgot all the rules drummed into his turning head and the car swerved dangerously before he got it under control.

'Watch the road, mate,' Johnny yelled.

'Sorry, kid . . . '

Johnny bent forward, tapped the man on his right shoulder. 'Don't call me kid,' he snarled. 'I'm . . . '

'Old enough to vote,' the driver smiled.

'Christ, I ain't that bloody old!'

The man scowled, avoided a mini darting from a sidestreet in the opposite direction to that which its direction signals showed. 'Women!' he snorted and then, as the long-haired youth grinned and gave him a two-fingers 'Up You' sign: 'Long-haired git!'

Johnny didn't care. He kept jabbing the driver with a stiff finger. 'You do your job, mate - we'll attend to our business.'

'All I wanted to say, kid . . . er, Johnny . . . '

'That's better!'

The interruption didn't stop the driver's flow of thoughts. 'You watch yourselves,' he mentioned. 'I ain't running down show business but I get an awful lot of 'em for customers an' I'd wager most are queer.'

Suddenly, Johnny showed an interest. 'Yeah?'

'Especially the bleedin' television crowd,' the driver said with more assurity. 'A bunch of fags . . . '

Johnny winked to Peter. 'Name some,' he challenged.

The driver concentrated on getting their vehicle onto the motorway approach through a jam caused by a slow, overladen dump-lorry which had no legitimate right to paralyse traffic here.

'Are you going to name some?' Johnny asked.

The driver sighed. 'I don't like causing trouble for people. Even if I gave their names you probably wouldn't know 'em. I wasn't just meaning the stars, you know. I'm talking about the blokes behind the scenes. Producers, directors, administrators . . . '

Johnny's interest waned and like the moon he sank back out of sight, content to bask in the reflected glow of his final word.

'Innuendo . . . '

CHAPTER SIXTEEN

A LARGE, hand-lettered sign attached to the saloon bar door of the 'Royal Oake' public house said what the majority of villagers within ten miles of the pop concert were whispering in private. NO HIPPIES. TIES MUST BE WORN. Down the street, the landlord of the 'Woodman's Arms' got into the act after trying to view the situation with a profit-calculating mind and reluctantly placed a sign of his own inside the foyer opening onto both saloon and public bars. It read:

SORRY - HIPPIES, DOGS AND UNESCORTED MEN NOT PERMITTED. That, to his way of thinking, excluded the London-Birmingham heavy mob dressed in their colourful uniforms with the sinful word 'Security' on shoulder flashes. The ones leading vicious dogs around and making out to be doing a duty all would appreciate.

Stragglers still stood by roadside throughout the Midlands, thumbs waving frantically now as the 'great day' drew frighteningly close. In less than twenty-four hours the first entertainer would mount the stage and sound would blast from the one hundred and fifty speakers dotted round the Thurlow farm.

Watchful police from three counties kept an eye on the hitch-hiking flood, doing nothing to stop the fans from reaching their destination but not being very helpful either. All leave in Warwickshire had been cancelled and the same applied to Worcestershire's eastern regions. A combined drug squad set up headquarters outside the festival's 'sacred precincts' and rumour had it that many of those holding tickets were, indeed, undercover fuzz.

Other organisations were in evidence, too. Church groups seeking converts: trusting in the Jesus movement to sway weary, musically-satiated fans into loving arms. Do-gooder factions about to cope with homeless girls, hungry teeny boppers, stagestruck idiots, drifters looking for yet another handout. And there were the off-beat ones - international cults preying off the ill-treated, the aimless, the unsure.

Like mushrooms springing from fertile, shaded soil, the caravans and tents and coaches formed a ring round Thurlow's farm. Outside the high barbed-wire fence. Beyond the 'authority' of the festival's promoters. Supposedly protected from the unofficial guards . . .

When Steve Morash reached the site with the 'Jolly Green Men' he felt a shudder of revulsion creep down his spine. He'd heard about other shows and what happened when the Hell's Angels cut loose. He didn't like the number of leather jackets hanging about nor the familiarity they shared with tough-looking security men. He deplored the lack of uniformed police near the gates, in the crowds camping rough inside the grounds. If he'd been running this operation he'd have paid a fantastic sum to have all policing done by the established, official law.

'Christ, there must be a hundred thousand of 'em here,' Bruce gasped, face pressed against their car window.

'Ten thousand anyway,' Steve grinned.

'A bleedin' lot of hairies an' Angels,' Mick said cautiously.

He scanned the throng. 'Can't pick out any skins . . . '

'They'll he here,' Bruce remarked with a wink hidden from Steve. *They'd better be,* he thought, *or, Johnny'll do his nut.*

'Where's our pad?' Mick asked.

'In Birmingham,' Steve told them. 'I just wanted to make certain arrangements for tomorrow first. And don't any of you get out of this heap unless I give an order! Okay?'

Johnny got a report from his mates that same night when they met up in their hotel. Not far away, less than two blocks, Narcissus held court to hear from his 'agents' how the situation looked.

'Gerstein's beggin' for trouble,' Blaine said as he lit a cigarette. 'Nobody told me Hell's Angels would be actin' as peace-keepers.' He poured from a pint bottle into a glass, glanced at the label. *Watney's Pale Ale.* He nodded satisfaction, sampled the drink.

'Can you handle your end?' Narcissus growled.

'Yeah - easy as cutting cheese.' Blaine laughed. 'What I want to know is how your queens will react once the fun starts.'

Narcissus glared, tossed his head. Anka Shippe paled, concentrated on his pink-gin and avoided being brought into matters. Only McGovern seemed able to voice an opinion. He snarled, 'Less of the queens lark, man. Some of us could tear the hair out of your heavies.'

'That you surely could, ducks,' Blaine smiled. Suddenly, his face menaced and he jabbed cigarette and a stiff finger in McGovern's direction. Behind his cold eyes burned a viciousness that, for once, scared the hard Irisher. 'One false move by you or your bloody mates an' I guarantee to personally plant each six foot under!'

Narcissus sweated. He wondered if Gerstein knew what type of man Blaine really was? And how deeply they were all becoming involved in what could possible result in serious injury - even a killing?

Shippe sighed a decade away as fear trickled cold perspiration down from under his hairless armpits. The old face looked positively ancient, awfully white and pasty.

'How about the Hell's Angels?' Narcissus asked.

Blaine chuckled. 'Let 'em come at my boys and they'll discover what it's like being on the receiving end of a bikechain,' he mentioned too casually.

'Jeeze,' McGovern breathed, 'don't start a war!'

Laughingly finishing his drink and dropping a still burning dog-end into an ashtray, Tom Blaine got to his feet and walked to the door. There, pausing, he idly said, 'If only you knew what that meant,' and burst out of the room roaring his head off . . .

Becky Wilmott basked under a sun-lamp, absolutely starkers. Steam filled her bathroom, drifting across her gorgeous body in misty waves. Faintly, through the partially open door into her bedroom, the sweet music of a nightride radio programme kept her mind active. She knew the dangers of over-exposure to the lamp's rays and her own desire to get a bronze tan, not a tropical browning. All she wanted was a sun colouring to make men take a second, or third, glance. To make them heap attentions on her.

An announcer broke into the almost continuous music . . .

'The Midlands police ask us to broadcast the following warning to those fans who have not yet arrived at Thurlow Farm for tomorrow's pop festival. Stay at home. Or, if you happen to be on the road, turn back. All tickets have been sold and no-one else will be admitted to the concert.'

The music started again only to have a second interruption as the announcer made his own request . . .

'Kids, pay attention to the men in blue. They're doing a job you'd hate *but it is in the interests of the majority*. Facilities for sleeping and food are stretched to the limit as it is. According to the public health officials on the spot there is a grave risk if another five hundred fans are allowed within the festival area.

'Don't be foolish. Please. Stay at home. Or go back before you're caught up in the excitement at close range. It isn't worth a broken heart or ill-health. I ought to know, kiddies. I caught a bad attack of Spanish tummy once by not listening to advice from those who knew the situation better than I.

'Okay? Good. And don't forget - for all who miss the big show - we're presenting a recording from this station on Friday night's 'Pop Explosion' show. So - keep tuned and make Friday a date with Joe Robinson . . . '

Becky struggled upright, switched off the lamp. Steve would be delighted by the news of a sell-out crowd. Not that he had ever doubted the success of this venture. The score or more top names on the bill had been an automatic guarantee. She only hoped that Jasmyn and her efforts had brought quite a few Johnny Holland fans to the 'pearly-sound gates'.

The bath had a shower attachment and she stepped into the porcelain tub, adjusted the temperature and ran water. Shivers goose-pimpled her tender flesh as a rush of cold cascaded over her but before she could leap from the needlespray, the hot came through and she twisted in ecstatic approval with the fine tingling jets playing sensuously on her skin.

She adored showers. People she knew who had been in America spoke of the shower with downright reverence. Steve thought Britain uncivilized not having a shower in every home. And, she had to admit, she joined him in this unpatriotic condemnation. When one thought of the daily dirt clinging to one's skin it was much better to have the grime gurgle down a drain than scum bath water and adhere even as one rose from sudsy, filth-stained static pools.

Using her towel with a vigorous swipe she thought about Steve and Johnny.

Steve wanted her to make the big-time.

Johnny didn't even consider her as a rival. Not that she was, really. The teeny bopper fans screaming Johnny's praises were hardly interested in a 'girl'. They wanted some attractive, sex-symbol bloke to heap their praises on; to gaze at his picture and imagine themselves deeply in love with this 'current' knight in musical armour.

Dry now, she walked into the bedroom, lowered the radio's volume. She wasn't addicted to loud noise. She believed in the experts opinion that too much sound tended to deafen one before the age of fifty. Since she hoped to live beyond that limit she didn't want to be forced to wear a hearing aid. Or, worse, to be totally deaf.

Ray Stevens . . . *'Everything is beautiful . . . '*

She felt weak, jelly. She loved Ray . . .

If he'd been at the festival she'd have offered Steve a contract for a year's intimacy just to appear on the same bill as *her* idol . . .

She laughed bitterly. Steve hadn't asked for anything. They'd shared a few hours together but she knew this wasn't the reason for his effort to make her a star. Steve wasn't such a bad guy. Maybe ruthless when it boiled right down to plugging his 'product' but, underneath, he was all heart. And softness.

A sudden thought struck her. What if Steve could convince Johnny that SHE deserved a chance . . . A try out in front of a critical audience!

God, wouldn't it be terrific! The urge consumed her. She grabbed her telephone . . .

'A bird? A bleedin' bird singing with us doing the background? No, thanks, mate!'

Johnny kicked his legs out, let his heels flop on the bed. But for his underpants he was naked. The others wore street garb, sat on chairs and the twin bed. Only Peter Acroyd stood and he was by the window, watching Birmingham's traffic enter the Bull Ring in perpetual amazement.

Bruce gestured with his hands, repeated, 'No birds! I mean it.' His face twisted in confusion. 'Any roads, why does Steve think we'd do this?'

Johnny Holland shrugged, scratched his stomach. 'He's givin' her a break like he did for us. She's got a good voice . . . '

'No bleedin' use to us!' Bruce insisted.

Turning from the window, Peter grinned. 'We could *arrange* for her to get a spot . . . '

Johnny frowned. 'How?'

'Give *Tavern* the boot!'

Bruce jumped to his feet. 'Man.'

Johnny silenced the immediate enthusiasm in the room. 'Bloody hell, can't you blokes think about anythin' 'ceptin' using your boots?'

Peter returned to his window, saying over a shoulder, 'You're getting to be a bore, Johnny. Christ, what's come over you? Don't you ever want to do the things we used to do? Don't you even feel like aggro now?'

Johnny lay back on his bed, hands behind his head. The ceiling intrigued him. A crack formed a face - just as evil as the devil's. Discolouration around the crack seemed to make the face outline alive.

'I bloody asked a question,' Peter roared.

'And I'm considerin' it,' came Johnny's reply.

'So?' an exasperated Bruce asked.

Shutting his eyes to block out the face, Johnny tried to sound offish whilst getting his message across in no uncertain manner. 'I don't forget the kicks we had. If somebody aggravated me I'd boot 'em . . . *but we've got a nice thing goin' for us in showbiz.* We're making lots of lolly and we've got fame. Isn't that a scene worth keeping?'

Bruce grunted, picked his nose. 'I'm not bleedin' livin' in a big house,' he began.

Peter glared, watched as Johnny sat bolt upright. 'If my buying a house gets up your bloody nose then for crissakes fork out some bread and get your arse outta Acton.'

'I like Acton,' Bruce affirmed in anger.

'So what's the beef?'

Peter interrupted with a slow smile. 'He's jealous. He hasn't the bleedin' guts to move and he's green-eyed 'cause we did!'

'Not true!' Bruce yelled.

'Listen to me, mate,' Johnny said evenly, eyes fixed on his group one by one. 'You show me a good reason to clobber some bastard an' I'll be there. But I ain't going to ruin everything we've got just to satisfy some stupid urge. Bloody hell, ain't we got enough aggro from those newspaper blokes and the fancy glams?'

Peter removed his jacket, slung it over an arm and went to the door. 'I'm for keepin' our noses clean but I'm with Bruce, too. It's about time we did something exciting. It doesn't matter what, long as we can rid ourselves of this bloody frustration . . . !' He waved nonchalantly and departed.

For a moment the room was silent. Then, suddenly, a babble of sound shattered Johnny's desire to rest. Disgustedly, he grabbed his gear, waved his arms like a crazed windmill. 'Screw it,' he roared. 'Leave me alone. Lemme think eh?'

Bruce grinned behind Johnny's back. He had the feeling he'd won. He could remember when Johnny used to blow his cool. And, always, it meant an aggro coming up. Nodding to his mates, Bruce got moving towards the door. 'You think, Johnny,' he advised. 'We'll be downstairs in the coffee shop . . . '

CHAPTER SEVENTEEN

JULIUS GERSTEIN arrived at Thurlow Farm shortly after 10.00 a.m. It had not been his intention to visit the festival but pressure from fellow-agents and an important executive for one of the large recording concerns made it imperative he attend.

He was in a foul mood. Pop concerts gave him a pain in the neck. He couldn't stand the racket, the screaming fanaticism of girl fans nor the big-headed antics of those professing to be entertainers. In Julius's opinion most glamour stars and teeny bopper idols were just so many loud-mouthed, lesser-talented individuals than his rag trade dress designers and salesmen. If it hadn't been for the money he accumulated from pop he would willingly have sold out his interests in Discodrome and those performers he handled on a percentage basis.

Within minutes of his arrival at the security gate, Julius confronted Narcissus and Tom Blaine. 'Well?' he asked menacingly.

'*All* set,' Blaine assured.

'We've worked out a scheme to . . . ' Narcissus started.

Gerstein held a hand up. 'I'm not interested in details. Just results.'

Blaine smiled sarcastically. 'It's a two-pronged attack. If his guys don't succeed in ruining the act we're gonna destroy the bastards!'

Gerstein shuddered mentally. The way Blaine spoke meant violence. Something he had to avoid.

Blaine dropped his sarcasm, accused, 'You didn't tell me the Hell's Angels would be here.'

'How the blazes do I know who buys tickets to these things?' Gerstein shot back righteously.

'I'm not speakin' 'bout 'em coming for the show,' Blaine cut in. 'They're workin' with your security mob - freelance guards!'

'I didn't . . . ' Gerstein frowned, bit off the excuses. It wasn't for anyone to question his methods even if, truthfully, he had not directly issued orders regarding the use of outside provocateurs. He didn't try to hide the fact he had great influence with the promotion staff. Nor that any suggestion coming from him would be acted upon verbatim.

'Can you have 'em called off?' Blaine asked.

'I'll see . . . ' Julius turned on his heels, strode away. His mood turned more sour now. He didn't want a repeat of events that had taken place in other outdoor concerts. No Hell's Angels running loose and bringing the police into action. No clamour for money refunds. No adverse publicity and an enquiry linking him with the use of force again.

'You guys get backstage an' leave me to handle the outfront situation,' Blaine told Narcissus, eyes boring into Gerstein's retreating backbone. A premonition filled him with something approaching dread. If anything went wrong he could be sure Julius would set the dogs on him, disclaiming any involvement or responsibility. Even now, he sensed, Gerstein was probably working out a scheme to extricate himself should the plot backfire.

'Me old mate!' Narcissus grunted. 'The right bastard!' He winked with an over-blued eye and let golden stars flicker.

Tom Blaine swung, face stoney. 'Get lost, chum!'

'Hmmmm - ain't you uptight,' Narcissus muttered, tossing his head. Without waiting for the other's retort he flounced off into the thickening crowd of admirers hanging out near the caravans reserved for entertainers. As the third act due to appear he had certain adjustments to make to his costume, more cosmetics to put on. And, for courage, a few belts to take . . .

'Don't worry,' Steve Morash told Becky Wilmott as they stood near the single turnstile which gave admittance to the festival. Not far away, like Nazi guards in a prison camp, security goons waited with impassive faces and huge, savage dogs straining at their leashes. Beyond the gate, dotted forlornly amongst the 'outside' caravans and police cars, the late arrivals wandered aimlessly in silent rebuttal of a SOLD OUT sign attached to the wire fence.

Becky drew a deep breath, forced a pathetic smile. 'I'm scared stiff if the truth was known,' she admitted. 'Johnny won't get the guys to agree. I feel it.'

Steve grunted, took her arm and moved towards the stage rear. He wished to heck he had a bottle of *Hundred Pipers* handy. Not for Dutch courage but just to satisfy a desire to sit down, relax and enjoy the fine taste of a drink. 'I'm not entirely depending on Johnny coming through,' he told the girl. 'I spoke to "Salt" Winds. He's agreeable to accompanying you on his harmonica.'

Becky sighed. 'I can't see us being a raving success.'

'God, don't let him hear you saying that,' Steve laughed. 'Salt isn't exactly the type to let criticism go unoathed . . . ' His laughter deepened. He liked his coined word 'un-oathed'. He'd have to remember it for future occasions.

'Is that why they call him "Salt"?' Becky asked.

'Partially.' Steve recalled a fan magazine's explanation but alienated it as a publicity gimmick. In reality, "Salt" had been nicknamed in school because he would insist on carving model ships under his desk when others were being taught their '3-R's'.

'Can Salt play my kind of music?' Becky was more worried than she cared to admit.

'Sure he can. Some professional musicians swear he's a genius on the harmonica. A budding Larry Adler. And don't be put off by his act, either. Those sea-dog numbers are catchy and go with his pseudonym but, at home, he's a classical buff.'

Becky felt more relaxed. Steve's comforting hand on her arm warmed her flesh, provoked a sense of well-being. 'Maybe we should tell Johnny to forget me and just agree to having Salt?'

'No, thanks,' Steve said firmly. 'I've got to find out how far Johnny and his guys will go to help me.'

The girl could almost taste Steve's bitterness. She had liked Johnny Holland once but, of late, his egotistical rejection of Steve's advice had left her cold. Especially after the way he'd avoided a direct commitment to provide backing for her. She accepted, partly, his explanation that the blokes wouldn't go on stage with a bird. But she still felt he could order them.

'Come on,' Steve said sharply. 'Let's go see Mister Teeny Bopper in person . . .'

Narcissus clung to his mike, gear shimmering in spotlight produced 'sunshine'. A chilly wind came down from distant hills, washed-over the huddled fans. Here and there, near the back of the forty thousand crowd, applauding 'friends' tried to offer their particular hero encouragement. But, for the most, Narcissus felt he was but a name doing a fill-in act. A 'glam-boy' heating up an audience for the really big turns. Like Johnny Holland. Or Bacon and Rind. Or Scrambled.

Danny La Rue would not have been pleased as Narcissus took off one of his numbers. The fans certainly weren't going mad.

In the wings, Tavern waited and watched their mate dying. McGovern shuddered. 'Christ,' he said aloud, 'this is bloody bad!'

'Why the hell didn't he stick to his hits?' another enquired.

'What hits?' McGovern asked with typical showbiz jealousy.

'Naughty-naughty,' came the grinning retort.

McGovern blocked his ears to Narcissus's voice, his mates' chatter. He searched the tented gloom surrounding backstage. He could just about make out figures moving there. People readying themselves for the nerve-shattering occupation of the wings. Performers dreading to know they had forty thousand critical voices out front. Guys whose reputations hung in the balance of a first-ever mass public exhibition. Tried and tested acts feigning indifference to the rising stars this huge crowd had come to hear. And see. And worship.

'Where the hell does Holland come?' McGovern asked.

'We're next . . . '

'Tell me somethin' new,' the Irishman snarled.

'After us,' his mate continued unabated, 'is Scrambled. Then, Mort and Bart. I think they're followed by "Salt" Winds and Safari Park . . . '

'Holy Mary - that puts Holland in with the top bhoyos!'

'Right!' his mate snapped viciously, adjusting his gymslip. 'If you'd been with us when we discussed the bill you'd have known.'

McGovern wiggled his shoulders and wet a finger to fashion an eyebrow. All the actions contradicted the man's attitude, his inborn savagery. It was as if he had a split personality. A viciousness and a softness fighting for supremacy.

'Hey,' another mate exclaimed suddenly, coming from the background to stand beside McGovern. 'Did you hear that?'

The Irishman frowned, whipped a small mirror from his schoolgirl's purse, studied his make-up. 'Hear what?'

'One of the big - and I mean BIG - groups have just arrived. They asked if they could do a special number for their many fans! What a flamin' cheek!' Eyes rolled wildly. 'I wouldn't mind but they're saying they'll go on next!'

McGovern dropped his mirror. The glass smashed.

'Oh!' the annoyed performer said, hand clasped to open mouth just exactly as a distraught girl would do.

'You bloody bitch!' McGovern hissed. 'That's seven years bad luck!'

'I'll buy you another, dear,' the Tavern said.

McGovern pushed him aside, stormed off-stage. His anger rose with every step and when he finally reached the stage manager's cubbyhole he was fit to tackle a pack of wolves.

Or Irish giants.

'McGovern,' the stage manager said, beaming. 'I was coming to see you. We've had an unexpected . . .'

'Shit on 'em! We're next and our contract says so!' McGovern squared his shoulders, glared.

The other sighed. He'd fully anticipated an objection. It wouldn't have mattered which act was replaced they all believed nobody had the right to step into their time. But . . . He kept his beaming face happy. 'Narcissus hasn't helped your act any, McGovern. A group with top appeal could get this bunch worked up to a frenzy. Enough to make your boys go over real fantastic . . . '

McGovern lost some of his ire. What the stage manager said made sense. Narcissus had died. And slain their audience to boot. Anything to liven 'em up would be most welcome. 'Okay, if that's how you see things - I agree. We sit this dance out . . . '

As he began to walk away the Irishman suddenly paused, asked: 'Who are *they?*'

Before information could be given four young men filtered past the cubbyhole. Each face had a familiarity born from over-exposure on stage, television and films. From being on record sleeves for the past three years.

'Them?' McGovern whispered.

'Them!' the stage manager said reverently.

The enormous crowd clapped out of boredom as Narcissus finished his performance and shashayed off stage. Not all his glitter, his desperate attempts to rouse the throng had met with what could legitimately be called success. He knew why, too. His act had suffered from a large dose of Julius Gerstein and a burning hatred for Johnny Holland. He'd been all geared-up to cause trouble, not entertain. And it had shown disastrously.

Ignoring Tavern and the M.C. stalking happily onto the platform, Narcissus shouldered past a group wearing ordinary street gear and vanished into the backstage gloom.

'Now a surprise treat,' the M.C.'s voice roared from the speakers with undisguised enthusiasm. 'I don't have to find praise-worthy words to introduce our next . . . '

Narcissus swore. Jealousy filled him. Tavern didn't deserve such a build-up. He refused to listen to more of this crap and clapped hands to his ears. Even that, though, didn't blot out the tremendous roar of approval from the forty thousand music-lovers out front. They drowned the announcer's voice completely. Roared louder and louder. Kept yelling and screaming . . .

Slowly, Narcissus dropped his hands, made a circle round a pile of instruments and went back towards the stage. He couldn't - wouldn't - believe that Tavern had ever been acclaimed to such a sky-lifting extent.

Then . . .

He saw McGovern and the others standing in the wings. Saw a slice of stage with daylight and spots illuminating M.C. and . . .

Now he knew what was making the fans go hysterical! *No wonder!* he thought and quickened his step. Even he had to catch this performance . . .

' . . . from our latest album . . . '

At full volume the speakers had a job reaching every ear. The crowd response would not let the spoken word get through. All they wanted was *that sound. Those voices* joined in singing. Anything would do. Just so long as their favourites, their heroes, their real idols got down to the serious business of entertaining.

A momentary hush fell over the vast arena.

Then, bedlam!

Standing with Becky and Johnny, Steve Morash watched the magic one of his publicity cohorts had conjured up. And marvelled. And mentally heaped praise for a job so well done that no power on Earth, no earth-shaking series of exposes concerning each could destroy. This was a publicity created image that could not die. That would live for eternity.

The music was no better than Johnny's. No individual voice came through as good as Johnny's. Yet, there was that something extraordinary special about the 'whole' that sent this group soaring into a stratosphere of adulation unequalled in living memory.

Moving slightly to get a fuller view of the fans, Steve could see where the security men would have problems. Already, the wire fence bulged and shook as those outside tried to break in. And, too, the ticket-holders were far from being satisfied to stick to their appointed few square inches of ground. The mob thrust forward - making like a gigantic tidal wave for the stage. Anguished screams rose side by side with those specifying delight.

'It's getting ugly out there,' Steve shouted above the music.

Johnny grinned. He didn't mind. He was used to football terraces suddenly surging this way and that as the crush became almost unbearable.

Becky pressed against Steve. Frightened by his tone. And the scenes she witnessed.

'If it gets worse I'm calling off your number,' Steve yelled into Johnny's ear.

Johnny shook his head in the negative. 'No!' he replied at the top of his voice. 'I love it!'

Steve shrugged, grabbed Becky and began to push against a solid wall of performers coming from their caravans. 'You will be safe inside the trailer,' he shouted.

With Steve and Becky out of his way, Johnny let himself be carried forward on the rush to get backstage. Like the others, he wanted to experience this worship. To capture the emotional explosion.

Once, in the press, he caught sight of Bruce and Peter. Ahead of him. Borne on the chests of those following. And McGovern already standing on the platformed back of the covered stage area. Narcissus, too. A sad, dejected performer.

In the bone-breaking crush, Johnny didn't notice how he was being carried straight to McGovern. Or how, by some fluke, were Peter, Bruce and Mick. What he couldn't see was the way Tom Blaine and a few of his heavies kept close behind, forming a spearhead, separated by but four or five performers in Johnny's rear.

Already, the stage overflowed. Those coming into the covered area couldn't help being propelled out front. To join the delighted group in the middle of their impromptu performance. To become targets for the worshipping fans.

Lifted almost bodily on the surging wave, Johnny brushed past Narcissus, felt a hard fist snake between those round him and land in his groin. He felt sickened. He wanted to vomit. Wished he could double and erase the terrible pain stabbing upwards from his injured parts.

'Bastard!'

Moistened eyes fixed then on McGovern, on the way the Irishman clung to a stanchion to keep himself from being swept aside. He didn't see the foot lashing out. He heard an expletive erupt from the youth on his left, then . . .

They're getting at me!

Limping now, McGovern's kick having hurt more than Narcissus's fist, Johnny staggered through the crowd, punching and kneeing until he reached the stage front.

I'll get the bloody bastards!

Amplified music made it impossible to hear. Even seeing was blurred by the constantly shifting heads bobbing and weaving between him and his attackers.

A heavy hand clamped on his shoulder and strange eyes laughed as the fingers dug into nerve-ends.

For once, Johnny Holland came near to outright fear. His enemies were legion. Surrounding him. Getting at him under cover of the confusion.

I've got to find a refuge!

Suddenly, he knew where safety lay . . . Tearing from those steel-like fingers he plunged onto the stage. Straight to the group. Right up to the microphone. He didn't give a damn about the fans yelling abuse at him. This wasn't a gimmick to steal another act's thunder.

The music dropped to a plaintive twang of a single guitar. Accusing eyes focused on him. Eyes with fandom behind their 'don't dare' challenge.

'Roundheads . . . get up here fast!' Johnny roared into the mike. 'Up the skins!'

Grinning now, his groin hurting less with each passing moment, Johnny grasped the microphone and swung in time to see Blaine charging.

'You've asked for it, bastard!'

Right to the fence Johnny's words went.

Fans who a split-second previously had wanted his blood stood silent, immobilised. Watching. Listening . . .

Johnny's arm moved like a darting snake jabbing. Thrusting the mike into Blaine's face. Splitting grinning lips. Breaking front teeth in amplified glee. Letting the mike fall, Johnny smashed at the man with hard fists, feet finding a joy in other targets.

Yelling encouragement, Peter and his mates stormed the stage. The famous group, smiling apologies, moved artfully into the background. This wasn't their scene. But it was a performance to applaud.

From his viewpoint, Steve Morash watched the public slaughter as a sleepwalker would a policeman upon being awakened. He couldn't believe his eyes. Nor did he want to accept what was happening.

The stage area had miraculously cleared of performers except those engaged in the actual battle. There was Johnny, Peter, Bruce, Mike, Narcissus, Tavern in their outrageous gym-slips and other assorted characters from the security force and audience.

It didn't seem possible for the contestants to recognise their opponents or friends yet, strangely, both sides were doing a remarkable job of eliminating foes.

Narcissus went down, bleeding.

McGovern hurtled from the stage, arm flailing like a broken reed.

Bruce sank to his knees, head in hands as blood spilled from his nose.

Johnny slammed a right to Blaine's face, grabbed a guitar and smashed the instrument over - and around - the injured head.

'Oh, God,' Steve moaned . . .

CHAPTER EIGHTEEN

WORLD POPS editorial comment read:

Disgusting. Shameful. Tragic.

Words alone are not strong enough to describe the horrendous climax of the Thurlow Farm affair.

Show business cannot ever have witnessed such scenes of downright brutality, such monstrous behaviour from those supposedly 'up there' to be examples for all fandom.

Whilst we must accept mitigating circumstances for Johnny Holland's viciousness we cannot excuse the manner of his incitement for those who came to watch a spectacular festival.

We hope that we never see the likes of this again. And we draw attention to Julius Gerstein's role in the brawl. Had it not been for Discodrome's ex-owner none of the shocking scenes viewed by some forty thousand pop buffs would have happened.

Glad to be rid of you, Mr Gerstein!

Pop is better off without your sort!

Steve Morash sighed and placed his newspaper beside his glass of *Hundred Pipers*. The police were satisfied with Johnny's evidence. Although they, too, deplored his participation in what had become a mass riot, they did not intend to charge him. The same, Steve thought gratefully, did not hold for Narcissus, Blaine and McGovern. The latest word coming from police headquarters was that each could expect a stiff sentence.

Sipping his drink, Steve considered the outcome of the affray. Johnny's popularity had risen like a shooting star. He was the 'bloke who knocked the stuffin' out of all his enemies'. As WORLD POPS said in another section of the magazine . . .

'Roundhead Johnny Holland confirmed that his backing group are now to be known as 'The Knockers'. We think this is carrying the Roundhead-Cavalier image too far but admit the aptness of their new title.'

Steve laughed silently, finished his drink. He had a date. And afterwards, a front row seat to catch Becky's first Discodrome performance.

Slipping into his velvet jacket, Steve nodded to his mirrored reflection. 'You're doing terrific, pal,' he told the speaking image. 'The top idol in your stable and now - a real golden doll ready to burst onto the scene. Lucky for you the Discodrome belongs to you, eh?'

He was still beaming as the door closed behind him. As he climbed into his Rolls and let Simon, his personal chauffeur, touch his cap before driving off to the Big Smoke . . .

THE END

Also available from S.T. Publishing

THE COMPLETE RICHARD ALLEN VOLUME ONE
Skinhead   Suedehead   Skinhead Escapes
SKINHEAD portrays with horrifying violence all the terror and brutality that has become the trademark of these teenage malcontents. SUEDEHEAD sees Joe grow his hair and swap his boots and braces for a velvet-collared Abercrombie coat. His aggro days are over - his city slicker days are just beginning. Joe's exploits of violence and anti-social behaviour were cut short by a prison sentence. But in SKINHEAD ESCAPES Joe Hawkins is on the loose again.

THE COMPLETE RICHARD ALLEN VOLUME TWO
Skinhead Girls   Sorts   Knuckle Girls
SKINHEAD GIRL gives a girl's eye-view of living for kicks. Joan Marshall was a skinhead at fifteen with all the savagery and excitement that went with it. SORTS are the Smoothies' girls. On the run from home, her skinhead lover and her memories, Terry Hurdy finds herself in a world of sex, drugs and - murder. And finally, meet Glasgow's Ina Murray in KNUCKLE GIRLS. Her violent upbringing taught her to fight for her rights - with a bicycle chain and copper wire!

THE COMPLETE RICHARD ALLEN VOLUME THREE
Trouble For Skinhead   Skinhead Farewell   Top-Gear Skin
When Joe's sent to Dartmoor prison for killing a cop, he's got new problems to face - like the arrival of his old enemy, Charlie McVey. It all adds up to TROUBLE FOR SKINHEAD. In SKINHEAD FAREWELL, Joe finds himself blazing his way across Australia to nail down Charlie McVey once and for all! In TOP-GEAR SKIN, meet Roy Baird, the leader of a skinhead gang who needs more excitement than pulling birds and putting the boot in has to offer.

THE COMPLETE RICHARD ALLEN VOLUME FOUR
Boot Boys   Smoothies   Terrace Terrors
First there were skinheads. Then came suedeheads. Now there are BOOT BOYS, ready to do battle on the terraces every Saturday afternoon. SMOOTHIES are the new villains of the peace, born out of the skinhead-suedehead cult. The aggro is always present - until they go too far! Then comes TERRACE TERRORS. Who better to tame the hooligans than Steve Penn and his crew of skins from another era?

THE COMPLETE RICHARD ALLEN VOLUME FIVE
Mod Rule   Punk Rock   Dragon Skins
MOD RULE welcomes Joe Hawkins' bastard son, Joe Watson, to Allen's pulp fiction world of sex, crime and aggro. London mods rule okay as the bikers roar their engines and head straight for Joe's crowd. In PUNK ROCK, the clash between teds and punks can mean nothing but violence. And in DRAGON SKINS, Steve Penn is back to combat a criminal mob of Kung Fu fighters.

The above books are available from selected outlets and can be ordered from most bookshops. They can also be ordered by post. For a free copy of our our street music and youth cult book and magazine catalogue please write to S.T. Publishing, P.O. Box 12, Lockerbie. DG11 3BW. Dumfriesshire. Scotland.